HOUSE OF FAT MAN

RULES IN THE GOLDEN TRIANGLE

M. GERARD-ALESCO

House of Fat Man: Rules in the Golden Triangle

ISBN: 978-1629672625
Library of Congress Control Number: 2023917483

v23-10.26

Three may keep a secret if two of them are dead.

Benjamin Franklin

DEDICATION

For Gregory, Matthew, and Nicholas

Kachin State
CHINA
Yunnan
Province
Mandalay
Bagan
Shan
State
Huay Xai
Chiang Rai
Luang Prabang
BURMA
LAOS
Chiang Mai
Rangoon
THAILAND
VIETNAM
Pakse
Bangkok
Pattaya
CAMBODIA

PART ONE

CHAPTER ONE

Sunrise clawed along the wooden shutters.

Mama Pajama placed the Singha beer next to Greg without a word and collected the two empties. It had been a long night for him. She had seen it for years with Wes, more recently with Albie, and now Greg. Greg could not recall when drinking beer at dawn had become the norm. Wes said that there was nothing left to do now but wait. And wait, they did.

Albie and Wes sat at their usual table in the corner. Wes smoked. Albie anxiously shuffled the deck of playing cards. No gin rummy today. Greg preferred the bar. No one talked. Greg wondered when it all went to hell. He watched as Mama began unlatching and opening the heavy wooden shutters, hooking each by the ropes suspended from the overhead crossbars. *Tuk-tuks* backfired on Suthep, the main road, and rattled past.

The morning train from Bangkok had arrived—almost on time. Tourists and world travelers and hippies would soon arrive at Mama's. Before *Fodor's Asia on $5.00 a Day* made Mama's a must-stop for visitors, and even before the legend spread among the WTs that Mama's was the top-ranked destination for the munchies after savoring Chiang Mai's opium-dipped Thai sticks, the local expat community had long ago anointed khun Mae, aka Mama, the Queen of Bake for her fruit pies. Pies baked daily in an oversized, commercial oven that only Wes knew whence it came.

Mama turned on the three ceiling fans, and the fresh smell of the pies spread past the open windows. The aroma—*more fragrant than perfume*, Albie used to say—drifted past the mango trees near the entrance, rose above the cacophony of Chiang Mai's traffic, and floated over the chanting of the temple monks in the wats throughout the city. Gently, but inexorably, like a daily offering, the ambrosial scent glided toward the sacred Doi Suthep mountain and Chiang Mai University nestled at its foot, wafting past the School of Medicine and the

University Hospital, where just a few hours ago, they had left their good friend Nok in a coma.

***

Greg found Nok at the abandoned Research Station, which Albie had built two years ago in the valley almost five kilometers from the hill tribe village of Ban Su. If there was a center for the Golden Triangle, it would be Ban Su. Someone had beaten Nok. She was bleeding and barely conscious. There was little question about who was responsible.

Nok had been Albie's closest friend in this mountainous hill tribe region. She convinced others in Ban Su to help him build the Agricultural Research Station. She tried to convince her grandfather and other village leaders that growing something other than poppies was possible and profitable. Now, after the project had been abandoned—*sabotaged,* if you asked Albie—Ban Su was once again in the crosshairs for control of the product and the traffic.

She shuddered and moaned when he touched her shoulder.

"Nok, it's me. Greg." He spoke in English and then repeated it in Thai.

She clutched at her pregnant belly. Seven months. She was crying. Her swollen eyes were closed, but he could see the tears slipping down over the dried blood on her bruised face.

He tried to reach around her to lift her, but she withdrew even more into a fetal position.

Greg knelt next to her and tried to give her a sip of water from his canteen, but she did not respond. He wanted to hug her, but there was no time for that. He lowered his head next to hers and spoke softly in Thai.

"Nok. Listen to me. We must get you help. Get you to Chiang Rai. To the clinic."

She was too quiet, and Greg thought that perhaps…, but he could see her body move ever so slightly with her breath.

"I am going to lift you. Listen to me. You are going to have to help me. We have to get you on the motorcycle. We have to get down the mountain to Chiang Rai. And we must do it now."

***

Chiang Rai was little more than a village in the late sixties and early seventies. The northernmost city in Thailand remained an outpost even as the first attempt of paving Highway 1 from Chiang Mai ended last year. A border town pressing against the frontier of Thailand and Burma and Laos. The legal borders of those countries were only twenty to thirty miles away. Tourists made their way to Chiang Rai for day trips, stopovers for lunches of sticky rice and chicken, shopping at the River Market, and then brief excursions on dirt roads for a few miles to visit the more accessible hill tribe villages.

A scarcity of suitable lodging limited the traffic, as *farangs,* white foreigners, had little tolerance for what passed as a hotel in Chiang Rai. *Quaint* was the term tour guides used to describe Chiang Rai. *Believe it or not*, they would say, *this is what Chiang Mai was like not so long ago*. The Wild West was the description Wes and Albie preferred. Opium moved easily down the mountain by mules and packhorses into Chiang Rai and then onto speedier transportation. But times change. National soldiers arrived to complement the corrupt local police. Expenses went up, so alternate routes had to be developed.

A Catholic nun named Mary Peyton ran the clinic. She was more of a midwife or a nurse than a doctor, but she was the most qualified medical professional in the village. For those who preferred to wait, a doctor from Chiang Mai made bi-weekly visits to a polyclinic in the city center. The locals trusted Mary Peyton with all their concerns, and Albie would tell you that her work in the more remote hill tribe villages was life-changing. If Nok was Albie's best friend among the hill people, then Sister Mary Peyton was his dearest *farang.*

***

It was almost midnight when he finally arrived. He had used a cloth wrap to tie her close to him and to keep her from slipping off the motorcycle. She rode in front of him—partly on the gas tank—with her face nuzzled against his chest. She was such a tiny person that her short legs hanging over each side did not impede his ability to shift and navigate. The greater problem was when she lost consciousness and slumped. Her listless body would shift as he twisted down the narrow path, and with every rutted patch, she would begin to slip off the bike. He used his forearms the best he could to keep her situated. If Thais could manage three and four people on one motorcycle, Greg convinced himself that he could carry Nok.

***

The clinic was dark, but he hoped the nun would still be awake. Perhaps reading in the back. He had Nok in his arms and kicked at the door several times.

"Okay, Okay. Just a minute. I am coming." Her Thai language skills were poor, but few foreigners spoke Thai as well as he could.

"Mary Peyton, hurry! Please."

Lights appeared in the main clinic area. The door was finally unlocked and swung open.

"Greg. What happened? Who is that?"

"It's Nok. She's unconscious."

"Oh, my God. Place her on that table. What happened?"

"I don't know. I found her at the Research Station. Someone beat her savagely. She's still breathing, isn't she?"

Mary Peyton turned on the additional lights and began examining her, while Greg stood on the other side of the table.

"What do you think? Is she going to be, ok? What about the baby?"

"Greg, stop. Please. Get a glass of water and sit down. Give me a minute. Please."

He slumped in a nearby chair, while Mary Peyton used her stethoscope and then a penlight to look into her eyes. Her hands worked across Nok's head, neck, and eventually her stomach. She then turned to Greg.

"Greg, are you all right?"

"I am fine. What do you know?"

"We must get her to the hospital. The sooner the better, both for her and for the baby."

"Ok. Can we get a car at this hour?"

"Probably, but she shouldn't be in the back of one of those trucks. Call Albie. Have him come up in the Land Rover."

"But it will take several hours for him to get here, and you said sooner is better."

"I know. I know."

She was thinking. Calculating the risk to Nok and the baby in a local taxi—a mini-pickup truck with wood benches in the back for seats. That versus the time for Albie to make a trip here from Chiang Mai and then back to the University Hospital. Add the risk of driving on Highway 1 in the dark—even one-way—and nothing about this situation was promising.

"Call Albie. It is the best option. She can't take any more abuse. It is not good for her or the baby either. Bouncing and shaking in one of those trucks. Her heart is weak, and she has slipped into a coma. A concussion, for sure."

She cleaned up the dried blood on Nok's face, and Greg went to the back-office area and phoned Albie's house. Ping answered as usual, and she sounded annoyed until Greg explained quickly that there had been an accident, and he needed to talk with Albie. It took a few minutes for her to get him from upstairs and for him to make his way down to the phone. He had been asleep by the sound of his voice.

***

When he re-entered the examination room, Mary Peyton was connecting Nok to an IV.

"He's on his way. He did not want to talk about anything. Just said he would try to get Wes on his way out of town and hung up. How is she doing?"

"The same. The IV should help. Any idea how long she was there before you found her?"

"No."

"Who do you think did this?" she asked.

"Isn't it obvious? The Fat Man."

"But he can barely get around anymore."

"That's a farce. Besides, his son is the hammer. Fat Boy has been threatening Nok's grandfather for the longest time. I just never thought he would stoop to this."

Mary Peyton adjusted a sheet around Nok.

"You should clean up. I will put water on for tea. When was the last time you ate?"

"I am not hungry, but I will rinse off. I suppose I don't smell particularly good."

Sister Mary Peyton smiled as if to agree.

"I need to get out of this robe and put clothes on as well. Clean up and we can talk."

Greg went outside to his motorcycle, where he had items in a side pouch. He found a clean tee shirt. The street was quiet. He could see the night lamps by the entrance to the temple to his right. Wat Po was a simple village temple with only thirty or forty monks at any one time and paled compared to Wat Rong Khun, the White Temple. Located just past the city's center on the other side of Chiang Rai, the pristine White Temple was a profitable tourist attraction, with a massive reclining Buddha and beautiful gardens.

Near the temple were the river and the market area. The River Market would be closing by now and even the massage parlors would be attending to the last patrons of the day.

It occurred to him that Fat Boy could be in Chiang Rai as well. Probably drinking at the River Market with his Chinese friends or whoring in a massage parlor. It would not take much to find him. Then what? Confront him. To what end? He was a thug. They were all the same. Bullies. Yet, what could he do? Hit him. Teach him a lesson. Then what? Nok and her grandfather would not be any safer. No. Something else had to happen.

***

The clinic had an office area, minimal storage space, and two bedrooms beyond the large examination room. The kitchen area was the last room at the very back.

Greg had stayed in the visiting bedroom multiple times when it was too late to drive back to Chiang Mai. The clean sheets and a mosquito net without holes were a luxury. The toilet and bath area were typical Thai. Mary Peyton kept it as clean as possible, but the toilet was little more than a hole in the ground that led to a septic tank. The shower was a rain barrel and a bowl to scoop the water. She left a clean towel for him on the sink.

The mirror had a crack along the top. He needed a shave and a haircut too. He had always cared for himself that way, starting in high school and college. As a football player at the University of Michigan, he had little choice. *If you were not clean-shaven, you were not clean.* However, repeated injuries and two knee surgeries ruined his athletic career, and somewhere along the line, he became an actual student, an academic. A linguist. Something he never took seriously until his senior year, as his Oriental language skills were more a product of his ancestry than his acumen.

He could still taste the dirt in his mouth but had failed to collect his toothbrush from the saddlebag. He knew better than to use the tap water from the faucet to rinse. She would have boiled water in the kitchen.

He brushed his shaggy, sandy-brown hair with his fingers, disentangling the curls as best he could. He was convinced that a receding hairline was only a matter of time. Women said that they loved his hair. He never knew what that meant, and like many other things that women said, he learned not to ask for an explanation.

Where did all the years go? Can you feel old at twenty-nine? Thirty was just around the corner. He had a sinking feeling that his boyish good looks were already vanishing.

***

Sister Mary Peyton had changed into her religious garb—a long navy-blue skirt and a simple white blouse. She had not worn the customary veil since her arrival in Thailand and no longer wore any head covering while working in the clinic. But for her trip to Chiang Mai, she tied a small navy-blue scarf around her head. A small crucifix made from wood, rather than a precious metal, hung on a leather string around her neck.

When Greg re-entered the examination room, he found her talking with Prawaite, the owner of the automotive shop next door. Prawaite placed his hands together in prayer fashion, positioned them high near his face, and greeted Greg.

"*Sawadee krap*," he said and bowed slightly. The elevated position of his hands was a sign of respect for Greg.

Greg reciprocated the greeting, but his hands were much lower. He had grown to accept the distinction of status. It was far easier to get along by simply accepting the mores, regardless of whether you agreed with them.

"Khun Prawaite is going to monitor the clinic while I am away," she said, turning to Greg.

Prawaite was looking past her at Nok's body on the table. He wanted to ask about the patient, but he knew better. He smiled politely at Greg again.

"Can I leave my motorcycle with you?" Greg asked him in Thai.

"Absolutely. Anything you need. I can take care of it. Does it need any repair?"

"No. I just need a safe place for it."

In Thailand, you did not leave a vehicle unattended or unlocked. Sometimes, even that is not enough. Greg lost his first motorcycle while he was sleeping upstairs during a rainstorm. He was staying at a house in Tak and had not only parked the bike inside the house on the lower level but had chained it too. The pounding rain on the corrugated tin roof gave the robbers, *camoys*, all the cover that they needed.

Sister Mary Peyton's request to Prawaite to watch the clinic spoke to her clear understanding as well. She knew Prawaite would take the responsibility seriously to the point of sleeping on one of the examination tables at night and leaving his wife and family next door in their building.

While the two men left to move the motorcycle, Mary Peyton prepared the tea and had it ready when Greg returned.

"He is a nice guy. You are fortunate to have such a good neighbor. He will change the engine's oil, which is probably a good idea. I don't recall the last time I had that done."

"Prawaite is a mechanical genius. He repairs the *tuk-tuks* and taxi trucks, and everything imaginable. He is so clever. The tea is almost ready."

"Any change?" Greg asked.

"No. However, I looked at her lower body more carefully while you were next door, and I think her leg might be broken. Someone did a number on her. How did you find her?"

"Albie asked me to check on the buildings when I was in Ban Su. Her grandfather, T'ang, said that he had not seen her for a day or so. I am never sure what to believe from him when he has been working his opium pipe. He mumbles so much nonsense. I thought she was off with the others working in one of the more distant poppy fields."

"You saved her life. She would have died up there had someone not found her. I am amazed that you managed to carry her on the motorcycle and down that path in the dark. You have already had more than a couple of spills on that route. The last one was nasty and in the dark as well. Do you remember? You did not have a helmet on. Now that I think of it, I did not see your helmet tonight."

The look on her face conveyed her admonishment.

Greg caught himself before rubbing the back of his head where the twenty-plus stitches had been. He could see the helmet on the floor of the Research Station right now. After balancing Nok on the bike, he decided to forgo the helmet. She was right. It was foolish.

He tried to downplay the danger. "It was dry, and I think that there has been more four-wheel traffic than usual, so the dirt was firm."

"There are still *camoys* up there. Sabotaging the road by digging trenches and dropping logs to upend vehicles."

Greg thought it was amusing how she dropped Thai words into the middle of English sentences.

"They haven't bothered us for quite a while. Not since Albie became friends with them. He would make purchases for them and deliveries on his way up. And besides, they all know Nok and would help her anytime."

"What would any of us do without Albie? He is a saint."

"Part of that is true. Albert Saint Clair."

She smiled. "You know I didn't mean that. And besides, his full name is Albert Saint Clair IV."

"Yeah. I am staying at number four's house now and trust me, *saint* is a bit much."

They both laughed. Just a breath from the brutality that placed Nok in their hands.

"How do you do it, Mary P? Deal with the sick and suffering every day?"

"Not everyone is broken. We have plenty of healthy mothers who simply need help with their pregnancies. And scratches, bruises, and bellyaches that aren't so life-threatening."

She was minimizing her impact and her presence.

"I am going to check on Nok. I think I will place a splint on her leg, just in case I am correct, and the bone is cracked. X-rays will tell them at the hospital, but it will be safer while we are moving her. She is so tiny, but I think we can lay her comfortably on the back seat of the Land Rover, don't you?"

She declined his invitation to help and left him to tidy up the cups.

Greg looked at his watch. He hoped Albie was driving safely. He did not want to consider what they would do if something happened to him while trying to get here. What a mess. There was no other way to look at it.

CHAPTER TWO

Elliot had his non-governmental office in the same compound as the U.S. Consulate. He was packing boxes, preparing to leave Chiang Mai, when Greg and Albie arrived. Mary P had called Mama's Bakery Bar from the hospital to tell them that nothing had changed. Nok was in a coma and the baby seemed to be normal at this point. Nok's leg was broken as the nun suspected.

Albie had had enough and insisted that Greg arrange this meeting with his American friend Elliot. Albie was out of options. Everything he had tried had failed. He was convinced that if the Research Station had remained open, then Nok would not be in the hospital and certainly not in a coma. Her decision to help him had changed the paradigm in Ban Su, and Fat Man wanted his opium back. Only the Americans could help him now. Or so he thought.

Elliot was the consummate listener, so he sat quietly in the disarray of his own office—the shades forever drawn closed—and waited for Albie to finish. Greg wondered for a moment how old Elliot was and guessed forty, but in the shadows of this cloistered office, he could have been an undergrad at university. It was his patience, Greg thought, his unflappability that set him apart. That and his grasp of details.

"Look, I am sorry about your friend Nok, but what exactly do you think I can do?" he asked Albie.

"Get the Thai Border Patrol to return there. Step up the drug interdiction program in Ban Su. Stop Fat Man from regaining control of the region. He is getting more pernicious by the day."

"Albie, be serious. We cannot tell the Border Patrol to do anything."

"Bullocks! You trained them. Wes and his lot trained them. They use your planes."

Greg could see Elliot being Elliot. No emotion. Albie's suggestion about the Border Patrol was risible, even Greg knew the Border Patrol was the most corrupt of all the military and police. The planes that the Americans had indeed given them and then trained them to fly were logging more hours transporting large shipments of narcotics from the

Golden Triangle over to Northeast Thailand, Laos, and Vietnam than securing the border.

"You have a better chance of getting your Thai friends in Bangkok to help you. This is an NGO. Water purification is our expertise. Go next door to the State Department. They can lean on DEA. I have no standing here. I am packing right now to leave Chiang Mai."

"Bullocks," Albie repeated. He was undeterred and began detailing the precise crux of the problem, the history, and the demise of his project.

When he settled on Ban Su, Albie had the support of the Thai government made possible by his family connection to the Royal Palace. The region then saw an increase in Thai National Army personnel to ensure Albie's safety. Across the border, in Burma and Laos, and a little farther north in southern China, the renegade Chinese Nationalist Army of Chiang Kai-shek made their home. When additional Thai police and Thai army personnel appeared near and around Ban Su, the locals could no longer sell their opium to Fat Man and his Chinese mob for transport through Thailand. It was one thing for Fat Man to bribe a handful of Thai police, but quite another to buy off an entire regiment. Fat Man was flummoxed, and the locals found a new buyer in one of General Chiang's subordinates—General Xu, who, as Nok explained to Greg, paid better than Fat Man did.

However, maintaining a prolonged military presence along a nebulous border also presented too many opportunities for mishaps, confrontations, or brush fires with the Fifth Army led by General Xu or the ever-antagonistic Burmese army. It was better to do what Thailand had done for centuries. Avoid conflict, give the frontier its space, and let the opium warlords conduct their affairs as they had for so many years.

The result was a decision that maintaining the Agricultural Research Station, despite its lofty intentions, was not pragmatic. The Provincial Government ordered Albie out and reduced the presence of national soldiers. Now Fat Man wanted Ban Su to return to his control. Ban Su was in Thailand, and General Xu and his cronies had copious sources on the other side of the border in Burma, Laos, and China.

Elliot knew all this and more.

What Elliot could not tell Albie, however, was as far as the U.S. was concerned, the more opium that Chiang Kai-shek and his generals had, the better it was for their mission. The U.S. had already been supporting the Kuomintang and the Nationalist Army for years. Their interests had aligned. The moral conundrum of supporting heroin production bothered no one on the seventh floor at Langley, or if it did, they certainly did not let it stop them. What has always been clear was that instead of doing what is right, the important thing is not to be caught doing what is wrong.

Elliot offered neither solution nor suggestion and Albie, after more pronouncements about our moral responsibility, left in a huff, leaving Greg alone with Elliot.

"He needs to let this go," Elliot told Greg.

"I know."

"He is a great man. Accomplished. Successful. I get it. OBE from the Queen. He does not need all the torment that comes with this. Call it a loss. One rotten hand. Never lose everything on one bad bet."

Greg shrugged his shoulders. What could he add? Albie and three of his wealthy friends had created the International Conservation Institute headquartered in Stockholm. Each scientist had started a special project somewhere in the world: the rainforests in the Amazon, the Serengeti in Tanzania, the Great Barrier Reef in Australia, and the teak forests in the Golden Triangle. Albie, the geophysicist, had spent almost four years of his life on this project. From its conception to its endorsement from UNESCO and the London-based World Geographic Association to the collaboration with a shaky Thai government. He almost died during the initial exploration for an appropriate site. Even the sheer physical challenges of transporting building materials and the first plantings up the mountain to a desolate location did not deter him. Let alone the expense. All to save forests. All to convince indigenous tribes who had been slashing and burning the teak and bamboo forests of these rugged hills for decades, if not centuries, to enhance the soil for their only source of income—opium, that growing fruit trees was better for the long-term well-being of the planet's environment.

Why would anyone so foolish to embark on that mission, to spend tens of thousands of dollars of his own money, now stop because others did not agree? Right or wrong, as far as Albie was concerned, he was still the dealer, and he held the cards.

"I am on the first plane tomorrow morning to Bangkok. We can grab a beer at the Night Market and talk some more. Talk to him, Greg. Before something more serious than the injuries to that woman occur.

You know better than most that the Golden Triangle is a ticking bomb and Albie does not need to be the fuse."

Elliot was not one for hyperbole. At least in Greg's experience with him, it had always been just the opposite.

Greg agreed to meet Elliot around nine near the restaurants along the klong. He then headed out to find Albie, stop at the hospital, and then get back to the house for a power nap. He was exhausted and knew that a beer with Elliot would not end with just one.

***

Sister Mary Peyton was still at the hospital when Greg arrived.

"You just missed Albie," she said.

"How is Nok?" he asked.

"Not good. The doctor is worried about her heart."

"What have you been doing?"

"I have been helping where I can. Cleaning in some cases. I do not think that I have ever seen Albie this upset."

Albie and Sister Mary Peyton first met when one of the hill tribe members cut himself badly during the building of the Research Station. Albie took him to Chiang Rai and the clinic, and Sister Mary Peyton patched him up. Unbeknownst to most, he had been subsidizing her clinic ever since.

"He will be all right," said Greg. "Nok means a great deal to him. Do you know how often he tried to get her to leave the hill tribe village and move to Chiang Mai? He said that he could get her a position at the British Consulate. She could translate or do something. If not that, then something else. Anything to break the cycle. Get out of the mountains and improve her station in life."

"She would never leave her grandfather, would she?" Sister Mary Peyton suggested.

"No. Nok told me that maybe when he was gone, she would consider it, but T'ang relied on her."

"Do you have any idea who the father of Nok's baby might be?" she asked.

"No. I thought you might. I figured you examined her over the last few months."

"I saw her twice since the pregnancy began. The first time she came with Albie and the most recent was about a month ago. She walked down from the village. Can you imagine? Took her the entire day. I know she had to leave at first light to get to Chiang Rai before dark."

"How long are you going to stay in Chiang Mai?" Greg asked.

"I will go over to St. Michael's for the night and leave tomorrow," she said.

"Are you going to play any tennis?" he asked.

It was a standing joke between them. St. Michael's was originally the residence of a wealthy French diplomat who built a clay tennis court behind the house. It remains in excellent condition and the priest who lives at St. Michael's plays on it regularly.

"No. I think I will pass this time," she said, smiling. Greg loved her smile.

"How will you get back to Chiang Rai?" Greg asked.

"Albie said he would take me. Do you want to go? Your motorcycle is there."

"No. Not tomorrow. I will use Albie's motorcycle for now. He never rides it here in Chiang Mai, and he is always offering it to me. If I miss you tomorrow, then I will see you in a few days. Thanks again for everything, for all your help."

She hugged him, then pulling back slightly, gripped him on both shoulders.

"Father will say a Mass at five this evening. You know you are welcome."

"Thanks. Once was enough."

CHAPTER THREE

Scooters, increasingly ubiquitous, scurried past on the narrow road that separated the *klong* from the outdoor tables on the sidewalk. Working-class men sat smoking on the edge of the waterway's concrete embankment. Everyone in Chiang Mai must have decided to patronize the restaurants that lined the Night Market, or so Greg thought as he hunted for a place to park his motorcycle.

"It's the weather," said Elliot as Greg sat down. "Reminds me of Boulder, Colorado. Shorts and sweatshirts. Beer?"

Elliot signaled the server.

Greg had never been to Colorado, but their university football team, the Buffaloes, had played in Ann Arbor. He was in between surgeries then. He played in that game, as well as in a fair portion of the season before another helmet to the outside of his good leg sent him under the knife.

"Did you win?"

"We did." And he never played again, although he expected Elliot already knew that.

The server who arrived with the beers knew Elliot and unsurprisingly settled into the empty chair at their table. The server's dialect was unmistakably northern Thai. Elliot's language skills were more than adequate and he leaned into the conversation, leaving Greg to watch the scooter traffic and a truck with a large sign and ancient loudspeakers blaring a promotion for tomorrow night's *Muay Thai* fight.

The server eventually asked Greg if he wanted anything to eat and both men ordered the *Pad Thai.* Greg had chicken and Elliot tofu.

"Always get the house's specialty, right? You seldom go wrong with that."

Greg did not respond. The bright fluorescent lights strung above the tables were suddenly annoying him. The Thai music, scratchier and louder than usual, blared from inside the shop. The onset of a headache. He looked down at his beer and rubbed his eyes. Elliot's voice reached him as if it were across the *klong* and not at the table.

"You need to go home. I am not sure why you are staying in Chiang Mai anymore."

"Albie asked me to stay. Offered me a place to live behind his house in a guesthouse."

"Servants' quarters."

"They are nice quarters and compared to the huts and hovels you had me stay in, I would call it the Ritz. Albie wanted a translator for his meetings with the Thai officials. He no longer trusts anything they say, let alone some poor translation."

"I cannot help you anymore. You are off the payroll. The Fulbright grant is over and so is the cover. It was perfect. Only one cut out. You were great. Did a fantastic job. Stayed safe. Now go. Go home before you become like Wes, or one of these other expats, or even worse, like me."

It was always so simple for Elliot. Just move people around like chess pieces. Everything planned. Nothing left to chance. Except perhaps when he played cards.

The server brought them their food and a tray with condiments including the fiery *nam prik,* along with more beer. Elliot piled on the hot pepper. Greg's headache eased once he had something to eat. They were becoming more frequent, but he kept that to himself.

Greg considered Elliot immune to such ailments. Elliot did not appear any different, any older than when they first met. Healthy and handsome. Charming with well-timed smiles. An easy rapport that engages strangers and invites servers to join you at a table. A soft, almost melodious timbre in his speech—regardless of which language he chose. A pied piper. Always dressed nicely, never over the top, but unmistakably fine dress shirts and well-tailored slacks.

Elliot's recruitment of Greg started at the basketball court in the old gym at Oxford's Christ Church College. On Tuesday and Friday nights, a group, mostly graduate students like Greg, played full-court pickup basketball. Visitors popped in now and then, so the arrival of another American was not surprising. What was surprising was how good a player he was. Most of the *lads* had played sports in their youth, and these basketball runs served mostly to burn the calories they would consume at the pub after the game.

Elliot did little to set himself apart from the level of play. He had no reason to exhibit his prowess. As Greg realized later, it was just the opposite. He wanted nothing more than to blend into the flow and facilitate the success of others. Except once, when Greg was convinced that he alone saw the magic act.

During a fast break, a two-on-three, when good judgment would suggest that Elliot pull back and reset the offense, Elliot dribbled the ball directly toward Greg, who was standing in a defensive position in the lane. It seemed foolish to risk an offensive charge, but as Greg held his ground, even reached to swat away the ball, which was immediately between him and Elliot, the ball disappeared, and Elliot slithered past Greg without touching him and softly laid the ball up against the backboard and into the hole. The ball did not go around his back, a move Greg had seen many times, but disappeared on the dribble itself.

Later, at the pub, Elliot told Greg that he saw Pete Maravich do the same thing. Rather than collect the ball in front of you after your last dribble, you dribble it backward between your legs and grab it with your opposite hand and bring it back around, and then simply up against the board. *Not that difficult*—except if you are at full speed.

They talked little that first evening at the pub. The Quill was extremely popular and noisy, especially on Friday nights. Elliot left after only one pint with an attractive redheaded woman, a teaching don, whom Greg recognized but had never met. Mathematics, if he remembered correctly.

He did not appear at their next game on Tuesday, but on the following Friday, Elliot arrived after the game had started and waited for his opportunity to rotate in. This time, he played on the same team as Greg. It was then that Greg realized how easily the game came to Elliot. Neither Greg nor Elliot left early from the Quill that night, and as the evening wore on and more pints arrived, they found themselves alone at a table, talking at length despite the din of the place.

Near the end of the evening, he asked Greg if he played poker, and if he might be interested in playing in a *garage* game the following night. A friendly game at someone's house nearby. Greg was non-committal. It was then that Elliot suggested drinks at eight. He could decide after that either way.

They met at the Governor's, a pub on Joyce Street. A bearded man—not much older than Greg—was wearing a placard over his chest near the entrance. *Repent. The end is near.* Last chance to walk away, but he knew that once he had agreed to meet Elliot, he had already decided.

The pitch came after the first pint.

"Your Rhodes scholarship is expiring, if I understand the timing correctly. Do you have any plans? Perhaps you will go back to the States and teach somewhere? Maybe you want to work on a Ph.D.?"

Greg had little interest in teaching and even less in continuing for another degree. He had barely engaged himself with his studies at Oxford. He spent more time chasing women, drinking, and occasionally exercising than he did at his tutorials or lectures. The School of Oriental Languages had introduced him to all types of linguistic experts, but his proficiency in any of the languages that he possessed arrived from some God-given gift to hear the mellifluous jangle of syllables but a few times and then assimilate them into his consciousness. He did not learn languages. He absorbed them. *Osmosis* was what one teaching fellow said. A few beers with his classmates or dons taught him more than hours of lectures, tapes, or books.

He was like those musicians who hear the music before they touch the keys on the piano. He had an ear for languages. That was all. No big deal. He dismissed all characterizations of genius. Child prodigies abounded in Oxford, wizards of every sort, and he was never one of them. In fact, he considered himself a bit of a phony by accepting the Rhodes, but he settled into a dissolute, debauched, and amoral lifestyle, and such thoughts dissipated.

Elliot was correct. He would soon have to find gainful employment.

***

It was simple. Nothing nefarious. No cloaks and daggers. No subterfuge or sabotage. In fact, by all appearances, boring and mundane.

He was to be a recipient of the prestigious Fulbright Scholarship with a plan to study the hill tribe people of Thailand—focusing on the western regions of the country. Visit them, take pictures, and then author a book about their customs, mores, their history, and their current condition, whatever resonated most profoundly with him. Then go home and become a published author.

There was little training even required. How to use an SLR camera, drop-off locations for his film and his notebooks, and strategies for sending messages if anything went sideways. The carapace of deceit almost non-existent. Two years. No more. Not unlike a Peace Corps volunteer, except with a hefty payout.

***

In the beginning, Elliot arranged escorts for him, guides to take him up the mountains, and even introduce him to the tribal leaders and elders of the villages. He would stay a few days or a week and return to a nearby city, where arrangements had been made for a place to stay. He edged his way northward toward the Golden Triangle. After several months, his repeated and expanded trips became common knowledge among the tribes. Their initial hesitancy to consider him yet another spook poking around the border regions faded.

Even the real spooks thought he was a harmless academic, as their own research and physical tracking of him never proved otherwise. A perfect backstory. No fiction needed.

He became a welcome guest in one village after another by endearing himself with his ability to converse so easily as he sat for hours around a fire, or opium pipe, or bottle, listening and telling stories. Doing precisely as Elliot directed. *Watch, listen, and report.* It was his only job. *Anything more and you will get yourself killed. You don't have to make sense of anything. Gather fragments. Let the analysts put the picture together. Take pictures. You cannot take enough pictures.*

After a while, he moved as easily as the hill tribe people did between the porous borders, photographing road constructions, military movements by the Burmese and the Chinese Nationalist Armies, even snaps of other spooks, and, of course, the beautiful indigenous people at work, harvesting their poppy fields.

Elliot's advice was *never stay too long* in one place, and now he was repeating it yet again.

CHAPTER FOUR

"Jack has a new dealer. She is a knockout. It is his latest strategy to entice some of Fat Man's clientele to his place. I told him I would stop by tonight."

Lewcharlemwong was Jack's real name but attracting *farangs* with a less Thai appellation proved easier. It was the same reason Fat Man embraced his nickname for his gambling den.

Jack's was crowded. Six poker tables and not an empty seat. Eight blackjack stations with a robust business. The roulette wheel teeming with enthusiastic gamblers. And a raucous craps table. Only the bar had empty seats. Jack found them there as they settled into their first drink.

As one might expect of a gaming house owner, Jack was a convivial sort. Greg knew he spoke English, but tonight he spoke to them in his native tongue.

"I have been looking for you all night. I am so happy you came."

"You are packed tonight," said Elliot.

"Yes. We have made tonight a special occasion, and like foreign establishments, all drinks are free tonight. Until midnight. I had to draw the line somewhere." He laughed loudly at his own humor and then leaned closer to Elliot, almost whispering.

"Are you truly leaving tomorrow for good?"

"I am afraid so. I will miss you and Chiang Mai."

"Then we must make your last night memorable. I have been saving you a place at the table in the back. Others, who wanted entry grumbled, but what can they do? I am still the boss, yes. Come. I want you to see Preeya."

The back room was for high rollers, and Jack charged a sizable cover to enter the room and gain a seat at the table. The house also took a rake of two percent from every pot. His dealers extracted that more deftly than a pickpocket could. Drinks were always on the house back here—even past midnight.

The smoke that choked the main hall did not filter back here, nor did the din and bright lights. Here the light was soft, welcoming, and warmly fixed over the main table.

Your eyes went right to her when you entered.

She wore a sleeveless white dress with a modest décolletage. A white amulet hung around her neck. Long, wavy, black hair curled around her slender shoulders. Her face was angelic, incandescent. She was everything that made Northern Thai women the most beautiful in the world.

Jack ushered Elliot to the promised open seat, but now with Greg's arrival as well, he created an additional place directly on her left.

Greg had no business playing poker at this table, but Elliot had staked him to five hundred dollars in chips and insisted that he enjoy the evening as his treat.

Greg was bewitched. He would steal a glance at her face whenever he could but tried not to stare. He fixed his eyes on her hands, as they seemed to deal the cards without touching them. He could smell her perfume—spiced, feral. He felt himself tremble when the curve of her slender bare arm crossed near him to reach for discards. He wanted to grab it. Touch it. Just once. Brush his hand against the smooth, immaculate skin.

She was serene the entire time. When she spoke, it was a whisper, a sigh, for the gamblers to make their bets, pass, request cards, or fold. No one dared to disturb her calm. She was too perfect. Unblemished. Untouchable. And with every passing moment was exponentially more beautiful.

Any chance that he had of concentrating on his cards was lost. In less than an hour, he was out of chips and relinquished his seat at the table. Meanwhile, Elliot was the same Elliot that Greg had seen since their first game in England. Patient. Unruffled. Moving chips in with little emotion and collecting them with even less. Not a gesture, never a tell. Just Elliot being Elliot.

Greg did not note the other gamblers until he busted and was sitting next to Jack at the small bar. The server at that bar spoke in hushed whispers to Jack as different gamblers won or lost. Two *farangs*, one blonde Dutchman and a pock-faced Australian, seemed to hold steady. A gaunt, Chinese man was losing big, and a drunk Thai was doing just as poorly. Meanwhile, Elliot's stacks of chips grew ceaselessly.

Greg was content to watch her.

***

It was three in the morning when they left. An all-night noodle shop welcomed them.

"What did you think of the dealer?" Elliot asked.

Greg did all he could to keep a straight face.

"I thought she was," and after a long pause, "efficient."

They both laughed.

"Have you ever heard the Chinese expression, *Qí hǔ nán xià*?"

"No. Not that I can recall," answered Greg.

Elliot repeated it and asked if Greg could translate it.

Greg put down his chopsticks and answered.

"When you are riding a tiger…"

"That's right. It is the beginning of one of hundreds of Chinese forewarnings. Do you know the rest of it?"

"No idea."

"When you are riding a tiger, the hard part is getting off."

"Your point?"

"Go home, before you find yourself on that tiger."

"So, you said, more than once. Where are you going from here?"

It was a bit out of line to ask such a question of Elliot, but even more surprising to Greg was when Elliot answered.

"I am going to the Northeast. It's a nightmare over there. Refugees pouring across the Thai border to avoid genocide in Cambodia. Some assets, some of them pretending to be, and so many others are just afraid. Everyone knows that the ones who are sent back to Cambodia will probably die."

"What will you do?"

"Interview people. Try to decide who stays and who goes back."

"How?"

"I am not sure. I will tell them that whatever lie they told to get past the first hurdle, to make sure that they keep telling the same lie."

"Why do you do it?"

"I ask that more than you think. Mostly, you do what you are good at."

They were quiet for a moment, and it suddenly occurred to Greg that he did not see Elliot leave with his money.

"Where are your winnings? I never saw you cash out."

"I left it all with Jack."

"Jack?"

"Yep. Safer than any Thai bank I know. I must go. I still have items to pack and the plane is at eight a.m. I will get one of the *samlors* to take me. Look, if you get in trouble, or if you need something, then see Jack."

"Jack?"

"Yes. He will help you. He will get you what you need. Just tell him I sent you. No code words, no tradecraft, no spy stuff. Just tell him I sent you."

"Is he an asset?"

"No. Not at all. He is a good friend. A good guy too. You can trust him. There is no one else in Chiang Mai that you should trust. No one."

"And you?"

"I am off the grid once I leave here. As I said, I cannot help you."

They walked out of the noodle shop, and Elliot signaled for the *samlo*r driver who was across the street.

They shook hands and Elliot was gone.

Greg headed up the street to the main road on Albie's motorcycle. He stopped at the intersection as three loud scooters approached from the right. The driver on the second scooter was the thickset Fat Boy, easily recognizable by his physique and by his partially shaved head and braided pigtail. He recognized Greg immediately, and as Fat Boy drove through the intersection, he smiled malevolently and made a slashing movement with his thumb across his throat.

Just minutes ago, Greg had left his drink half-filled on the table. Now suddenly, his throat was dry, and he realized it was fear.

CHAPTER FIVE

For the last few months, since moving into Albie's guesthouse, Greg had lapsed into late nights—mostly talking and drinking with Albie or Wes—and late mornings, recovering. Beautifully crafted teak shutters kept even the most persistent morning light at bay, and the single-unit air conditioner—although noisy—created a comfortable sleeping environment. Therefore, absent any pressing commitments he made the previous day to assist Albie, he again indulged in the indolence that marked his Oxford days.

It was not surprising that he woke thinking of Preeya. If he lacked for anything these days, it was the carnal pleasures that he had grown so accustomed to in England. However, his trekking in the hills for the past two-plus years somehow restored his sense of purpose, and he had become a bit of an ascetic, a celibate. Massage parlors abounded in even the smallest of towns where he landed. Bangkok, where he rendezvoused frequently and made deliveries to dead-letter boxes, offered an almost infinite number of lascivious and salacious opportunities. Yet, he abstained. He convinced himself that he loved all the women he knew, even the ones whose names he could not remember, and believed a visit to any den of iniquity spoke of turpitude and not love.

The mountains had changed him. He found himself genuinely engaged with the hill people and their circumstances. He disagreed with those who called it their plight. They had a hard life, but it was a viable lifestyle, and they persevered with a joy that he had never witnessed. If he ever wrote the story, he would explain that they were a special culture, valuable, like any small indigenous tribe or ethnic group. Albie understood this as well, and their burgeoning friendship was, at least in Greg's opinion, borne of this.

That is why the attack on Nok distressed them both so much. She was so blameless.

He shook himself awake and showered, suddenly determined to get to the hospital immediately. Running water and a water heater were yet other luxuries available in Albie's residence. In the downstairs kitchen, he found fresh fruit—papaya and pineapple—sliced and on a plate in his refrigerator, compliments of Ping.

As a courtesy, she never entered the second floor of his bungalow when he was there and would clean only when she knew he was away. Albie roamed as he chose, so it was no surprise to find a note on the table explaining that he had borrowed Greg's camera equipment stored in the den upstairs. Greg then looked in the refrigerator where he kept his unused film and discovered it was gone.

The note said nothing else.

***

Ping stopped him as he was rolling Albie's motorcycle out of the shed.

"*Bai nai*?" she asked. A typical friendly Thai greeting and an inquiry as to where he was going, but today fraught and troubled.

Her daughter Dao was in her arms and greeted him, but she used her newly learned English salutation with a beaming smile of satisfaction. Greg said *hello* back to her and then answered Ping in Thai.

"To the hospital. To see Nok," he explained.

"Albie left early this morning to go there."

"Did he say anything? Where else he might go?"

"He said he was taking Sister back to Chiang Rai."

Dao squirmed out of her mother's arms and ran to her Aunt Dang, who came into sight, walking up the long pathway from the entrance gate. One of the security guards carried her packages.

"No running," her mother shouted after her.

Greg learned of Ping and her relationship with Sister Mary Peyton shortly after he arrived in Chiang Mai. Mary P persuaded Albie to take in Ping. She was barely eighteen years old and pregnant. The nun convinced Ping to have the baby. Ping became the housekeeper and caretaker of Albie's new house in Chiang Mai. When the baby girl was born, Ping's older sister Dang appeared at the door to help. She never left. The three of them have been living with Albie ever since.

"Only that. Just Chiang Rai?" Greg asked.

"No, nothing else. He left in a hurry. He did not sleep well last night. I was not happy."

Greg squinted as sunlight glistened on the shards of broken glass that covered the top edges of the estate's walls, and he put on his sunglasses. He knew that Albie and the much younger Ping had long shared the same bed, but that was of little interest to him right now. What he wanted to know was why Albie took the camera and where he was going.

Beyond the walls that encircled a house so grand that guards were at the front gate and patrolled the perimeter, and beyond those same walls topped with glass shards to deter intruders and to protect Ping, Dao, and Dang—but could not protect Nok—the distant clatter of Chiang Mai traffic sounded. Somewhere in that traffic was Albie.

"Everything will be fine," he lied without hesitation, lied because somewhere in that traffic was not only Albie but also the malicious Fat Boy. He started the motorcycle and headed down the gravel path past a waving Dao.

CHAPTER SIX

Students were crisscrossing the campus as he navigated his way on the narrow, two-lane road through Chiang Mai University. U.S. students would have cut paths on the well-manicured, grassy lawns, but the Thai students conscientiously used the paved sidewalks. The young Thai men sported crisp, white shirts and short haircuts, clinging to the rule that defined their early schooldays. Long dress pants had replaced their khaki shorts. The Thai coeds, however, seemed more willing to discard their schoolgirl regimen, eagerly abandoning their long navy skirts for shorter versions, as well as their modesty for their budding sexuality.

The CMU campus and enrollment were small and paled compared to both Oxford and Ann Arbor in size and scope of study. The student protests occurring in Bangkok and at the sprawling Thammasat University did not resonate with this mostly Northern Thai student population. Greg would have characterized it as an ivory tower, except for Elliot's cautionary notice. *The place is a rat's nest of spooks. Brits, Germans, French, even Canadians, and that Russian couple pretending to be Dutch. Stay away from there. Academia is the most overused cover. One more reason to applaud what you did.*

Three young women at a crosswalk waved at him in unison as he passed through an intersection. He could hear their laughter as he revved his engine in response. He remembered why he enjoyed graduate school so much and pulled away slowly from this dangerous, unabridged, female sexuality.

The hospital took the smile from his face. Modern in every way, he thought, but the antiseptic atmosphere spoke more of illness, even death, than healing. Nok lay motionless, connected to tubes, cords, and sensors. Monitors measured her heart rate and other vitals. Only an oxygen clip under her nose distracted from her tranquil countenance. The nurses attending Nok were exceptional. They were in and out of the private room, which Albie had arranged for her, multiple times every hour, but in their absence, a sepulchral silence reigned. One gray-haired nurse encouraged Greg to talk to her. *You can read to her from one of the books that the nun left if you like. She needs encouragement.*

The book on top was *The Selected Poems of Thomas Merton.*

The doctor's name was Somchai. He arrived in mid-afternoon with a medical resident, whose name Greg heard, then forgot immediately. At first, the doctor was reluctant to discuss anything with Greg, but when Greg explained his relationship to Nok and to Albie, who was paying the bills, as well as Greg's obligation to travel back to Ban Su and inform her grandfather, the doctor seemed to understand.

He asked Greg to leave the room and allow them to complete more tests. After which, he would be happy to talk with Greg.

Greg wandered the halls and then thought about getting a drink in the canteen on the main floor. His head ached again, and he thought coffee and sugar would help. A pleasant woman was alone in the room working behind the counter chopping vegetables near her *wok* and seemed disappointed that Greg wanted only an iced coffee. She mixed rich coconut milk and sugar water with the dark coffee, and poured it into a plastic bag with ice, before tying it off with a rubber band. A plastic straw was squeezed through a small hole near the top. Greg assured himself that ice from a hospital had to be safer than ice from a street vendor.

The tests took longer than Greg expected, and he sat impatiently near the nurses' station with his eyes fixed on Nok's door. He hated hospitals. Everyone here wants to be healed, everyone wants to be saved, and everyone is failing. Survival must be possible. He had scars—across his scalp, on both his knees, so maybe Nok can awaken with just scars as well. He squeezed his eyes shut, trying to press the throbbing from his head. There is a scar inside there too, he considered, and a sense of hopelessness invaded his soul. We are all falling apart, slowly, and inescapably, and do not need help from men like Fat Man and Fat Boy to speed up our demise.

***

Dr. Somchai sat in his office chair and unbuttoned his white lab coat, revealing his blue and red Chicago Bears logo tie. Greg commented immediately, and Somchai happily explained that his connection to the Bears began during his residency at Rush University Hospital in Chicago. He spent one season on the sidelines, which luckily coincided with Gayle Sayre's first year on the Bears. *Those were exciting times. All that seemed long ago*, he mused, and he has been here in Chiang Mai for the last five years.

"Nok is stable. She remains in a coma, and that is not ideal, but her pregnancy creates possibilities for complications. There is considerable stress on both the mother and the child."

He paused, clearly searching for the correct words. He certainly would not speculate on hypotheticals.

"In time, the baby will come to term, and we will have to make decisions. One question that I have for you or Mr. Saint Clair would be who directs us in these decisions. Is there a family member or father of the child with whom we can speak? You said the grandfather lives in the northern hills."

"He does. I don't see him making the trip here for a consultation. He is…elderly and infirm," Greg lied, more about the infirmity than the age.

"And the father of the baby?" Doctor Somchai asked.

"Don't know."

"Very well. My suggestion is that you visit the office downstairs and establish a point of contact for us. In the United States, there would be multiple legal hurdles, health care power of attorney included, but we are more flexible here in Thailand, and there is a clear understanding for us to deal with itinerants."

The word *itinerants* upset Greg. He considered it pejorative, demeaning.

"Do you have any idea how old Nok might be?" Dr. Somchai then asked.

"No."

"Any previous children? Any illnesses or diseases?"

Greg knew the doctor was trying to do his job, but either his tone or Greg's headache was getting the better of him.

"She has no other children that I know of and no diseases either," he said, raising his voice slightly.

The doctor missed or ignored Greg's irritation.

"She is not a young woman, and that presents challenges as well. The hospital has an excellent maternity ward and exceptionally good obstetricians, and my recommendation is to move her from the ICU to that wing of the hospital."

"Fine. Great. Thank you."

Doctor Somchai smiled weakly.

Greg went downstairs to an oversized business office occupied by an oversized ego, where he signed poorly translated documents, not the least of which was one naming him Nok's executor and caretaker. But, as he walked out of the building, started his motorcycle, and then placed his sunglasses over his tired eyes, it occurred to him that the hospital had misspelled *executor* using *er* and not *or,* and the dyspeptic hopelessness that had abated while reading poetry to Nok now returned.

CHAPTER SEVEN

Wes drove languidly, but fast. Sunlight reflected on his customary aviator sunglasses as he sped past a farmer's cart pulled by a water buffalo. Minutes later, he passed a wobbling truck filled with passengers in the rear bed, and although he came close to hitting an oncoming scooter carrying a woman, who rode sidesaddle behind the driver, Wes remained unfazed. The retrofitted army jeep shouted U.S. Army despite its changes, and Greg knew Wes had absolutely no problem with that perception.

"I am going to tell you something, schoolboy. You might think it's insane, but I swear to God it is the truth."

Greg stared out through his dark sunglasses at the rice paddies that lined Highway 1. Wes had been talking nonstop from the time that he collected Greg at Albie's house just before daybreak. When Wes arrived, Ping was outside the entrance gates making merit with donations to a quintet of local monks, who paraded with their rice baskets each morning from Wat Doi Kham through this affluent section of Chiang Mai. Unlike Albie, Ping disliked Wes. She would never say anything to Albie, and she would always be as polite as she could be when Wes was at the house, but Greg had spent enough time with her to understand her true feelings.

Wes was a "know-it-all" and had an opinion—if not an outright bias—about most everything, which he shared unfiltered and unfailingly with anyone within hearing distance. He was a large man, with thick hands and muscular arms, burly, but not overweight. His short, salt and pepper hair, always freshly trimmed, declared former military, and if anyone had any doubt, then he only needed to read the dagger tattoo on Wes' right forearm. *Si vis pacem, para bellum.* He had not shaved this morning and at sunrise already sported a five o'clock shadow.

When Greg first met Wes, he felt much like Ping did, but after spending time with Wes, and especially with Wes and Albie together, Greg's opinion softened. Wes displayed a profound respect for Albie.

His nickname for Albie was *the Professor*. Greg also came to know that Albie trusted Wes implicitly and confided much in him.

Greg never reached that level of trust but settled on a benevolent tolerance of Wes' voluminous assertions and jokingly characterized him as the original expat.

Ping was entrenched and would have none of it, and Greg wondered if her reasons went beyond Wes' verbosity to something darker, to something she knew about his past, something that blackened his soul, or worse, signaled some capacity for evil. Did the shadow on his face speak to something darker or more sinister?

"Heroin," Wes continued, "was originally considered a miracle drug. Bayer pharmaceutical products in Germany created the name heroin for the chemical compound diacetylmorphine, which is the organic morphine from the opium poppy bonded chemically with acetic anhydride, a common industrial acid. I am being serious. In the early 1900s, the American Medical Association approved the use of heroin in place of morphine. Not for everything, mind you, but for certain medical instances."

One of the best things about Wes and his lectures was that he did not require engagement. You never had to answer. He enjoyed occasional questions because they enlarged his opportunity to pontificate, but he was equally content to continue uninterrupted, convinced that everything he had to say was of importance and or of interest.

"Do you know how they make heroin? There are two stages. The first step is to get the opium converted into morphine. This process is not overly complicated, but you still need a chemist of sorts. Most any hack can learn this…"

A local farmer carrying a basket on his bicycle approached them in the opposite lane, followed by a speeding truck, which when passing the bicycle veered close to Wes' jeep before returning to his side of the highway. Neither the truck nor Wes slowed down. A forever game of chicken on Highway 1. Wes took a cigarette from the glove compartment. Greg could see multiple packs of French cigarettes and knew a gun was at the bottom of the storage unit. Wes lit the cigarette and kept talking. His voice was tedious and distant.

Greg was not listening. His thoughts turned to the first time he saw poppy fields and the many times since that he watched, even photographed the hill tribe people—men and women and children, descendants of mountaineers, tough, rugged, stubborn, a mixed race of Thai, Burmese, Chinese—planting their crop in the early fall and then harvesting the crop some three months later. Wes was talking about chemists, but there was no science for Nok and her friends—only backbreaking work, tilling the soil on rocky hillsides and removing boulders, when possible, to expand the plot before scattering tiny poppy seeds. No measured distribution—just experienced hands casting the tiny seeds that would provide their income.

Bright pinks, vivid purples, and stunningly beautiful white flowers bloomed on the green stalks. Nok told him she sometimes grew sad watching the colored petals mature and fall off, leaving a small green seedpod, a bulb about the size of an egg.

Those were extraordinary days for Greg, alone on remote mountainsides with his new friends. Away from the chaos of civilization. At T'ang's urging, Nok taught Greg how to use a specially designed, curved knife to slice parallel incisions across the surface of the bulb. The plants had tubular stems and ranged in height from two to four feet, so the cutting required a deft touch and constant bending, leaning, twisting, and inevitably sweating. The jagged terrain, more suitable for slighter bodies—like women and children—made the chore even more strenuous. They laughed and joked with Greg as he fumbled with the task. After less than an hour, he was exhausted. He could not decide if his back or his fingers ached more. He collapsed in a heap on a steep grade, and they laughed and continued working.

A white sap oozed out of each incision, and as it congealed on the surface of the pod, it changed color to a deep brown, the recognizable hue of opium. Nok and her crew scraped each bulb carefully using a different tool, a dull knife, and patiently collected the opium into sacks hanging on leather strings around their necks.

"Morphine to heroin, on the other hand, requires an expert chemist." Wes was talking at the windshield. "Not just a hack, but a chef, a pro, a real cooker. This process is not overly complicated either, but it is dangerous and needs to be precise. Albie knows all this. You know he studied chemistry at Cambridge…"

Wes detailed how the chemist meticulously mixes equal parts of morphine with acetic anhydride in a glass flask and then heats it at exactly one hundred and eighty-five-degrees Fahrenheit to create an impure form of heroin, called diacetylmorphine.

"After that, there are three stages to purify the heroin…"

Nok said that one of her earliest memories was as a child, five or six years old, riding on a packhorse carrying sacks of opium down the mountain to Chiang Rai. Her grandfather led her horse and taught her the names of trees and birds. Such trips ended when she was quite young. Now they cook the opium closer to home. It made it easier for them and for the Chinese buyers. No one has to carry opium as far, and the morphine, once dried and packed for processing, was only a fraction of the weight compared to the opium, so transporting morphine is easier too.

"The last step creates the treasure, and it is the last step that is the most dangerous. After the water and chloroform, and then the sodium carbonate addition, and then a delicate process with a suction pump, followed by alcohol and charcoal purification, comes the final mix. If the chemist makes any mistake now, then he will blow up the entire lab. The danger comes with the ether gas.

"You start by mixing the heroin you have at this point with alcohol in a large flask—again carefully measured. Then you add the precise amount of ether and hydrochloric acid to the solution. Slowly white flakes form, and the scientist filters out the flakes and dries them. Then bingo, you have the infamous no. 4 heroin. A lily-white powder that runs eighty-to-ninety percent pure." Pretty flowers transformed into death.

CHAPTER EIGHT

Sister Mary Peyton was busy when Greg and Wes arrived. A mother and her two young boys were in her examination room. The older boy complained of chest pains, and both had been vomiting, and judging from the stains on their teeth, they had been experimenting with betel nut chew. Mary P was explaining to the mother and to the boys that kidney disease, abnormal heart rates, and other side effects are possible with this stimulant.

"Your teeth and gums will be ruined as well, and you will lose your beautiful smiles," she said.

She made them promise her they would not use the chew anymore before dismissing them from her presence and giving the mother instructions for their diet over the next few days.

"If they are not feeling better in two or three days, or if any other symptoms occur, come back immediately. However, I think they will both be fine."

***

Looking back, Sister Mary Peyton regretted not stopping Albie. Wes was irate, insulted even, that Albie had embarked on such a mission without consulting him and without his protection, and Greg lamented he lacked Elliot's perspicacity to piece together the obvious.

Albie detailed his plan to Mary P while driving back to Chiang Rai earlier that week. After dropping the nun at her clinic, he then headed up the mountain. He knew that the Research Station was the perfect transit intersection and the ultimate objective for Fat Man. Set in a low depression—not quite a valley—the modest building had a view of the narrow dirt path that led to Ban Su. Another road snaked around hills and led down the mountain to Chiang Rai, and finally, two slightly wider paths led toward Mae Salong in one direction and Mae Sai in another. The level and once-tilled field to the west of the building stretched low and flat for just enough length to land a small aircraft once his dying plants and trees were gone. Albie had selected the site after an arduous survey precisely for its geographic and strategic location.

For all of Wes' talk about expert chemists and labs that transformed morphine into heroin, the Fat Man's immediate need was a nearby locale and makeshift lab to cook the opium into the morphine first, and then transport it to a sophisticated lab environment for the heroin-making process. General Xu had such labs neatly positioned deeper inside Burma and Laos, but Fat Man needed his makeshift lab in Thailand, away from Xu's Fifth Army and Burmese warlords, like Zhang Qitu. Those groups were building roads and airstrips and more labs, but Fat Man could more than thrive if he could move his processed morphine down Thai jungle trails to his Chinese chemists and secret labs. He had to stay in Thailand, shielded and protected by his corrupt police friends in Chiang Mai Province. However, he needed Ban Su, or somewhere like Ban Su, to reduce the transport load. Morphine was easily eighty to ninety percent less than the bulk weight of opium. Therefore, absent Ban Su, his enterprise required another place nearby to cook the opium—and Albie was going to find it.

Albie's plan, at least in his mind, was simple. Photograph and expose the process. Catch Fat Man's crew in the very act of drug production. Fat Boy was the ersatz chemist—that was common knowledge. How an idiot like him could even count to ten was another matter. They could make do in an accessible area, but they needed enough space for large oil drums and a place for a wood fire along with a ready supply of lime fertilizer and concentrated ammonia. With any luck, Albie could capture all of it on film. His friends at the *Bangkok Post* would have a headline story, and then finally, a greater authority would step in and halt the criminal operation. His only challenge was to find their current arrangement.

Albie was doing exactly what Elliot predicted—lighting the fuse.

Upon hearing all this from Sister Mary Peyton, Wes ignored the company and let out a string of profanities.

"I will go to Mae Salong to start," he said. "You go to Ban Su and work toward the border. Someone must have seen him. For a smart guy, he might be the dumbest son-of-a-bitch I ever knew."

Greg said he would start with T'ang. He needed to update him on Nok. Greg then collected his motorcycle from Prawaite, paying him more than necessary for attending to his motorcycle.

Before he left, Sister Mary Peyton stopped him.

"Greg, there is something else. More."

"What is it?"

"Albie just told me the other day, and I promised not to tell anyone, but I think he is in danger now, and I am not sure what to do."

"Mary P, for God's sake, what is it?"

"Nok was trying to help him," she said. "Albie believes that is why she was beaten."

"I can't believe he involved her in something like this. Her people already live on the edge dealing with those thugs. What the hell was he thinking?"

"He did, and there is more."

"Go on."

"Albie is the father of Nok's baby."

"Are you shitting me? Sorry. I didn't expect that."

"No. Please, do not be sorry. I am the one who should apologize. It's just that I promised to keep the secret. I should have stopped him from going up there."

"I doubt that you could have. Looks like he decided a long time ago. Let's just hope we can find him before Fat Boy and his gang do."

"I will pray."

"We all should."

CHAPTER NINE

Greg spent four days looking for him before returning to Chiang Mai. Wes would not return for another week. Ping was convinced that something awful had occurred.

"You must go back and look. He could be hurt like Nok and needs help."

"Wes isn't back yet. Maybe he had success, maybe he found something. Let's wait for his return and see what he tells us."

"I don't like him."

"Ping don't be ridiculous. He and Albie were best friends. Wes was more upset than anyone else that he went alone. Like him or not, he knows that area as well as anyone."

Greg knew from Elliot that Wes had long ago been Military Intelligence—back before so many other spooks showed up in the Golden Triangle. *They would parachute him into China and wait for him to make his way back to Thailand. No support, no radio contact. Solo recon. Pretty crazy even for us.*

Greg knew he trained the pilots for the Border Patrol, but not that other business.

He was good back then, no doubt about it. He speaks Mandarin and other dialects better than he does Thai. At some point, enough was enough. He hit the sauce hard, and they cut bait. Put him on the shelf. That Thai woman he lives with sobered him up.

Greg could not tell Ping any of this, and considering her frazzled condition, it would not have mattered. All she cared about was Albie.

She started to cry. Greg knew he was useless and was not providing her with any consolation.

Greg held her in his arms. He had forgotten how young she was. Just in her early twenties, with a child to care for and now a missing husband. That was how she saw him. Albie was her husband. She was the wife. It didn't matter that he was twice her age. It was normal to have such marriages in Thailand. Unions of convenience. Wes had the same with Mama. Greg wondered why he didn't have one too.

Ping then surprised him.

"I went to the hospital when you were gone. I went to see Nok."

"Really?"

"She was special to Albie and so she is special to me."

"How was she? Any change?"

"No. The nurses say she is in a coma."

Greg, of course, knew that, but he was proud of Ping for going to visit Nok.

"Thank you for going," Greg said.

"She has no one without you and Albie," replied Ping.

"She has her grandfather."

"Albie says he is very old and not healthy."

"That is true, but he is still alive and is worried about her. I saw him and told him about her condition."

Ping had regained control of her emotions. Perhaps she was thinking about how desperate Nok's condition was. How similar it was to her situation. She apologized for crying and making a scene, leaving Greg to wonder how he could ever tell Ping that Albie was the father of Nok's child.

***

For the next three days, he went back and forth from the house to the hospital twice a day. He quickly found the quietude of the hospital a welcome break from Ping's constant angst and questions. He took turns reading and talking to Nok. He asked her about her love for Albie, and not hearing a response, told her about his first true love. Heather. How she had broken his heart, and he spent his time in England filling the vacuum. *A lacuna of love.* He had read that somewhere.

"You already know how Albie and I met, but did I ever tell you about the time that we drove the Land Rover on that dirt road toward Mae Fa? I don't remember why Albie even wanted to go over there. Something about a type of tree. The path was so narrow that we should have taken the motorcycles, but he wanted to collect cuttings and try to replant them. The vegetation was thick, and the path disappeared into the full jungle and then suddenly Albie slammed on the brakes, and not twenty yards away was a Burmese tiger. I mean a behemoth. He just stood there staring at us with eyes from Hades.

"The path was officially gone, and the tiger was not inclined to move. I told him to blow the horn, but he said that he wanted to see what the tiger would do, and why should we scare him? I said *because he is scaring me.* The animal was magnificent, and I kept thinking thank God we didn't take the motorcycles. Then the tiger walks at the car and Albie realizes the only exit is reverse, so he puts the car in gear and starts backing up, but the tiger keeps approaching. It was hard enough to go forward on the path and now Albie is looking out the back and trying to avoid trees and bushes and the tiger keeps coming. I could see the beads of sweat forming on the side of that colossal head of his and feel them under my shirt and along my side. When suddenly Albie hits a tree. You know, he swears *bullocks* like he always does, and so we stop and can only go forward. The tiger is now only yards away, and we are going toward him, and he looks like he is going to pounce on the hood of the car when Albie finally leans on the horn. The big cat became startled and disappeared into the brush. That's when Albie says *so much for a picnic today.* I don't know if he was talking about the tiger or us."

Nok said not a word but remained as silent as light.

"Nok, I am more than a little worried about Albie…we could really use your help. Where did he go and where would he go to look for that lab? I talked to T'ang. He was looped the first time, so I went back later, and he was better, but still confused. He didn't understand where you were or why you weren't back home by now. Nok, why did you even go to the Research Station?"

Greg waited, but nothing.

"You are going to have to wake up soon."

Greg leaned over to the side table and shuffled the pile of books.

"We finished the books that Mary P left. We even finished that long dictionary of saints. Albie didn't have much to choose from other than books about geology, physics, and scientific texts, but I found one book of fiction that he must have liked because of all the dog-eared pages. It's titled, *One Hundred Years of Solitude*. Let me know what you think."

CHAPTER TEN

He had been at the hospital since nine a.m. on that third day, and as he was leaving the wing, which had the private rooms, he saw Preeya. She was talking to a nurse. She had traded her all-white wardrobe for a typical Thai dress—a flower print with short sleeves that barely covered the tops of her shoulders and exposed her lovely long arms. She was taller than he realized, certainly taller than the nurse with whom she spoke, and with her hair tied back in a short ponytail, her striking features were on full display.

He stood motionless, waiting for her to finish her conversation, and then interrupted her path to the exit.

"Preeya," he said. "*Sawadee krap*, I am Greg. A friend of Jack's."

She seemed to recognize him. Then, placing her hands in prayer fashion, she bowed slightly and replied.

"Sawadee ka."

There was an awkward silence for a second, and Greg continued in Thai.

"Is everything all right? Are you all right?"

"I am fine," she replied. "I am visiting a friend."

She was searching her memory to place him. At least that is what Greg hoped, and he tried to help.

"I met you on your first night at Jack's. I sat next to you for a brief time at the table."

Greg imagined he could still smell her perfume.

It clicked, and she smiled.

"Yes. I remember now. You were a poor player."

He laughed loudly. Laughed for the first time in days, if not weeks. He explained that his friend on that night was the experienced card player, and he was with him to celebrate his last night in Chiang Mai. Jack arranged for them to sit at the table.

"I remember him as well. He was a skillful player. You speak Thai very well. Have you lived here long?"

She seemed very self-assured.

"I have been in Chiang Mai for about a year and in Thailand for three. Where are you going? Can I give you a ride? I have a motorcycle."

She looked at her skirt and looked at him yet again, more carefully. Greg wanted to believe she even smiled.

"I have shopping to do near the old market."

"I can drop you there."

"Is that on your way?"

"It is now."

"Thank you. That would be nice."

She rode sidesaddle. He could feel the shy weight of her hand on his back. He wondered if she could feel how he was trembling like a schoolboy. She steadied herself with her other hand on the seat while he drove slowly and carefully—more so than at any other time in his life in Thailand. He no longer had to imagine her scent.

He made his next decision when they crossed over the bridge, and he parked the motorcycle.

"I know you work in the evening, but maybe we could get lunch one day."

She smiled. This time, he was certain.

"Jack does not like for us to see customers. He says it is a poor business practice."

"I am hardly a regular customer, and I was more like a guest than a client that night."

"It is probably wise that you are not a regular," she giggled and never finished the thought.

"So?"

He was hanging by a thread. His chest was pounding louder than the honking traffic. He stared at her smoldering, seductive eyes and held his breath.

"Do you know the movie houses on Wattana? Across the street is a noodle shop called Kulap's Garden. You can't miss it. There are roses painted on the front glass. I can meet you there on Friday around this time."

He repeated the name and street just to make sure and to lock it in his memory and then drove there immediately after he said goodbye. It was an actual place, and he had an actual date.

***

They had lunch twice over the next five days. He told Preeya about Nok—never mentioning his suspicions about Fat Boy—but who Nok was and how she had helped Albie over the years on his project. He talked about his research in the most academic terms and how his path crossed with Albie's in Ban Su. He refrained from telling her about Albie's disappearance as he held out hope that he would return shortly. When he asked her about her friend at the hospital, she dodged the question and said that she was already back home, that it had been a quick visit to the ER, and all was fine.

For their third date, she prepared a basket lunch, and they had a picnic at the park near the Angkaew Reservoir, close to the zoo. She told him she was born in Chiang Mai province but grew up and went to school in Bangkok. She and her mother lived there with her uncle Sarathon and his family. Her uncle, like Jack, operated a gaming house called the Tiger's Den. *It was very fancy*, she said *and had visitors from around the world.* In the evenings and on weekends, only after all their schoolwork was completed, she and her cousins would do minor tasks around the casino, but the gambling rooms were off-limits. *So, of course, we peeked at every chance that we had.*

Greg was falling in love with her voice and her lightheartedness. The Thais have an expression about attitudes and responses to conflicts or demanding situations. People are *jai yen*, cool-hearted, slow to anger, and calm under any duress, or they are the opposite with hot hearts, *jai ron*, and have fiery tempers. Greg loved the expression *jai yen* and transmuted its meaning with the American slang of cool and smooth. Preeya embodied that connotation.

They kissed for the first time on that date. The next evening, she did not have to work, and they had an early dinner at Kulap's Garden and slept together for the first time at her tiny apartment. He was nervous, even hesitant. He had not been with a woman for more than a year. The last time was with a Peace Corps Volunteer in Tak. Cassidy or Cassandra, he couldn't recall. He remembered she had a long body and sad brown eyes on a pretty face. She was a vegetarian and teetotaler. He was neither. She had been enthusiastic in bed with the drive of a long-distance swimmer, and when they finally fell asleep to the sound of the pounding rain on the corrugated metal roof, *camoys* came and stole his motorcycle. That would not be the case tonight with Preeya, because she too reacted as if it had been some great time, and with sleep abandoned, the ardor of each carried them through the night and sustained them to the dawn.

***

For the next week, he triangulated from Preeya's apartment to the hospital and to Mama Pajama's Bakery Bar, where he talked incessantly with Wes about Albie and what to do next. The conversation was always the same.

"Ping is becoming frantic," Greg explained to Wes. "I think we should go to the police."

"What do you think they will do? Send a patrol up there. To talk with whom? T'ang? The other villagers? Albie is not sitting in someone's hut exchanging stories or smoking a pipe. He is not in any of those villages. We went to all of them."

"He must have found something, and he was caught, or he is trapped or something worse. Maybe he crossed over the border and the Chinese or Burmese have him?"

"The Chinese do not need to hold a British scientist. They would spank him and escort him back. Xu has bigger issues, and I don't think Albie would get deep enough into Burma for Zhang Qitu's group to hold him. He wasn't interested in Burma. Fat Man can't go deep into Burma either, so why even look there? Albie would know that."

"We have to do something," Greg said.

"We'll go back up and look again. I will tell you what worries me. Swamp grass. If he slipped and went over one of those ridges and fell into a swell or valley with those sinkholes, then no one will ever find him. Ever."

Later that day, he returned to the house and told Ping that he and Wes were heading back to Ban Su. She was pleased, but all this waiting had taken its toll on her. Her eyes, once bright and cheerful, were sullen and bloodshot from crying, and she had dark circles underneath them much like an older woman.

"What is going to happen to us? Where will we go?"

She kept asking the same things repeatedly, and Greg had no answer for her. She asked him if he wanted dinner and commented that she had seen little of him this past week. Greg then told her he had met someone. He elaborated only to say that they had dinner together and were planning to do so again tonight.

Ping smiled and said it was about time that he had a *fan*, a girlfriend. Greg agreed, although he kept that comment to himself.

CHAPTER ELEVEN

At first, he tried to sleep in the jeep as Wes drove, but when he leaned too firmly against his back, the welts from her scratches woke him. After their first night, they met as her schedule allowed—late nights, early mornings, or afternoons. Each time seemed more fervent, even desperate, than the last. She often fell into a deep sleep and nestled her soft body next to him, sometimes hooking an arm around him and often draping at least one leg around his. She could have slept completely on top of him, and he would not have minded. Last night, she was restless and caressed him unceasingly. In bed, she was modest, almost shy, but untiring, and last night more determined than ever.

Every woman he had known had something special about them, some wonderful quality—a way of expressing herself, her touch, her kindness, her generosity. The list goes on—but none had ever been as beautiful or as vital as Preeya. Her arrival at a time in his life when grief, uncertainty, and anger raged may have even saved him from himself. She was more than a peaceful oasis. A respite from the fight. She was love incarnate, and her love was transcendent, even if tragically ephemeral.

He finally explained to her all that he could about Albie, Nok, and even his suspicions about Fat Boy. She said that his repeated trips to Ban Su were dangerous. *Let the authorities manage it* and pressed her supple body against his.

Despite her lighthearted banter on the motorcycle as they traversed the city, even giggles as they frequented shops, or shared drawn-out meals, her demeanor in her tiny and carefully ordered apartment was subdued, more intimate, and gently tranquil. The whispering mystery of human desire, no longer notional and prosaic, but actual and romantic, murmured and exposed their deep loneliness—even isolation—as she clutched, embraced, even clawed to deny that we deserve such lonesomeness because of something we have done. They were tumbling fast, and he did not care.

***

"Let's be sensible. On the one hand, we know he is not staying in any of the villages, but he needs food, water, and a place to stay."

Wes spoke a bit more slowly than usual and his driving mirrored that as well.

"There are no Wimpy hamburger places, no fish 'n chips shops, and certainly no local pubs, so he must have someone helping him and providing for him. It has been over two weeks. Look at how much we are carrying in the back, and we aren't planning anything quite that long."

Wes was accurate in his assessment.

Greg squirmed in his seat and pulled at his shirt, which was sticking to his tender back.

"Who would he find to help him?" Greg asked as much of Wes as to himself. "Nok was always his contact, even his guide when we weren't with him. T'ang certainly likes him, but they can barely speak to each other."

To describe Albie's Thai language skills as rudimentary was generous, and T'ang spoke his own dialect, a strange combination of Thai, Burmese, and various Chinese dialects, often mumbled with betel juice dripping out of his mouth or opium clouding his brain.

Greg opened the window as Wes lit another short, stubby, Gauloise cigarette. Sweat was forming on Greg's back, and the breeze helped. Greg kept talking.

"I don't know any others with whom he spent any considerable time. The villagers in Ban Su, who helped him build the station, were skittish even with me if Nok was not around. Why would it be any different with him? In addition, we do not know where he parked the Land Rover. The best way to get around up there is by motorcycle or walk, but for crying out loud, how far can he walk?"

"He is in better condition than he looks," Wes offered in Albie's defense.

"No, I am not saying he isn't fit, but trekking for two weeks straight would be much for any of us. No, something godawful has happened. Something ruinous."

Greg waited, but Wes did not answer. It was as if Greg's last gloomy pronouncement had unsettled Wes. Had Wes truly not considered that Albie was dead? *Something* was on his mind, Greg reasoned. Garrulous even in the most tranquil of times, a quiet Wes was out of character, and suddenly the silence in the jeep hung between them like a shroud.

When the ride first began, he was on a tirade about the world travelers and hippies, who were, in his words, *littering Mama's with their presence.* He grabbed and threw one hapless WT out the door and onto his backside because he was sermonizing far too loudly on the U.S. brutality in Vietnam and the intervention by the U.S. in what this hippie called a civil war. Wes' diatribe soon moved to the *queers* and *fagots*, both *farang* and Thai, who were growing like a pestilence in Chiang Mai.

"Niggers might be the only thing worse than fags," he said, "and I am certain that there is a special place in hell for nigger fags."

None of this was new to Greg. Wes announced his bilious racist, homophobic, and misogynist views without compunction. Greg had heard it all in one form or another more than once. This was a man, he thought, who would be easy to dislike. People like this feed on hatred, arousing aversion and antipathy, but Wes nurtured and cultivated it. The best strategy was, as Albie so often did, to change the subject as quickly as possible.

"I did not think you believed in heaven and hell," said Greg.

"No. I don't believe in heaven, and I don't believe in that enlightenment bullshit either, but I have seen enough to believe in hell, and if you want to start one of those conversations that Albie liked so much about good and evil or some stuff that the nun likes then good luck."

All of that passed as it usually does with Wes, and after a cigarette and a break on the side of the road to answer a call from nature, the conversation in the jeep shifted to discerning Albie's whereabouts. Until just now, when Greg's grim declaration quieted Wes.

Greg waited and adjusted himself in his seat repeatedly. He was content to stare out of the window across the rice paddies stretching to the horizon and think about last night with Preeya. He imagined the taste of strands of her long black hair in his mouth. Her searing gaze into his eyes as she arched backward and pulled him ever closer. Where was he going? Why was he driving in this direction and not toward her?

It didn't take long for Wes to shatter the moment.

***

"We go to Mae Salong first," Wes said. "That is the largest village and a bit of a grand central station. The Border Patrol has a small airstrip there and the pilots who I know might be around as well. I brought liquid incentive in the back. Real whisky. Not that Mekong crap. We are going to have to do our hunting on foot, and that's as good a place as any to leave the jeep and supplies to start."

Wes was clever. Greg had known that for quite some time, and despite his bigotry and intolerance, he was a war vet, a patriot, a man of courage, and strangely generous. Greg had seen him jump out of his jeep on a crowded street to help an old man push a broken down *tuk-tuk* off the road and heard that he cleaned out the stench in Mary Peyton's septic when it backed up last year. It was difficult to call him altruistic, but his bursts of charity to those in need were evident. Albie trusted him, and for that, so did Greg, but somewhere in the back of his mind, he could hear Elliot's last cautionary words. *There is no one in Chiang Mai you should trust. No one.*

It never occurred to Greg until that moment that he and Wes might each be looking for something different.

"One more thing," Wes added as they approached Chiang Rai. "We stay together the entire time. No wandering off on separate paths. No one goes into the bush without a gun or a rifle. If we are going to poke around outside of the main villages, then anyone we bump into will be carrying, which means you will be too."

"I will not carry a gun."

"You damn well are and if no other reason than to protect me. So, get with the program or keep your ass right here with the nun."

***

They spent ten days in the Golden Triangle and found nothing of Albie. A Border Officer thought he saw the Land Rover about a month ago but could recall nothing more recently. No one in Mae Salong had seen anyone resembling Albie or talked to anyone who had. A pilot, whom Wes had trained, told them that the Chinese were moving product in enormous amounts eastward through Tachileik, which was due north of Chiang Rai. Xu had built a road in Burma for that eastern track. Labs were scattered throughout the area and the finished product moved to Northeast Thailand, Laos, and Cambodia.

Wes was convinced Fat Man was using a similar route in the northernmost part of Thailand, but just south of the Burmese border. It made perfect sense, and if you had a lab in that area, you simply stayed in line toward the point of sale for heroin or a jumping-off spot for shipment to Vietnam. The pilot didn't disagree but said the jungle was too thick to see a trail in that area.

With that in mind, they worked their way north into the Mae Fa Luang District and to Tambon Thoet and ran into two separate groups of hunters. The first group of four was tight-lipped and offered nothing, but the second group was much friendlier. This group had set up a small camp, and they were skinning their kill—three monkeys, all hanging with their arms spread wide above their heads on a cross rope between two trees. One man was peeling off the hairy skin and another was gutting the animals. The skinless monkeys looked much like tiny human beings hanging by their wrists. No hands. Monkey claws sell. A third hunter was crouching and tending a fire.

They invited Wes and Greg to stay and have a bite to eat. And to Greg's chagrin, Wes said yes and opened a bottle of whiskey. The friendly hunters became even friendlier, but in the end, had nothing to share of any consequence.

None of them believed there were any proper paths leading eastward. They said that they have hunted in this area often and the jungle was too thick through here, and there were too many quick drop-offs. They did acknowledge, however, that this clearing was about as far north as they went. Soldiers patrolling the frontier shoot first and ask questions later, so the hunters avoided going north too far and never crossed the northern ridge that was part of the Burmese frontier.

Something still convinced Wes that this had been, and still was, one of Fat Man's most efficient routes. He reminded Greg that Fat Man would have no respect for any border and likely had his people move along whatever path was available. However, that was the rub—availability. Greg quietly disagreed with Wes. If Xu's enterprise was growing as everyone attested, and he was active in the same area with equally the same disdain for borders, then Fat Man had neither the firepower nor the wherewithal to challenge him. By default, he had to find other routes. And those routes would not be near here.

Greg and Wes decided not to test the zone beyond the northern ridge and backtracked on a more southerly path that the hunters suggested, before heading due south dangerously close to the western Burmese border. The monkey killers reminded them that tigers were abundant and to keep their rifles ready. *Watch out for snakes too—cobras, especially*, was their parting advice.

They stopped at any village regardless of size to talk and to ask about any visitors in the last few weeks. If you include Burma and Laos with Thailand, the Golden Triangle was easily 350,000 square miles of mountain terrain and the area in Thailand was the most rugged. It was becoming more obvious with each conversation that they were looking for the proverbial needle. Eventually, they returned to Mae Salong, where they managed a decent shower and ate from the provisions that Wes brought in the jeep.

Greg wondered if Albie might not have looked more to the west of both Ban Su and Mae Salong and then southward along the border. Here again, there were few roads, but more paths and opium fields that ran along the mountain ridge on both sides of the border. Wes was skeptical because not far south you had to cross the Kok River and its tributaries, and the terrain leading up to the river, and in all directions from the river, was treacherous, so much so that not even the hill tribe people had a single village anywhere in that area.

"Just ask any of the people here in Mae Salong," Wes said. "It's uninhabitable and veritably impassable. We can look, but I don't think anyone is heading extremely far in that direction, let alone a caravan of horses or mules carrying dope."

"Let's look," said Greg. "The only other possibilities are the paths that lead south from Ban Su toward Chiang Rai and Chiang Mai, and I covered that section the first time."

"I know. Those are the old routes, and they are tricky and like a spider web, but they were once the most dependable ones for Fat Man. He could protect the package that way. Buy off enough provincial police. Chiang Mai and Chiang Rai didn't become what they were because of the weather. Chiang Mai first, and then Chiang Rai, were the original capital cities of contraband. If you are selling this shit, you have two choices—you go east to Tachileik and cross over into Laos, or you go south through Chiang Mai province and then transport it to the northeast."

Greg again disagreed but kept quiet. What Wes said might be true about parts of the Golden Triangle, but he had learned long ago, when he first started visiting the hill tribe villages well south of the Golden Triangle and along the eastern border of Thailand, that all their shipments slid southward toward Bangkok. He wondered why Wes refused to recognize this option now. There was no reason not to suspect that Fat Man would find circumventing Chiang Mai City and trucking product along a similar route to Bangkok viable. Granted today, the most lucrative and currently hottest market was the eastern track toward Vientiane and Vietnam, where heroin was flooding to U.S. soldiers, but if Xu controlled that route and if the DEA and others were clamping down in Chiang Mai, then redirecting south made sense. Maybe Wes was right, and this passageway was too treacherous, but once across the river, it would not differ from all the other routes that the traffickers used on the eastern side.

To Wes' credit, he humored Greg, and they set out on foot in the direction that Greg suggested. It was rough going from the very beginning, and Greg's headaches had begun again. The first arrived with a roar during the monkey meal and others were sporadic as they trekked along. He plied himself with aspirin and cautioned himself to drink more water, but that was tricky as they only carried two canteens with them.

As Wes predicted, this trek was a slog. They trudged along slowly on a narrow but definitive path, climbing steep slopes, and looking for any sign that Albie might have followed a trail in this direction. What did they expect to find? Greg finally wondered. Albie camping in a clearing cooking monkey meat. His dead body in the thick brush just off the track. Not a single trace or sign of any open area where Fat Boy could cook opium into morphine. No residual barrels. No detritus. It was a fool's errand, and as foreseen by Wes, they finally reached an impasse, a place where they needed to climb, not walk, but to scale a jungle mountain wall. Greg relented and apologized to Wes.

"I am sorry, but there must be another way. We are missing something."

"Common sense," replied Wes, removing his sunglasses and wiping the sweat on his face with the back of his hand.

Greg sat on the slope of the hill, and Wes noticed how uncomfortable he appeared and questioned him.

"I have a headache. It is nothing. I don't think I have been drinking enough water. Happens whenever I get dehydrated." Some of that was true. "What I cannot understand is how Albie went undetected in these hills. Not a single person even saw him. He sticks out like a bowling ball, a *farang* bowling ball."

"A bald *farang* bowling ball," said Wes, suddenly discovering a sense of humor.

Albie was short, five feet, eight inches, but his no-neck, barrel-chested figure made him look even shorter next to average height *farangs* like Greg and Wes. Albie lost a bet to Wes in one of their gin rummy games and had to shave his head like a Buddhist monk. He purported to like it and continued with the appearance, lauding the ease of grooming.

They were both tired. Wes looked it as well. Neither had shaved for a week and Wes' salt and pepper beard made him look even older. Absent his aviator sunglasses, which were now in his shirt pocket, the dark circles under Wes' eyes, the grime on his face, and the dirty red bandana wrapped across his forehead all added to the picture of lassitude.

"Now what?" Wes asked.

"We need to go to Ban Su. I have to talk with T'ang and give him an update on Nok. After that, we head home."

***

From Mae Salong they drove over to Ban Su, where Wes spent the time drinking with the villagers, hoping one or two might remember or share something. Greg reminded him to inquire about Nok, too. *Had anyone seen anything before Nok was beaten?* Greg meanwhile sat in the hut with T'ang, and for one of the very few times in Greg's experience, T'ang was lucid and sober. He had been working with the others, tilling, and clearing rocks, and by the time he got back to his hut in the late afternoon, he was physically exhausted. Greg was with him just after he returned that day.

A woman by the name of Kanda, the wife of Arthit with whom Wes was drinking, prepared a meal for T'ang, and he invited Greg to share it with him.

T'ang ate loudly with a quick, rhythmic motion of his chopsticks as he slurped his watery rice dish. He held the tiny clay bowl near his mouth while he ate, but constantly stared at and listened to Greg. Greg reviewed Nok's condition and her current location in the hospital in Chiang Mai. He avoided any description of the beating and focused on her present state. It seemed as if T'ang remembered most of this. When he told T'ang that he was worried about Albie and that Albie had now been missing for three weeks, T'ang set down his bowl.

"People disappear in these mountains. One day my son, Nok's father, was here, and the next day he was gone. No one ever knows what happened. They go to a city down below, they go to China or Burma, or maybe they fall into the river, or even the swamp grass. No one knows, and no one asks. You are chasing smoke."

T'ang ate again and then stopped.

"Fat Man was here not too long ago. He was looking for the summer crop. It was not very much. It never is. We should not even bother, but Arthit says *better a little than nothing.*"

Arthit was T'ang's successor as the village elder.

"Look," T'ang continued, and he opened a metal box that had money in it. Thai baht. Greg had seen more in one hand at Preeya's gambling table than in that box. "It is not much. It never is, but it will buy rice."

"Fat Man or Fat Boy? Which one?"

"Fat Man."

"What did he want?"

"He came to make a deal. For the next harvest."

"Did you see our friend Albie? He said he was coming here. Was he here when Fat Man was here? T'ang, please tell me."

"Your friend came long after Fat Man was gone. I told him too. He had a piece of paper with a drawing on it. I think Nok made it."

"Why didn't you tell me this the last time I was here?"

"I don't remember. I thought I did. Your friend doesn't talk like you. He is difficult to understand."

"Where did Albie go? Do you know where Albie went?"

"No. He wanted to chase the opium. I told him it was too late. It was gone. There was only a little, but it was gone."

"Which direction did he go when he left? Someone must have seen that."

"No one will say. Your friend outside can drink whiskey all night and no one will say. Fat Man and the General are like the hills that make people disappear. They are all afraid of the Fat Man and the General."

"Why aren't you afraid, then?"

"I am an old man. What good will it do to kill an old man? We spread the seeds tomorrow for the winter crop. It will be a good crop. The soil is good. I have seen it. I hope Nok is back for the harvest."

"T'ang, listen to me. Please. You are my only hope. You are the only one who is not afraid of Fat Man. Just tell me which direction Albie went when he left here. If we don't find Albie, then the police and the army and many people are going to come up here and look for him. They will chase you right out of Ban Su."

"Thai men and police and others have come here before and told us not to grow poppies. What else can we do? No one bothers us. If they make us move, we will move. We have been moving for a long time. I cannot remember where I lived as a boy. Ban Su is just one more place."

"The only thing Albie wanted to do was to help you. He was a friend to everyone in this village. He brought them food, medicine, and even clothing. I have been a good friend to you. I have been a good friend to Nok. We are trying to help Nok right now. I will do everything I can to help Nok and help you. Just please tell me, when Albie walked out of this hut, which direction did he go?"

"Fat Man and the Chinese General say the same thing. *Be quiet.* The less we talk, the more they pay. Everyone in the village knows that, and it is the way to keep everyone safe. Fat Man said he will be back at the harvest in three or four months, and he will bring his weights and scales."

"Don't tell me one word about Fat Man or the opium or money or anything else. You can keep that to yourself. Where did Albie go?"

"He walked back on the path to his building, and I never saw him again."

CHAPTER TWELVE

Wes and Greg agreed that T'ang's confession told them little to nothing. They expected Albie started at Ban Su, and that he walked back to the Research Station meant little. If there was anything to take away from the talk with T'ang, it was how much Fat Man, as well as the General, exerted terror and fear on these people.

They slept that night at the Research Station and began early the next day, re-examining the routes that led away from the station just in case T'ang's comments were credible. Greg marveled at Wes' familiarity with all these trails. He knew the hills as well as he knew the hill dialects.

Four obvious options presented themselves, but each of those had two or three detours, and those divergences had their own alternative routes, sometimes within a kilometer or two. The brush was thick, not as dense as the jungle that they encountered last week, but the hills were equally steep, with treacherous ridges, scarps, and dead ends. If you went close enough to the rim, you could occasionally see a patch of high elephant grass stretching a hundred yards in a deep ravine. More than once, they lost their bearings in the labyrinth, and on one occasion, when they tried to backtrack, they found themselves deeper in the jungle, with no path forward. On still another lane, they walked at length down a steep winding incline that ended with a sudden precipitous escarpment and a view of swamp grass.

"We are being stupid," Wes finally declared. "It makes no sense to go this distance with the raw opium. It defeats the entire purpose of lessening the load. It takes more work, more horses, and more people to go this far."

"I agree," said Greg. "Let's get out of here."

They left the Research Station late in the afternoon, hoping to get down the hill to Chiang Rai before dark. Neither had much to say. Defeat and silence have long been companions. Greg couldn't help but recall his ride down the snaking path with Nok. She was the one they needed. Greg was certain that if anyone could find Albie, it would be

Nok. Nok was the key. A key that was slowly slipping away like one more unanswered prayer.

***

Moonlight illuminated their way down to Chiang Rai, and as the ground flattened, Wes started another conversation.

"I heard your buddy Elliot left town."

How Wes learned things amazed Greg, and why was he mentioning this now?

"Yes. He left the same day that Albie left."

"You two became quite chummy, didn't you?"

"I am not sure what you mean by that."

"Just seems like you became buddies pretty fast, as if you knew each other from an earlier time."

"If you remember, you were the one who introduced us. You and Albie. At poker one night at your place. That was the first time that I met him," he lied. "And if I remember correctly, Mama won big and cleaned us all out of cash that night."

Deny, deflect, and change the subject. Never admit or concede anything. Never. Elliot whispering in his ear.

"Yea, I remember, but you two got pretty friendly, pretty fast."

"We played basketball two or three times a month at the outdoor courts at the university. Sometimes twenty or twenty-five players would show up for the late-night games. *Farangs* and Thais from the various consulates and local businesses. The guy who owns the shipping company organized it."

"Yea, I know that guy."

"He played on the national team in the Asian games. He is the tallest Thai man I have ever met. Albie even played occasionally. That was a joke. So, I am not sure what you are getting at."

"You know he is a Company man, and that water purification thing was a cover."

"Well, you know more than I do, because I don't know anything about any of that." *Admit nothing—not a single item.* "Do you think that everyone who works at the embassy or in a government office is a spy?"

"Yes. Did he try to recruit you?

"To do what? We played basketball, and we played poker and shared beers, and most of those beers were at your place." Another lie. "The only nefarious thing he ever did was take me to Fat Man's gambling house and introduce me to that SOB, and then get us both thrown out when he started an argument with Fat Boy."

"Okay, let me ask you this. Do you think it was a coincidence that Albie and Elliot both left Chiang Mai on the same day?"

"Now I am completely confused. Albie drove to Chiang Rai. We know that because he saw Mary P before he headed up to the Research Station, and Elliot flew out of Chiang Mai airport to Bangkok and parts unknown. What are you getting at?"

"Look, we both agree that it was gutless to beat Nok. Cowardly, to batter any woman. And I know you think Fat Boy was the one who hurt Nok, but that's the problem with our thinking. What if it wasn't Fat Boy?"

"That's ridiculous and you know it. Who else could it be?"

"I don't know, but that is what I am getting at. Perhaps someone else hurt Nok and that is the same person who knows where Albie is."

"And you think it was Elliot?"

"You said Elliot introduced you to Fat Man, and you said they didn't like each other. Maybe it was a ruse. A misdirection. Or more likely, Elliot was trying to cut Fat Man out. To keep the dope going to Xu. Maybe he was the one trying to convince Nok to help him and help the Company support Xu rather than feed Fat Man."

"That's ridiculous."

"Why? Because he is your friend? Because you played basketball and poker together?"

"Are you listening to yourself? Fat Boy had been threatening T'ang ever since the Research Station closed because T'ang is content to keep selling to General Xu. The only way to get to T'ang was to leverage Nok. Send a message. What is the Chinese expression? Kill a chicken to scare the monkey. People like Fat Man believe that type of garbage. And Fat Boy does whatever he is told."

"I know, but it doesn't serve Fat Man to bring more attention—let alone hell and chaos down on his operation. And if something connected him to either of these incidents, to Nok's beating or Albie's disappearance, then how does that help him? Ban Su isn't his only source. Why risk everything? Elliot—or his people—could kill two birds. He could get Fat Boy to look guilty, bring scrutiny and damage to Fat Man's operation, and still arrange for the dope to go to Xu. T'ang doesn't care who gets the opium as long as he gets paid, and if it looks like Fat Boy hurt Nok, if T'ang were to believe that it was Fat Boy, then he would have even more incentive to sell to Xu."

"T'ang said he and Fat Man have a deal."

"Only time will tell if that happens but answer this. Why couldn't we find a single trace of Fat Boy's cookout anywhere we looked? No debris, no empty barrels, nothing. What if T'ang is still selling to Xu? T'ang said the Fat Man was *looking* for the summer crop. That is exactly what you said. He didn't say he sold him the summer crop. What if T'ang sold the summer crop to Xu, then Xu and his boys would cook the opium and make the morphine, even the heroin itself, in Burma and not in Thailand, and we were never looking in the right place?"

Greg was stunned. Some of this made sense. He didn't believe it, but that didn't mean it wasn't true. Greg finished Wes' argument in silence. *And, if Albie thought that same thing, or somehow learned that Xu bought the crop, then he might have tried to photograph General Xu's operation, in which case, if caught by Xu, then we will never find him.*

Elliot had gone dark, *off the grid* in his words, and Greg recalled Elliot's words of advice for the refugees. *Whatever lies you tell the first time…keep telling the same ones.*

As they arrived in Chiang Rai, Wes suggested they go to The Heavenly Flower Massage Parlor for a hot bath and a rub. Greg declined, even though the idea of a hot bath and a legitimate massage sounded good. Wes persisted in saying that Greg didn't need to avail himself of the entire menu of amenities but that he could keep his virginity intact and still enjoy the basic services. Greg said nothing more and had Wes drop him at the clinic instead. They arranged a pickup time for tomorrow morning.

Sister Mary Peyton was in her kitchen when Greg arrived.

"I am so glad to see you. You were gone for such a long time."

"We stopped by when we first arrived, but you weren't here. I left you a note."

"I saw it. I must have been in the town running errands. Judging from your appearance, it doesn't look like you had any luck finding Albie."

He couldn't get his head around the idea that Elliot had anything to do with the attack on Nok or Albie's disappearance, and considered for a moment saying something to her, but then refrained, knowing it was neither prudent nor pragmatic. He would have to work this out by himself.

"Nothing. Not a trace. T'ang spoke to Albie but had no other information. He could be anywhere up there. I just can't imagine how he could survive this long on his own."

"This is awful. I feel so responsible. What are you going to do now?"

"We must go to the police. Report him missing to the authorities in Chiang Mai and notify the British Consulate too."

"Where is Wes?"

"He is going to spend the night at a hotel in town. I thought I would stay here if possible."

"Absolutely. I have dinner started. It will be easy to add more vegetables in the wok."

"Thanks. Let me clean up. Do you have anything for a headache?"

"I am certain that I do. I will get it for you."

"Thanks, again. I will get it after I shower."

CHAPTER THIRTEEN

They sat in the kitchen at a small wooden table and ate steamed rice with vegetables. Greg thought of Elliot as he splashed the fiery *nam prik* on his plate.

She wanted to know how the search went and where they looked, and Greg detailed the journey as best as he could. He said that trekking in the thicker jungle areas was challenging, and he never could have done it without Wes. Greg's previous experiences in the hills entailed hiking or walking, but it was often on well-established paths. Carrying a rifle for the entire time was also a new and uncomfortable experience.

"Did you ever use the rifle?" Mary Peyton asked.

"No, thank goodness. Wes made a big deal about it and gave me lessons on shooting and cleaning the weapon, but I must admit I was purposely a poor student."

"We had all types of guns while I was growing up," said Sister Mary Peyton. "Rifles, shotguns, pistols."

"Really?" Greg exclaimed. "I can't picture that."

"My father and younger brother loved to hunt deer, and we lived far enough outside of the city, where shooting rabbits and wild turkeys was common in the area. We learned to shoot while we were still in grammar school. We had targets set up in the field next to our house, and Dad would supervise and teach us. I can remember him insisting that we always wear ear protectors. He said that he regretted not doing as much when he first shot. I spent more time as a child with my dad shooting than anything else. His favorite expression was *point, shoot, pray.*"

"I never would have guessed. I expect you were good."

"Annie Oakley, good," she laughed. "I lost interest around middle school, and by the time I was in high school, I don't think I ever picked up a gun again. *It was not appropriate for a young lady*, at least that is what my mother said, and by that time, my brother and dad were the ones going deer hunting, and I had little interest in that."

"That's amazing. I guess I should tell you about the monkeys."

***

After dinner, they remained at the table and talked about Albie. It was obvious that she knew him better than anyone else did. She told him that Albie had been married, but that his wife had passed away at an incredibly early age. She didn't know any of the details but knew that Albie somehow felt responsible, that he believed he failed her.

"I believe," she said, "that is why he has been so generous to so many. You know he is very wealthy. We talked a great deal about religion. He was quite astute, as you may have imagined. I considered him a true polymath. He knew far more than I did about Christianity, Buddhism, and Judaism. He was well-informed about Islam too. I remember one time over a dinner like this one, he spoke about the meaning of suffering and detachment in all those religions. Sometimes, he would talk about death as if it didn't matter, and I was worried that he might be depressed or feeling despair, but he told me that was not the case and quoted one of the Psalms. *Man is like a breath; his days like a passing shadow.*"

Sister Mary Peyton rarely proselytized. A nun she met in India told her *to preach the Gospel, and if necessary, use words.* She understood that almost everyone in Thailand was Buddhist in one fashion or another and often in dinner conversations like tonight talked more about other Christians or her saints. She believed she could please God with a simple life and grateful spirit, and if she could be generous with acts of charity, then she would serve some useful purpose in this world and be an example of Christ. She said she loved the Thai custom of bowing and greeting.

"Every person is carrying God," she said, "and when I bow to another person, I bow to the holiness in that person."

Greg struggled to accept that all men were holy. He had plenty of examples that showed otherwise, and Mary Peyton did not disagree. However, she insisted all men know what is right, even the most depraved have the laws of truth and justice embedded in their hearts.

"What I never could understand," said Greg, "was why he was so obsessed with the Research Station. It was not only ill-conceived, but it was also untenable. Unsustainable. He was smart. He must have known that, and yet he persisted like one of those Greek characters rolling the rock up the mountain. His expertise was science, oxygen, carbon dioxide, deforestation and environmental degradation, and everything that goes into that, and here he was muddled in opium trafficking. It never made sense to me."

"He believed that the Research Station was for research in the truest sense," she said. "This was a project that would take years of study, and the idea was not to create a farm or an orchard of olive trees, oranges, or apples, but the beginning of a solution, something to break the cycle of this death crop. It began as a first step and then it changed. He saw what he perceived to be the squalor and suffering of hill tribe life. He saw them as a lost people, cut off, isolated, bordering on desolation and desperation and hopelessness, and he wanted to save them more than save the planet."

"They don't want to be saved. I spent two years with dozens of distinct groups, and I can't think of one who wanted to abandon their lifestyle. Occasionally, one or two people from a village would make their way to a life elsewhere, but they were the exception and not the rule. I know Albie understood that. He said as much to me."

"It was the exploitation that infuriated him. The hill tribe people are pawns and victims in the heroin process. He detested that the drug kings and opium warlords, driven by unchecked avarice, were not only killing people with their drugs, but they were corrupting civilization, bribing government officials whose duty it was to protect society, all on the backs of these gentle people, who were scraping the soil to make enough to buy rice."

"I get it, but do you risk your life for that altruism?"

"He was Don Quixote."

"Honest to God, Mary P, I don't think Albie is alive."

"I pray constantly that he is, but I am worried too."

***

The phone was ringing, destroying more than their sleep. He could hear Mary Peyton's muffled voice through the thin wall, and then he was certain he could hear her crying.

Nok was dead. She died of cardiac arrest even as her baby survived. Her last dying breath gave the child life. She died alone and, according to the doctor, never regained consciousness. Neither friends nor family were there. They were all chasing a ghost. *Chasing smoke* was how T'ang described it.

The hospital contacted the house looking for Albie or Greg. Ping took the call and phoned Sister Mary Peyton. Ping was distraught and barely coherent, according to Mary P, and the details were uncertain. However, the child lived. Premature by a month, but stable in neonatal care. Ping begged Sister Mary Peyton to come to Chiang Mai.

They were packed and ready when Wes finally arrived. Hungover and still drunk, he reeked of whiskey and stale tobacco. The booze and other foul odors came off him like heat from an oven. He made no apologies for his condition even as he heard the news about Nok. Instead, he tossed the keys to Greg and crawled into the back of the jeep, and promptly fell asleep.

As far as Greg was concerned, it was a blessing. He would have had zero tolerance for any of Wes' diatribes and was struggling with his own grief, fighting back his own tears. The driving helped to calm him. Sister Mary Peyton huddled in the seat next to him. She had her rosary out and fingered it methodically, without a sound.

In the dismal silence, he searched for meaning in Nok's death and saw only the mordant mayhem, and his spineless cowardice for his failure to act. Certainly, he could have done more. Isn't that why he stayed in Chiang Mai in the first place? To help Albie and Nok. Now a litany of responsibilities, for which he had neither the aptitude nor appetite to manage, confronted him.

What will they do with Nok's body? How will he tell T'ang? What do they do with the baby? It's Albie's baby too, and he is not here, so what is the right thing to do? They needed to go to the police and the British Consulate. Albie wanted to keep his parentage a secret, but what do they do now? Ping. How does he tell Ping? What does he tell Ping about Albie? Was the baby a boy or a girl? Should they take the baby up to T'ang? Holy shit.

He thought of his private talks with Nok in the hospital. The prayer book that Mary P left at her bedside from which he read with uncertainty if not cynicism. Passages about faith, hope, and charity. Passages extolling the virtue of accepting good with gratitude, and evil with patience. Passages about a loving God and an Old Testament God whose wrath was so great that only the crucifixion could placate it. Was Sister Mary Peyton praying for forgiveness for those who killed Nok now? How do you forgive the unforgivable? He wanted to ask her, but she sat there, silent, praying on her rosary beads, telling herself repeatedly that *Christ died for everyone—no exceptions,* even as they drove toward the inexorable confrontation with the sons of perdition.

CHAPTER FOURTEEN

If anyone had any reason to feel adrift, even forsaken, it was Ping. Albie was not only her husband, her love, but also her sole means of support, and now he was gone. Yet, in the concatenation of events over the next month, even as Greg fell deeper and deeper in love with Preeya, it would be Ping who provided the most unforeseen act of love, and not Preeya.

Greg deposited Wes at his place, consigning him to the care of Mama and telling her he would return the jeep later that day. He drove to the house, where Ping and Sister Mary Peyton consoled each other while he showered, and then all three headed to the hospital. Sister Mary Peyton knew many of the nurses on this maternity floor, and a cheerful aide led them to the neonatal unit, where Nok's baby was receiving, according to the aide, the best possible care for premature infants. They passed by the main ward, which seemed overly crowded with mothers and babies and two busy nurses attending to them, before crossing a hallway into a smaller room, where a large glass window separated them from the babies.

The aide explained that as a safety precaution, the premature babies remained in this isolation room and only the neonatal nurses and doctors could enter. Four white bassinets held the four tiny infants, and Nok's child was the second one from the left. Greg pressed his face against the glass as he read the nametag on the front of the bassinet. *Baby Robber Saint Clair.*

"What is that name all about?" he exclaimed, far too loudly.

"Oh, that is so precious," said Sister Mary Peyton.

"Likely, that was the name we had on record for the deceased mother," answered the aide, referencing Nok's death with what seemed to Greg a chilly indifference. "If you like, I can ask the head nurse."

"Please do," answered Greg, as he watched the young woman retrace her steps and exit the room.

"Greg, there is nothing to be concerned about. It is just a temporary measure," explained Sister Mary Peyton.

"It just threw me completely. I wasn't sure what to expect. I never considered that."

Ping remained quiet and peered through the glass, while Greg and Sister Mary Peyton continued their conversation about hospital protocols and procedures. The aide returned to tell them exactly what she had said earlier. Absent the name of any father, those two names were the names that the office had for Nok, and as Sister Mary Peyton had explained, it was a temporary designation.

"When you sign the official documents, you can indicate the name. The head nurse wanted to remind you to see the administrator regarding the deceased." Her tone was more reserved as she delivered this message. "If you like, I can take you to that office now."

Ping wanted to stay a little longer, so Greg and Sister Mary Peyton departed for the administrator's office, where they spent the next hour discussing the matter of Nok's cremation, the baby's care in the hospital, and adoption procedures for whoever would assume that responsibility. Albie had made financial arrangements with the hospital through the agency of his local bank, so those matters were not an issue.

As Greg expected, so much needed to be decided, but at least the infant was healthy and receiving the needed care. The administrator could not speak for the doctor, but all indications were that the child should remain in the neonatal unit for at least two or three more weeks.

Ping was waiting for them in the lobby, and as they walked slowly to the jeep in the parking lot, Greg took on the same business-like approach as the hospital administrator.

"I will go over to the mortuary and find out what the next steps will be, and then I need to go to the police station. You two don't need to do that. I can drop you at the house first."

"Something we should consider," said Sister Mary Peyton, "are regular visits to the hospital. I am happy to go while I am here, but I cannot stay in Chiang Mai for too long of a time."

"I will figure something out," said Greg. "I have time. I need to see T'ang. So as soon as we complete the cremation, I will get the remains to him, and he can decide about adopting the baby."

"Do you think that is the best thing?" Sister Mary Peyton asked. "T'ang adopting the child…"

There was no need to finish the sentence. They both knew that Albie would not want the child doomed to a hill tribe life, but Albie's return was more questionable than ever.

"I would like to adopt the baby," said Ping suddenly. Her voice was softer, calmer than ever. She often spoke in nervous, rapid bursts, but now she was measured and more composed.

All three stopped walking. Greg, stunned and speechless, looked at Ping and then at Sister Mary Peyton. The nun extended her arms and placed both her hands softly on Ping's shoulders.

"You are a wonderful, generous soul, but you have your baby and your own life to consider, and you do not need to do this."

"I want to do it. The baby has no mother and no father. The boy has no one, and I know Albie would take care of this baby like he took care of me and Dao."

"Can that even happen?" asked Greg.

"I don't know, but I don't see why not. The adoption process here is not at all like that in the States. I have placed children with families more than once."

Ping continued, her staccato bursts returning.

"I want another child. I asked Albie for another child. It is a better life for a child to have a brother or a sister. My sister means everything to me. A sister is more than a friend. I would die for my sister. She means that much to me. Dao will love a little brother for her entire life. After I am gone, she will have him, and he will have her. Sister, you can make this happen."

"Ok, Ping, slow down. Greg, what do you think?"

"I think Ping has a great idea."

CHAPTER FIFTEEN

Ping needed to shop, and Sister Mary Peyton agreed to accompany her. Greg was going in a different direction to the mortuary and then to the central police station, so the two women waved down a *tuk-tuk* and headed to the market. As Greg drove Wes' jeep to the city center, he wondered if Ping knew about Albie. Did she see something in the bassinet that the others could not see? Albie's broad forehead, his brooding eyes. Did she know all along how Albie loved Nok, and yet she was not jealous? Ping knew Albie loved her, and if he loved someone else, then all the better for that person. Treasure what you have, not what you want. The only thing that mattered to Ping was that Albie loved her and took care of her, and took care of Dao, and even took care of Dang. If Albie's love did not stop with one person, then why should hers?

The business at the mortuary was straightforward. They required a last name on the death certificate and absent any other, Greg provided his. Greg needed to contact one of the local temples that performed cremations and then the mortuary would release the body to that temple. They gave him a printed list of temples from which to choose. He could pick up the death certificate tomorrow and let them know which temple would conduct the ceremony. Greg did not recognize any of the temple names but hoped Ping might suggest one.

His attitude toward Ping had changed. In his own failed way, he never quite understood the relationship between Albie and Ping. Albie never struck him as one of those desperate expats purchasing, and when so inclined, replacing Thai wives like a garment in a wardrobe. Greg never saw him display any outward public affection for Ping or Dao—he attributed that to his British disposition—yet a constant fondness and respect emanated always. She was not his pet, and Ping was not a striver. In the beginning, her arrangement with Albie was a matter of expediency. She may even have romanticized the situation and viewed herself as a young girl accepting an arranged marriage, but somewhere love replaced both expediency and the picturesque revealing a remarkable woman—an abandoned woman, who could be homeless and penniless soon—offering now to adopt another child.

And it occurred to Greg that he had nothing but his own self-absorption. No one of any lasting meaning in his life. No one for whom he would sacrifice his own contentment or gratifications. Just the same, buoyed by Ping's generous spirit, he entered the police station believing others too would care, or at a minimum, create the appearance of such. After waiting for an hour, the police sergeant was less than helpful, surprising Greg with not only his disinterest but with a level of derision that struck Greg as completely out of character for Thai people.

Sergeant Somsak was the liaison to *farangs*, the *farang* police officer, no doubt because he spoke passable English. He became annoyed when Greg offered to speak in Thai. He knew about Albie and his failed attempt at the Research Station and hinted that he knew something about Wes and even Greg. He wasn't surprised that Albie had had a problem. *Wasn't he told to stay away from Ban Su and the area?*

"Why look for problems?" he asked rhetorically. "You don't go into a tiger's den and not think a tiger will eat you. You *farangs* are all the same, always the same problems with *camoys* or prostitutes."

Greg filled out a missing person's report and left, remembering that Wes had predicted such a response by the local police. Disenchanted, Greg delayed the trip to the British Consulate and opted to see Preeya. He had already waited too long for that reunion.

He veered through traffic more recklessly than was his custom, trying to remember the last time he saw her face and to recall the things she had said and the expression in her eyes as she said them. When they kissed goodbye, she had placed both her hands on his chest, her fingers tugging ever so gently on his shirt, pulling him closer, but preventing their bodies from a full embrace. Now, his mouth was dry as he knocked on the door. He did not doubt that this next kiss would be without restraint and reached for her even as the door opened.

***

Some moments stay with you, moments that are too big for all they contain, and find their way back to you not as hazy shadows or faded memories but with remarkable clarity as perfect images. For Greg, his first vision of Preeya was one such moment, and it seemed improbable that another could be so closely linked.

Greg was convinced that he looked the fool and told Preeya later that he was certain he made an embarrassing sound in place of words, when a woman, who was very much not Preeya, answered the door.

She was older than Preeya, with fulgent streaks of gray in her long black hair. She looked directly at Greg's dumbfounded expression, her face and demeanor unfazed. Not a smile nor a frown. Neither his reaction nor the interruption itself had had any effect on her. She remained silent, and Greg stumbled for the words of introduction. Much later, what remained with Greg was her steady stare. She was not pretty, though in fairness, most paled to Preeya. And although she was not beautiful, she possessed an unforgettable face. A face that had seen an unspeakable tragedy. And now, unbearable sorrow welled out like an unstoppable fountain.

Greg finally found the words to introduce himself and learned her name was Jaz. She invited him into the apartment, and Greg, seeing the cast on her other arm, knew immediately that this was Preeya's friend from the hospital. Embarrassed by the cast, she pulled a wrap around her shoulders and arms as they settled into chairs. Greg ignored her discomfiture and discussed the hospital and his good fortune to meet Preeya there. He was recounting the details of the meeting when Preeya arrived, carrying bags from the market. Her greeting to Greg was cool, restrained, only how surprised and pleased she was to see him, and far from what Greg had long been expecting. Greg wondered immediately if Jaz was aware of Greg's relationship with Preeya. Or was Preeya embarrassed by Greg's appearance at her residence? Did it speak to an inappropriate familiarity? Or even something else?

Preeya suggested they go out to get something to eat, even though she had just shopped, so they headed to a new restaurant nearby called Spice Market. Preeya's demeanor changed immediately as they walked down the street, and as they settled into their seats at the Spice Market, Preeya began asking Greg about his trip to Ban Su.

With little background, Greg explained to Jaz that his British friend was missing in the Golden Triangle area and that he had spent two weeks looking for him. He mentioned the places where they looked and, recognizing that the village names meant little to them, he switched gears and told them about the encounter with the monkey hunters. However, neither one of them found that amusing, so Greg retreated into his *khao-soy*, careful not to embarrass himself by splashing curry noodles onto his shirt.

Jaz remained quiet but became animated when Preeya began talking about the latest developments at Jack's. She was a huge fan of Preeya's success. Patrons packed the casino nightly and the big attraction was Preeya. The local heavy hitters, even those who most often frequent Fat Man's gaming house, were coming by and paying a hefty fee to get into Jack's back room. However, the biggest news was that starting next week, gamblers from Singapore and Macau, as well as Bangkok and Penang, were to arrive at Jack's for a big game. Jack was renovating the back room to accommodate more than just one table and the standing joke was how he would duplicate another Preeya or two!

The barrenness and grief which Greg imagined he saw in Jaz's face seemed to fade in Preeya's presence, and as they laughed and congratulated Preeya on her success, Greg's anguish of the last few days dissolved as well. Preeya even touched his arm once while talking about the renovations—their first physical contact since his return—and his concerns about Albie, Nok, and Ping waned.

Preeya described how Jack had given her a tremendous bonus to buy new outfits for next week and that she wanted Jaz to help her pick out the clothes. They laughed about the charade of wearing all white. *Here they were, two peasants in a noodle shop, and now they were planning to buy expensive clothes at Chiang Mai's most exclusive stores.* Preeya refused to see herself as a great beauty. She took more pride in her card skills than she did in the glamour.

Jaz said that despite the cast on her arm, she had been practicing shuffling, and she wanted to resume the card-dealing lessons that Preeya was giving her. Preeya was singing praises of Jaz when Fat Boy walked into the restaurant. His venomous eyes settled on them immediately, and he headed directly to their table.

Ignoring Greg and Preeya, he leaned close to Jaz and tugged at her arm.

"Go home."

Before Jaz could move or answer, Greg responded.

"Keep your hands off her."

"What are you going to do?" Fat Boy asked. He spoke Thai poorly with a thick Mandarin accent.

Greg stood and towered over him. Unlike Fat Man, whose height as much as his girth distinguished him, Fat Boy was small in stature but broad as an ox with thick arms and heavy legs.

"Leave her alone, or you will see!" Greg shouted.

Everyone in the restaurant was now looking at them.

"It's ok. I am going," said Jaz.

"You don't have to go. Who the hell is this fat midget to tell you what to do?"

"Now!" ordered Fat Boy.

Preeya grabbed Greg's arm.

"Let it go, Greg."

"No, I won't let it go. This slime ball killed Nok. You know that, right? She's dead. You beat to death a pregnant woman. Quite the man, aren't you?"

"I don't know what you are talking about."

"Bullshit. You killed her."

Jaz stood and bent over to hug Preeya and left.

Fat Boy let her pass and then sneered, shaking his head at Greg.

"Big mistake, big, big mistake," he snarled and walked out of the restaurant.

"You shouldn't have done that. You made him lose face," Preeya said.

"Why did she have to go with him?"

"Jaz works for Fat Man. She has for quite a while. She is like a slave to him for a great debt. Like an indentured servant."

"Was Fat Boy the one who broke her arm?"

"Yes."

"That's great. Now I have made it worse for her."

"No. Don't worry about that. I don't think he will hurt her again. Jaz said Fat Man was not happy that Fat Boy beat her and said as much to her. Fat Man promised it would never happen again. I think Fat Boy will never stop bullying her, but he won't defy his father. No one does."

"How did you become friends with her?"

"It is a long story, and I must get ready for work. One day I will tell you."

CHAPTER SIXTEEN

Unlike the Chiang Mai Police, the British Consul was deeply distressed to hear about the disappearance of a British national, and given that the missing person was Albert Saint Clair IV, the concern was even greater. Greg had little difficulty gaining an audience. He moved quickly from the receptionist to a polite, low-level functionary, whom Greg believed to be even younger than he was. Then, after a brief stop in an empty waiting room, a chubby, friendly, and effeminate man named Irving Raleigh, who had the thinnest mustache Greg had ever seen, escorted Greg to the third-floor office of a tall, string bean of a man, who introduced himself simply as Fowles and offered a seat to Greg.

Fowles leaned forward on his desk, resting his left elbow on the polished wood. His manicured fingers spread apart against his clean-shaven face, which rested in the palm of the same left hand. He listened attentively as Greg summarized the disappearance. Greg found it difficult to decide which details to include in his narrative and outlined the timeline of the disappearance and his own failed search efforts, sparing Fowles the reason for Albie's journey and the various speculations that Wes advanced.

Irving Raleigh interrupted Greg's report when he reappeared and delivered a green file to Fowles. With his back to Fowles, Irving smirked lewdly and winked an eye at Greg as he was leaving. Greg dismissed the gesture as he was more interested in whether the file was his or Albie's.

Greg concluded his report by detailing the response or lack thereof he received from the surly Sergeant Somsak.

When Greg had finished, Fowles picked up the phone and spoke to someone requesting his or her presence in his office before turning to Greg.

"Mr. Robber, we will take it from here. There will be an investigation, and we will immediately notify the family in England. Thank you again."

The response was terse, but not discourteous. Greg considered the brevity typically British and left feeling better now that he had reported the matter. He wondered what exactly they intended to investigate and what resources they could employ to locate Albie. He drove to Mama's dropping off Wes' jeep and regretted excluding Nok from his report. It was as if he too had accepted her death as a non-event, just another insignificant hill tribe person gone. His guilt continued to swell, yet what could he or anyone do?

***

The following morning Greg and Ping visited Wat Doi Suthep to arrange the cremation and a funeral ceremony. At Ping's urging, Greg made a hefty donation beyond the required payment. He then took Ping to St. Michael's to meet Sister Mary Peyton, leaving the two of them to discuss the adoption. At the mortuary, he signed the death certificate, paid the administrative fees, and gave them the name of the Wat for the funeral.

The morning had gone without incident until he arrived at Mama's.

Wes was not around, but the tables and bar were crowded, swarming with tourists and expats. The place was abuzz about Albie. There was no doubt the word was out, and the locals began besieging Greg with questions. *Do you think he is dead? Why would he go up there alone? Where did you look? What did the police say? Did you talk to the Brits?*

He understood why Wes was not around, and Greg left word with Mama that the funeral for Nok was the day after tomorrow. He was one step out the door when Joe Hardy cornered him. Joe was a freelance writer and wrote the weekly column "Hey Joe" in the *Bangkok Post*, a long-standing newspaper for English speakers. Joe was the tiresome sort, who welcomed himself into any conversation, ordered drinks freely, and seldom paid the tab. Greg did not know for just how long Joe had been living in Chiang Mai but knew that in the world of Bangkok expats, Joe was *persona non grata.*

The story was that Joe had tried to make a go of it in Bangkok, but with all the freelance expats searching for a way to survive in one business or another in the nation's capital, he found himself with too much competition.

Bangkok was teeming with foreign journalists covering the war or the foreign embassies, as well as breaking news and dedicated events.

Joe flipped the script on feature articles, and rather than writing about the newest restaurant in Bangkok, or the hippest bar, or even an interesting cultural experience, he began writing about the expats themselves. As a habitué of the Madrid Bar and other well-known Patpong watering holes, he ingratiated himself with fellow barflies—*farangs* and expats. He mined their experiences, their stories, and, if lucky, an extraordinary exploit, and then published it in his *Bangkok Post* column.

In the beginning, the expats saw his column as an opportunity to promote whatever their interests might be, and travel writers, gem dealers, and ambitious entrepreneurs, who thought their enterprise could profit by promotion to the English reading population in Bangkok, flocked to him. However, even Bangkok's vast expat population had its limits, and Joe ran out of stories. Then it occurred to Joe, as he listened to one narrative after another, that he could duplicate in print what Paul Harvey was doing on the radio with *The Rest of the Story*.

He had already become a master of the cliché and a purveyor of the tantalizing. He never quite twisted the truth but had no hesitancy in exaggerating, embellishing, mixing metaphors, and politely plagiarizing. So, with little effort, he dipped into the more salacious, scandalous, and titillating with what he called "The Back of the Story." Whatever line the editors of the *Bangkok Post* drew, Joe Hardy made a point of not crossing it, but living on it.

In no time at all, he betrayed so many trusts that only strangers and tourists would talk to him. Then, after he went as far as to call *Bangkok, a city of dark shadows, abounding with brothels, gaming houses, and saloons, where mobsters and cops fraternized and boasted openly about their exploits, and girls, thousands, and thousands of young girls, sold themselves for the promise of a future*—a shabby simulacrum of Raymond Chandler's LA noir—certain figures in Bangkok, both prominent and shadowy, encouraged Joe to relocate.

He started over in Chiang Mai. His first column from there was a confession. A mea culpa of sorts. He characterized his departure from Bangkok as *his luck had not just run out, but jumped on a motorcycle to head out of town.* Wes said that he had stolen that line from a famous author. Regardless, the apology and self-deprecation worked, and he plowed on. He returned to the mundane, comparing noodle shops, philosophizing on the merits of mango, and waxing sentimental or reveling in various annual festivals and Thai celebrations. Quietly, he confessed to Wes that he would one day collect all his sordid stories and publish a book.

However, tragedy and breaking news have always been journalists' bread and butter, their meal ticket, and Albie's disappearance was the stuff of that, so Joe pressed Greg for information, any information whatsoever.

It was noon when Greg arrived at Preeya's apartment. She seldom returned home, let alone made it to bed before two or three in the morning, and she tried to sleep until late morning. She said her neighbors were abundantly kind, but they were busybodies, who loved to talk and who had asked her questions about the *farang*.

Greg understood it all too clearly. He learned that oriental eyes were always watching him. Even in daily life, when the Thais seem busy with the mundane of selling, cooking, or shopping, their eyes were still scanning and following the *farang*. They knew the difference between a WT and an expat. Every Thai knew the difference, and everyone knew never to trust either.

Fortunately for Greg, Preeya was the exception. She had been waiting for him. She had bathed but remained undressed beneath a robe and neither wanted to talk about anything.

CHAPTER SEVENTEEN

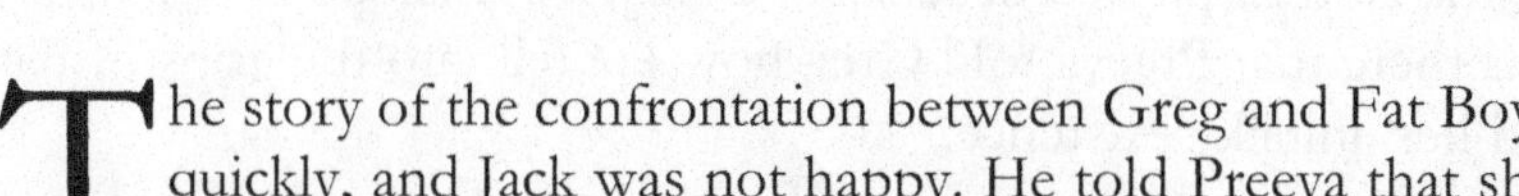

The story of the confrontation between Greg and Fat Boy spread quickly, and Jack was not happy. He told Preeya that she was a public person now, a celebrity, and people would scrutinize her every action. This was not the time to jeopardize their enterprise. Next week will be especially important, not only for next week but for both their futures.

"Jack knows who you are. He said it doesn't look good for me to have a *fan,* a boyfriend. It diminishes the allure, and it does not look good if the *fan* is a troublemaker."

"Is that what you think? That I am a troublemaker?"

"No. No. You are wonderful. You are genuinely kind, helpful, caring, and attractive, but this is what others think, and right now, we need to be careful."

"I am not afraid of Fat Boy."

"I know you are not, but this is not about Fat Boy. This is about all of us. You, me, and Jack, and Jaz too."

She curled even closer to him, wrapping her arm across his chest. Her long black hair covered part of her face, and he brushed aside the strands to look at her. She smiled at his soft touch.

"I don't have to work tonight," she said, "and then only tomorrow night for the rest of the week. Jack has work to do in the room and wants to create anticipation. He is quite a genius when you think about it."

"Let's go to the house tonight after dinner. You have never been there and maybe it could be a safe place for us. Away from the eyes around here."

"I would like that," she whispered.

He rolled onto his side and kissed her, wanting only to bury the turmoil and himself into her flesh.

***

They stayed in bed through the afternoon and even slept a little. For dinner, they went to the Night Market and ate tofu soup and a lotus-stem curry. The market was not as vibrant at this early hour but suited them perfectly. Across the klong, groups of schoolchildren in their blue and white uniforms were heading home. Lottery sellers were setting up shop nearby, arranging collapsible tables covered with charms and hanging the clothes-pinned tickets *for the lucky* on small poles.

It was there that Preeya told Greg how Jaz fell into the grips of Fat Man and her unlucky existence.

When Jaz was just fourteen or fifteen years of age, she lived in a small house next to Jack's residence—not the casino, but Jack's actual home. Jaz's father was a gambler and not a good one, and he accrued significant debt at Jack's gaming house. Jack helped him out more than once, and then they made a deal with the last bailout. Her father would no longer gamble at Jack's. Jaz said she remembered her mother being so pleased that she made a special meal for Jack and his entire family to thank Jack for all that he had done. Her father promised to devote all his energy to his job at the furniture factory.

However, once a gambler, always a gambler, and bad gamblers never get to be good gamblers. He avoided Jack's and started going to Fat Man's gaming house, and it wasn't long until he had debt again. Fat Man had businesses throughout Chiang Mai, and one of those was a popular mahjong parlor that his wife managed, and women—both Chinese and Thai—packed regularly. He would ridicule Jaz's father and tell him he belonged there and not with the men.

Fat Man covered his debt to others for a brief time and then had Jaz's father do menial work for him to pay off the debt. It was a hopeless cycle. Besides his job at the furniture factory, he now was working a second job for Fat Man, and unfortunately, kept trying to gamble his way out of debt.

One night at Fat Man's, he was in a game of poker with Fat Man and three others. Fat Man, unlike Jack, had no qualms about gambling in his own place. Back then, they did not have dealers either but would rotate the deck, so you can only guess what Fat Man may have done. Jaz's father had been drinking too much Mekong and was losing big yet again, and on that night, he bet the services of his daughter. He thought she could work at the mahjong parlor for Fat Man's wife, or at least that is what he told himself. Fat Man's vile laugh, full of derision and scorn, echoed in the room. Everyone there that night told the same story. The others at the table told him not to make the bet. They even offered to pay part of the debt, but no one had enough, and the greedy Fat Man made sure that everyone knew that too.

"So, he lost his daughter in a card game?" Greg asked.

"Yes."

"How is that possible?"

"What could anyone do?"

"And she has been there all this time?"

"Yes, like a prisoner for over twenty years."

"And the father did nothing to reclaim her?"

"He tried, once. I know you have heard about the game Russian roulette. There is another game in Thailand or a type of bet that is illegal but happens at places like Fat Man's. I have heard of it in other gaming houses too in Bangkok."

She was struggling now to finish the story. It was as if she knew too much, and the same unbearable sorrow, which he had seen in that stare of Jaz's, was now in her muted voice. Preeya looked so different in places like this market. Not the alluring beauty, just a pretty girl with kind eyes and a beguiling smile, turned somber now, as she explained the wager.

"It happens when you run out of money, chips to bet, acceptable IOUs, even promises, but you do not want to fold. You think your cards are winners, and you do not want to be bullied out of the game, and your adversary offers you an option. You can wager your life."

Greg wanted to stop her. He could see the heartache in her eyes. Hear the anguish in her voice. It was as if she was placing them both in the same room with the menacing Fat Man.

"Fat Man took out a revolver and removed all the bullets from the chamber. He spun it clean and then with a sibilant hiss said, *one bullet for the money and one for your daughter.* Jaz's father did what all gamblers do. He looked at his cards for an answer. Who knows what ran through his mind? It is not likely he had any chance to calculate his probability of winning, and less to calculate his odds with one, let alone two bullets in a revolver. The inimical Fat Man sat gloating, filling the room with his sickness.

"Jaz's father nodded his head and Fat Man spun the chamber, now loaded with two bullets, and set the gun in the middle with all the money. *Lose the game and you pull the trigger.*

"He lost," Preeya said.

"Did he shoot himself?"

"No. Even worse.

"He held the gun to his head, with a shaking hand no doubt, and collapsed in tears on the table sobbing like a child. The loathsome Fat Man laughed and laughed, the flesh quivering on his face. He called him many names, including a coward. Shame beyond shame."

"What happened?"

"He left the gaming house, and no one ever saw him again."

Horns blared and *tuk-tuks* backfired on the road. The tables were filling up, and the server asked them if they wanted anything else. Greg paid the bill.

As they drove to the house on his motorcycle, weaving through traffic along Suthep, he asked her how she met Jaz.

"Jack had always done what he could for Jaz since those early days. Like I told you, I grew up in Bangkok, and my mother and I lived with my uncle who also ran a gaming house. He knew Jack. Jack came to Bangkok every so often, and it was Jack who gave me my job here."

"I think I owe Jack an enormous debt for bringing you here, and if Jack wants me to be low-key, then that is the least that I can do to show my gratitude."

She hugged him with both arms and pressed her chest even closer to his back.

"Thank you. See, I knew you could be a good guy when you weren't being a troublemaker."

CHAPTER EIGHTEEN

The comfort and luxury of Albie's house surprised Preeya. Greg introduced her to Ping when they first arrived and, much to Greg's amazement, the two of them settled into a lengthy conversation, sometime during which Preeya declared to Greg her desire to attend Nok's funeral ceremony. Greg sat idly by as the two women talked for an hour, and it was only when they finally crossed the covered breezeway to his bungalow, did Preeya turn her attention to him.

"This is a beautiful house. I cannot believe you waited so long to bring me here. Were you afraid that I would steal the artwork?"

"Yes. That is exactly the reason."

"Ping is very distressed about your friend Albie."

"We all are."

"I wish I could have met her daughter tonight. What was her name, again?"

"Dao."

"Yes, Dao. How sweet. It means star, but of course, you know that."

"She is a lovely child and brilliant. Albie was teaching her English, and she loved it. Loved spending time with him."

"Tomorrow, I will see her. You should have told me she had a daughter; I would have brought a gift. Children love receiving presents. Are you helping Ping adopt that baby?"

"You and Ping seemed to have covered quite a bit this evening. I don't know what is happening with the adoption. Another friend of ours is helping her. I would have asked Ping tonight, but she was too busy talking with you."

"Do I sense some jealousy?"

"No. I was happy that you hit it off. I have brought no one here before, and I didn't know how Ping would react."

"She is not your wife. Why should she mind?"

"I don't know. I am culturally sensitive," he said with a smile.

"Yes. I noticed that." She leaned forward and kissed him.

"So, I am the first woman you have ever brought to your home. Should I be nervous or flattered?"

"Why don't we find out?"

CHAPTER NINETEEN

Greg sat on the ground facing T'ang in the decaying light of the hut and listened as the old man talked about the place beyond thunder. Nok's ashes were in a ceramic urn next to the cross-legged T'ang. The old man's hands were shaking as he tried to remove a rolled betel leaf from a small silver container, tarnished black over the years of use. Greg guessed Kanda rolled the betel mix for him, and cooked for him as well, now that Nok was gone. T'ang dropped it twice before placing it in his mouth. What teeth he had left were black from the constant use of the plant.

Greg made no pretense about understanding death. Sister Mary Peyton cried as she sat next to him at the funeral ceremony earlier that morning. She had spared him any theological lesson, but he knew she believed that death was a portal to life everlasting with God. She also believed that Christ had destroyed death. He had no idea what that meant and wondered why she was crying if she believed that.

T'ang said you had to be quiet to hear the voices from beyond the thunder. His hands were still shaking, and he asked Greg to light the wick in the small glass bottle. Greg had never heard voices and considered those who claimed as much to be charlatans or simply crazy. In T'ang's case, he leaned toward the latter, but also recognized how sad the situation was for him. The wick floated in a clear liquid and lit easily. In the flickering light, Greg could see the black juice slipping from the old man's mouth and dripping across his craggy chin.

Ping hugged Greg when he left. She wrapped the urn carefully in a silk cloth and packed it into the saddlebag of his motorcycle. She reminded him to be careful as he drove and to be as compassionate as possible with T'ang. *Nothing is worse than losing a child.* No pain can match that. And that pain never goes away. Never.

Greg told T'ang that he would spend the night in Ban Su and leave tomorrow. He could see the old man rocking ever so slightly. Greg asked him if he could get him anything, and T'ang then asked him to load his pipe. Greg had performed this task often throughout his travels in the hill tribe regions. He had little affection for the black pill. He found opium too much like a sledgehammer. When he sobered up, he invariably had a massive headache—and he had enough headaches already without the Big O. Given a choice, he preferred weed, but the pipe was, as Elliott explained, more than a custom, more than an icebreaker to draw close to his guests in the villages, it was a type of bond, a communion of sorts.

He did not need to get any closer to T'ang tonight, so he arranged the viscid substance, a resinous pill, in the black bowl of the long, slender ivory pipe, but abstained, merely attending to the flame for T'ang. The old man worked to inhale and coughed repeatedly.

While they were at the temple, shortly after the ceremony, he saw Preeya approach the monk who conducted the ritual as if there were throngs of mourners. The monk sat imperiously on the elevated platform with his legs crossed. Preeya approached from the side, knelt, bowed deeply, touching her forehead to the floor, and passed an envelope toward him. He did not reach for it. They spoke together in hushed voices, and then Preeya rejoined Greg.

Greg told her she didn't need to do that. He had paid for the services already. She acted surprised by his comment. *I thought you understood Thai customs.*

T'ang's eyes grew narrow and glassy, and his voice, now muffling slurred, unintelligible words, made it clear to Greg that he had nothing left for another child. Greg considered giving T'ang the death certificate, but to what end? The old man couldn't read, and he didn't need a piece of paper to tell him that Nok was dead.

In the darkness outside of T'ang's hut, he recalled standing in the same place with Albie, looking at the myriad of stars, commenting lamely on their beauty, on their stunning brightness from this mountain height, and Albie portraying the sight as a great jigsaw of space and particles, *a swarm of ephemeral quanta, an infinite arabesque of reality*. He stood alone again tonight and looked heavenward, scanning for the place beyond thunder, searching for something, anything, to stop the inexorable, slithering nihilism from polluting his soul, but all he could see were the tears sliding down T'ang's woeful face and his own utter isolation.

***

Jeeps had a wide enough path to climb from Chiang Rai to the split in the road that took you either to the Research Station or else to Mae Salong. From the Research Station, jeeps could navigate the one narrow trail that led to Ban Su, but it was fraught with seasonal challenges. For that reason, motorcycles were the preferred mode of transport for *farangs* like Greg and Albie when they journeyed from village to village. If you drove a jeep up the mountain, you invariably had to park it somewhere and make your way on foot, otherwise, you risked the chance of damaging the jeep or worse.

Of those considerations, neither one concerned Sergeant Somsak, who at first light could be heard outside Nok's hut swearing and cursing at his men, the path, and their entire enterprise. His discovery of Greg in Ban Su only heightened his vitriol.

Their lead jeep had become immobilized when the path narrowed to such a degree that the passenger side of the jeep slipped over a washed-out section and left the vehicle teetering on a ledge with two wheels on the path and two suspended in mid-air. The rocks blocked the driver's door, compounding the situation and compelling the driver and Sergeant Somsak to jump out of the jeep and over the ledge, before tumbling safely to a flattened area. It was all very comical to the villagers who witnessed the fiasco.

"What are you doing here?" Somsak wanted to know.

"I came up to deliver the ashes of a deceased villager."

"Whose ashes?"

Greg explained and made the mistake of reminding Sergeant Somsak that he had shared the news of Nok's death with him when last they met.

"I told you then, and I will tell you again, you don't know how to stay out of the way."

Greg wanted to answer, but Somsak was already onto a full rant about the British Consulate and their meddling and the entire senselessness of everything involved with this Albie character. The shouts of his men cut his tirade short when the jeep slipped even more while they were trying to lift it and carry it backward to regain enough path. Fortunately, no one was injured as the vehicle tumbled first to its side and then upside down. Somsak stormed down the path toward the other vehicles in the search party.

Greg had hoped to get an early start back to Chiang Mai, but with the path blocked by a cavalcade of police jeeps, an early departure was not possible.

Somsak soon calmed down and exhibited genuine leadership skills, directing half of his men to traffic management and the reclamation of the upside-down jeep, and the other half to interviews with the villagers. In a matter of hours, Somsak completed both assignments and remarkably, at least in Greg's opinion, his men even started the engine of the damaged vehicle and backed that one down the path along with the other jeeps.

Somsak didn't learn anything about Albie as far as Greg could discern, and Somsak did not seem willing to share what other villages he intended to visit. The list of villages scattered in the hills was long. Greg discovered these troops were a combination of provincial police from both Chiang Rai and Chiang Mai, and while they conducted themselves with professionalism during the interviews, it grew clear to Greg that Somsak viewed these humble hill people with derision. Greg could almost hear Wes's voice and his description—*a rabble breed.*

Greg left before the noon hour, and as he negotiated the serpentine path slowly, even a bit more carefully than usual, it occurred to him that Sergeant Somsak and his men never once made any inquiries about the poppy fields or opium. Perhaps they believed those fields were just as likely in Burma as they were in Thailand, but their indifference seemed odd. What he wanted to tell the Sergeant was to talk to Fat Boy, but the slim possibility that Wes' story was correct, and somehow Elliot had his hand in all this, kept him quiet.

CHAPTER TWENTY

The front page of the *Bangkok Post* was dedicated completely to the student demonstrations in Bangkok. It was the headline on the second page that sent Wes into a tirade. British Scientist Missing in Golden Triangle—presumed dead.

"If Hardy so much as steps foot into this place, I will beat him to a pulp."

Hardy's story did not reveal the source of his information. He only wrote, "according to sources in the Chiang Mai Police." The British Consul had no comment and would not even confirm that an investigation was taking place, yet Joe Hardy had Albie dead and buried.

Greg felt awful. He had returned to Chiang Mai in the dark and driving the last hour of the trip on Highway 1 had left him frazzled. He tossed all night with a pounding headache. His only solace was the scent of Preeya, which still lingered on the pillows. In the morning, he went directly to Mama's for a cup of strong coffee but found Wes, and in Hardy's place, received an earful of invectives. He had a beer instead and explained to Wes that despite Joe Hardy's interrogation, he had not divulged the least bit of information to him. He wanted to tell him that Elliot had taught him well. When Wes had calmed down, Greg reported his visit with T'ang and his surprise meeting with Sergeant Somsak and his investigative team.

"What a joke. Those cops couldn't find their ass with two hands on it. Especially up there."

Greg told him about the overturned jeep.

"They will be lucky if someone doesn't get hurt. I will bet you anything they don't go close to any of the border areas. Hell, Ban Su might just as well be in Burma, and I am surprised they even went there."

"They had to go there. If for no other reason than I mentioned it to Somsak."

"You are right. It's a miracle they even found it. It's not like there are road signs anywhere up there. It's hundreds, no, thousands, hundreds of thousands of square miles."

Wes was right. Greg had taken it for granted how easily he and Wes made their way from one tiny village to another, as well as the advantages of being on motorcycles or on foot.

Wes put his hand on Greg's shoulder. His grip was powerful, and he pressed his thumb against him.

"You need to stay away from there for a while. There is no reason to go back up there. Let the cops, or whomever, poke around, do whatever they think they are doing, and not get involved anymore. We did everything we could do. It is time to lie low."

Greg just nodded. Here he was again, listening to yet another person telling him to mind his own business. The problem was that Albie was his business. How could he just stop?

***

Preeya and Greg spent the next three days and nights exclusively in each other's company. Neither had any tug in their lives other than the anticipation of the big gambling game next week. Before he left to pick up Preeya, he told Ping that T'ang placed no claim on the baby, and Ping shared that Sister Mary Peyton was making progress with government officials for the adoption. The multitude of issues, which worried him only a brief time ago, seemed to find resolve.

He and Preeya took a day trip to Mae Thien Waterfall and hiked up the trail toward the summit. It exhausted Preeya in little time, and Greg made fun of her sedentary life. As they sat on a ridge watching the rushing water in the gorge below, she remarked how strenuous it must have been for Greg to wander the hill tribe regions for these past two years. Greg told her about his knee surgeries. He said he was grateful to walk and hike. After the second surgery, he wasn't sure he would be able to do anything very demanding, but his rehab went well, and he was continually inspired by teammates who had even more crushing injuries and fought back. Preeya said that Jaz inspires her in much the same way. *Nothing defeats her.*

She slid sideways, stretched her legs, and settled her head on his thigh. Her long hair spilled across his lap, and she stared up at him, smiling. Greg brushed a strand away from her cheek. She sighed and relaxed her weight against his leg. She closed her eyes, concealing the dusted brown of her irises. He didn't want this picture to end, ever. He had never been this happy. And if he weren't so afraid, he would have told her.

His eyes settled on the white amulet around her neck. He stroked her neck and touched the polished stone.

"Where did you get this necklace?"

"It was a gift. A long time ago from a friend."

"It is beautiful. The stone is so white. What does the inscription say?"

"My name is on one side and R 3:5 on the other."

Her hand reached up and tenderly covered his hand and the amulet.

"What does R 3:5 mean?" Greg asked.

With her eyes still closed, she evaded his question and answered with another question.

"Do you believe in karma?"

"Buddhist karma? The sum of your actions in this life decides your next life?" he asked.

"No, not that. No. I know most Westerners don't believe in reincarnation."

"Do you mean fate and destiny?" he asked.

"Sort of."

"What goes around, comes around," Greg said.

She sat up, resting on her elbows.

"Say that again."

"What goes around, comes around. A cliché. You hurt someone or do something bad, and it comes back like a boomerang to hit you. What you do to someone, or someone does to you, particularly something not nice, always comes back to haunt you or bite you. I had a coach who used to say *the people you step on while climbing up are the same ones you see when you are falling.*"

"Do you believe that?" she asked.

"I do. Yes."

"So do I."

And she leaned back as before, resting her head in his lap. She closed her eyes yet again and now crossed both her hands on top of her amulet, shielding its cryptic secret. Greg placed his hands on her shoulders, content to watch her breathe and wait for an answer.

***

On their last night together, he woke to find Preeya sitting in the dark at the table in the adjoining room. A makeshift desk for Greg to organize his photos and notes. The surface recently cleared for the appearance of neatness, as well as for an abundance of caution. Silhouetted against the window and leaning straight back as she shuffled a deck of cards, she looked taller, stronger, and even more erotic and alluring, if that was possible.

"What are you doing?"

"I couldn't sleep. I guess I am anxious about this week and wanted to practice. It calms me."

Greg drew up a chair and sat next to her. Her white tank top almost covered the curve of her breast. He could see the cut of her silk undergarment on her naked legs. Slants of moonlight graced her nimble hands, riffling and strip cutting. He knew their softness, marveled at their dexterity.

He must have asked her how she learned to handle cards as she did, but reminiscent of the first time he sat next to her he could barely speak, bewitched by the magic of her voice, the musky scent of their carnality, and the hypnotic deftness of her hands.

***

Her first lesson came from her cousin Mali. It wasn't so much a lesson as a card trick. For as long as she could remember, Mali was always shuffling cards and practicing card tricks. She would interrupt Preeya while Preeya was doing her homework to show her a trick. Preeya would smile, pick a card, bury the card, and pretend to be amazed when Mali showed her the card. She would then return to her task. School was her focus, and games would not distract her. She was an honors student with an exceptionally excellent memory and had every intention of going to university. Until she discovered just how expensive and exclusive the university was, and she realized her mother would never have the financial wherewithal to support her.

Her teachers told her she could win a scholarship, but even a thirteen-year-old can do the math on the vast number of schoolchildren in Bangkok and the admission rate at the universities. One evening, she and Mali decided they would become dealers and built up the courage to ask their mothers for permission. It was more of a teenage pronouncement during dinner than a formal request. Neither of the mothers was inclined to allow it. Undeterred, the girls turned to Mali's father, Sarathon, whose Thai name means tiger.

The eponymous owner of the Tiger's Den agreed with the girls. He thought career aspirations were good, and he said that he would arrange their training to start the next day—after they completed their homework.

The girls were ecstatic, and after completing their assignments, they sat and waited anxiously in the small storeroom next to the kitchen. Their hearts sank when Thaksin, the stone-faced croupier of the roulette table, walked in. He was their least favorite person in the entire gaming house. He was always scolding the girls for being in the wrong place, talking too loudly, or just being pests. He called them the mosquito twins.

He sat across from them at the table and shook his head. The natural set of his face was oriental disdain. Preeya was certain that the Tiger was punishing Thaksin as much as he was punishing them.

"Where are the cards?" Mali asked.

"Cards. Did you come here to play? If you want to play, go back to your room with your dolls and toys."

"I do not have any toys," said Mali. "I am thirteen and do not play with dolls."

"Hah!" Thaksin scoffed. "Tiger said I am to teach you to be dealers. Is that what you want?"

Both girls said yes in unison.

"Ok. First rule. No talking. None. No questions and no talking. If you talk, then the day's lesson is over. Is that understood?"

Preeya caught herself before answering and grabbed Mali's arm. She put her finger to Mali's lips and both girls then nodded their heads. They thought they were clever.

"Good. You are not so stupid after all."

He collected two large, empty pineapple crates from the storage rack and instructed the girls to place them under their chairs solidly and resume their seats. The result was that they now sat quite higher than the table and both giggled a bit at their new stature.

"No laughing either. No laughing, ever. You should not even smile, but that is for another day."

Once that was clear, he instructed them to sit up as straight as possible and to suck in their tummies to support their back.

"Place both your feet on the box beneath you. One day that will be the floor, if you don't get squashed by a fly swatter before then. Now, place your hands on the table with fingers slightly spread."

The girls did precisely as instructed and looked at each other proudly, like soldiers lined up and standing at attention.

"If you decide to come back tomorrow, leave your fancy rings and bracelets. Dealers should have nothing on their hands."

He studied them. The scene was risible, but he did not even smile. Two teenage girls—one with a ponytail, the other with pigtails, sitting like statues, feet on pineapple boxes.

"Finally, you must look straight ahead. You must be able to see everyone at the table while looking straight ahead. In time, you will learn to move your head properly. Questions?"

Mali caught herself before answering. Preeya could hear her faint utterance.

"Good."

He pulled out a black and white alarm clock.

"For the first day, we will try for twenty minutes."

He could read the dismay on both their faces.

"Yes. You are to sit as tall as you can, feet planted, and hands resting as they are for twenty minutes. When you are too tired to do that, then you may leave. One day, you will learn to relax in such a posture as you sit there for hours on end. Questions?"

Preeya could see the scowl on Mali's face.

"Good."

The routine was the same for weeks. The only variation was an incremental increase in the time until they reached one hour. After that, nothing changed. Preeya was convinced that it was nothing more than a test, but Mali was furious with her father. Called him diabolical. She was certain it was some type of cruel punishment. The girls consoled each other and pledged not to let Thaksin break them. They knew monks sat and meditated for hours on end and gained enlightenment. If old men could do that, then so could they.

***

Preeya fanned the deck of cards across the table. She was sitting just as he remembered that first night in Jack's, except now he could see the round of her breast on the side of the sleeveless, white tee shirt.

"That is how we learned. Eventually, we practiced opening a new deck of cards properly and fanning them on the table, and after two or three more lessons, we flipped them over in one motion to reveal all the cards."

With a deft touch of her finger on the lead card, she did exactly that for Greg.

"Every lesson was exactly one hour, no more and no less, and Thaksin never once changed character or disposition. Lessons were suspended for exams or special occasions like festivals or holidays, but the format never varied. After a year, he stopped insulting us.

"Mali was becoming quite a beauty and boys were calling her, and even the exacting Thaksin could see her blossoming. She was statuesque, and the training no doubt contributed to her graceful bearing.

"I cannot recall when, but eventually we dealt the cards to imaginary players and to Thaksin as one of such players."

"Did you ever talk?" Greg asked.

"A few times. One of us broke the code for one stupid reason or another, and as promised, the lesson ended immediately. He never ceased trying to trick us."

"Is Mali still a dealer?"

"No. She never was."

"Really? All that and she didn't continue."

"Mali never wanted to be a dealer. She liked the idea, but not the actual work. She loved the magic acts and the tricks and kept practicing those things, but that had a bad ending."

"What happened?"

"One day, when we were older, we learned about betting and about rakes and how to extract them. Mali was the dealer and when she distributed the cards to our fictitious players and Thaksin, she did a bottom card deal. I thought it was good. I never saw it.

"Thaksin sat there for a long time and said nothing. Just waited. Remember, we still were forbidden to speak. Eventually, we would learn when to ask *how many cards.* Or how to move the game along with *your bet* and other short phrases. But not that day.

"Thaksin got up and went into the kitchen. He came back with a handful of peanuts, lettuce leaves, and a hammer, along with a small culinary hatchet.

"He wrapped the peanuts into a long leaf, looked at Mali, and said *this is about the size of your pretty finger.* He then smashed the leaf with the hammer. The blow was so loud you could only imagine the sound of the cracking nuts.

"*This is what will happen the first time.* Mali did everything she could to keep back her tears.

"He then wrapped another leaf, and using the hatchet, chopped it into tiny pieces. *This is what will happen after that.*

"Mali broke down, sobbed, and sobbed, tried to say it was just a joke. A trick. *Why can't we just have fun?*"

"*You are to be a dealer and not a mechanic.*"

Preeya collected the cards into one hand and fanned open the entire deck with the brush of her thumb and fingers.

"What is a mechanic?" Greg asked.

"Someone who manipulates the cards. Arranges them or selects them and deals them with his design. The first one I ever met dealt me four aces on every hand. I watched him shuffle, cut, deal, and each time I had four aces."

"So, it's card tricks. A magic act."

"Yes, and no. Unless you are gambling and then there is nothing magical about it."

She closed the fan, and with the entire deck still in just one hand, split it into two and then shuffled them back into a single deck.

"Have you ever played with good poker players and no dealer? A friendly game. Chances are the winner manipulated the cards in some manner during his deal."

Greg thought of Elliot's constant success but then considered that he had success when Preeya dealt too.

"Gamblers, pros can spot a cheat a mile away. They watch every action of the dealer."

"So how can you ever cheat, then?"

"The magic comes with misdirection. Another mechanic I met used his talking, his banter to create the misdirection. Questions, anecdotes, jokes. Nonstop chatter. He was the expert in the second card deal and I could never see him do it."

"Second card deal?"

"He could hold the cards right in front of you and deal the second card and not the top card to whomever or whenever he liked."

"But why? What's the point? It's just another card."

"He knew where certain cards were in the deck. He could arrange them during the shuffle. Memory is part of the mechanic's magic."

She spread her hands apart and, bending the cards in her right hand, propelled them rapidly one by one into her left hand. The flourish was flawless. Magical.

"And observation is the consummate skill of the professional gambler.

"That is why we learned to sit up straight, hands and arms out front always and on full display for the players.

"This week, every gambler is a pro. Everyone will watch my every move, always. No one will be distracted by the sound of broken glass, or like you, by my perfume.

"If you want tricks or magic or want to cheat, then you need misdirection. That was Mali's mistake. She failed to provide that misdirection."

"Can mechanics get away with cheating with pros watching?"

"I don't know. I suppose if they are fantastic. There was one man I met in Bangkok. He came to Mali's wedding. He was a *farang,* an American, a bit of a talker, I remember, and when he learned I was a dealer, he asked me to show him how I shuffle the cards. I thought it was amusing, but he was a friend of Tiger's and he seemed nice.

"We sat alone at a table outside on the veranda. We then played a few hands of five-card draw. Just the two of us. No money. Just dealing, drawing, and some imaginary wagers. He said I was good. Wished me good luck, and I asked him if he would like to deal a few hands. He agreed.

"As he shuffled the cards, he asked me if I ever gambled myself, and I said no. He said he was surprised. *You could win quite a sizeable sum of money. You could even learn to win every time. Doesn't that interest you?* I said no, and that I doubted that winning every time was possible.

"He suggested we play five hands and promised that he would win all of them. Or ten even, if I was so skeptical. I laughed. I said what if I catch you cheating, and he said that would never happen."

"What happened?"

"He won all five, and we played five more and he won those."

"And you didn't catch him?"

"No."

"How did he do it?"

Preeya didn't answer. Another secret. She placed the deck of cards in a stack in front of her and folded her graceful hands.

"Whether he could do that at a table full of professionals, I don't know. I heard that in Singapore there is a man named Bao. Supposedly, the best mechanic in the world. Gamblers purposely play him to catch him. He would never admit to being a cheat, but everyone knows and wants to be the one who catches him in the act. Gamblers are crazy."

"And you…?"

"For me, the most important thing is the rake. Real gamblers are smart, and no one likes to be cheated. So extracting the exact amount or even a little less is what keeps everyone calm at a game. Remember, unlike you, these men are not familiar with losing very often, and in gambling, someone is always losing."

"Maybe people like me are just unlucky in cards," Greg suggested.

"Gambling is not about luck. You are confusing chance and probability with luck. Everything is calculated in cards, and it is not good fortune. So, there is always tension and suspicion. The last thing Jack and I want is someone questioning the deal and taking his frustration out on us. No. No one will ever catch me cheating."

Greg thought her words sounded much like Bao, the Singaporean mechanic.

"Here," she said. "Cut the cards. High card wins."

"What's the wager?" Greg asked.

"Loser gives the winner a back rub."

"Are you going to cheat?"

"Maybe, but you will never know."

CHAPTER TWENTY-ONE

Their honeymoon ended the day before the big gambling event. Greg began to miss her even as she started packing the sundries that had accumulated at his bungalow. She would be busy for long hours during this upcoming week and sleep would be at a premium whenever she could get it. Greg said he would have to take cold showers regularly. They were walking out the door toward his motorcycle when a telegram arrived by courier. Someone by the name of Anthony Blackledge was arriving in Chiang Mai this afternoon and wanted to meet Greg at the British Consulate in matters regarding Albert Saint Clair IV.

Greg dropped Preeya at her apartment and went directly to the Consulate. Fowles was expecting him and offered him a cup of tea.

Fowles maintained a composed exterior despite his displeasure with the Joe Hardy story, which was not at all flattering of the British Consul. He told Greg such sensationalism was frequent in the British press, but he had hoped the editors of the *Bangkok Post* would have had a bit more restraint if not courtesy than those on Fleet Street, then commented that compassion never was a trademark of journalists.

Greg sipped his tea. The assurance that marked Fowles' manner when first they met was waning. An already troubling matter had become a public embarrassment. The British foreign diplomatic hierarchy was not unlike the U.S. arrangement. The Consulate in Chiang Mai was an outpost, a satellite office for the British Embassy in Bangkok. Career diplomats like Fowles, already cast as permanently middle-ranking civil servants, have their aspirations quashed by scandals. Solving problems without fanfare or publicity is the only desired outcome.

According to Albie, Fowles had arrived in Chiang Mai in the wake of another discomfiting scandal. His predecessor, it seems, had an over-fondness for massage parlors. A proclivity, which, unsurprisingly, to all familiar with Thailand, did little to damage his standing in the local community. In fact, unlike Fowles, he was a bit of a fan favorite. A bon vivant. Fluent in all things Chiang Mai.

And had his predilections not competed so strenuously with his other priorities, including three-martini lunches, overspending, and accounting errors, then even his growing appetite for the more salacious in the shaded, sordid, side streets of Chiang Mai may well have been overlooked. But as the Chinese are so apt to say. *Fame brings trouble.*

Fowles was here to reassert the dignity of the Foreign Office. Commissioned to steady the ship. He needed the Albie quandary to go away.

"Before Mr. Blackledge arrives, I should share with you other news. Not exceptionally good news, I am afraid. One of the Thai police officers, who was investigating in the Golden Triangle, was lost."

"What do you mean, *lost*? Dead? Missing?"

"Do you know anything about something they call swamp grass?"

"Sure. They are death traps, sinkholes, a version of quicksand underneath the guise of long, waving elephant grass. From above, it looks like an open field with tall grass. From a high vantage, it would appear as a straightforward way to cross over to another hillside. Don't tell me one of those police officers waded into it?"

"I am afraid that is precisely what occurred." He spoke with a despondent voice, his career no doubt drowning in the same swamp grass.

"Why would someone be so stupid to do that?"

"I don't know. I am not sure who can answer that either."

Greg did not recall seeing any locals with Somsak's police team. They were all city boys, making their first trip into the area. He shook his head in disbelief and dismay. Death was mocking everyone.

"Sergeant Somsak called me two hours ago. He was exceedingly distressed, as you might imagine. He said the newspapers have it. We will see it tomorrow."

Greg wondered if Somsak had ordered the officer to go down there. How awful for Somsak if that were the case. What an awful way to die, he thought. To drown in dirt.

They were both silent. Each lost in his thoughts. The sound of footsteps and chatter in the hallway and anteroom broke the spell.

The same foppish Irving escorted Anthony Blackledge into the office, much as he had Greg on his first visit, and thankfully spared them all his veiled theatrics today. Introductions were made, and

Blackledge apologized if he had kept them waiting. The plane from Bangkok was late and there was little he could do.

He thanked Fowles and Greg for making themselves available on short notice and acknowledged Greg's apparent friendship with Albie.

Fowles offered him a cup of tea, and Blackledge readily accepted. Greg thought Blackledge looked like an Oxford don, only better dressed. A tall, imposing figure, neatly groomed, trimmed mustache, and outfitted in a well-tailored, dark gray suit—Savile Row, no doubt—with a white shirt and a blue silk tie. His facial features were set somewhere between dour and stern.

In an assured voice, he informed Fowles of his recent arrival in Bangkok and his good fortune to speak with the British ambassador yesterday afternoon.

Fowles said that he was aware of the appointment and added without sincerity that it pleased him the two of them could meet. His tone doing little to assuage the tension in the room.

Blackledge settled into his chair, tasted the tepid tea poured from the same pot as Greg's cup fifteen minutes earlier, and, feigning a smile, set it aside. He listened as Fowles took time to explain the status of the investigation and that, unfortunately, there was no added information regarding Albie. Fowles reported the recent probe by the police, leaving out the bit about the dead police officer, and took it upon himself to report that Greg and another American friend of Albie's had also searched.

Blackledge wanted to know if anything further could be done, to which Fowles replied that from the perspective of the Foreign Office, he saw no other measures. Greg knew immediately that citing the FO was an overreach and might work with locals, but not with Blackledge. His face radiated impatience and disdain.

"I certainly appreciate the inconvenient situation presented to this office," said Blackledge frostily. "My"—his tone and the emphasis on the word *my* was not subtle—"conversation with the Foreign Office in London, and with Her Majesty's ambassador in Bangkok has led me here, and may I add, here on behalf of the Saint Clair family, hoping the Queen's Government might utilize its full cache of resources. Unless, of course, I have mistaken this office for a quango here in the Orient."

Fowles was peeved, and despite the insult to his office, maintained his unflappable manner. Blackledge may have summarized the hierarchy of power, but Fowles refused to be cowed and remained evasive and appropriately diplomatic.

"I believe we have exhausted our resources, but since you requested Mr. Robber to be here, perhaps you would like some time alone with him?"

"Thank you. Yes. I need to speak with Mr. Robber, but if you don't mind, could we have a moment first?" His razor-blade smile made it clear this was not a request.

Greg smiled secretly. He excused himself and waited in the anteroom with Fowles' secretary.

It wasn't difficult for Greg to guess what Blackledge wanted from Fowles. The British Consulate existed in Chiang Mai to house Fowles and his crew, as well as the secret services contingent on the other side of the building. Blackledge was sufficiently informed that the Head of Visa Section, or another nonsensical cover name, had a stable of Thai assets, contacts in Mae Salong at a minimum, who were monitoring the Border Patrol reports and making excursions into Burma. Matters with the Kuomintang and the drug interdiction programs in the Golden Triangle were U.S. and not British concerns, but Elliot had shared enough for Greg to understand that the gem industry, particularly the massive excavation of jade in certain areas deep in Burma, was of international importance, and the Brits were not ceding those interests any time soon.

When the conference ended, Fowles vacated his office, allowing Greg and Blackledge to have their privacy. Greg then, for what he hoped was the last time, detailed the events surrounding Albie's disappearance, and included the death of Nok and his own belief that Fat Boy was the perpetrator. He closed with the latest news about the swamp grass accident.

Blackledge had been taking notes as Greg spoke, and when Greg had finished, Blackledge set his pen down and asked Greg pointedly if he thought Albie was alive.

Greg said he didn't know.

Blackledge closed his notebook and sat back. He rocked in his chair as if collecting his thoughts. "If you don't mind me asking, what are your most immediate plans?"

"I don't have any. I wrapped up my research and I was only staying in Chiang Mai to assist Albie."

"Yes. I understand that part, but now what will you do?"

"I don't know. I have hardly had any chance to think about it. There has been so much going on. We looked for Albie. We had a funeral and then I went back to Ban Su with Nok's ashes. It's been hectic. And there is still no certainty about Albie."

"Quite. Yes. I can only imagine." Blackledge crossed his legs and, with the back of his hand, wiped imaginary dust off his dress pants. "We would like you to stay in Chiang Mai longer, if that is possible. I am instructed to give you money and to ask you to give additional money to the woman who has been living with Lord Saint Clair. I understand she has a child."

"Yes. That's right. Did you call Albie, *Lord?*"

"Yes. Albert Saint Clair IV is Lord Albert Saint Clair IV. The 15th Baron Lynn. Did you not know that?"

"No. I don't know why, but no. He was always just Albie to me. I saw something in the *Bangkok Post* article that called him *Sir*, but I guess it didn't register."

"The use of the appellation *Sir* is currently acceptable but covers others who are not nobility. I expect it is all very confusing to you as an American. Nevertheless, would you be willing to stay at the residence, take care of it as needed? We will cover all expenses."

"How long?"

"Well, that is stickier, isn't it?"

Blackledge talked about international law, foreign property situations, and the sensitive imbroglio of determining if Lord Albert was deceased—a matter that would be difficult in Great Britain, but was a veritable quagmire in a foreign country, particularly a developing or third-world nation. The Declaration of Presumed Death takes seven years in England, but overwhelming evidence, even without the remains, can shorten that period. He said that if one was to include the caveat that Thai laws, the government, and its bureaucracy are sometimes confusing, opaque, and even corrupt, then it was safe to say that a resolution might take an indeterminate amount of time.

"Can we simply agree for now that it would only be for a brief period? I know that is vague, but it would be an immense help to us if we had someone here with whom we could communicate and transfer documents for us. We can compensate you, and you would do the Saint Clair family a great service."

"Why not just use the British Consul here?"

"We will need an intermediary for all matters relating to Lord Saint Clair. I am afraid this office might find it unseemly to indulge in business matters for the family. And I have every reason to believe from Lord Saint Clair himself that he regarded you with the highest of esteem."

CHAPTER TWENTY-TWO

How do you measure success? For Michigan football, success meant beating Ohio State, and every day of the year and at every practice and every workout in the weight room, everyone was reminded of that. For Ping, it was about security for herself and her child. For Sister Mary Peyton, something to do with God. For Elliot, it was hard to say. For Greg, harder yet.

But for Jack and Preeya, it was, as it became known around Chiang Mai, *The Game*, and it was an enormous success. It lasted three nights. Gamblers filled the three tables on the first night and every few hours they rotated, so different gamblers played each other, and all had at least one session with Preeya as the dealer. On night two, the leading ten money winners played, and they split their time at two different tables, leading to the last night when the five biggest winners circled Preeya for the final showdown.

The betting limits of the first two nights disappeared, and the no-limit pots on the last night were often massive. Jack could not have been more pleased and said that even the early losers professed to have had an enjoyable time, all except the Fat Man, who lost big and early and witnessed the event with envy.

"Fat Man was there?" Greg's hand eased on the accelerator of his motorcycle, and he turned slightly toward Preeya, riding behind him.

"Oh, yes. For the first night. I did not see him leave, but Jack said he was not as sour as you might imagine. He even complimented Jack. Fat Man has amassed a fortune with all his businesses, but gambling is his great weakness, and he is not good. Certainly, not in the same class as those others who were there."

"Well, I am glad he lost. Everything I hear about him is unpleasant, if not vile."

Elliot told Greg to stay clear of the Fat Man. He said that no form of depravity, no vice, was below him. He owned the gaming house but also massage parlors and employed an army of pimps, robbers, and pickpockets. He amassed his wealth from the heroin scheme, but he persisted in these ancillary crimes for his amusement. Elliot called him *scabrous*, but Greg did not know how to translate that for Preeya and just said that Albie always called him *indecent, vile, wicked.*

"Everyone in Chiang Mai knows what he is like, but no one can do anything except enjoy the fact that this time he lost," she said, laughing.

He smiled. It was her laughter that he enjoyed the most, that and the feeling of her arms around his waist.

"It's so nice today. Let's drive up the mountain. What do you think?" she asked.

"Anywhere you want to go is fine with me."

***

Greg's headaches were occurring more frequently and with greater intensity and started waking him during the night. After their day at Doi Suthep Mountain, they drove to the Night Market, but the bright fluorescent lights hanging over the booths and the incessant cacophony from the haggling conspired with the hissing, crackling, and sizzling from the fish-frying woks to drive him and Preeya to the quiet and almost empty *kao tom* shop across the street from Wat Po.

The following morning, Preeya suggested he visit a doctor she knew, an acupuncturist. She had never consulted him for herself but had gone with Jaz, who swore by the results.

They navigated the crowded narrow streets of Chinatown on the southeast side of Chiang Mai Central. Ethnic Chinese vendors of all types had their wares on full display in front of their respective shops. Most striking were the groups that they adopted. Five, six, and even seven shoe shops were side by side with each other. Rice sellers, all hawking the same product, lined one entire block. Jewelers peddling ever-popular jade pieces had their own neighborhoods. And on it went. The Chinese way.

They drove slowly, as shoppers laden with bags crisscrossed the street at random, fearlessly dodging the pedi-bikes, *tuk-tuks,* and four-wheeled vehicles, all of which were blaring their horns, or in the case of the bikes, tinkling the bells on their handlebars.

Preeya sat sidesaddle behind him. Her left arm wrapped lightly around his waist while she gave him directions. She dressed in stylish jeans and a pretty lilac-colored blouse with short sleeves to keep her shoulders suitably covered in public. One-way streets complicated the labyrinth of the district. She pointed out the best shops, including which jade shop was trustworthy and who had the best shoes, although to Greg all the displays looked identical. He thought the price would be the only difference. She loved to shop, always hunting for a bargain or something special.

He squinted behind his dark sunglasses sensing the approach of another headache and then felt a sharp and impulsive desire to be somewhere thousands of miles away—in a British university lecture hall or walking in Ann Arbor on an early morning or sitting on an unknown, deserted beach. Unexpectedly, everything seemed foreign to him, unsafe. He let go of the handgrip with one hand and held Preeya's hand, registering her presence. He could feel reassurance in the squeeze of her hand, but something ominous inhabited these streets, and he was not remotely surprised when they drew to a brief stop and saw the mahjong parlor on the right, and Preeya telling him Fat Man's gaming house was on the other side of that same building.

Two, three blocks farther on, as they turned down another one-way alley, Preeya pointed out the building where Jaz lived, and one block later, they arrived at the doctor's office.

A friendly Chinese woman in her early thirties greeted them and said the doctor was with a patient, but if they could wait, then he could see them next. Preeya told Greg that she was going to see Jaz, even shop a little, and gave him the name of the restaurant only blocks away that had the best tofu soup. They could reconvene there. As Preeya exited, the comely receptionist also left the waiting area through the door that he guessed led to the examination area. Now, unexpectedly alone in this small anteroom, whose walls were covered in Chinese characters, lithographs of bamboo plants, and charts of exotic teas and unrecognizable herbs, the same disorientation that he felt when he first arrived in Thailand and stumbled around in Bangkok—culture shock—came creeping back. Preeya took it for granted that he could find his way in this oriental maze as if he were one of them. A torrent of panic seized him, certain that something awful was drawing near when, thankfully, the affable receptionist reappeared and invited him back into the inner sanctum.

Doctor Qiang could not have been kinder or more gracious, and he put Greg immediately at ease. Diplomas from various universities and institutes graced the walls of his large and comfortable examination room. Bespectacled and in his mid-fifties, he spoke perfect Mandarin, Thai, and even English. He complimented Greg on his Mandarin. He said that he had not met many *farangs* in Thailand who spoke Mandarin. They settled on Thai, though Greg used both English and Mandarin to explain his ailment.

Greg described as best as he could how the pain arrives slowly in one eye and works its way to his head. At times, not always, it feels like daggers in both eyes.

Doctor Qiang asked him what he knew about Chinese acupuncture or other non-traditional medical practices, and Greg pleaded total ignorance, and they both laughed.

The initial examination was quite simple, but as the doctor explained, it was not simplistic. He held Greg's arm and placed three fingers along the inside of his wrist as if he were taking his pulse. He adjusted them more than once and then did the same with the other wrist. He then asked Greg to stand up, and he looked closely at his face, his skin, and then his tongue.

After both resumed their seats, the doctor talked about *qi* and life forces and the flow of energy in the body. The need for balance. If Greg would allow the doctor to insert needles into different areas, the doctor believed he could help Greg's condition. He explained that re-establishing the proper flow of energy sometimes takes more than one or two sessions, but he would be surprised if Greg didn't feel a difference after one treatment. He showed Greg one of the slender needles, and he assured him he would barely feel the insertion.

Greg had no hesitation.

As Greg rested comfortably on his back on the table, the doctor chatted easily about pathways and meridians, and with almost no discomfort at all to Greg, inserted needles into Greg's shoulder area, his legs, his feet, and then five more into his forehead.

He asked Greg about his knee surgeries. He no doubt could see the scars and commented that the feet are often a target area for those who suffer from headaches.

After he had finished all the insertions, the doctor asked Greg to do the best that he could to relax on the table.

"Just close your eyes and breathe. Place your attention slightly below your navel and concentrate on the rising and falling of your abdomen. If you get distracted, simply acknowledge that distraction and return to your breathing awareness. Nothing more.

"I will be in the next room, and if you become uncomfortable, just say, and I will return. Otherwise, I will give you fifteen to twenty minutes of quiet before I remove the needles. Not too difficult or painful, right? Do you like tea? Of course, you do. We can have a cup after. Now just breathe."

***

The pleasant receptionist was the doctor's daughter, and she prepared the tea that Greg and the doctor now shared in the adjoining room. The room was quite remarkable, with two of the walls lined with teak shelves from top to bottom and filled with glazed ceramic canisters, all of which were of the same dark hue, and each one gracefully marked in bold, white Chinese characters.

Pictures of distinct types of leaves lined the third wall and served as a backdrop to a wide preparation counter. The fourth wall, which framed the door, was completely bare, but painted in a peaceful, deep green shade, and defined the calming ambiance of the room.

Greg struggled with his cross-legged position, and as they settled into the floor cushions, he quietly lamented his lack of flexibility in his knees and hips, even after almost three years of sitting on floors in huts throughout the hill tribe regions.

"My daughter Mei Li is quite an expert in the ways of tea. She has spent the best part of the last ten years, even a bit more, if you include her university time, studying the effects of fresh teas."

"This room is amazing," Greg commented. "And this tea is excellent."

"Storage of tea, my daughter tells me, requires precision to maintain shelf life. And we must take steps to limit light, heat, and moisture and control the odor and the air. Personally, I enjoy the quiet of this room, but she is so active in and out while serving as office manager, receptionist, and purveyor of herbal medicines that I scarcely can enjoy it. I use excuses like this one to secure time. But tell me, how did you come to be in Chiang Mai?"

Greg recited his most well-rehearsed and abridged version.

"That is quite a noble exercise you have undertaken. What discoveries have you made in your research of the hill tribes?"

The question was innocent and obvious, but it unsettled Greg as he realized how he had squandered much of his time. He had interesting photos, anecdotes, and even cultural observations, but what *did* he discover after all these years? He defaulted to clichés.

"People are the same everywhere you go. Some are nice, some are not so nice. Most everyone I met in the hill tribes was very much in the first category. I don't know if I can recall any hill tribe villager who wasn't welcoming even though I was a foreigner."

Dr. Q pressed the question. "So, the *not-so-nice* seem to be elsewhere. Not in the hill tribes?"

Greg smiled slightly at the doctor's astuteness.

"Yes. I suppose that is correct." Then, searching to expand the thought, Greg added, "Maybe it is the larger cities and populations that create the issue."

"Are you asking me? Or is that one of your discoveries?"

Mei Li saved Greg from a continuation of Dr. Q's questions. The next patient had arrived and was waiting for the doctor.

"I will see you next week," said the doctor. "I look forward to learning more from you. Mei Li can provide you with a selection of tea based on my notes."

CHAPTER TWENTY-THREE

He drove up and down the unfamiliar streets, and after getting turned around, ended up near the front door of Fat Man's gaming emporium. Unlike Jack's entrance, which hovered somewhere between discretion and invisibility, the sign above the twin, metal doors proudly and loudly announced *House of Fat Man* in Thai, in English, and to the far right in blood-red Chinese characters, the same. Legends abounded about how and why Guo Hsiao-sheng not only adopted the moniker Fat Man but embraced it. Elliot said it came from the sullied sages on the streets, who cautioned others *not to fuck with the fat guy*, and upon hearing that cautionary exhortation, the Fat Man elected to remind all who crossed his path of its accuracy. No windows on this fortress. Gaudy-colored dragons painted on the solid concrete walls. One fat rooster stepping on the neck of a smaller cock. A bunker or a mausoleum. Take your pick.

Fat Boy was out front, leaning on his jazzed-up motorcycle with its low handlebars. He and his cronies were smoking cigarettes—or something else—and if he noticed Greg, he didn't show it. But Greg knew he was not invisible. Not here and not anywhere in Chiang Mai.

He drove around lost, and then finally asked a *tuk* driver where *Sukhothai* was. After that, it only took him five minutes to reach the restaurant.

Jaz sat to the right of Preeya, leaving the other seat next to Preeya open, while the fourth seat had packages on it.

It was clear to Greg that the two were in a serious and intimate discussion. As he approached the table, they broke off immediately to adopt a welcoming attitude toward him. Jaz showed off her cast-less arm and commented about how much smaller it seemed to her compared to her other arm. Greg searched for the Thai words for muscle atrophy, which Preeya provided. He said he went through the same with his knee surgeries and the subsequent healing period. The conversation remained light, and they all broke out in laughter when Jaz told him that yesterday the Thai police had arrested a man as he was being ordained a monk on charges of stealing two water buffaloes. Crime in Chiang Mai was under control.

Greg foolishly destroyed the mirth when he mentioned he had just seen Fat Boy. The announcement prompted Jaz to comment about happenings at the casino.

"I heard Fat Man arguing loudly with your friend yesterday."

"My friend?" asked Greg. "Who?"

"The American with the Thai wife and bake shop."

"Wes?"

"Yes."

"Where did you hear them?"

"At the gaming house. He has become a regular. Always playing blackjack. I see him when I am cleaning up the bar area."

It baffled Greg. About Wes being a regular. About the argument. And how did Jaz know Wes was his friend?

"Everyone knows you and the scientist, and the grouchy guy were friends. He owns the place where all the *farangs* eat cookies."

"Pies, pastries," Greg corrected her.

"Cookies too," said Preeya, and the two women laughed.

Greg let it go.

"What were they arguing about?" Greg asked.

"I don't know. They went back to Fat Man's office, and I heard them yelling at each other."

"But about what?"

"I don't know. It's not smart for me to stand nearby and listen. But I could hear them. Lots of words that you don't repeat."

Preeya grabbed Greg's hand.

"Let's enjoy our soup. Talk about other things."

Greg relented outwardly because he knew Jaz had little more intel to share, but the scene of an expletive-filled argument between Wes and Fat Man unnerved him, and he chastised himself silently for his gullibility and his failure to see the obvious.

CHAPTER TWENTY-FOUR

The door was locked when Greg arrived. Wes was on the floor working on something underneath the oven. Greg could see his shoes extending past the end of the bar. He imagined Wes was swearing and cursing at whatever inanimate object was confronting him. For a moment, Greg considered not knocking on the door, but he had delayed as long as he could.

After lunch with Preeya and Jaz, he spent the afternoon driving around the city trying to think of anything except the incident Jaz had described. He failed miserably and thought of little else. Finally, deciding that regardless of the conversation between Wes and Fat Man, Wes's frequent trips to the casino were in themselves a betrayal. He knocked at the door and watched the rest of Wes appear piece by piece as he wiggled out like a snake from under the bar.

Wes placed the wrench that he was using on the bar and unlocked the door. Before Greg could say anything, Wes turned his back and retrieved two cold Singha beers from the refrigerator.

"It's always one effing thing or another breaking in this damn country. If they would spend more time making something of quality rather than making fakes of anything and everything, everyone would be better off. Do you know who makes the best counterfeit passports in the entire world? You guessed it. Just do that with the other shit people use day after day. Is it that difficult? You look serious. What's up?"

Greg left his beer unattended.

"I hear you were in a big argument with Fat Man at his casino."

"Where did you hear that?"

"What does it matter? Is it true? What was it about?"

"I am not sure it's any of your damn business."

"It is if it concerns Albie."

"Don't give me that crap. When did you become the sole caretaker for Albie?"

"You know exactly what I mean. I don't know about you, but I know Fat Man was involved, might still be involved, and besides, I haven't given up hope Albie is still alive."

"Who said I have given up on him? You were connected to Albie's hip these last few months. Weren't you the one playing as his guardian angel? And who the hell are you, schoolboy, to question where I go and who I talk to? I don't need to explain myself to anyone, least of all you."

Wes had a long drink of his beer and Greg waited. Wes was doing just as Greg would. *Deny whenever you can, and if you lie, then stick to the lie.*

"I'm sorry," Wes said. "You don't deserve that. Look, we all care about Albie." Wes took another drink. "We didn't discuss Albie. My argument—as you call it—with Fat Man was only a business disagreement."

"So, you are in business with him."

"No. I am not *in business* with him, but I do business with him from time to time. He supplies this place with certain products and even equipment now and then. We discussed the costs and the payments. It was about money. What else? He owes me money and says that I owe him. It's money. It's always about money. You know that, right? That's all it was. Nothing more. I went there once to straighten it out."

Had he not added that last part, then Greg might have believed him, but he knew then that he was lying. *Stick to the story, stick to the lie. Never amplify. One lie on top of another is always a tip-off.*

Greg remained silent, even as Wes raised his bottle toward Greg and asked, "We good?"

Lying was a talent, and Wes' skill was slipping. Greg lifted his bottle, and the clink of the glass did not announce an indistinct truce so much as a strategy for each. *Keep your friends close, and…*everyone knows the rest.

CHAPTER TWENTY-FIVE

Several weeks passed, during which Greg settled into an everyday routine. He unpacked his notes and photos—those that Elliot returned to him—and spent part of the day writing and organizing his manuscript after a morning walk or even a jog. Doctor Q's question about great discovery begged for a response, and he wondered if he could discover an answer in his notes and memory. He saw Preeya as her schedule permitted, and they would share a meal, time in bed, and occasionally an entire evening at his place if she did not have to work.

Over time, in small doses, he told her more about Albie and his aspirations, the circumstances that led to the closure of the Research Station, and the opium. He realized as he recounted these stories just how much he admired the scientist. While Albie was full of his own self-esteem, he was also funny, curious, and empathetic. Greg bemoaned Albie's disappearance but lauded his courage. He was a man of action and was not afraid to fail and did not readily accept failure. Greg agreed with Mary P that Albie had a towering intellect, but what made him so likable was that he was also a dreamer, someone who looked into the future and imagined a better world, and unlike Greg, tried to make that envisioned future a reality.

He visited the acupuncturist weekly, as much to talk to the doctor as to have a treatment and buy tea from the pleasant daughter. The headaches were not as severe, nor were they occurring as often. He refused to enter a self-debate about the legitimacy of non-traditional medicine. He was feeling better. Period. And if acupuncture was only a placebo, so be it.

The good doctor was not always available for a lengthy conversation after every treatment, but he insisted Greg sit and have a cup of tea each time. He explained that the tea session served as a post-treatment recovery period that allowed patients to collect themselves and to adjust to the re-balancing of their life forces before heading out.

On Greg's most recent visit, the doctor invited Greg to join their early morning *T'ai Chi Ch'uan* class at the nearby park.

"It is exceptionally wonderful exercise. We have practitioners of every level, new ones every week, and others who are ancient in both their age and their wisdom. You are very athletic. I think you would enjoy it. There is no charge. No commitment."

"How long have you been practicing *T'ai Chi*?" Greg asked.

"Many years. When I was young, I studied *Wing Chun Kuen*. It is a style of kung fu, and it is beautiful, but once I began to study medicine, I was more attracted to the *T'ai Chi Ch'uan* style. It, too, is a style of kung fu, something many Westerners do not understand."

"Well, count me as one who didn't know that, either. I thought *T'ai Chi* was more like dancing, not fighting."

"Dancing, fighting, meditation in movement. It is all the same. Until it is not."

Greg told him he would consider it but confessed that he was not good at waking up so early in the morning.

"That just takes some practice," noted the doctor wryly.

Greg started to leave and picking up his small parcel of tea, which he purchased before the treatment, he asked the doctor about the notes and quotations that Mei Li placed in his package.

"Does she include these postcards in all her bundles?" Greg inquired.

"I am afraid so. She is an avid reader of the *I Ching* and the commentaries that Confucius wrote about the *I Ching* and she shares those too. I hope you were not offended."

"No. Not at all. I had read nothing about the *I Ching*. I found the quotations interesting."

"Good, I am happy to hear that. Her regular customers in the neighborhood would never say anything. I appreciate your perspective and forthright response. I will tell you something if you promise not to tell her."

"Sure."

"A while ago, I told her she was too smart and successful to succumb to a Chinese fortune cookie stereotype. She became so incensed that she did not talk to me for a week. Raising a daughter is not without drama now and then. And then one day, she marched up to me and answered. *The truth is never a stereotype.* I wanted to suggest a new aphorism to her. *Raising a clever daughter dispels most drama and enlightens the father.* I left well enough alone."

Both men laughed.

"You are a wise man, doctor."

"Fortunate, yes, but a long way to go to become wise. Thank you for being such a good patient. Think about *T'ai Chi*, please. I look forward to our next appointment."

***

Since *The Game*, Preeya was doing a bit more for Jack by giving instructions and conducting practice sessions with aspirational dealers. She refrained from the severe tactics that Thaksin employed to teach her and Mali, but fundamentals such as posture and hand positioning were obligatory, as the wannabes riffled and split cut and dealt their cards.

Some afternoons, he stopped by to see Wes and Mama, but since his confrontation with Wes and Wes' lying to him, the conversations were mostly topical of the latest goings-on in and around Chiang Mai. He learned that another group from the National Army, rumored to be at the request of the Palace, investigated the Golden Triangle. They discovered no new leads.

It was also at this time that Greg made his first venture into Albie's office. The space was meticulously well-organized, and Greg couldn't help but admire the large teak desk with its elaborate carvings on the lower drawers, and the elegant hutch set back and above the shimmering flat writing surface. Ping continued to dust and polish this room regularly.

There were two trays on the right with letters on each, and Greg took the liberty of examining them. A recent letter from his colleague in Peru caught his attention. He wrote to Albie explaining his departure from Brazil and his decision to go to nearby Peru, where he was encamped upstream at one of the last villages where the unbroken jungle begins. His reception by the indigenous people here was lukewarm. Their distrust of outsiders was clear. *Gun-laden drug traffickers, illegal loggers, as well as oil companies wishing to extract petroleum, had victimized these people for the past decade; but more troubling was that they had recently begun warring with their neighbors, other indigenous tribes, over the dwindling resources, like turtle eggs and musk hogs.*

Greg skimmed to a section near the end on the second page. After a scathing critique of governments for their utter ignorance of deforestation and their repeated refusals to end the growing loss of forests, the writer now was explaining how the lack of immunity from

Western diseases also plagued this population. His host family told him they were certain that their grandparents died from a pathogen a visiting scientist brought here years ago. *Little wonder they were hesitant to accept me.*

He returned the letter to the tray and picked up a small, unmarked, black book, a diary, resting on three larger notebooks in one nook. It contained a daily reflection or commentary by Albie, although there were gaps in the daily sequence. Albie's minuscule script was unmistakable. Greg had just settled on one page, one sentence when Ping appeared at the door.

"This is his private space," she declared in a matter-of-fact tone.

"Yes. Of course, it is. I just thought I could find something, anything, to help."

"Maybe, but it is still private, and..." she was searching for the words.

"Yes," Greg said. "And if he returns tomorrow, I will apologize for violating his privacy."

While unspoken, they both knew Albie would not return tomorrow and maybe never.

Greg replaced the diary and then continued. "Let's talk about it. If we are going to do everything that we can to find him, then this is part of *everything*."

Ping just shook her head to say no, and she closed the door decisively as they exited. She was spending a portion of each day visiting the preemie ward and told Greg that Baby Saint Clair was doing well. She believed it was only a matter of days before they would clear the baby to leave. Just then, the ringing phone downstairs interrupted her narrative, and Dang's excited voice called for Ping.

The call was from Sister Mary Peyton with news that they finally approved the adoption. There were papers to sign, of course, but Mary P would arrive tomorrow and accompany Ping to the administration office. Ping was already hugging her sister as she handed the phone to Greg.

"How excited is she?" Mary P asked.

"She is dancing with her sister and now they are running back to Dao's room to tell her."

"How great. I don't know if she heard me, but I will come down tomorrow. Khun Prawaite will bring me. He needs to buy parts for his shop and is planning to leave at dawn."

"I can collect you when you arrive."

"No. Thank you. That is unnecessary. He will bring me over there or I can grab a *pedi* or *tuk*, depending on his schedule."

"Do you need me to do anything?"

"I don't think so. Ping will need to settle on a legal name. You might remind her about that, so it goes smoothly tomorrow. Other than that, I think everything should be set."

"Are there any more expenses?"

"Hmmm. That is a good question. There shouldn't be. You paid plenty the first time, but you never know, right?"

"I will give Ping additional cash, just in case. It's not a big deal."

"You are a saint."

"We had this conversation once before about Albie."

"You are right. Let's leave it, and just call it good thinking."

CHAPTER TWENTY-SIX

Greg headed to the acupuncturist with plans to go to Preeya's afterwards. He knew Ping and Dang would want to have a celebration when the new baby came home, which could occur in the next few days. It would be nice if Mary P could stay for that. And it would be nice too if Preeya could find the time. She was working more hours than ever. Going in earlier and not taking days off, even after long nights. He wondered how long she could keep up such a demanding schedule.

Traffic was light today, and as he drove toward Chinatown, he felt untroubled for the first time in quite a while. Albie was still out there, somewhere, but other parts of life, his life, were not too bad. The joy in Ping, Dang, and Mary P brightened his days. And his headaches, once annoyingly recurrent, were nonexistent. So much so that he even considered canceling today's appointment, but he knew from rehab years ago to stay on the recovery plan, even if you think you are ready to go. He was convinced that the needles had worked. Besides, he enjoyed talking with the doctor, and his explanation of life forces and balance made sense to him. He did not see it in any religious context but viewed it all as a matter of health and energy.

He had always liked the way he felt after a good sweat. He remembered athletic trainers telling him rigorous workouts and practices are the best medicines. Exercise increases brain chemicals, dopamine, and adrenaline, and other chemicals whose names he couldn't recall. You become more confident by working out. Most importantly, it is a stress buster.

So maybe it was the needles, or maybe it was his morning runs. Regardless, he was feeling better. What's next? He wondered. *T'ai Chi?* It was then that Albie's words, the sentence he was reading when Ping interrupted him, suddenly came back to him. *Most people live their lives as if they will never die.*

That might easily have been a maxim from Mei Li. But it wasn't. It was Albie in the secrecy of his room. Was he talking about all those he knew and exempting himself? He would be arrogant enough to do that. But was it even true? Do we live like that? What prompted him to write that? Greg knew at that point that he would read that diary again.

A car in front of him suddenly screeched to a stop as a jaywalker entered the street. The car's driver blasted his horn, but the person wobbled across the street unfazed. Greg was slowly learning his way around the maze of Chinatown's densely populated streets. A warren with few two-way streets and an abundance of side alleyways so narrow even a single vehicle could barely navigate.

One stumbles upon Chinatown if you are new to Chiang Mai. And for those who live here, necessity drives you to this district. The Thai people, for all their grace and charm, are, as a race, as bigoted as all the other Asian people. Wars, occupation, and subjugation throughout history have fueled their racism, mostly veiled, but easily manifested given sufficient provocation. People are judged by the color of their skin, the roundness, or lack thereof, of their eyes, their ethnicity, their size, appearance, dress, and speech. It was no different here than it was in the States or other places. Ironically, Greg discovered, the hill tribe people were the most tolerant because they co-mingled and co-existed with various ethnic groups for hundreds of years.

The sessions with the doctor were always the same. First, questions about his current condition and then a brief examination. Sometimes, the doctor spent a bit more time looking at his tongue, and other times, he focused on checking his pulse. Greg soon recognized that the doctor applied different amounts of pressure with his fingers each time he checked the wrists, seeming to push a bit more with one finger or another at any of the nine spots he had earlier described. The doctor did a scan of Greg's entire body, occasionally touching part of his back or neck, and Greg had a distinct feeling that the doctor used this opportunity to smell him, but the idea seemed absurd, and Greg hesitated to ask lest he insult the doctor. Finally, the doctor always asked for permission before he inserted any needles.

The number of insertions was decreasing with each visit, and today marked a first when he placed needles in the lobes of each of Greg's ears.

***

"I would like to think about it, but on first blush, I don't think I agree with that at all. Do you mind repeating it?" the doctor asked Greg.

"Most people live their lives as if they will never die."

Greg waited for the doctor, who immersed in thought, sipped his tea, holding his cup with two hands, as was his custom.

"I disagree," he finally replied and set his cup aside. "The sentiment that most are happy-go-lucky, reckless, or even lacking rectitude does not mean that they believe they are never going to die. I would argue the opposite. A carefree attitude comes because you recognize that someday you will die, so live for today. The now is all that matters."

"You mean like the *Eternal Now* in the *Book of Sayings*? Mei Li gave me a card with that phrase on it."

"No. I think Tsiang Samdup was providing guidance for a path to Enlightenment. To immerse yourself in the existing moment, not to cling to the past, not to cling to your lost pleasures, not to fret about the future, but to develop awareness in the ever-changing present. Your saying is clever but specious. What do you think?"

"I think death gives life its meaning. Death reveals itself every day. And some people are more afraid than others. It's the difference between those two groups that I find most baffling. Why are some less afraid? Why are some people brave and others not?"

"Questions such as those are more helpful than pithy dictums. I like questions. Questions encourage discernment and start you down a road to self-discovery and even truth with a capital T."

The shouting of Mei Li in the reception area shattered their conversation. Her voice was loud and resolute, but fraught with danger.

"Get out. Get out and stay out. Don't you come near me again!"

The doctor and Greg rushed into the adjoining room to see the loathsome Fat Boy standing in the center and Mei Li safely behind the counter.

"What's going on, Mei Li?" the doctor asked.

"He got his money and wanted something else, something more," she said, now visibly shaking.

"What are you doing to my daughter?" he asked the menace.

"Nothing," snorted Fat Boy, staring now at Greg, who stood just behind the doctor.

"Then, if your business is finished, please leave."

"Too good for a Chinese boy, huh? Looks like you prefer *farangs*. Good luck with that."

Mei Li cried after he left. Her father held her in her arms.

"Are you all right, my child?"

"Yes, I am fine." She was still trembling, but she left his arms and tried to regain her composure. "I am sorry, Mr. Greg, if I caused you any uncomfortableness."

"Are you kidding me? No. No, you have done nothing wrong, not to me, not to anyone."

"Mei Li, what was this all about? What happened?" the doctor asked.

"I gave him his money like always, and then he started leaning on the counter saying that he wanted me to go out with him, and when I said no, he said ugly things about what we could do, what he could do. It was awful. I kept telling him no, and then he made gestures and I screamed at him. I am sorry, Father, if I have caused you more problems."

"No. No. No. Everything will be fine." He placed his arm around her again. "Let's go inside and have some tea. You are safe. No one will harm you. You need to rest. Mr. Greg and I are finished for today. We will lock up and have tea."

"Doctor, please let me know if there is anything I can do."

"No, thank you. We will be fine but thank you for your kindness."

Greg started his motorcycle and scanned the street for any sign of Fat Boy.

None of this was surprising. Fat Man was extorting money from his own neighborhood businesses. Should have seen that a mile away. Like a Chicago gangster or a Boston mobster demanding protection payments, and Fat Boy acting as collector. You can add *bagman* to his disreputable resume.

CHAPTER TWENTY-SEVEN

As he drove to Preeya's, he decided not to say anything about this latest incident with Fat Boy to her. Fat Boy's unseemly behavior toward Mei Li and Fat Man's extortion of neighborhood businesses could wait. Greg had good news to share.

"Ping is going to adopt the baby. It has all been arranged, and she is signing the papers this afternoon."

"That is fantastic for everyone."

"Yes. Sister Mary Peyton was the difference maker, as far as I can tell."

"You are both so lucky to have good friends."

"Once she gets the baby home, then I would like to have a small celebration. I know she would like to have you there."

Preeya was suddenly quiet. Pensive. She moved over to the rattan-framed couch and sat down.

"Thank you. Thank you for thinking about me," she said.

"What do you mean? Of course, I would think about you."

"Please sit down. I have something to tell you."

Despite the soft cushions, Preeya was sitting up as straight as she could. Much as she did when she was dealing. Her sculpted hands were folded and rested in her lap. He loved her hands. So soft, tender. Loved them even more because they were so graceful and efficient. For the first time that Greg could remember, her voice was labored. The words came out as if rehearsed.

"I am leaving Jack's."

"Really? What will you do?"

"I am going to work for Fat Man."

Greg jumped up from his chair.

"What? Are you serious? You are kidding, right?"

"Greg, please sit down and please talk softly. Please."

Greg did as she asked, and as if in a bad dream, listened as she explained how she and Jack reached the decision. Fat Man's jealousy of Jack's success, especially the success of *The Game*, drove him to make repeated overtures. Finally, she and Jack laid out the terms. Jack will receive a huge payment, and Fat Man will release Jaz from her debt so she can work for Jack.

"This is crazy. You can't just trade people like they are merchandise."

"Your voice, please."

Greg groaned. The terror of the brutish Fat Boy invading Preeya's world was too much for him.

"You know how evil Fat Man is. Why would you ever agree to this? He is a criminal, a gangster. He extorts money from his people in Chinatown."

Preeya did not speak, but Greg pressed her.

"Preeya, please. You are putting yourself in danger whether or not you realize it. Maybe not directly at first, but by the mere association with that character. I know you like Jaz, but you can't sacrifice your life for her. There must be another way to get her release from him."

Preeya still did not speak. Tears welled in her eyes, and she closed them tightly, trying to hold them back.

"I will tell you something," she said. "I will tell you one thing, but you must promise me you will never repeat it or tell anyone. Not anyone. Ever."

"Sure. What is it?"

"No. Greg. Not *sure.* It is my deepest secret and if you betray me, then my life has no meaning. I want you to promise with all your heart."

Greg got up from his chair and sat next to her on the couch. He put his arm around her shoulder and pulled her close even as she remained in her stiff posture.

"Preeya, I promise I will tell no one. I will never repeat it. Never write it down or never admit anything to anyone, ever. So help me, God."

She dropped her head on his shoulder and cried. He placed both arms around her, but she kept her hands folded and merely leaned into his embrace. After a few minutes, she collected herself and sat straight up again. She unfolded her hands and held Greg's hand with both of hers and took a deep breath.

"Jaz is my sister. My older sister. Everything I told you about her and me is true, except I never told you we were sisters. I was four when our father made that gamble and that bet with Fat Man. Jaz was around fourteen when my father gave her away…when she was lost to Fat Man. My mother went to Fat Man after my father disappeared and offered herself for Jaz, but Fat Man mocked her and asked why he would want an old car when he could have a new one. It was Jack who found a place for my mother to work in Bangkok. Tiger's wife is Jack's sister. Tiger is his brother-in-law. Everything I told you about Bangkok was true. My mother raised me there. Only Jack knows who I really am. No one in Chiang Mai could ever recognize me. I changed my name to Preeya a long time ago when I became a dealer. That was Tiger's idea. I was only sixteen when my mother died, but that is when I decided that one day I would come back to Chiang Mai. I didn't know how I could help Jaz, but I knew we needed each other. Fat Man does not know who I am."

Silence. Deafening, terrifying and ruinous.

"Fat Man laughed at Jack when he said he wanted Jaz as part of the deal. *Preeya for Jaz.* Jack said he said the same thing to him as he said to my mother. Jaz was now an old car, and I was the new one."

"But he will destroy you."

"No. He can't. I am the treasure, and we have a written contract. Signed, witnessed. If Fat Man touches me, if anyone ever places one finger on me, if anyone does anything to harm me, then I walk away."

"You make that sound so easy. Do you think men like Fat Man care about contracts?"

"Maybe not. But I have it. Fat Man jeered at me when I told him about my demands. He said he had an abundance of women. *I don't need you.* I am not his employee, his servant, or his minor wife. We have a business agreement, and I am a partner. And that means something."

"What kind of partner?"

"I will receive one percent of every rake. It may not seem like a vast sum on the surface, but it will be enormous over a short period. Jack had over a million U.S. dollars land on the table over those three days alone. The rake comes out of every pot, every game, and every time. Losers are still losers, and the winners just don't go home with as much. That is how the rake works."

"I don't know. It is too dangerous."

"Like Jack, I also receive an immediate large payment and will have enough money to move to another place, a larger, nicer place that Jaz and I can share. And Jack is going to let Jaz be a blackjack dealer, and she can start a new career. It is all going to be fine. It is good business. Jack wins. Jaz wins. Fat Man wins and so do I."

All this time, she had been holding Greg's hand, and now she squeezed it even tighter.

"Tiger was kind to my mother, but she worked hard every day of her life. She cleaned, cooked, and took care of me, and even Mali much of the time, and never once complained. I know she wanted to go back to Chiang Mai to see Jaz, but she was afraid someone might find out about me, and that somehow Fat Man would steal me, too. She spent her life protecting me, so I knew I had to come back here to do what she always wanted to do. Help Jaz. My mother died of a broken heart, and when I first came back and found Jaz, I could see the same sadness in her I saw in my mother every day. My mother tried to smile and be happy when I did well in school, but a great sorrow had settled on her, and as I became older, I understood…" and her voice, filled with melancholia, trailed off.

Preeya reached for air with another long, deep breath.

"Speaking English was the key. I learned it in school, and Tiger thought it would help me be a good dealer too, so he encouraged me to keep practicing my English. *Farang* visitors are more comfortable. And Fat Man does not have many who speak English."

"Ok, I get all that, but why the tears?"

"There is one more thing. Fat Man doesn't want you around. Fat Boy especially. They want me to break up with you, not see you anymore. Fat Boy hates you. Ever since that day at the restaurant, he carries a grudge. He lost face that day. He said if you walked into the gaming house, he would kill you."

"What did you tell them?"

"I told them, no."

"They insisted. Then Jack stepped in. He told Fat Man that he had told me the same thing. You were a troublemaker, and to keep it low key. He said to Fat Man that we both did that and that there was no reason to believe that we couldn't keep doing the same while I worked at Fat Man's."

"And?"

"Fat Man agreed, but cross the line even once, and then either you go completely, or our deal is rescinded. Jaz will go back to Fat Man, and I will have to repay everything to Fat Man. The bonus, the rakes, everything. We can do this, but you cannot fail me. I will never be able to pay back everything, and I will end up like Jaz if you fail me."

She was squeezing his hand tighter than ever now.

"That is so bullshit."

"It is a contract."

"How long is this contract?" he asked with contempt.

"Fat Man wanted four or five years."

"I bargained for one or two."

"And?"

"We settled on three years."

"Three years of sneaking around."

"We don't have to sneak. We have to be smart, and we are both good at that. I know you are."

Greg felt defeated and his sigh revealed as much. He slouched back on the sofa.

"Greg, Jack said it to us as advice, and it proved to be good advice," Preeya continued.

"This is not advice. This is a threat. He has leveraged you, me, Jaz. He is despicable, and this is repulsive."

"Maybe it is, but our lives are in the balance and Jaz especially. You must trust me. You must trust that I know what I am doing. Greg, please!"

Greg got up and stared out the single window in her tiny apartment. The dirty brick wall on the other side of the alley stared back.

Preeya was now repeating herself. She kept telling him it was a win for Jack, for Jaz, for her. She sees it as working in a slightly different hellhole. She said that she had worked in a hellhole before. A friend of Tiger's was trying to get a casino off the ground and asked if he could borrow her from Tiger. It was in a dangerous part of Bangkok, and the business was a long shot. It was not well financed or operated, and it was only a front for illegal activities.

"I have seen hellholes. I went to two or three other places and eventually went back to the Tiger's Den. I have seen unpleasant places and the Fat Man's place is not like that. Three years and we will be rich and can do whatever we wish. No one expected the cult of the woman in white to be so big. It surprised everyone, but it made this transfer even easier and more lucrative."

Greg remained unconvinced. She was on the precipice of something awful, and he felt helpless to convince her to do otherwise. If she breaks the contract, she will then be so indebted to Fat Man that she will become a lifelong slave to him. That was the real danger. Not him. She will spend the bonus money and make more money and spend that, and at some point, Fat Man will make the situation intolerable, and she will be trapped.

"Yes, I know. I realize all that. I have considered all that. We have to be careful. Nothing else."

"We can go away. Leave Chiang Mai."

"I cannot. Just like you cannot abandon your search for your friend, I cannot abandon my sister."

"I don't like it. I understand everything you are saying, but I don't like it. There must be another way. We can leave here. We can go to the States."

"Greg, I will not be your Thai trophy. One of those trinkets. A Thai doll paraded around on the arm of a *farang*. A woman desperate for a better life."

"Is that what you think I am? Just another *farang*."

"For heaven's sake, no. You know what I mean about those types."

Greg realized now why she rejected all public displays of affection. She did not want to be seen as an ornament.

"We can get married. We can go back to the U.S. We can have children."

"The U.S. is not *back* for me. It is *back* for you. And what about Albie and your search? What will happen to Ping, and now two children? And my sister? I told you—I will never abandon Jaz."

"I don't know. I haven't figured that out, but I will. I can. Nothing good will come of your going to Fat Man's. It's doomed. It doesn't make sense. There must be another way to buy your sister back. He will end up destroying you like he has Jaz, like he has everything he touches."

"Jaz is not destroyed. Hurt, scarred, but not destroyed. And you can't save me. So, stop trying to save me. No one needs to save me. I know what I am doing. If you love me, you will believe me."

They had never used the word *love* in all their interchanges. There was never any doubt that he loved her, and she knew that, but why had they never said it aloud?

She was exhausted. She no longer sat upright in her place, and as she slumped back into the full of the couch, she reminded him one last time.

"Remember the promise you made? Never a word about Jaz. Never, ever."

CHAPTER TWENTY-EIGHT

In the days leading up to the homecoming of the new baby, Greg saw Preeya only once to give her the details of the event. She was already moving to her new workplace and spending whatever available time she had with Jaz, looking for a new place to live. Preeya and Jaz were inseparable, at least for the time being, and Greg tried to be happy for them. Mary P had expedited the adoption papers as expected, and the doctors released the baby two days later.

Without revealing the parentage of the baby, Mary P made it clear to Ping that she could not legally use Saint Clair for the baby's name, even though she, with Albie's permission, had unofficially adopted it along with her surname. It made no difference to Ping. Her focus was on his given name, one that she debated about with herself, Dang, and even Greg, before settling on Klahan, which, of course, means *brave.*

It was at the celebration that Mary P told Greg that she had been making frequent trips to the hill tribes and checking on as many villages as she could. When Greg asked her if she thought it was wise to be up there in the wake of Albie's disappearance, she said that nothing had changed for these people. They would not come down to her clinic in Chiang Rai unless they knew her and trusted her; and by making these visits, she could detect health-related problems before they became more serious, even fatal. Khun Prawaite had recently outfitted her with a well-used Datsun pickup truck, that despite its beat-up exterior, ran well and was remarkably dependable.

Preeya and Jaz arrived with presents for Ping and the baby but also made a point of bringing gifts for Dao as well. Greg played host as best he could, circling the room and providing refreshments for everyone, so Ping did not have to occupy herself in that role. Ping, and Dang especially, were reluctant to let anyone else hold baby Klahan, but after a little prompting from Mary P, they relented and allowed Preeya and Jaz a moment, and then allowed Mary P to feed him a bottle when he became restless. Mary P settled on the couch and enlisted Dao to help hold the bottle, which pleased Ping to no end. Ping used the opportunity to take photos with the Polaroid camera which Greg had given her.

Greg took stock of the room filled with women. Lucky Klahan, he thought at first, and then considering the different struggles all those present had, he wondered if *good luck Klahan* wasn't more appropriate.

It seemed as it should have, like a new beginning. No talk of Albie, even though all of them were in his house, and all knew each other because of him. Greg felt a twinge of guilt because he did not invite Wes and khun Mae, but Wes' lies about his visits to Fat Man's casino continued to give Greg pause. And even dismissing the growing chill between them, he knew that this was Ping's celebration, and given her long-time suspicions of Wes, he believed it was the wisest choice.

A certain inevitability also loomed. Wes knew Greg and Preeya were intimate, and she was now going to be at Fat Man's, meaning Wes would soon need another cover story to explain his regular presence at Fat Man's place.

At one point, Preeya and Ping secreted to the kitchen area. Preeya's visits to the house had never been furtive, and while she and Greg were content to spend their time together in his bungalow, Preeya seldom missed the opportunity to seek Ping upon arriving or departing to say hello and visit together. It was while Preeya and Ping were out of the room that Mary P told Greg that Ping had agreed to have the child baptized.

"But Ping is not Catholic. She is Buddhist through and through."

"It makes no difference."

"If it makes no difference, then what is the purpose? Ping will not raise him Catholic, even Christian. Isn't that one condition for baptism?"

"Yes, and no. I am not a theologian, but baptism brings Klahan into the family of God, the Christian family. At least one parent, in this case, Ping, must agree to the baptism, but if she cannot raise the child as a Christian for a compelling reason, then the baptism can still take place."

"I am surprised she agreed to it."

Sister Mary Peyton was unusually quiet, and then it clicked for Greg.

"You leveraged her, didn't you?"

Sister did not answer.

"You did," Greg realized. "You told her you would help her with the adoption, but you had some conditions."

Sister still did not answer.

"Albie!" Greg exclaimed as if he finally understood. "You had a deal with Albie. He was always making secret deals. He made you promise, even when he thought Nok would be the one raising the baby. You would keep his secret, but…"

"Albie was not a Roman Catholic, but he was a Christian. He would want the boy baptized. I have a responsibility to the soul of that child. Ping will be a splendid mother and the child may be a lifelong Buddhist, but that is not for me to decide. I can only do what I can do."

"You are clever, Mary P. I will give you that. Resilient and resourceful. It must be wonderful to believe in something so completely."

"It is, and I hope someday you will find out just how amazing it is."

***

Preeya and Jaz left first. Both had to be at work later that day. Preeya at Fat Man's and Jaz at Jack's. Greg then drove Mary P to Saint Michael's. When she dismounted the motorcycle, she stood next to him, straightening her skirt before thanking him and saying goodbye.

"By the way, Ping told me you and Preeya have become quite a couple, but the two of you acted like you hardly knew each other today?"

"She is very reserved in any public setting, and to be honest, we just had a bit of a tiff."

"Oh? Sorry to hear that."

"It's not a big deal—well, it is a big deal. What she is doing is a big deal, but the argument, if you can call it that, is not a big deal."

"Glad you cleared that up," she said with a smile.

"She is changing jobs, and I don't think it is a good idea and it has created some friction."

"How so?"

With a sigh, Greg explained Preeya's move to Fat Man's and her rationale. He excluded Jaz from the conversation completely. It was easier to explain her move based on the financial benefits, rather than the deeply personal and underlying reasons. He would keep his promise to Preeya. When he got to the part of the story where he implored Preeya not to make the change, that it was too dangerous, and that they could get married and start a new life together somewhere else, Mary P interrupted him.

"Gregory Robber, did you really say that?" she asked, her voice filled with astonishment.

"Yes. I told her we could get married and go back to the States," he answered flatly, not at all understanding her tone or the question.

"That might be the worst marriage proposal that I ever heard. You really know how to sweep a girl off her feet."

"I…I…I was trying to make a point. I was trying to convince her to find an alternative. I was offering her one."

"Like I said, the worst proposal ever. Is that what marriage means to you? The best alternative to avoid a difficult situation."

"No. Of course not. And the situation is not just difficult. It is downright dangerous. You know that as well as I do. Everyone knows that, but her."

"Is it possible that Albie's disappearance has you overly anxious? You are worried about my trips to the hill tribe people, whom I have been seeing for years already. You are worried about Preeya doing the same thing she has been doing for years."

"Are you forgetting Nok is dead? Someone beat Nok and killed her!"

"No. I haven't forgotten. But we can't all put our lives on hold, either. We can't live our lives in fear. We must keep doing what we have been called to do. We must abandon ourselves to the will of the Father, and while that may sound like it takes heroic confidence, it just takes Faith."

"I don't see it that way. I see someone driving the wrong way on a one-way street. And with their eyes closed, no less."

She leaned across the handlebars and kissed him on the forehead.

"Let's pray that the traffic is nonexistent that day."

CHAPTER TWENTY-NINE

The days crept by uneasily. His morning runs had taken on more purpose. Once or twice a week, he would drive over to Doi Suthep and run up the mountain for a short distance. The incline was steeper than he imagined, and on the first few attempts, he tired quickly after only a mile or so. He took care to walk down the road rather than to run to protect his fragile knees. Occasionally, he would see young *Muay Thai* fighters on the same road doing their early morning training. There was no walking for these young combatants. They would wave and shout encouragement to him, as they sped past him with an energy Greg could only recall and no longer replicate.

He helped Preeya and Jaz move boxes into their new place, which was only three blocks from Jack's house. Set in a compound with two other houses, which the owner's family occupied, ensured that the two sisters had trustworthy security. They were taking their time with furnishings, choosing to do without until they could afford exactly what they wanted. New household items for the kitchen area were a priority, so Greg's housewarming purchase of new knives was met with great appreciation. Greg confessed it was Ping's idea, but he made a point of buying the most expensive German knives that he could. *Guaranteed to last a lifetime.*

Both women were determined to have new bedroom sets before any other major purchases, so their immediate sleeping arrangements could best be described as spartan, and as a result, any romantic time that he spent with Preeya was at his bungalow. Unfortunately, even those nights together were dwindling, as Preeya had only one night off from work each week, and what time she had available during the day was now spent painting the interior of her new place.

His visits to the acupuncturist continued with regularity, improving his familiarity with Chinatown's maze of streets. He circumnavigated the area close to Fat Man's casino, giving a wide berth to the entire block. He prided himself on avoiding any accidental run-ins with Fat Boy. Shortly after the incident between Mei Li and Fat Boy, he pressed

Doctor Q about the extortion payments. The doctor was dispassionate regarding the shakedown. Doctor Q said such practices are the norm, and the people in the quarter have more security and safety with and by Fat Man than they would ever receive from local authorities. Chiang Mai police seldom patrolled here. He would be foolish not to pay Fat Man. He has never had a single robbery or break-in. *How many other businesses in the city can say that?* And other than that one silly overture by Fat Boy, Mei Li walks around Chinatown with no hesitation or qualms. *We look after each other.*

This day's tea conversation was a lesson about the meridian system and the concept of *yin* and *yang* to define how *qi* flows and maintains balance. The principle of duality—*yin* and *yang*—can be seen in everything. Hot and cold. Light and dark. So too are the organs in your body. The *yin* organs are solid—heart, spleen, kidney, liver, and lungs. The *yang* organs are hollow—the stomach, bladder, gallbladder, and small and large intestines. Ten of the twelve meridians are associated with these organs.

"And the other two meridians?" Greg asked.

"The other two meridians are the triple-warmer meridian, which controls metabolism, and the pericardium meridian, which is linked to emotional and spiritual well-being."

Greg sipped his tea as he processed yet one more lesson in traditional Chinese medicine, pondering this last meridian and speculating where the needles would go to balance the *qi* of one's innermost being.

"May I ask you a personal question, Mr. Greg?" asked the doctor.

"Absolutely. You are my doctor. Why not?"

"You have gone weeks with no serious headaches and your *qi* is flowing properly through the meridians, providing you balance and harmony. I do not think we need more sessions. I am extremely impressed by your current health, and I am curious about what you do."

"I have been running most mornings."

"No. I can tell that you are exercising. I mean, what is it you do for a job? For a career?"

Greg's face fell into a shadow, and he scratched his neck and chewed on his lip.

"I understand it is personal, and if you care not to answer, then I completely understand. You told me about your research in the hills when you first arrived, but now you are here, living in Chiang Mai. You are too young to be retired. Are you one of the fortunate rich?"

"No. I am not one of the fortunate rich. I don't do anything now, so I am idle. A friend of mine has gone missing and I am waiting for his return."

"Missing? That sounds terrible. Ominous."

"It is. It is distressing. His family asked me to look after his house, so for the time being, that is what I have been doing. It has given me the chance to collect all my notes and photographs and to organize them for publication."

"So, you are a writer."

"No. Far from it. A collator better describes me. I have not written an original word in my life."

"I asked, in part because your life forces are strong. Not all have such vitality. You had an imbalance, but that happens to everyone throughout his or her life, and now that we restored your balance, I can't help but observe your vigor."

"I do feel much better and am grateful to you for your help."

"I would like you to keep taking the tea that Mei Li has selected for you. It will continue to fortify you."

"That sounds good."

The doctor then said the most remarkable thing.

"I suppose it is the father in me, and seeing you are very much near the age of my child, I venture to offer additional advice. Your life forces are potent, stronger than most. No one has an expiration date stamped on the bottom of his or her foot. Even when a patient arrives with a terminal illness, we can ease the pain but can only speculate on the timing of the result. I believe you will have arthritic pain in your knees as you age, but your demise will probably be from an outside force rather than from within. I would caution you to go slowly with whatever career path you choose."

Greg did not respond. There was simply too much to digest.

Doctor Q then stood, thanked Greg for being such a diligent patient, and said that it was an honor to have been able to assist him before excusing himself to deal with his next patient.

CHAPTER THIRTY

"Why do you like going up to those places like Ban Su so much?" Preeya asked as she moved the stepladder to the other side of the windows. Greg held the paint can and brush.

"It's quiet. The weather is crisp, the air clean," he replied, sidestepping any discussion about Albie.

"It's dangerous. Ok. Hand me the paint. Why are you pushing your luck? Tempting fate?"

"I don't see it as tempting fate or any type of gamble. I am not exploring dangerous areas. I have been going to the same types of villages since I first arrived in Thailand. I was in Mae Salong two weeks ago. It has grown so much that it is almost large enough to be on the map. For the longest time, the only buildings up there were the hangar and barracks for the Border Patrol, but now there are actual houses and a handful of makeshift places to eat. It looks like one of those towns in old Western movies." He did not add that a whorehouse was also fully operational.

She and Jaz were nearly finished with the painting. Preeya said the yellow walls in this room are for good luck.

"You went up there last week as well. Should I be worried that you have a new *fan*?"

"No," *but why are you mentioning this?* He asked from deep inside his thoughts.

"Hand me that rag, please. Those kinds of mountain dwellers have their own way. You said as much. Maybe leave them alone. I don't want anything to happen to you."

Now he was baffled. And disappointed. Her words were racist. Not even remotely cryptic in her denigration of hill tribe people. Such bigotry was out of character for her, and the sentiment for his safekeeping, warmly received in most any other context, was now a late add-on. *Too much information is always a tip-off.*

She looked down at him, expecting a response. The blue scarf around her hair outlined her perfect face. She was his passion. He wanted nothing more than to be with her, and yet they were spending less and less time together. And now this.

"Did you hear me? I don't want you to get hurt."

"I don't either. You can go with me the next time as my bodyguard."

She tossed the rag at him. "You make a joke out of everything. Keep it up, and I won't be going anywhere with you."

"Not even dinner?"

"Ok. Dinner, but I get to choose where we go."

"That's fine. You might even get to pay."

"I am warning you. The next thing I throw at you will be the paint."

And there it was. *Stay away.* Another warning. But from whom—Preeya or from her new boss, Fat Man?

CHAPTER THIRTY-ONE

Just after the turn of the century, the Royal Family of Great Britain gave the King of Thailand a car as a gift. As a result, the Thais have been driving on the left side of the road ever since. However, the Thais, in their own practical manner, were astute enough to recognize any bargain that came their way and had throughout the years welcomed vehicles with steering wheels on either side of the car, which, as one may surmise, did nothing to enhance safety on the roads in the Land of Smiles, and even less on Highway 1.

If you drove along Highway 1 in the daylight, as Greg was now doing once a week, and maintained constant caution and a clear understanding that tour busses and trucks shared the narrow two lanes with the locals on bicycles, mopes, and rickety carts pulled by water buffaloes, then your odds of going unscathed were improved. But, if your attention wandered, or if you became distracted by the biblical sunrises over the vast rice paddies stretching eastward, then all bets were off.

His mission today was simple. A quick visit to Ban Su with a gift for T'ang. He had spent yesterday cataloging the rest of his photos. His initial attempt to keep everything—notes and photos—in chronological order had gone awry somewhere along the line, but the last few weeks and yesterday especially had been productive, and his photos were finally organized and stacked neatly across the table. The negatives were another matter altogether. Deposited haphazardly, but safely sealed in an airtight container to keep them incorruptible, they were a hodgepodge. His notebooks, with pages missing courtesy of Elliot—*human intelligence (HUMINT) was gold dust*—were in equal disarray, but for now, at least the company-sanctioned photos were organized.

The prize of yesterday's effort was a portrait of T'ang and Nok in the opium fields. Shoulder to shoulder, sweat beads across T'ang's brow, and a laughing Nok set against a resplendent background of purple, white, and green flowers, and a pristine blue sky. As good fortune would have it, he even found the perfect handcrafted teak frame at the photo shop near the Rincon Hotel.

He considered bringing one or two Polaroid photos of baby Klahan but held that thought for a later visit. As he navigated easily in the cool of the morning, he wondered if he could someday convince Ping to journey to Ban Su with the baby for the great-grandfather to see. T'ang would never leave the hills. Not at this point in his life.

Once, a year after he began in Thailand, Greg transported an elderly hill tribe man to the small city of Uthai Thani. The old man, already crippled with a severe limp, had developed dreadful styes on the edges of his eyelids and had aggravated them with a deleterious local ointment. It was the old man's first visit to a city. The traffic and noise frightened him, and he clung to Greg's arm. The ophthalmologist's office was on the third floor of a medical building and, given his ambulatory limitations, it made sense to take the elevator.

They approached the single elevator, watched people enter ahead of them, filling the small cubicle, and witnessed the door closing. They waited patiently for the elevator to return to the ground floor, and when the doors opened, different people emerged. The old man was petrified. There was no way he would enter the magic box. He was convinced the compartment had transformed those people. Greg tried to explain how an elevator operated and what had happened, but to no avail, and they walked up the three flights of steps.

No. Despite anything Nok might have done over the years or attempted to do with her grandfather, T'ang would not be coming to Chiang Mai, or not even to modern-day Chiang Rai. All of which reinforced why Mary P made so many visits to the hill tribes.

He went directly to the clinic when he arrived in Chiang Rai, and finding the doors locked, he wrote a note. Khun Prawaite must have seen or heard his motorcycle.

"She has been gone for almost a week."

"I saw her just last week."

"Yes. She left the day after you did. The day after you went back to Chiang Mai, we gassed the Datsun and loaded it with rice and other food and supplies, and she left."

"Did she say where she was going?"

"Sister said a girl in a village not too far from Mae Salong was having difficulty. She was going there. She has never stayed away this long. She has had many local patients come by since she left."

"Bandits," said Greg, thinking aloud.

"No. She said there are four bandits, but not on the path toward Mae Salong. Just the same, she takes extra rice and even cigarettes in case she sees them and says that they never bother her. She even knows their names. One bandit had an infection, and she took him medicine too, she told me."

Just like Albie, thought Greg.

"Maybe the truck broke down?" suggested Greg.

"Maybe, but I check it every time before she leaves, and it is a reliable machine."

Greg left immediately. His goodwill mission was now a search operation, and he knew from the outset that he was not good at such enterprises. The path up toward Mae Salong was dry and with panic pushing him, he drove far too fast and too recklessly and only slowed down after a near spill. He debated whether to search out the village in question or go to Mae Salong and opted for the latter. It proved to be the right choice.

He found her in Mae Salong at the barracks of the Border Patrol.

"It was here or the new house with the red curtains," she told Greg, trying weakly to make light of the situation.

Her face was bruised, and her breathing was labored.

"What the hell happened? Are you all right?"

"I was in a village north of here. A young girl is pregnant and having a challenging time."

"Mary P, there is not much north of here in Thailand. You were in Burma. What happened?"

"You must promise not to get too angry."

"Enough! Tell me."

"Fat Boy stopped my truck when I was leaving. He and two of his friends blocked my path with their motorcycles. He pulled me out of the truck and hit me. He told me to stop poking around up here. Lots of cursing."

"Holy shit."

"He was pulling things out of my engine when the father of the pregnant girl came up and the two of them got into it. There was some more pushing and yelling, and then Fat Boy and his buddies left."

"I tried to walk over here, but he broke some ribs and breathing was difficult. The father went to Mae Salong, and an agent from the Border Patrol came back in a jeep and here I am. They pulled the truck here and are fixing it now."

"That father saved your life."

"Yes. He was a godsend. But Fat Boy wasn't trying to kill me. Just hurt me and threaten me."

"I told you it was dangerous, but you wouldn't listen. You could have ended up like Nok. Fat Boy is a psychopath."

"He must have thought I was asking about Albie. I don't know. I was only helping that girl. And her mother was not well either. She needed antibiotics."

"Why didn't the Border Patrol take you back to Chiang Rai?"

"That was my choice. Probably not a good one, but I didn't think it was necessary. The mechanic thought he could get the truck running in a day or two, but one thing or another has disrupted that. The agents don't live here either. They work here. They fly in and fly out. So, it's not like they can take a day and drive down to Chiang Rai if it isn't something serious. I didn't think it was that serious."

"You look pale. Can you ride on the motorcycle? I will take you back to Chiang Mai and have you checked."

"No. I am ok. The ribs will heal. There is nothing anyone can do. I can go back to my place. We can get the truck another time."

"We can discuss all that in Chiang Rai. We need to get going before it gets too dark. Where are your things? Your medical bag."

"In the back room of the barracks."

"Sit tight. I will get them."

The barracks were little more than a weather-beaten wooden shell with paper-thin walls separating three small rooms. The entire place was a complete pit, a dark and dismal pigsty. Not even daylight could penetrate the two dirt-stippled windows. Her bags were on a cot, which appeared both filthy and uncomfortable. The cot's only redeeming value was to be off the ground and provide limited protection from the visiting snakes and scorpions. He shook his head in disgust. He couldn't imagine how she got any sleep in here. Get her to Chiang Rai for now and tomorrow to Chiang Mai, whether or not she likes it.

The ride down was thankfully uneventful, mainly because Greg had grown so familiar with the serpentine route and its most acute turns. He could hear and feel her labored breathing behind him and insisted she hold his midsection tightly. She rested her head on his back. If her grip lessened, he would slow down, talk to her, and have her reset. In the back of his mind, he was terrified that she would lose consciousness and fall off. As often as he could, he released one hand from the handlebar grip and touched her arms. The ghost of Nok rode with them.

She could barely walk when they arrived at the clinic, and with her reluctant permission, he carried her to the bedroom. The room was sparse as the nun within her intended it to be. A table, a lamp, and a narrow bed with a hard tatami mat rather than a mattress. A mosquito net hung above the bed. Her only concession to comfort, he thought. The crucifix on the wall gazed down at them. She insisted on cleaning up a bit, so he put her on the bed and excused himself.

"I will be in the visitor's wing," he said, winning a smile from her drained and bruised face. "Do you need anything?"

"Water. Would you fill my pitcher here with water, please?"

"That's it. Are you sure? I can prepare hot tea. You are always giving me hot tea."

"No. Just the water," trying to muster yet one more smile.

He collected the pitcher from the table and went into the kitchen. He cleaned the pitcher first and then filled it with clean, cold water, which she always kept in the refrigerator. When he tapped on the door and entered the room, he found her already asleep on the bed. He placed the white sheet over her and lowered the mosquito net. He wanted to kiss her goodnight.

Before he went to bed that night, Greg visited Prawaite next door. The two of them decided that Mary P must go to the hospital tomorrow. Prawaite told Greg how his cousin had cracked ribs and a punctured lung from a *Muay Thai* fight. He never completely recovered and still struggles with breathing today. Prawaite would drive her to Chiang Mai tomorrow, and Greg would follow on his motorcycle.

CHAPTER THIRTY-TWO

Ping and Dang ushered Sister Mary Peyton into Dang's bedroom, where she was finally resting comfortably. She had had a tough morning during the drive to Chiang Mai, and then over five hours at the hospital with examinations, X-rays, and consultations. Three cracked ribs and a small pneumothorax, which in lay terms meant a small lung puncture. She was lucky; the doctor explained. The puncture was minuscule, barely visible on the X-rays, and the lung should heal with no surgery or invasive action. The same for the ribs.

"Rest, rest, and more rest," emphasized the doctor. "Only a few years ago," he said, "we would have wrapped the rib cage to stabilize the ribs and help them heal, but that is no longer the best practice. Ice for the next few days, although you should have done that immediately after the injury."

When Mary P said that there was currently a shortage of ice machines in the hill tribe villages, the doctor did not smile. He prescribed painkillers and an anti-inflammatory drug, with strict instructions to return immediately if she was not feeling better in the next three to four days. Greg was to look for pale skin, rapid heart rate, and shortness of breath.

She said the pale skin might be a good thing compared to the darkening bruises across her face. Once again, the doctor did not smile.

Nor was Greg smiling now as he navigated through Chiang Mai traffic. He left the house just after four p.m. and headed for Chinatown. His anger had been building since he first found Mary P in Mae Salong. Enough was enough. He had never had close friends until he came to Thailand. Classmates, teammates, and an assortment of women filled his early years, but Albie, Nok, and Mary P had been different. They acted with an unbridled, unsolicited generosity that he had never experienced. No negotiation, no reciprocity. Mary P told him she endeavored to show charity in the small things in life as much as the important things. *God has not called us to immortality*, she said, *but to holiness.* She treated everyone with that same love. And Albie. He had opened his home to Greg with no expectation, just as he had for Ping and her sister. Greg knew no one from his past life who would have done something like that. And Nok. Dead because she too helped others. Helped her friends. Had helped him when he was in Ban Su, when he needed a place to stay or food to eat. On it goes with her generosity. No. Enough was enough, and it stops today.

He parked his motorcycle next to Fat Boy's sleek machine. The teenage boy on the stoop said that he should not park there. Greg told him nicely that it was fine. He had an appointment. He gave the kid a hundred baht note and told him to keep an eye on it. He pulled open the outsized red door and entered a circular hallway with another door at the other end. Two hefty bouncers, both smoking cigarettes, barely acknowledged him—just another *farang*—as he passed by and walked into the large gaming area. The long bar running against the wall on the left had only two patrons. Lights shone on the empty roulette tables with their green baize tablecloths. A sizable number of intransigent gamblers, a mixture of Chinese, Thai, and *farangs,* occupied the blackjack tables and the other gaming tables that filled the rest of the room to his right. There was no music, just the murmur of voices and the click of chips changing hands.

Scanning the room, his eyes settled quickly on the back of Fat Boy. He lacked the stature and girth of his father, but his distinctive *queue* hairstyle, the bare forehead with a single, long braid in the back, along with his round body were unmistakable from any viewpoint. He was talking to two other Chinese men when Greg walked up behind him, and as Fat Boy turned, Greg punched him in the face with his best right hook. And before anyone could intervene or Fat Boy had the chance to react, Greg hit him a second time with his left hand. Fat Boy staggered backwards, and then, doing his best to shake off the blow, came charging into Greg with a tackle and a roar. Bigger and stronger men had hit Greg plenty of times in football, and while Fat Boy's attack pushed Greg backwards, it failed to knock him off his feet. Entangled now in each other's arms, Fat Boy tried to wrestle Greg to the ground, but Greg managed one last blow, by freeing his right arm from Fat Boy's grasp and landing a solid elbow punch to the hoodlum's jaw, about knocking him out. It was then that the bouncers and others finally intervened, pulling both men apart.

As with football, one rarely heard the roar of the crowd as the play took place, and it was only in the aftermath that the shouting registered.

The loudest came from Fat Boy himself, with a string of obscenities. Blood seeped out of his mouth, but he kept yelling, screaming at the bouncers to let him go. Greg was in a bear grip by a *farang* from behind, the dagger-tattooed arm and the voice of Wes recognizable.

"What the hell are you doing? Are you completely crazy?" Wes shouted. His voice was hoarse, and his breath smelled of whisky.

Greg tried to shake him loose.

"Get your hands off me. Let me go."

"Like hell." And his grip tightened.

The shouting in multiple languages continued. Then the room became suddenly quiet. The sea of people surrounding both Greg and Fat Boy now parted for Fat Man. Slowly, as if he could move in any other manner, Greg would recall much later. He waddled through the crowd like a massive penguin. His moist and empty eyes, which had never looked on anything without evil intent, were now fixed on Greg.

Fat Man reached his son first. Lifted his great right hand to the devil-child's face and examined the damage and the blood. Turning toward Greg, he flicked his fingers of the same right hand, waving off the grip Wes had around Greg. The entire place was still silent. The oxygen was sucked out of the room.

He drew close to Greg, so close that his massive midsection touched Greg's torn shirt hanging loosely around him. His breath rancid. He placed his right index finger ever so closely to Greg's chest, and with a sibilant hiss, an almost inaudible whisper that only Greg and those who stood behind him could hear, promised to kill him the next time he saw him in this place or in any other place where he does business.

Before Greg could say anything, Fat Man turned in the direction whence he came, and everyone, Greg included, was now looking at the resplendent Lady in White, standing motionless in the doorway to the back room, the sanctum for high rollers. A gasp from those who had never seen her lambent beauty. A vision and revelation for those less fortunate gamblers who, lacking the wealth or courage to afford a game with her, had only heard the stories. She surveyed the scene, her eyes finally resting on the interloper, and with that finding confirmed, gently touched the white amulet around her neck with her right hand and walked back into her unhallowed domain.

PART TWO

CHAPTER THIRTY-THREE

Daybreak pierced the bedroom shutters and his lingering desires. The incandescent events of his time with Preeya were over. Vanished. A memory and nothing more. Neither Ping nor Mary P had questioned him, and he offered nothing.

For two weeks, he threw himself into the care of Mary P. Initially, serving her morning and afternoon meals in the upstairs room, and then walking her up and down the stairs for dinner with Ping, Dang, Dao, and baby Klahan, who took in the conversations from his nearby bassinet.

Ping and Dang assisted Mary P with her showers, and Dao took delight in brushing Mary P's hair, but the nun soon tired of the attention and pressed Greg with her intention to return to Chiang Rai.

She was improving daily, and Greg implored her to remain patient for at least another week, even as he too experienced a similar ennui, plagued by his meaningless and desultory existence. He had overstayed his welcome in Chiang Mai—Elliot's admonishment realized. Now trapped by his promise to Blackledge, he was growing frustrated by the absence of communication, other than the bi-weekly checks for Ping, the household expenses, and a sizable payment for him.

When not attendant to Mary P, he retreated to his bungalow with no purpose other than to be alone. His photos and notebooks lay dormant. He sat in the same place where she shuffled cards in the dark, convinced that the room retained echoes of her presence.

He paced the chamber, searched for a whit of regret for his actions, and found none. He refused to believe that he had sacrificed his relationship with Preeya for Sister Mary Peyton. It was Preeya. She had made the choice. Not him. He stretched out on the bed, measuring his life as before Preeya, and after Preeya; and like a fragment in a fleeting dream, he could hear the rush of the waterfall. He could see her hair falling around him and onto the ground, and her hand clutching the amulet.

He sat up quickly. Stared across the room. She stood in the casino, unaffected, impassive, clutching that talisman. Did she choose to remain in character or had Fat Man's cacodemonic influence already polluted her soul?

Mary P roused him from his indolence.

The kettle whistled in his kitchen, and she stood guard over the teapot.

Before he could ask her what she was doing in his bungalow rather than resting in her room, she began her reprimand.

"I cannot believe for one second you were so foolish to confront Fat Boy! And to attack him, no less! Are you completely out of your mind?"

"How do you know anything about what happened?" Greg asked.

"Wes told me when I called him this morning."

"Wes! Why are you calling him?"

"I need a ride back to Chiang Rai, and he seemed like the best option."

"I can take you back. We don't need Wes."

"On the motorcycle. Seriously."

"No. I would have arranged something."

"Wes was more than willing. He did not even know that I was here or anything about my mishap."

"Mishap? It was not a mishap. It was an assault. In any civilized place, Fat Boy would have been arrested," Greg insisted.

"But being that we are not in *any civilized place*, you took it upon yourself to be judge, jury, and executioner."

"He was not executed." A darkness inside of him wanted to add *yet.*

"Humph. I had a brother. I didn't need him to fight my fights for me, and I don't need you barging into casinos and punching people."

"He is barely a human being," he carped.

"Be that as it may, I will have no more of it. Wes is picking me up tomorrow morning, and I am going home."

"What else did Wes tell you?"

"Nothing. What else is there to tell? He seemed relieved to know why you attacked Fat Boy. He thought you had simply lost your senses."

"Well, he can think what he likes."

He struggled to change his tone but wisely stopped there rather than expand on Wes' presence in the casino. Or anything about Preeya. *Change subjects as soon as possible.*

"Do you think you are well enough to travel? You know you won't rest at the clinic. You will go back to work immediately, knowing you."

"I feel so much better. I do. If I get tired, then I will rest. I walked around the grounds earlier today for almost twenty minutes and felt fine. It was only a nick in the lung tissue. I can build up my strength slowly."

She poured the tea into two cups.

"Greg, you need to promise me you will not wage war on Fat Boy. Let's leave it alone. For both of us. I have forgiven him. You need to do the same."

"Like hell."

"Greg, we can't give in to the darkness. We can't fight evil with evil."

"I have no interest in forgiving either Fat Man or Fat Boy. They are criminals and reprobates. Scourges on society."

He paused for a second, before adding, "I will promise you this. I will stay on my side of the street, but that's it!" Thus, making the same worthless promise he gave to Preeya and then broke at the first provocation.

She shook her head gently, and sipped her tea, while his vanity prepared the answer to the expected but unasked question. *What if they cross the street?*

CHAPTER THIRTY-FOUR

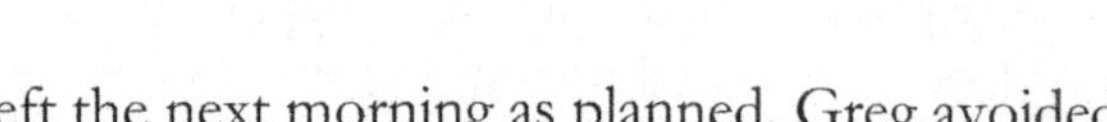

Sister Mary Peyton left the next morning as planned. Greg avoided Wes, and Wes did not rouse him from his bungalow.

He was in his kitchen area when Ping knocked on the door and entered. She had Klahan in her arms, and she was anxious. Every dawn, without fail, she met the parade of barefoot monks on the street when they passed. She made merit by depositing a daily donation into their begging bowls, and every week she went to the temple, chanted, prayed, and clung to the hope that Albie was still alive. She understood Blackledge was supporting them, and now another *farang*, another stranger, had arrived.

"What is it?" Greg asked.

"There is a *farang* woman at the front gate. She is asking for you."

"Who is it? Do you know?"

"No."

Greg's heart raced. He had been thinking about Heather recently. Their time together. Even how they first met. They had not seen each other nor talked or even written since that day he traveled from England and arrived at her German apartment as a surprise. Only he was surprised. How could Heather have found him here?

"Who is it?" he repeated.

"She gave me this card."

A white business card. *Crissa Bradley* with two addresses in England. One in Kensington, London, the other in Cambridgeshire.

Greg exhaled a bit.

"Ok. I will need to change my clothing. I will be right out. Tell the guards to let her in."

He had beefed up security since the incident in the casino with Fat Boy. No one gained entrance without the expressed consent from Greg or Ping. One guard saw Fat Boy on two separate occasions on the road in front. Out of an abundance of caution for Ping and her family, Greg doubled the number of guards and increased the pay of all the workers as a sign of loyalty. The money from Blackledge was more than adequate for such measures.

He slipped on jeans and a tee shirt and then ran a brush through his unkempt, curly hair, but it made no difference as far as he could tell.

He crossed the breezeway from his residence behind the main house and entered the house through the back. Through the open shutters, he watched a black car make its way through the main gate and into the gravel courtyard. Greg recognized it immediately as a British Consulate car. The woman who emerged from the back seat was in her thirties, he guessed. Slender, attractive. She wore oversized sunglasses. Dang was playing in the courtyard with Dao, and Crissa stopped to greet them. The little girl placed her hands high on her head and bowed politely. Greg could easily imagine her soft voice greeting the visitor. Crissa smiled broadly, entertained by the gesture, and tried to reciprocate.

Greg joined Ping and baby Klahan at the opened front door.

"Hi," she said. "I am looking for Mr. Robber." Her voice was distinctly American, fresh, sassy even.

"I am Greg Robber. How can I help you?"

"Great. My name is Crissa Bradley." She extended her hand to shake and then looked back at Dao. "What a lovely child! Is she your daughter?"

"No. Ping here is her mother."

"Well, she is darling. So nice to meet you."

Greg translated for Ping, but he knew she understood. He also knew that Ping would not engage in English with a stranger. Ping spoke to Greg.

"Ping said thank you. Please come in."

"Thanks. Should I remove my shoes?"

"It is customary, but unnecessary," Greg answered.

"Well, when in Rome…"

Greg led her back through the great room into a smaller room, which Albie had used as a library.

"Wow. Air conditioning. This is quite a house you have here, Mr. Robber."

"There are multiple rooms with air conditioning units, and this house is not mine. I live in a building in the back. A guesthouse. Ping and her children and Ping's sister live here. It all belongs to Albie. Albert Saint Clair. However, I expect you already know all that."

They sat across from each other, separated by a teak coffee table. Hand-carved like all the teak furniture in the house. Engraved elephants and tigers on the table waited for her to answer.

Crissa crossed her slender legs. Her yellow skirt with thin black lines just barely covered her knees. Greg could not help but notice her wriggling her toes as she took in the surroundings. She was more attractive than Greg first realized. She had replaced her sunglasses with wide-framed, tortoise-shell glasses, which were both stylish and bookish. Her auburn hair had a red tint and natural curl, cut shoulder length, and pushed back, revealing her gold earrings. Her radiant smile from the courtyard traveled with her easily. She settled her slate-blue eyes on him.

"Mr. Robber," she began.

"Greg. Please, just call me Greg."

"Very well. As I said at the door, my name is Crissa. Crissa Bradley. I am the personal secretary to Lady Guinevere Saint Clair, who is Lord Saint Clair's sister. She is in Bangkok. We just recently arrived, and she asked me to come to Chiang Mai to meet with you."

Before Greg could say anything, Ping entered the room with a pitcher of water and glasses. She asked if they would like something else, something to eat. Both declined and Ping stared at Greg for a second, then left. She knew that this woman was not here on a social call. There was something more. Something about Albie. And if it had to do with Albie, then it had to do with her.

Crissa could not help but notice Ping's glare but continued without comment even before Ping had left the room.

"Her ladyship is trying to learn as much as she can about Lord Albert's disappearance. We have seen the reports, and it is very frustrating. We were hoping you could enlighten us."

Greg finished pouring the water.

"I told the lawyer from England months ago everything we knew. Hell, I never knew that Albie was a lord or royalty until the lawyer told me. Albie left the day after we found Nok. He took my camera equipment and went somewhere near Ban Su. He never came back. It was not unusual for any of us to go up to the hill region for a week or longer, but after two weeks, when he had not returned, Ping became nervous. We all did. Ping said that he left in a rush. He did not take everything that he usually took. So, I went up to Ban Su to look for him."

"And?"

"And nothing. We couldn't even find the Land Rover."

"We?" she interrupted. "I thought you said you went to look for him."

"I did. Wes was with me when we drove up to Chiang Rai for the first time. He had a look around as well in the area. Wes was, is, a good friend of Albie's." And currently not mine, he did not add.

"I apologize for interrupting, but how many times did you go look for him? I am a bit confused."

"Wes and I had a quick look days after Albie left. Wes was upset, and we were concerned, so when we were in Chiang Rai, we had a look around Ban Su and the other villages. We found nothing. I went over to the nearby village where Nok and her hill tribe live, and no one there had seen him either. Wes went over to Mae Salong and came up empty.

"After a couple of weeks, he still hadn't returned, so Wes and I went up there again. This time we hunted for ten days and found nothing. It was more than strange. I came back and reported it to the authorities, and they made their investigations over the next few weeks and found nothing. I told all this to the lawyer."

"Blackledge," she said.

"Yes. Anthony Blackledge, if I recall."

"He is Lord Saint Clair's solicitor. He made arrangements for you, if I understand correctly."

"Yes. He asked me if I could remain here. He said that this was a complicated matter. What with his disappearance in a foreign country and his estate and his will and all his business interests and foreign property."

"Did you know Lord Albert called him the day he left for Ban Su?"

"The correct pronunciation is Ban Su. It is a soft *a*. No. Blackledge did not tell me that."

He felt a twinge of embarrassment correcting her. It was out of character for him, but her interrogation was bothering him. And now, this latest information about a phone call was emerging from her side.

"He did. Lord Saint Clair called Anthony and left him detailed instructions. Gave no explanation. He then posted a letter to Blackledge with even more details and rewrote his last will. And at some point, before he left this city, he stopped at the Consulate and had it witnessed and countersigned."

"I was unaware of that. Mr. Blackledge asked me to stay on while he sorted issues with the Thai government and gave me two checks. One was for me and the other was for Ping. I was to receive bi-monthly checks for Ping and checks for expenses here at the house for an indeterminate future. I was to make sure that Ping received her money."

"Which, of course, you did."

"Yes. Absolutely."

"And your checks? You never cashed them."

"No."

"Why?"

"Miss Bradley…"

"Crissa, please."

"Crissa, no one has to pay me to help a friend. Albie did plenty for me already and for a lot of other people. I explained this to Blackledge when he gave me that first check. He insisted I take it. He asked me to stay while he sorted issues and that has taken longer than any of us hoped, but as promised, I am still here, and I expect you are about to bring this chapter to a close."

"Greg, I am not trying to upset you. Believe me, that is the last thing I want to do. I am just trying to get as much information as possible so I can report to her ladyship. Do you understand?"

Greg nodded.

Then she asked about Nok, who she was, and what had happened. They talked for another twenty minutes, during which Greg explained to her that Ban Su was not even on the map. It was so small. A tiny, nondescript, hill tribe village situated so close to the hilly geographic border it might be in Burma. That is why the Research Station was purposely located several kilometers away from the village—to make sure that it was in Thailand. He wanted to explain that the location of Ban Su was the root of the problem. It was the source of the conflict among all the competing parties, but it was too complicated. He avoided all discussions about opium, heroin, and drug trafficking. Instead, he pointed out that the authorities were limited in their search and investigation. They could not meander as they chose across borders like the locals. No one, absolutely no one, wanted to engage with either the Burmese authorities or the rebels about a missing person in the Golden Triangle. *Limit facts. Eschew specifics. Persist with vagueness.* The typical cultural and historical minutiae followed.

As Greg slowly steered the conversation away from Albie's disappearance, she relaxed a bit, and dropped her interrogator's temperament, recognizing the reluctance of the witness. Greg thought her initial perkiness returned, and he pushed the conversation into comparisons between Chiang Mai and Bangkok.

Finally, Greg asked her if she would like to see the house, but she declined, looking, as if on command, at her expensive wristwatch.

"I need to be going. I was uncertain I would find you here and have other scheduled meetings in Chiang Mai."

He assumed they would be at the British Consulate.

"Can we meet again this evening? Perhaps dinner?" she asked.

"Sure. That would be fine."

"I am staying at the Rincon Hotel. I assume you know it?"

"Yes. It is about halfway between here and the center of town. We can go into the city and eat."

"Should we say, seven? Pick any place you like. It is my treat."

"Any preferences?"

"Something not too fancy. I would like to get out of these clothes and into a pair of jeans."

Greg thought she looked attractive in those clothes.

"Ok. I will pick you up at seven. I have a motorcycle, or we can use taxis."

"A motorcycle! That would be great." Her radiant smile re-emerged. "I can cut this driver loose, then."

Greg walked her outside to the waiting car. He recognized the Thai driver almost immediately. He was a staffer at the Consulate. Greg had seen him more than once when he and Albie were there.

"Tell Ping goodbye for me." Then, reaching to touch his hand, she added surprisingly to Greg, "Tell her she has nothing to worry about." She slipped gracefully into the back seat and closed the door.

CHAPTER THIRTY-FIVE

They dined at the Fish Garden just blocks from the *klong* and the Night Market. It was crowded, but the owner always found an available table for *farangs*, especially the ones he recognized.

Greg shaved for the first time in days and tried on two fresh shirts, before selecting the powder-blue batik, which Preeya had purchased for him. For a moment, he felt guilty wearing it on this date, but he liked the shirt and liked the way it made him look.

As announced, Crissa wore jeans, expensive and snug in all the right places, complimenting her long, slender legs. She looked stunning in a pink Thai-silk blouse that she said she purchased just this afternoon. Her eyeglasses tonight were ovate, the brown hue rims paired perfectly with her auburn hair and framed her luminous blue eyes. Diamond stud earrings and a pricey Bulgari wristwatch completed her ensemble.

There was little talk of Albie, at least not in the beginning, but about each other. Greg asked innocuous questions to keep the conversation focused on her.

He liked the way she smelled while riding on the bike and her firm and immediate grip around his waist, rather than holding on to the side of the seat or riding sidesaddle as Preeya did. He wondered if he felt soft in the middle to her, having abandoned his morning runs these last weeks. He smiled to himself as she pressed her chest against his back, wondering, even hoping, that he was on the precipice of something new and fresh.

"You like it here?" she asked.

"People are nice. Food is good."

"What is your favorite?"

"Sticky rice and fresh mango topped with sweet coconut milk. Albie calls it God's dessert."

"I am going to have to try that."

The server arrived with two bottles of Singha beer and two frosted glasses. Greg told him to take the glasses and that they would order shortly.

"What if I had wanted a glass?" she asked.

"Sorry. Habit. Why drink from a dirty glass when you have a clean bottle?"

"Ok. That makes sense."

"Cheers," he said, raising his bottle to hers.

"Cheers. Hmmm. This is good. I haven't had a cold beer in quite a while. The Brits prefer a warmer brew. But you already know that."

"This restaurant has the coldest beer in Chiang Mai. Even Mama cannot keep hers this cold."

"Mama? Who is Mama?"

"Mama Pajama. She and Wes own a bakery bar."

"A what?"

"A bakery bar. She makes baked goods. The best in Chiang Mai. Mostly pies and serves beer along with other types of drinks. A bakery bar. What else could you call it?"

"Mama Pajama? Really? Isn't that disparaging, if not outright racist?"

"I never thought of it like that. Her Thai name is Mae, which means motherly or ma or mama. Her husband, Wes, gave her the nickname. They have been together for quite a while. Married by longevity and public opinion. A typical arrangement here. Wes gives almost everyone a moniker. Albie was *the professor*."

"This is the same Wes that went with you to the hills."

"That's right," he said flatly. Now sorry he mentioned his name.

"Is he a westerner? An American?"

"Yes. An expat living here in Chiang Mai. Like many other *farangs*."

"I know what an expat is, but what is a *farang*?"

"A white foreigner. Like you and me."

"And do you have a sobriquet?"

"Not that I know of," he lied, refusing to acknowledge the condescending *schoolboy* handle Wes had occasionally used.

"Sobriquet. That is quite the S.A.T. word," Greg commented.

She smiled, shrugged her shoulders a bit, and took another drink of her beer. She asked him to tell her about Chiang Mai.

"I have only been here for about a year, but it is booming. There are two new luxury hotels, new businesses, and new houses going up all over the place. Traffic can get crazy. Not like Bangkok, but still wild just the same. Tourism is all that anyone talks about. Economic growth."

That, and prostitution, gambling, drug traffic, and a litany of other diseases, he pronounced silently into his beer.

The server returned and Greg took the liberty to order a spicy noodle salad, a spicy shrimp soup, and the house specialty, while also requesting that the *spicy* be *farang* style to accommodate his guest.

"And two more beers," Crissa added. The waiter understood her English and grinned.

"Tell me about yourself," she continued to Greg.

"Not much to say."

"Hardly. A football player at Michigan, a Rhodes Scholar, and then Fulbright. Multi-lingual. Quite a resume."

"You seem to know most everything already."

She smiled, slightly embarrassed, confessing that research and background had indeed taken place. Even commenting that he looked better in person than he did in photos. What she wanted to know, however, was how he and Albie met.

"We met at his Research Station, which was a short distance from the final hill tribe village that I visited for my Fulbright research. They shuttered his project for security reasons. The Thai government did not want soldiers patrolling up there, providing security to Albie, and risking a brush fire with the Chinese or Burmese or insurgent Shan State Army. At least that is what the government officials said."

"Blackledge told us, Lady St. Clair and me, that he took a liking to you."

"When Albie learned I had completed my research, and that I had a few months to write and organize photos before heading home, he offered me a place at his house. He said it was better than a hotel. I stay in the back bungalow. Then, as he tried to re-open the Research Station, he had frequent meetings with Thais and asked me to attend and translate."

Their food arrived. The noodle salad had just a touch of *nam prik*, and Crissa loved it. She struggled with the chopsticks, but Greg gave her a lesson. He moved his chair, sat beside her, and adjusted the sticks in her fingers. Her hair smelled like jasmine and his heart was pounding. He hadn't felt like this since his first night at Jack's next to Preeya.

"Now I understand why the people here are so thin," she said, and as she managed better with the chopsticks, Greg returned to his place across from her.

When the *tom yum goong* soup arrived, however, it had too much of the fiery red pepper, and though Crissa professed to like the prawns, she was quickly into her third beer.

The main entrée was an entire fish, more than a foot long, with the head and eyes intact, cooked and seasoned perfectly, and simmering in a tasty broth. Greg made the first carving and explained that, by Thai custom, the fish's head was for the guest of honor. Crissa laughed loudly in horror, apologized in the same breath, and eschewed the privilege. Greg said eyeballs are a delicacy.

"Perhaps you would like just one?" he asked teasingly.

"If you would be so kind as to share a bit of the yummy-looking, white meat on the body, below the skin you so expertly removed, then I would be grateful. As for the eyeballs. You can have both."

Greg filled her dish with the choice pieces and encouraged her to have rice as well.

"How did you end up working for Albie's sister? What is her name again?"

"Guinevere. Lady Guinevere Saint Clair," she replied through bites. "I met her when I was working at Sotheby's in London."

"You are not British, are you?" Greg asked.

"No, not at all. I am from Rhode Island, but I worked at the Tate in London after I graduated from Duke in art history. You know, the Tate Museum."

"Sure. I think I drove by it," he said, smiling.

"Funny. I only stayed at the Tate for one year, but while I was there, I met the DG of Sotheby's, sorry, the Director General, and he offered me a job, but I went back to the States to study international law. After I finished that degree, I contacted him, and he offered me an even better position. It was at Sotheby's where I met her ladyship."

"Where did you study international law?"

"Yale."

"The one in New Haven?" he asked, stone-faced.

"The same," she answered, shaking her head and smiling.

"Not bad. Duke and Yale."

She did not respond but continued.

"I had been at Sotheby's for little more than a year and loved it. I met the most interesting people. And the range of art rivaled most museums. Her ladyship asked the Director General if he could recommend someone to do an audit of her family's collection.

Paintings, antiquities, artifacts. An incredible myriad of *objets d'art* that her father had collected over the years. The insurance carrier, Lloyd's of London, required a more up-to-date and verifiable provenance report. Collections this vast are often accumulated in different manners."

Greg assumed the last sentence was code for illegal.

"The DG suggested that I do it, and he arranged a leave of absence for me so I could spend time at their various residences and complete the project. The provenance of certain pieces required more research and paperwork than anyone expected, and months turned into a year. We spent more time together, and it was during that period that her father died, and she assumed full responsibility for the estate and his business. She liked me, needed additional help, and asked me to stay on as an administrative assistant, a girl Friday. That role has grown, and I do more of everything every day."

They finished their meal, and the server cleared their table. She declined to order another beer, and Greg still had half of his left as well.

"Where was Albie? I thought he was the older sibling," Greg asked.

"His lordship wanted nothing to do with the family business. He loved his father, I am sure, but considered himself a man of science and chose a different path. Her ladyship was all business and liked nothing more than butting heads with the Neanderthal men of that world."

"I have a feeling that you enjoy that as well."

She refused the bait.

"I serve as her representative and voice as she decides. Often with her ladyship's lawyers, of which there are many, including the legal representatives from our subsidiaries and Blackledge, Lord St. Clair's solicitor. Now I am here to complete Blackledge's efforts with local officials and to bring you to Bangkok."

"Excuse me?" Greg said and sat back in his chair, suddenly creating whatever distance was possible from Crissa.

"We would like you to meet with Lady Saint Clair in Bangkok in two days."

"And here I thought I was beginning to like you," he said.

"Those two matters are not mutually exclusive."

Greg smiled but retreated to his training and remained silent.

She lifted her eyeglasses and rested them on the crown of her head. She leaned forward onto the table with her elbows and placed her chin on her folded hands. He had never seen eyes so blue, and something about her made him think he knew her from some long-ago time.

"Her ladyship's mother was dying when Sir Albert went missing. She would have come to Thailand when the Embassy called but simply could not. So, Blackledge came."

"And now?"

"Now, she wants very much to meet the person closest to her brother. She is in Thailand. She is meeting with family friends at the Royal Palace and with other business associates in this part of the world, but she is in the country to meet you."

"If she wants to meet me so badly, then why doesn't she come here? I don't work for her, and this feels like I am being summoned."

"I am sure she would love to, but her schedule simply won't allow it. I apologize if it sounds like a summons. It is a request. She wants to hear about her brother from someone she believes she can trust."

"Why should she trust me?"

"Probably because her brother did."

"I don't know. I don't like Bangkok. Never have." He also suspected that he was being drawn into something.

"We are not asking you to live there. Just visit with her ladyship. Albie's last communication, the one I told you about, included you, Ping, and others. Lady Saint Clair wants to understand as much as she can about the situation."

"Like what?"

"She has questions, and it is not my place to ask them or discuss those matters. I am just the messenger, so please don't shoot me."

Crissa extended her hand across the table and tapped the tabletop as an entreaty to his hand.

He hesitated and then uncrossed his arms, and when he touched her hand, she interlaced her fingers into his.

"You don't have to decide anything tonight. I am sorry I mentioned this just now. The last thing I wanted to do was to ruin this nice dinner with this not-too-unattractive young man, who seems to have forgotten to order that special dessert. Tonight is tonight. We can talk more tomorrow."

He recommended that they have dessert at the Night Market, but as they boarded the motorcycle, Crissa suggested they skip the Night Market and have a nightcap at her hotel. And without objection, he raced headlong into the seduction and a new liminal space filled with feelings of intense curiosity and dire forebodings.

CHAPTER THIRTY-SIX

When asked, Crissa said that the morning had been a complete success. First, Greg's acceptance of the invitation to visit Bangkok, and then a long morning at the British Consulate that could not have gone better. With the afternoon now free from additional business meetings, Crissa set her eyes on shopping.

"Jade. I have read and heard that Chiang Mai has great bargains on jade jewelry."

"I don't know about that, but I know where there are several jewelers who sell jade."

"Let's go."

As she seated herself sidesaddle on the motorcycle, Greg cautioned her to tuck her skirt tightly, so it wouldn't snag in the rear wheel. He could hear her chuckle at the thought.

"Where are we going?" she asked innocently.

"Chinatown," he answered and offered nothing else.

He knew that this early afternoon period was Preeya's shopping window, but the chances of seeing her or Jaz were remote, and he had nothing to be ashamed of. His greater concern was seeing Fat Boy and his associates and risking another confrontation. He selected what he was certain was the best route—one that would avoid Fat Man's casino and steer them to the row of Chinese jewelers and Preeya's recommended store.

Relieved to arrive with no sign of Preeya or Jaz, and not a glimpse of Fat Boy along the way, Greg was delighted to find Doctor Qiang in the store completing a purchase. A sixty-something Chinese face under a mop of white hair welcomed them even as he was handing Dr. Qiang his package.

"Doctor Q! What a pleasant surprise."

"*Sawadee krap*, Mr. Gregory," and he bowed politely.

Greg introduced Crissa, and in perfect English, the doctor explained that Greg was one of his favorite patients and a loyal customer of his daughter's teashop. Today, he said he was buying a birthday gift for Mei Li.

"I would show it to you, but my good friend, Zou Yang, has already wrapped it nicely. Jade is a great treasure. Jade cultivates both good health and good fortune. In our homeland, many believe it deflects evil as well. And Zou Yang has only the finest jade and the best designs. You must see his imperial jade. The translucent emerald-green color is without equal."

He then turned to Zou Yang and repeated what he had just said in Mandarin.

The shop owner bowed deeply in gratitude for the ringing endorsement and smiled proudly.

"Zou Yang and I are from the same region in China. We have known each other for years. I am certain he will take diligent care of you."

He then turned to his compatriot yet again, repeated the comment, and told him that not only was Mr. Gregory his good friend, but that he spoke wonderful Mandarin too.

This time the animated jeweler nodded his head and smiled unconvincingly, and as Dr. Qiang made his departure, Zou Yang watched his *farang* surcharge follow Dr. Q out the door.

Still, Zou Yang regained his eagerness when the price range of Crissa's hunt became obvious. He spoke halting English to Crissa and occasionally Mandarin to Greg to enhance the sales pitch as Crissa viewed and tried on a wide assortment of jewelry. She was looking for something nice for her ladyship, and then something smaller for herself. She enjoyed the hunt. Greg, clueless as ever in such matters, offered her little advice, and busied himself with surveillance of the pedestrians and traffic on the street. When asked his opinion about a specific necklace, broach, or pendant, by either Zou or Crissa, he offered only a hollow declaration that it—along with all the others—looked nice.

She selected a necklace for Lady Saint Clair and then a ring and earrings for herself. The total cost of over U.S. $3,500, reduced twice with half-hearted haggling, left Greg speechless. A broadly smiling Zou Yang, pleased with the sale even without the usual *farang* tax, insisted that Greg take a gift of a small jade Buddha as a token of his appreciation for bringing him a customer.

She slipped her arm into his as they exited.

"I like pretty things," she said, "and her ladyship would wear something from the thrift store if it wasn't for me. It is all part of the job."

"Must be stressful," Greg suggested.

And releasing her arm from his, poked him in the ribs.

It was too late for lunch and early for dinner, so Crissa suggested they escape to his bungalow—either that or more shopping.

CHAPTER THIRTY-SEVEN

A driver with a black Mercedes-Benz, appearing shamelessly oversized amid the typical Thai cars, had been waiting for them at the Bangkok airport, but lacking a police escort, they suffered the same indignities of traffic as all the locals.

She stared out the window and held his hand as if they were honeymooners. Was she clinging to the concupiscent moments of their past two nights together before their inevitable separation, or was she just making sure he didn't escape? What did she see? She was seldom at a loss for words. No. Not Crissa. She was erudite. Abundant in sentences. Did the snarl of Bangkok's nefarious traffic seize her vivacity? Did the black shroud covering the city—so apparent from the air as they circled for the landing—dim her hopes?

On the plane, she flipped through the Thai Airways magazine. She giggled, leaned her shoulder into his, and read the original name of Bangkok. *The city of angels, the great city, the residence of the Emerald Buddha, the impregnable city (of Ayutthaya) of God Indra, the grand capital of the world endowed with nine precious gems, the happy city, abounding in an enormous Royal Palace that resembles the heavenly abode where reigns the reincarnated god, a city given by Indra and built by Vishnukarn.*

Was she looking for those same superlatives in the black smoke belching from unregulated cars, trucks, buses, and *tuks*? A poster child for environmental decay. Where motorcyclists and their passengers wore scarves across their mouths and noses more often than helmets on their heads. A city of angels with smog-filled lungs.

This was Bangkok. A city of extraordinary opulence and abject poverty. He remembered the times, not only his first, when he walked to the safe house or the drop-off locations and witnessed the astonishing elegance and extreme depravity living side by side. One had only to turn his head to pass from one to the other.

Funny what you remember. Temples everywhere, outnumbered only by the food carts on each corner and the ubiquitous spirit houses occupying every available alcove. Singing girls, laughing girls. Passed a wrinkled man cracking coconuts with bludgeons. Serious old women fanning the flies from the Asiatic fruit slices on their tables. The whiff of satays and peanut oil—grilled chicken or another animal, if you weren't too particular. And pickpockets, not all of them the best in the world, but few cities could come close to the collective number.

The worst was the monsoon season. The streets would flood, as did the sidewalks in places. Your feet wet, always. Inevitably, you rolled up your pants to cross an eddy in the street. Unless, of course, you were Crissa. Crissa did not get her feet wet.

He was struck by the ease with which Crissa operated. Struck by how easily she slid into the limo. How seductive wealth is. She was unpretentious, nothing exaggerated about her appearance or manner. Attractive, yes. Straightforward. Perky. And despite her collection of eyeglasses, none of them were rose-colored. She was unabashed in describing her desires. She simply knew what she liked, and that included pretty things. And now him.

Last night in his bungalow, memories of his more shaming excesses in Oxford assailed him, and as he listened to her singing softly in the shower, he felt the old pull of his checkered past when he had so many women. Was his brief stretch of asceticism during his hill tribe treks just a mirage? Her hair was still damp. Her kiss was long-lasting, but then she laughed and smiled, even as she moaned and bit his shoulder. He tried to lift his weight off her, but she refused. She pulled him back and then turned him over. Falling asleep, he speculated whether this was a rebound from Preeya or if he and Crissa were truly more suited for each other. Did he have a secret need for another lover? No, he decided, one—two if you count Heather from a lifetime ago—had been quite enough. But in the inaccessible light, he heard her whispering, and he knew that there was something singular and extraordinary about Crissa that he had yet to discover.

CHAPTER THIRTY-EIGHT

Built on the banks of the Chao Phraya River—the River of Kings—in 1876, the Oriental Hotel was the oldest in Bangkok. It was also the most luxurious, and, if one were to believe the guidebooks, rivaled the opulence of any hotel in the world.

Crissa cruised through the lobby as if she were an undergraduate rushing across the quad—late yet again for class—waving to friends and classmates, or in this case, hotel attendants and bellhops. Many knew her name, and she remembered many of theirs, dispensing salutations and sharing her charming smile with all.

She was relieved to get out of the car and stretch her long legs, and eager for Greg to meet Lady Saint Clair as soon as possible. An unexpected dinner tonight at the Royal Palace compressed the schedule. The drive from the airport took far too long for her liking. The all-business lawyer in her was returning to operational form.

The royal suite was not a suite or a hotel room, but a multi-floor wing of the Oriental. Security, dressed in smart, blue suits, stood guard at the first set of doors, which opened to a long hallway. Paintings filled both walls, elaborately carved teak sculptures of elephants and tigers greeted guests on both their left and right sides, and fresh-cut flowers displayed in ornate vases perfumed the hall.

Two more oversized doors, also made of teak, awaited them at the far end, and Crissa pulled one open without hesitation to enter yet another anteroom, this one furnished as a small living space with all the amenities and occupied by a stone-faced, thick-necked, fifty-something-year old, with sandy-brown hair, flecked with gray in a military cut. He stood when they entered.

"You are late," he said with a heavy London accent.

"So nice to see you too, Rafferty," Crissa replied.

"She has to leave shortly for the Palace and is not pleased to be kept waiting."

"Rafferty, just once I wish you could tell me something I don't already know."

Turning to Greg, she introduced him to Rafferty, and the two men shook hands. Rafferty was about the same height as Greg, but significantly thicker and stronger, and his grip revealed as much.

"Rafferty is our bulldog and our protector. And despite his gruff demeanor, he is quite the cuddly Labrador at heart, if you can get close enough to scratch behind his ears. Just the same, don't let his faded film star good looks fool you. Former special branch with all sorts of skills. He can be quite the beast when necessary."

"Her ladyship is the one I protect. You, I am afraid, are already a lost cause."

"And lest I forget, his fealty toward her ladyship is unwavering. How did the meeting go this morning?" Crissa inquired.

"Well. We were back here before the noon hour."

"Did she eat?"

"A little. They set up a nice tea in the garden. You should go in. She has been on the piano for an hour. You know what that means."

Crissa left them and Rafferty addressed Greg. "Mr. Robber, it is a pleasure to meet you. If you don't mind, I need to check you and we can wait here until called."

Rafferty performed the pat down and offered Greg bottled water. He didn't offer much about himself and questioned Greg about the trip from Chiang Mai and the traffic. After only a few moments of conversation, Greg had the distinct impression he might just as easily be talking with one of Elliot's protégés.

Greg returned the favor in the same manner when Rafferty asked him about his work in Thailand and prior visits to Bangkok. *Vague. Evasive. Quickly change the subject.*

"How far is the Palace from here?" Greg asked.

"Not very. We will have a police escort, so traffic is seldom much of a problem. The recent protests have closed a handful of blocks, but that has not been an issue for us. Have there been student or worker protests in Chiang Mai?"

"No. It has been quiet in that regard." Now, if you want to talk about murder, missing persons, assault, and criminal enterprises, then that is quite a different story, Greg's inner voice added.

Crissa re-emerged before they bored each other to death.

"The redoubtable Lady Saint Clair will see you now."

***

By this time, based solely on what he could glean from Crissa, and the little he knew about Albie's background, Greg's imagination had painted Lady Saint Clair as a tall, imperious woman managing a complex, multi-national conglomerate, and vast personal wealth. Her presence amid the lavishness of the Oriental only reinforced that view.

He was quite unprepared for the grandeur of a royal palace when he accompanied Crissa and Rafferty into the next room. The space was abundant with teak furniture, silk furnishings, elaborate lamps, and oriental vases of fresh-cut flowers, most of which were orchids. A quite ordinary-looking woman sat on the bench of a grand piano near the large, glass French windows on the far side of the room, easily one hundred fifty to two hundred feet away. A wide staircase to his left led up to a second level.

She waited on her bench, Rafferty remained at the door, and Crissa escorted Greg past an L-shaped white sofa and twin elephant statues of hand-carved teak.

She stood and smiled as they neared. Greg guessed mid-forties, soft complexion, scarcely a wrinkle, and smartly coifed black hair, revealing her full face. Greg thought she even looked a bit like Albie, but as Crissa introduced them, and she extended her hand to him, he couldn't help but notice that she had one blue eye and one green eye.

"I am not sure," he said in complete seriousness as he took her hand, "if I am to shake it or kiss it."

Crissa let out a chortle, and Lady Saint Clair smiled yet again.

"If we start with kisses, then pray tell, how might we end? A shake will do for now. Let's go upstairs. There is a nice balcony overlooking the gardens and pools, where we can sit and talk. Rafferty will approve if he can keep an eye on me. It is one of his peculiarities."

"Would you like something to drink, your ladyship?" Crissa asked.

"Yes. That would be nice. The Dom will do."

"Gregory? Will Dom Perignon suffice for you, or would you prefer a Singha beer?" Crissa asked.

"Ignore her, Mr. Robber. She has been too long in the wild."

"Please, just call me Greg, your ladyship."

"Very well, but only if you call me Gwen. Anyone who could ingratiate himself with my brother is in a class of his own. Now, let's start with how you and Albert first met."

CHAPTER THIRTY-NINE

For the next hour, Greg and Gwen talked about Albie and emptied the bottle of Dom Perignon. As Greg narrated his account, avoiding embellishments but including more details than his previous versions, Gwen interrupted him to ask a question or add her own anecdote.

She was particularly interested in those people who formed Albie's closest circle, so Greg digressed more than once to describe the relationship with Sister Mary Peyton, Wes, and Ping. For the moment, he refrained from any detail about Nok beyond the attack itself—nothing about the birth of her baby or her death.

Gwen made no secret of the fact that she disapproved of Albie's project and his gang of five.

"Overaged hippies. Albert knew we had business interests in energy, coal, and oil, and this obsession as an environmentalist was just a rejection of my father's legacy and only began after Cat died."

"I am not familiar with Cat."

"Cat was Caterina Notari. A former fashion model, a runner-up to Miss Italy, Albert's first wife, and my close friend. They met at a function in Switzerland. She was a star. No one understood what she saw in Albie, but they fell in love. She gave up her career and moved to England. All she wanted to do was be a good wife. She threw herself into taking care of the houses. We had more than a few servants, and she managed all of them and treated them kindly. Far nicer than my parents did. Played host for all my parents' social gatherings, but given a choice, she preferred to root around in the garden, even though we had help for all that. Albert was still running off to conferences and symposiums, but she was content to stay at the Old House or one of our other properties.

"Mother was slipping by then, and Cat took care of her. Eventually, we needed a full-time nurse, but Cat resisted that as long as she could.

"Father became impressed with Cat and thought it was time for Albert to abandon his scientific pursuits and prepare to take over the family business. Albert refused.

"He was such a hypocrite with money. He liked it well enough and spent lavishly on these Quixotic projects but professed to have no interest in the business.

"Please don't misunderstand. I loved Albert. He convinced my parents to allow me to study piano. I was quite the prodigy. He always supported me, nurtured my career as a concert pianist, and even protected me, but then one day he came to visit me in London and said that Father was pressing him to abandon his scientific interests and join him in business. Father was not one to suffer refusal on any matter, but Albert was adamant. *I have no interest in the mercantile world,* he told me in my London flat. As if Father were a teller at the local bank. Albert insisted his was a higher calling."

Greg could hear him saying that.

"He convinced our father that I should take over everything. Of course, Father thought that was absurd. He was apoplectic. *A female CEO in the business world. How ludicrous?* Albert said for some women, even most women, but not for Gwen. Albert then played the most diabolical hand. He told Father that he had two choices. He could pass the mantle of leadership to Albert but know that the day Father dies, Albert will abandon the business and turn it over to an ill-prepared Gwen, or Father could take me under his wing now, mentor me, teach me, and prepare me to lead.

"My father doted on me but never saw me as his successor until that day. I balked. I had my career. Albert was so patronizing. I was good at music, so it followed that I would be good with numbers. He goaded me. *Was I afraid of the real world? Was I hiding in the arts? What do you believe in? Do you think you can make a difference by playing Chopin?* Such a hypocrite, as he professed his faith in science. He played Father, and he fueled my ego as well.

"I was, honestly, overwhelmed during the transition, and that was when Cat and I became close. Cat replaced Albert as my chief supporter. She had had her share of detractors and doubters and constantly encouraged me not to let any of them hold me back. To make matters more complicated, I came to understand not everything about my father was heroic.

"Father would say, *all things being equal, you do business with your friends, and if all things are not equal, then you still do business with your friends.* However, my father's friends were not nice people. Like my father, they gained massive wealth during the war. Or dare I say, because of the war. The government and the elite—call them the ruling class or royalty or Tories if you like—all were of the same ilk. Someone needed to make war materials. Guns and bullets, trucks and tires, helmets, and clothing. And after the war, for the rebuild, someone needed to supply energy, transportation, build homes, and provide food. Those *someones* made fortunes, and we were those *someones.*

"As I learned this, I shared it with Albert, looking for a reconciliation, a redemption, a way to move forward without the stain. Albert was no help. He threw himself into additional scientific quests and formed foundations and societies. Cat convinced me to talk to my father and try to understand the context. *Don't judge so quickly*, she said. Unfortunately, I continued to learn that other dealings of his were even less respectable, even borderline criminal.

"I resolved to dig out. *Atone for the sins of thy father.* But before I could even start, Cat died.

"Albert was in Stockholm. Father and I had just returned from London, and I went into her room and found her. The doctor said it was an anaphylactic shock, an allergic reaction to a medication. A medication that my mother used. It didn't make sense. Cat wouldn't have made that type of error. The doctor wanted to call it suicide, but suicide made even less sense. My father used all his influence to avoid that pronouncement.

"Albert didn't believe any of it. He was in denial, shock. Blamed himself and crawled into a hole. It took months before he returned to any work and then nothing else mattered but these pathetic, earth-saving ventures. No one asked about me, not once.

"So, I lost Cat, and a year later, Father died. Mother passed only months ago, just when Albert went missing. It has not been a good run as of late."

Gwen waved to Rafferty. She asked him if he could please bring her portfolio from the bedroom. She sat stoically as Rafferty crossed the upper area to the far side, where the master bedroom was located, and returned with a brown leather case.

Rafferty reminded her that the car would arrive within the hour.

"That is fine. I only need to throw something on."

She rifled through the bag, finally locating an envelope with a letter enclosed, which she handed to Greg.

"Please, look at this."

> Dearest Gwen,
>
> Something quite distressing occurred this week, and I am saddened by the violence and harm waged on yet another innocent. My friend Nok, the young hill woman, who, as you know from my previous missives, helped us when we first began, is pregnant and was beaten unconscious and left for dead. And had fate not intervened, along with the heroics of a young American researcher (whom I have come to know over the past few months), she would not be in our Chiang Mai University Hospital, but in a grave.
>
> I fear that I have had enough of this wilderness. My last desperate attempt to restore the Station was rebuffed yet again today. Summarily dismissed.
>
> I have attached a directive to this dispatch (and I will get a witness signature from that pompous ass at the Consulate, so Blackledge will be satisfied). It is self-explanatory, but as we agreed before I left England, we would make all the significant financial decisions in unison. I fear that without your prudent hand, I might have squandered a great deal more on the Group of Five. Oglethorpe and Addison have met with similar challenges in Africa and their prospects for any meaningful change or even meager success look bleak. Baker is, of course, no longer with us, but Crane seems optimistic about the rainforest project, and I think I could be of help to him—not just financially but supportive and collaborative in other ways if I were to travel there.
>
> The house in Chiang Mai and an annual stipend are to go to my housemates. (Please, do not make that face—scorn causes such a furrowing of your tender brow). The

locals refer to this place as a castle—what would they say about the Old House? I will never spend a shilling of Cat's legacy. That being said, the foundation's trust should be divided among these three people: a midwife of sorts (a catholic nun) (again, no furrowing) who operates a clinic on a shoestring—her miserly superiors don't appreciate her work; my young American hero, whom I think we can safely ask to execute the details; and if Nok can survive, then she makes three. So many times, I begged her to leave that village and go to Chiang Rai or to come here, but she would not abandon her opium-plagued grandfather.

I have but one last exercise in the mountains, and then I will head to South America. I believe the villain responsible for the attack on Nok is the same one that has forever been our nemesis. There can be no doubt, but civil justice is not available in the mountains. I am vaguely familiar with the terrain and imaginary borders that I must cross, as Mac and I spent considerable time in that frontier years ago. So, please do not fret. Per your good counsel, I am simply keeping matters organized.

You are the better part, always have been.

A

Greg returned the letter to her and waited. He had just read the outline of Albie's last will, at least that portion that dealt with his friends in Thailand, and a confirmation that Albie was indeed looking to do something in the Golden Triangle. The business of South America was new.

"He is not in South America," she said. "Blackledge has communicated with authorities there and he has entered none of the ports."

She leaned toward him, and it reminded him of Crissa, leaning across the table in the Chiang Mai restaurant when she held his hand for the first time.

"I would like for you to find Albert, and in the worst-case scenario, his remains."

"The authorities have looked," he answered quickly, as if expecting such a request. "I told you. I went up there, more than once, even while the police were making inquiries. It is not like looking in a city. It's 350,000 square miles of mountains and forests. There are no Oriental Hotels, or fancy restaurants, and hardly any roads. And there are drug lords and bandits and the renegade Chinese army."

"I understand all that, but I would like you to go again and look where the authorities could not."

"Excuse my insolence, but that is insane."

"Perhaps, but it can be quite lucrative."

"I don't want your money or his money."

She didn't blink but paused now. Greg sensed her measuring his disinterest, his obstinance, categorizing him in the manner of all her adversaries, his financial, social, and professional standing.

"Let me start again," she said. "Please, bear with me. I understand the danger. I know also that you are not a coward, and I would never ask you to do something like this on your own. But I must start with you because you are intimately familiar with the area—better than anyone else whom I could trust. There is another person who Rafferty tells me has a skill set that would make him ideal to assist you in this search. Albert trusted him."

Gwen reached again into her leather case and presented Greg with a plain manila file with a single name printed in black on the top. *Colonel Richard Macmillan.*

"We have friends in Whitehall, and when Albert began this escapade, they recommended a guide. A retired American soldier who was living in Bangkok. Albert met him. Liked him, despite the information in this dossier. Knowing Albert, it was because of the information. Regardless, Albert paid him handsomely, and the American cleverly negotiated permanent Thai residency and the right to property ownership for himself. He is living in Pattaya. The little I know about that place speaks about his appetites. What interests me are his talents, not his proclivities. And like any mercenary, we just have to find a price."

Greg opened the file on the colonel, courtesy of Rafferty and his friends. Richard Macmillan. West Point graduate, U.S. Army Special Forces, multi-lingual, French-Laotian mother, father an African American missionary, tours in Vietnam and Laos for much of the sixties, the Phoenix project, detail redacted, the Laotian details also redacted—covert no doubt—injured in battle, a lengthy list of medals and commendations. More pages, also heavily redacted. Greg didn't need to read anymore, and it didn't take much to guess that this Army Ranger was accustomed to crossing borders. Albie had mentioned him once or twice. He had been an excellent choice back then for Albie. Protector, guide, translator.

"What are you asking me to do?"

"Go to Pattaya. Find this colonel and get him to agree to accompany you."

"To do what?"

"To look for Albert."

"We already did."

"Blackledge learned from the secret services' report that their assets believed his trail led into Burma. The investigation by Thai authorities was limited, and we are not in a position to approach Burmese authorities, particularly in that region and under such circumstances."

She was looking directly into his eyes now.

"You were careful the first time not to cross any lines. This time, along with Macmillan, you can be less careful and look where you didn't look before."

"Why don't you send your own people?"

"Broached and rebuffed. You are better suited."

"If we hadn't already looked, had not already visited villages throughout the region, then ok, but what you are asking is too dangerous. Once you wander in the frontier, there are no rules. Government authorities don't go there because of the drug lords. The ethnic Shan, the Chinese, the Thai. No one has any regard for the law. And once you illegally cross borders, you are looking for trouble."

"Rafferty tells me you are not part of the intelligence community. You can feign research. No one can accuse you of anything nefarious. Colonel Macmillan helped Albert. He will be with you to protect you."

Not part of the intelligence community. He could see Elliot's poker face shielding a smile, but the file on Macmillan's clandestine adventures obscured little and left less for humor.

"Why? Why go to all this trouble?" he asked himself as much as to Gwen.

"I have lost my father, mother, best friend, and now my brother. Everyone that I have ever loved is gone. If he is alive, I want to know.

I am not naïve. I know this might be a wild goose chase. You will probably find nothing, but at least I will know that I have exhausted every measure. What would you do? What would you do for love?"

Greg shook his head and considered his losses. All paled compared to the loss of Nok and Albie. Both were proof of the carnage. A testimony to the anarchy of the Golden Triangle. With or without this colonel, he was not blatantly crossing into Burma to look for Albie. Elliot had made it clear. *Peak behind the curtain, no dilly-dallying, take snaps and get out. No one is coming to get you if you are caught.*

Greg felt a twinge of sympathy for her. Her sincerity was almost believable.

"It is getting late. I must get ready for this dinner at the palace. Albert's friendship with the royals is one reason he came to Thailand and received so much support, at least in the beginning.

"Crissa told me you might be reticent. What I am asking is not part of your academic world nor part of my commercial one. I had hoped to appeal to your affection for Albert. That you would understand."

Greg thought for a moment it was finished. They could go their separate ways. How naïve he was. Gwen, like her father, did not suffer rejection well. She abandoned her kind supplications, and with neither hesitation nor reluctance, transmuted her persona, and Greg had the distinct impression he might just as easily be sitting with Fat Man. Her heterochromia eyes were now as cold as those of the reptilian Fat Man.

"Blackledge explained to you the law. Seven years must pass before Albert is legally deceased. Seven years before his will takes effect. What happens to that woman Ping and her child in the interim? I have no obligation to keep that house or to support her. No reason to give money to that catholic charity nun, and certainly not to you, though you profess no interest in any of my money. You can do as I ask, be handsomely rewarded, and I promise to take care of those people immediately, as Albert would wish, or you can choose otherwise. It is up to you."

"You would throw them out?"

"I will do what I must. The question is, will you?"

"Ping and Dao were his family. That letter is proof that he wanted to provide for them."

"She was another stray that he took in. It is as simple as this. The midwife, the women in that house, that child, get nothing without my consent."

"There is another infant in that house, too. A baby boy. Ping adopted Nok's son."

"Nothing for them," she repeated cold-heartedly.

"What if I told you that boy is Albie's son? His heir."

"Maybe he is and maybe he isn't. It makes no difference to me. Albert has little bastards all over the world."

She stood, but Greg remained seated, ignoring all measures of protocol and politeness.

"Gregory, I like you. I can see why Albert liked you. Crissa too. You might think me a posh cow, or worse. I couldn't care less. The moral rectitude of our family resided with Albert. Not with me. I would like you to talk to this Richard Macmillan. Convince him to assist you in searching for my brother one more time. One last time. He has the requisite skills. He should be able to protect you as he did Albert in those early days—protect you from those cheetahs and Burmese tigers and whatever. I proffered the question. What would you do for love? For me, it is to find an answer. I will leave it for you to decide, and for you and Crissa to sort out the details. Do whatever it takes. Pay this colonel whatever he wants and find out what happened to my brother, and I will take care of your friends now, and in the future."

She turned and walked away like a deity. In her place now stood Rafferty. One cutthroat for another. He collected the files and portfolio, and without a word, handed Greg an index card with the address for Ret. Colonel Richard Macmillan. The American Bar. Pattaya.

CHAPTER FORTY

He remained at the table until Crissa arrived to escort him out of the royal suite. She read his temperament, and they proceeded in silence to the bar next to the lobby. He ordered a shot of tequila and a beer. Crissa had nothing.

He wanted to be angry. He had glided through life from one guardian to the next. Had never worked for a single day's wages. One gift after another. Once, a stranger in a strange land, and now an expat. *The good people left. We were never the good.* Only two decent ones left. Ping and Mary P, and now they will suffer. Have already suffered. Just walk away. He was no one's sordid savior. Nok was dead. Fat Man won. He was petty and mean. He could not control himself, and he saw no reason he should. Preeya had it right. Greg was a poor player. He never saw it. No misdirection needed. Gwen had every card. He never had a punter's chance. Not a blind spot. Only blind.

He ordered a second tequila, gulped it, and finally spoke to Crissa.

"Did you know about all this?"

"If you mean Colonel Macmillan, then yes."

"She wants me to go back up to Ban Su and the area near there."

"Gregory, you spent the last three years in the hill tribe areas. It doesn't seem like her ladyship is asking you to do anything that you have not already done. Many times, in fact."

"Proverbs 26:11."

"You are quoting the Bible now?"

"Like a dog returns to his vomit, so does a fool to his folly."

"Well, that is gross. Funny, but gross."

He ordered a third tequila, and she placed her hand on his arm.

"Why don't you slow down on the firewater and talk to me?"

No. He had already talked too much. He realized Crissa didn't know about Burma. She thinks he is only doing a rerun.

"Let's try this. Come with me now so I can show you your room."

"I haven't agreed to do anything for her yet. Why do I need a room?"

"Whether you go back to Chiang Rai or Pattaya makes no difference. You need a place for tonight. I have items I need to address, and I would prefer to know you are safely housed, rather than drunk in this bar, or worse, roaming the city. I don't want to lose track of you."

"Aren't you going to the Royal Palace?" he asked scornfully.

"No. I am not. Only Rafferty goes with her. I seldom make those appearances. I have things to do. We leave tomorrow as well."

"Where are you going?"

"Singapore. Now please, let me show you your room. You can clean up, rest, and consider your decision. We can get dinner later."

He chugged the last shot of tequila.

"She's a bitch."

"No. She is Lady Guinevere. She is royalty and accustomed to having her way. Royals differ from us, but she is no more damaged than we are."

"You don't appear damaged."

"I am not sure if you meant that as a compliment. Regardless, I have had my moments, which I prefer not to discuss, and most I pray that I never see again."

"How can you work for her?"

"It started with the challenge of something new, but quickly I respected her and her incredible energy. She is inexhaustible. When things seem bleak or overwhelming, she remains undaunted. Tough-minded. I admire that. Once you get to know her, she is funny and charming."

"She must be a great genius to make up for being so loathsome," said Greg, slurring his words.

"Let's go."

With a flick of her hand, she signaled the bartender, and the bill was covered. Crissa's secret language. What other secrets did she hold? Greg stood and stumbled a bit, wobbling from the tequila. The attendant near the door started toward them, but she waved him off, hooked her arm into his, and escorted him without further incident or conversation to his hotel room.

***

He passed out as soon as he hit the bed. They had had little sleep for the last two nights, and then a day of travel topped off with tequila. It was nine p.m. when he shook himself awake and found the shower. The bathroom, filled with every imaginable amenity and fresh-cut flowers, reminded him of the Ritz in London. Elliot's post-training graduation reward before Greg flew to Bangkok. The glass-walled shower had two separate showerheads to rinse your front and back simultaneously. He squinted through the shadow of a headache and was relieved that he had not done more damage to his brain cells.

He was brushing his teeth when he heard Crissa enter, and she called out to him.

"I am going to order room service. How does that sound?"

"What if I prefer to go out?" he asked through the foam and paste.

"I hear there is nothing to do in this city. Room service makes more sense."

He rinsed his mouth.

"Is everyone in this group accustomed to getting what they want?" he asked, sticking his head around the corner.

Crissa did not answer but was smiling as she spoke to the operator. She covered the mouthpiece to ask if he wanted more tequila with his dinner.

"Water. Lots of water. Sparkling water, too."

Crissa ordered the water, two Singha beers, and a bottle of Dom Perignon.

"I will not be shut out of the Dom," she said after hanging up and walking over to him. "I am also guessing you might want a cold beer later."

They embraced and kissed.

"Hmmmm. Nice. I am glad that you are feeling better, but this is going to have to wait. Her ladyship will be back shortly, and I need time with her."

"Do you pack her bags too?"

"No. We have someone who does that. Get dressed. Hotel staff will be here shortly to set up the dining."

"Isn't that over the top?"

"The attendant for her ladyship or the dining staff of the Oriental?"

"Both."

"In this world, neither. Have you had sufficient time to consider your response to her ladyship? She will want to know, and I will need to plan."

"What do you think I should do?"

"Greg. I told you what I thought, but it is your decision."

"Do you realize she is asking me to do more than just return to Ban Su? She wants us to follow up on intel that Albie might have entered Burma."

"No. I am not familiar with any of those details, but I am not surprised. I know a little about Mac, however. It started as a business relationship between him and his lordship. Lord Saint Clair paid him well, and arranged, with the help of his Thai friends here in Bangkok, to secure for Mac a visa for permanent residency and the property rights to a bar in Pattaya. However, they also became friends, and Lord Albert rewarded him even more when they completed their search. He bankrolled the bar in Pattaya. The place has been an enormous success and is a favorite watering hole for the U.S. Military. Pilots from the northeast air station in Korat go down there regularly. One group after another on R&R. When the navy began arriving in the bay, a deluge of U.S. personnel hit Bangkok, as well as Pattaya, and the American Bar has lines outside with sailors, soldiers, and pilots waiting to get in.

"The details in the dossier were redacted, but Rafferty told me that Mac was part of Project Phoenix. Deniable operations. Special ops and the CIA conducting interrogations and assassinations to dismantle Vietcong surveillance networks in South Vietnam. Mac then took a version of that into Laos with a smaller covert group. Rafferty says they were recruiting the Hmong people, arming them to fight the occupying North Vietnamese. It was all part of the secret Studies and Observation Group, an elite division of Special Forces. His language skills are like yours. Rafferty said his service record was exemplary, which tells you everything you need to know about how all of this was viewed. He has been out a few years, well before the drawdown and Paris talks.

"If I were looking for one guy to go with you, to take care of you and that pretty face, then despite the history, I would pick this colonel. And when you consider that he and Lord Saint Clair were friends, the selection makes even more sense."

"How do you know all this?"

"I am an expert reader and an even better listener. Look, if you don't want to do this, then just say so. Her ladyship will find someone else. She has already asked me to gather background on your friend Wes in Chiang Mai. He seems to have been a friend to Lord Saint Clair as well and has a military background. Rafferty, however, doesn't like the idea of two ex-military on this mission. Your sweet innocence makes you ideal."

There was a soft doorbell ring.

"That will be staff to set up dining. I will let them in on my way out. Do we have a decision?"

Greg nodded his head. He saw no other possibility. No way out.

"Good. I will be back as soon as I get her settled. When the food arrives, please start without me, but don't you dare touch the Dom until I get back."

She kissed him and left.

CHAPTER FORTY-ONE

Greg sat on a small balcony, his feet perched on the ledge, something he would never do in Thai company—pointing your feet at someone was a great insult. Past the hotel gardens and across the Chao Phraya River were the lights of Thonburi. The tourist boats were few this time of night, but the ferries were operating, moving faster than they could during the busy daylight hours. There was no reflection. The dirty brown waters of the Chao—dismal, dreary, and darksome, swallowed the lights from the new high-rise apartments along the riverside in Thonburi, and as if on command from Gwen, beckoned him as well into the murky and obscure perils of its depths.

What maddened him was that he knew this was a misplay. Elliot had preached as much from the start. *Information will come to you—it is a mistake to go out and try to find it.* But Gwen had obliterated his options. Her shameless exhibition of the super-rich on full display to intimidate, if not to taunt, had missed its mark. The expensive champagne, a droll touch to dull the fall, was equally off-target. Hollow and vain distractions. The biggest tip-off was the over-detailed narrative, filled with innuendoes and half-truths, marked with insincerity, and unconvincingly rendered. It had utterly failed to inspire in Greg, even a faint willingness to continue in his role as the Saint Clair family proxy in Chiang Mai. No. All her artifice was transparent. Her stratagems failures. What had worked was coercion. Hate-filled, contemptible threats to irreproachable innocents were forcing him to secure their safety, their well-being, and their futures by risking his.

He was drinking his second beer when Crissa returned. The prawns, a not-so-spicy vegetable curry, and steamed rice were untouched.

"That didn't take long," said Greg.

"No. She was tired, and we have an early departure. You look relaxed. Contemplative even."

"You look tired," he said.

"Thanks, just what a woman wants to hear. Do you ever run out of these compliments?"

"Sorry. You look great, but you should get off your feet."

"Good idea, but let's open this bottle of Dom first. Will you do the honors, please?"

Greg removed the wrapping, popped the cork, and filled the crystal flute. He passed on another glass of champagne and continued to nurse his beer.

"Santé," said Crissa and raised her glass to Greg.

"Fluent in French. Is there no end to your talents? Cheers," he replied, tapping his bottle against her delicate, tulip-shaped glass.

"Yum. Tastes good. I arranged your travel for tomorrow. A car and driver will be here at nine to take you to Pattaya. He will stay with you for as long as it takes and then get you back here to Bangkok. We set hotel arrangements in Pattaya in case you need a place. When you get back to the City of Angels, there will be a room for you here, and whenever you wrap up negotiations with Macmillan, then we will arrange your travel to Chiang Mai."

"What if the colonel refuses to do this?"

"We cross that bridge when we get to it. We hope that his friendship with Lord Saint Clair, as well as financial encouragement, will motivate him. It is a chance for you to show your prowess in negotiations."

"Negotiation is not one of my strengths. Just look at how effectively I avoided this assignment."

"You will be fine. He will have a price. All you need to do is find out what that number is."

"You seem so sure."

"History tells us to be hopeful. Not certain. Are you sure you wouldn't prefer this bubbly to that swill?"

"My beer is fine. How are we to stay in contact?"

"Here are the phone numbers to reach me. The first is the Raffles in Singapore, and the second is a London number. The people in London will always be able to contact me, so you can leave your number with them, and I can get back to you. You can always call collect. Likely, we will talk before we head to Sydney, so those two numbers should work for now."

"When are you leaving?"

"Tomorrow at seven a.m. One more thing. Here is the business card of the general manager for the Oriental. You should not have any issues, but just the same, he will be your contact. He is an American. A former Peace Corps volunteer."

"Have you thought of everything?"

"I do what I can. Her ladyship wanted me to tell you she is pleased with your decision and is appreciative."

"Swell. Her gratitude means the world to me."

"Don't be mean. She is very conflicted about Lord Albert."

"How so?"

"Despite their love for each other, they have not always seen eye-to-eye, and after Lady Caterina passed, things were very…difficult. For each of them."

"What do you know about Albie's first wife, Caterina?"

"Not much. I arrived shortly after her death. I saw wedding photos. She was stunning."

"Gwen told me she and Cat became close friends, but that timing seems so unusual."

"I can't comment on the timing, but I had the impression that her ladyship viewed Caterina as aloof or out of her element."

"Why do you say that?"

"After Lady Caterina passed, Lord Albert became a recluse at the Cambridge property. He was at the estate for the funeral, but months passed before he ever returned. My employment began about six weeks after the funeral. It was a challenging time because, besides the death of Lady Caterina, their father, Lord Albert III, began failing in his health—both in mind and body. He was a stone-faced industrialist, who, according to the servants, was terrifying behind closed doors. His wife was already in a nurse's care around the clock. Lady Guinevere was left to address all of that, the family business, as well as the estate itself.

"The Saint Clair House is a 175-room Jacobean estate built by the first Baron in 1645. Her ladyship lives in a private residence in a wing of the main house—they call it the Old House—but there are over one-hundred residential properties, which they lease, and thirty-nine acres of scenic gardens. Managing the estate managers was a sizable undertaking. Her ladyship was not always happy and resented her brother's overwrought grief and his refusal to assist.

"As I explained to you, I was establishing the provenance of each piece in the art collection, which was spread over four properties. The estate, the Cambridge house, a flat in Kensington, and a villa near Brighton. I spent long sessions with Lord Albert III, and those conversations were mostly lucid, but occasionally disjointed with wild digressions, especially when the history of a specific acquisition was clouded.

"On one occasion, he expounded on Lady Caterina, professing his everlasting love and heartache for her loss. It was as if he had been married to her—or imagined that he had. Another time, he was candid in expressing his anger with Lady Guinevere. We were all in the room together discussing a woodwork by Picasso when he suddenly chastised her ladyship for her disdain and resentment of Caterina.

"That simply is not true, her ladyship said. *I loved Caterina like a sister, but she was never one of us. Still, I did all that I could to make her feel a part of this family. This life overwhelmed her. We talked all the time. She struggled mightily. She was depressed by her inability to match Albert's genius, the wealth, the status. She was insecure. Why do you think she threw herself into the care of the gardens? She was hiding.*

"Her father was mean. *If you were so close, you should have saved her.*

"Sometime later, I traveled to Cambridgeshire to work on that part of the collection. The house was large, with forty or fifty rooms. The collection there was immense, magnificent. I was there for more than a week before I ever met Lord Albert IV. He came up to me while I was in a drawing room on the second floor with 17th and 18th-century artifacts.

"He was ever so nice. So polite and apologetic for not knowing that I was performing such an important task. He made me stop and insisted that we have tea, and we talked for almost two hours."

"That sounds like Albie," said Greg

"He eventually talked about Lady Caterina. I suppose it was cathartic. He left the room and returned with a photo album of the two of them. Pictures from the wedding and others from Italy. Mostly Florence.

"He said to me, *you would have liked her. Everyone did. All the staff, Father, and in time, Gwen too, would have come around.*

"He refused to believe it was suicide. *Why would she kill herself? She had everything. She had me. If we could only have had a family.*

"You could just see how much he loved her. He hated living with the lie of her suicide and lamented that no one heard her dying words."

Crissa collected herself and poured another glass of champagne.

"Then he asked me if I had seen the private library and the paintings that his father had placed there. I hadn't, and for a second I thought he was going to escort me there, but rang Mrs. Landau, and instructed her

I was to have access to every single room in the house, without exception. He was overly gracious. I was to be considered the queen of the house while I was there. That was it. I never spoke to him again.

"That was a long-winded answer to explain that I never got the impression that Lady Guinevere and Lady Caterina were close, any more than they were estranged in any manner. They were just living in the same orbit until Lady Caterina wasn't."

"Albie was always generous," said Greg. "A mutual friend of ours, Sister Mary Peyton, once told him: *it doesn't matter what you did, what matters is what you do.* And Albie repeated that often and acted on it."

"Do you think he loved Ping?" Crissa asked.

"I don't know. I know Ping loved him. Still does and still believes he is alive."

"And you? Do you think he is alive?"

"I don't know how he can be."

"Which is part of the reason you don't want to go look again?"

"I suppose. Not knowing is better than the alternative."

She took his hand and led him into his bedroom, where a new tenderness replaced the enthusiastic ardor of the past two nights.

"Why is your timing so poor?" Crissa lamented afterward as she nestled next to him.

"Mine? I was comfortably unemployed until you came along."

"It stinks. I am heading to Singapore and Sydney, and you are going to Pattaya and the Golden Triangle."

"Sounds like a directional matter more than timing."

"Don't be a smart ass now."

She placed her head on his chest and sighed. "What are we going to do?"

"I don't know. Just see what happens, I guess."

"That's a brilliant plan," she said.

"So, who is the smart ass now?"

She slapped him softly on his stomach and reached around his waist. "You are so skinny. You have the waist of a nineteen-year-old."

"I can't remember nineteen, and I am not skinny. I think the word you are looking for is sculpted."

She pulled him across to herself, lifted her head to his, and kissed him. He felt the heat of her face and the press of her body, as she lifted her hips and her legs coiled and overlapped with his. He could never remember her last words as they finally fell asleep.

In the crepuscular rays of the morning light, he awoke to find her gone and immediately missed her far more than he thought possible. With the memory of his breath caught in her hair, he rolled over and stared at the empty space. He wondered *what if* and even *why not*, before closing his eyes and settling on *once again*. The uncertainty of *what next* roused him from his musings, so he gathered himself and sat up on the edge of the bed. It was then that he saw the note on the lampstand and the money.

Dear Greg,

I didn't want to wake you. I didn't want you to see me crying. I don't know how this happened so quickly. It was as if I had been looking for you for a long time, and then suddenly there you were in front of me. I have always been careful. People have called me cold and calculating, but it seems so different with you, and I didn't want to waste another day.

I am sorry you have this search in front of you, but it brought us together, so maybe it is not such a dreadful thing.

I forgot to give you this money last night. Don't make a face. But you might need cash over the next few days. Don't worry about the receipts.:-)

I am too afraid to ask you how you feel, and I won't, but I will dream about tomorrows until I see you again.

All,

Crissa

CHAPTER FORTY-TWO

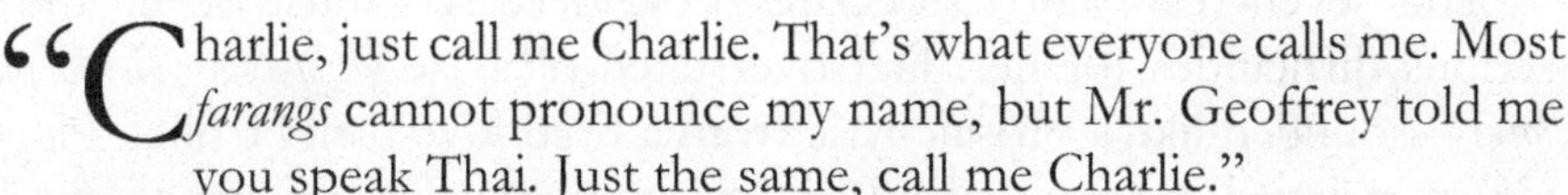

"Charlie, just call me Charlie. That's what everyone calls me. Most *farangs* cannot pronounce my name, but Mr. Geoffrey told me you speak Thai. Just the same, call me Charlie."

"Thank you, Charlie. My name is Greg."

Greg was in the back seat of a new car, which belonged to the Oriental Hotel.

"Have you ever been to Pattaya, Mr. Greg?"

"No."

The morning sun was already high, and Greg slipped on his sunglasses. A tourist bus passed them on the two-lane road and blared its horn. Charlie was driving carefully and too slowly for the bus.

"This route out of Bangkok is the most direct to the highway, but it can be crazy. How long have you been in Thailand?"

"A few years."

"I am surprised you haven't been to Pattaya. *Farangs* love it. It was a sleepy beach town, and not much happening until the war. I went there as a child, but now it's like nothing you have ever seen. New resorts all the time. More bars. You can hardly drive on Walking Road anymore. It makes *Patpong* look tame."

Patpong was the nightlife and red-light district of Bangkok, with bars featuring graphic sex shows, each one trying to top the next with outlandish lasciviousness. Greg had spared himself from the vulgar lechery, more so out of his disdain for public erotica and sex trafficking than even Elliot's advice.

"Mr. Geoffrey told me I am to stay with you until your business is complete in Pattaya, so you just tell me where and when you want to go. I will take care of you."

"You speak English very well, Charlie."

"Thank you. Mr. Geoffrey was a teacher of English a long time ago before he became manager of the Oriental Hotel, and he makes sure all of us take lessons and is not hesitant to correct us. He is the best of all bosses that I have ever had. So, whatever you need, you just ask Charlie."

"Thanks, Charlie. I hope it will be a short and uneventful trip, and we will be back in Bangkok in no time."

They merged onto the highway and the combination of more traffic and faster-moving traffic earned all of Charlie's attention, leaving Greg alone to reflect on his meeting with Gwen.

The seven-year wait to declare Albie deceased must be creating serious difficulties for her. Her overstated plea—*what would you do for love?*—sounded like a prosaic lyric from a tired love song. Unlike Ping, Gwen believed Albie was dead, and what she needed was proof of his remains. None of that was difficult to figure out, but her rendering of Caterina as her dearest friend flummoxed him. Assuming, of course, Crissa's version was accurate. Why create a fairy tale of friendship? On the surface, it wasn't all that important to what he was being asked to do, but it begged the question of truthfulness. What else in Lady Saint Clair's narrative was an imprecision, if not an outright falsehood?

CHAPTER FORTY-THREE

He was sitting on a bar stool with his eyes fixed forward on the Thai girl standing across from him behind the bar. She was shuffling a deck of cards. A revealing, white halter crop top exposed her bare midriff, as well as her narrow shoulders and slender arms. Her nimble hands separated the deck with split cuts and then riffle shuffles. She seemed adept, but not even close to the dexterity and proficiency that Preeya showed.

In the bar's front, just to the right of the doorway, an older Thai man in a sleeveless, white tee shirt straddled a stepladder, his dark-skinned legs dangled on each side of the ladder. His dirty, blue *pha chung hang,* a peasant man's loincloth, hiked high, exposed his muscular thighs as he stretched upwards to repair a ceiling fan.

He dropped his screwdriver as he made eye contact with Greg. It rattled on the hardwood floor, but neither the man at the bar nor the female dealer looked up. Greg collected the screwdriver and handed it back to the man on the ladder.

Posters of cars like the '58 Chevy Impala, the '62 Corvette convertible, and others were tacked onto the wall next to aerial photos of Yankee Stadium and Wrigley Field. Two large panels listed the current American League and National League standings. Greg could see prints of James Dean, Elvis, and Marilyn Monroe along the far wall.

As Greg passed more than a dozen wooden tables, he could hear the man at the bar speaking to the Thai girl in English. His voice was soft and melodious. An American accent Greg could not place. His long, curly, brown hair and the light from behind created the illusion of a nimbus around his head.

"There are only twelve notes in music, seven, if you don't count the flats, yet with those notes, look at all the combinations that have been created, and the musicians can remember those. How easy it should be to remember fifty-two cards, just fourteen hearts?"

"Excuse me. I am looking for Colonel Richard Macmillan."

The girl, who did not look over twenty, stopped shuffling. She set the deck of cards in front of the man and walked away toward the rear of the bar, where she organized items behind the counter. She remained there with her back towards Greg. Extremely short cut-off jean shorts hugged her hips, and Greg looked twice at her shapely legs.

"The bar is closed. There is a sign out front," said the man.

"I saw that. I am not looking for a drink. I am looking for Colonel Richard Macmillan."

The man at the bar picked up the deck of cards and slowly shuffled them as he spoke. From a distance, Greg thought he looked about the same age as Greg, but up close, not even the poorly maintained Fu Manchu mustache could distract from the cracks and creases on his weathered skin. Tattoos covered both of his forearms. A dragon breathed fire on his right bicep. Greg imagined his burly chest sported other ink patterns.

"He is not here. May I ask your name?" the man on the bar stool asked.

"Greg. My name is Greg Robber. I am trying to find the colonel. I believe he is the owner of this place."

"Greg as in egg. Robber as in thief."

Greg smiled. "Yes, I suppose so. Who are you?" Greg then asked.

"Who am I? Well, that is one of the great existential questions, isn't it? I am a little surprised that you would ask me that. I mean, we hardly know each other, and I would need to provide a context for whichever path I took to answer such a question. If I tell you I am the son of my father or my mother, or I say the child of both, then you know nothing more. If I explain where my father came from, what he did before he became my father, or what he did after he became my father, then I am providing a rationale that I am more than just a product of his procreative skills, but also a product of my environment. Isn't the word *product* demeaning in this case? Certainly, there are better words. I like words. When I was in prison, I kept a list of words. Words like *somniferous, incunabula,* and *eructation*; but people thought I meant *erection*, so I don't use that word so much. Now I simply say *belch*. *Lo...* and *lo.* What a word. *Lo.* You don't hear it except in the Bible. The born-agains in prison read the Bible. They had Bible meetings too, but they uninvited me, said that I talked too much, and insisted that I was fustian and had logorrhea.

"One of my favorites is *pulchritude*. That means beauty. You know who is beautiful. Ann-Margret. Have you ever met Ann-Margret? Now there is a beauty. That is her right there," he said, pointing to a framed picture behind the bar.

"She autographed that for me. See where it says, *All my love, Ann-Margret*. She hyphenates her name. If you look closely at the photo in the corner, that is me with her. She came to see me when I was in the hospital. Not just me, but the others, too. However, not all of them received an autographed poster and had their photo taken with her. She said I was cute. Imagine that."

"Ok. I get it. I meant what is your name?" asked Greg, trying to maintain his equanimity.

"My name? My name now is Miguel Arcangelo Sebastian Augustin-Rafael de Gabriel Jimenez, but now I prefer Raf, and everyone just calls me Pancho, except Mac. He calls me Wireless. Oh, and Ann-Margret calls me *Cutie*. No one remembers my original name, although if my parents had listened to the angel who said to call me Obadiah, then I could have had a cool name like that and might never have changed my name. People don't listen to angels much anymore. Or to God. Do you think God takes naps? I wonder about that sometimes, but if I wonder too much, or I wander too far, then I lose track of what I was thinking about when I first started wondering."

"You don't look Hispanic."

"I am not, but that should not restrict my options for a new name, should it?"

And before Greg could comment, Pancho continued.

"Why did I change my name? Of course, you want to ask. People say you change your name to get a fresh start. I don't know why they say that. I mean, what is a fresh start? Is there a stale start? Or do you change your name because you want to hide something? Maybe you want to hide from someone. Do you know how often characters in the Bible had their name changed? Jacob became Israel, Simon became Peter, and Saul became Paul. I always thought that the last one was a little non-dramatic. I mean, he only changed one letter. But in Aramaic, those two names were significantly different. Do you know any Aramaic? Few people do. Marilyn Monroe changed her name and so did Bob Dylan. Or was it Ringo? I don't think any of them spoke Aramaic. At least not Marilyn. It doesn't matter because they were artists, like the guy who wrote *Tom Sawyer*. He had a *nom de plume*, and artists do all sorts of things, but real people have real reasons—like needing a *nom de guerre*. I didn't need a *nom de guerre*, but it comes in handy to have one."

He leaned in and whispered now. "Spies have *nom de guerre* names too—they are called *cover names* and they have phony stories called *legends* to go with them, but we don't talk aloud about those types around here. You're not a spy, are you? Criminals too. They have aliases. Robber, are you a criminal, perhaps? I give all the girls who work here a *nom de scene.* It only makes sense because this is an American bar, we call it *The American Bar*, and these are Thai girls and it's difficult, especially for the sailors, to say Thai names like *Sasivimol* or *Ying-cheep*, let alone the ones with fifteen letters—and the girls like the American names like Savannah, Meredith, and Morgan. We even have one girl named L.A. You know, not La, but L.A., like Los Angeles, is called L.A. Thai people give their children nicknames all the time for good luck, but in business, you can't be successful with cute nicknames like Red, Skinny, or Bird. Business is serious stuff. I tell that to Sasinan over there all the time," he said, pointing at the electrician. "He was a fighter, a Thai boxer, and he had a boxer name too, but we don't call him that anymore because he wanted a fresh start and not at boxing. Do you wonder why a skilled athlete wouldn't want to take advantage of his name and accomplishments? Kickboxers are the sludge of Thai society, and like the girls in the massage parlors, they are reduced to those professions rather than aspiring to them.

"What about you, Mr. Egg Thief? Did you ever change your name? Or is it an aptronym with which you are comfortable?"

"No. Look, I appreciate your explanation, but I must speak to Colonel Macmillan."

"Mac is not here. Just call him Mac. No one calls him Colonel anymore. Have we met?"

"No. I don't think so."

"Really?"

"Yes," said Greg. "I am certain. I would remember."

Pancho shuffled the cards without looking at them. His hands displayed even more dexterity than the Thai girl had. The deck glided from hand to hand as he removed portions from the center and replaced them, alternating from top to bottom. Quicksilver split cuts faster than Preeya. Never a hesitation. Never a glance at the cards, as he kept his eyes transfixed on Greg.

"You look like someone I once knew. His name was George. I didn't know him as well as I knew his sister, but that was a long time ago. It was grade school. Her name was Rae—with an *e* not *y* like a guy's name. You remember names like that, you know. She was a good kisser."

He kept shuffling, only now for all to see. He flipped over the top card after cuts and slices. The ace of spades appeared, and he cut and sliced. He removed a section from the center of the deck and placed it on top and then another and another and then flipped a card. It was always the ace of spades, despite burying it repeatedly.

"But it might have been high school, now that I think about it, or maybe it was junior high school."

He shuffled the cards with only one hand. Fanning them out, closing the spread, adroitly moving cards from the top of the deck to the bottom, all with one hand.

"Anyway, we were just a year apart, so it wasn't weird."

"I am sorry. I am not George. If Mac is not here, can you tell me when he will be back?"

"You don't need to apologize. Are you certain you don't know Rae? Because you look like her brother, or at least what I think her brother would look like. He wasn't as pretty as Rae, but he was good-looking. Handsome. Not as pretty and as handsome as you are. Has anyone ever told you that you are magazine handsome? I imagine people turn around in the street to look at you, don't they? Still, she was pretty, the prettiest girl in the entire school. If no one is looking, I will close my eyes and think hard, and then I am sure she was impossibly beautiful. I remember I used to do push-ups at night thinking she would like me if I had big muscles. I must have done a thousand push-ups and then, before I got big muscles, she moved away. I never saw her again, but I remember her and her long hair. So black. Like a raven.

"I would offer you a drink, but the bar is closed. I could still offer you one since I am the boss. But if someone else comes in and sees you drinking, then I would have to serve him, too. And then, where does it end? That is why we put a sign up that says *closed.* Are you sure you didn't see that sign?"

"Look. I understand you are closed and that you might even prefer that I leave, but I have important business to conduct with the colonel, and if you are the boss, as you said, then it would be helpful if you could be more...helpful."

Pancho set the cards on the bar. He ignored Greg's gentle supplication. He spread out the deck in a continuous row and flipped the entire row back and forth, cascading in each direction. Greg knew he was what Preeya called a mechanic. Only a mechanic could shuffle the cards and make the same one appear on the top every time. Eventually, he stacked the cards neatly and caressed the deck as gently as you might a person. Then, with his large hands, he covered the deck entirely, and the cards disappeared.

"Have you ever been to Idaho?"

"No," Greg replied sharply.

"Neither have I. Do you know anyone who has? It's only that I never have met anyone from Idaho. I mean, I know it's there because of maps and books and the news and such, but it's just one of those places. It seems like everyone has been to Ohio and other states that end in a vowel. Even Alaska has visitors, but you don't hear about Idaho. And it's not like Rhode Island or other small states like Delaware—Idaho is big. I asked two different Navy guys last night if they knew anyone from Idaho. I am certain it was last night, but it might have been two nights ago. Not one of them knew anyone from Idaho. They knew people from Iowa, but not Idaho. Strange, isn't it?"

Greg closed his eyes and took a deep breath. He had to dig in, he said to himself. He had no other choice other than to suffer this circus act. He must find Mac.

"Are you one of those who believe that the cards can deal up your future?" Pancho asked.

Greg shook his head, seething to himself.

"Do you play poker? We have a big game tonight. Are you here for the big game?"

"No," said Greg yet again.

"That is good because you weren't invited, but you play poker."

"No. I mean, I have, but no, not regularly."

"But you know the rules. You know how the game is played."

"Sure."

"So, let's play a hand. It will be good for Pepper to practice."

He called Pepper. She arrived with unhurried steps. Her movements lissome, willowy. Greg condemned the distraction of his predatory eye as it gauged the scantiness of cloth and measured the enticing extent of exposed skin.

Pepper unwrapped a new deck of cards, removed the two jokers, handed one to Greg, and then shuffled the deck.

"Pepper is learning to shuffle. She wants to be a dealer and has skills. She wants to learn the Sybil cut, but right now, she is learning the perfect riffle. Have you ever seen that? It is not something she will ever use, but you must start somewhere. What is the perfect riffle shuffle? Is it a mathematical wonder? Not really. It is a simple mathematical permutation. She takes one-half of the deck into each hand and shuffles the cards one by one from each hand. Divides the deck evenly a second time and repeats. If she can do those precise shuffles eight times, then she can restore the deck to its initial position. She can reset the entire deck. It doesn't randomize the deck, but it is good practice and a fun thing to know.

"For our purposes, she will need to randomize, and six riffles are sufficient, particularly if they are not perfect in-shuffles. You should be concerned if there are less than three, and now you know what eight will do. You understand that shuffling is an art. Dealing is one as well. I met a guy from Madrid, or maybe it was Alicante, but he would deal you five cards and you ended up with four. Go figure."

Pepper did not appear to need any practice, but at Pancho's direction dealt five cards each to Greg and Pancho, and both received five cards each.

"Now, before you even look at them, I would tell you that the person who bets first and takes cards first is a serious matter. Would you agree?"

"I don't know," Greg said, not even trying to feign interest. "I suppose."

"Well, I will explain."

Greg lifted his cards and discovered that he had two pairs: eights and aces, and a lone queen.

"Now," continued Pancho. "Let's suppose you have two pairs."

Greg looked at him in surprise. "What the hell?"

"I am just observing the way you arranged the cards after you picked them up. I am simply saying, suppose you have two pairs. I don't know that to be a fact."

Greg looked at Pepper, but she was the picture of tranquility.

"Alluring, isn't she? Reminds me of Rae. Impossible beauty. Lambent. Focus on the game at hand. Now you must decide about a bet. You received the cards first, so you bet first. Here is where my point about betting and the first to take cards comes into play."

"I don't know. What if I check?" Not knowing if that was a good strategy or not. Greg was simply delaying the decision.

"Ok. Not a bad idea at all," said Pancho.

Pancho then began a tiresomely long discourse on gambling and betting, introducing Greg to the mathematical probabilities of drawing a single card to fill a full house or discarding three to get three or even four of a kind. Why and when you might choose one strategy over another based on what your opponent does. Greg did not know if any of the math made sense. He was trying to understand why Pancho was reluctant to share Mac's whereabouts and if this rambling oration was, as Preeya described, part of misdirection for card mechanics and magicians. But Pepper was the dealer, and Pancho was a droning lecturer. His voice was white noise.

So, I will bet first and my bet you notice—because you are a student of the game—is larger than my other opening bets.

Neither Crissa, Gwen, nor Rafferty had intimated that Mac had a business partner, and it occurred to Greg that Mac might not even be in Pattaya and that this trip was a total waste of time. If that were the case, then what would happen to Ping?

You might not be a math whiz, but an expert in psychology and instead you are studying me. You look to see if I tipped my hand by organizing my cards in the same manner you did, or if a crease of satisfaction appeared on the edges of my mouth or even my eyes, or a furrowing of the brow as you did when you considered your options. You might think my quick bet was heavy, meaning that I had something special or at least the beginning of something special. You are looking for my tell.

"Does all of that make sense?" Pancho asked, trying to engage Greg, sensing his antipathy. "You know what a *tell* is, don't you?"

"Sure." His attention had turned toward Pepper. Her skin, sleek. Her scent, musky like patchouli. Slightly slanted, seductive eyes. How easily lewd visions seethed beneath his courteous exterior.

But in all this, you are most concerned with your cards, your probability, and your choices, and understand that there is nothing you can do about mine. You must decide.

Decisions. Something his football coach had said at practice one day. Something about choices. But Pancho's voice would not allow him to remember, and the volume was mounting.

"You must go for a full house, so instead of discarding three, you discard one and hope. You don't hit and when I bet again, you are now faced with increasing your stake with your meager two pairs. You might bet once foolishly, but if I raise, then you fold. You never see my hand and you never know if I was bluffing. Do you consider bluffing after you get your single card?"

Preeya's voice now. *The best players never play the game too long. You don't have to worry about that, you are a poor player.*

"What if I hit the full house?"

"Ohhhh! Now we have something, don't we? Now the adrenaline rush. Do you venture a bet? Venture. Adventure. Do you bet slowly and keep raising, or push it? Are you so convinced that your full house would win? Remember, I stood pat. Did not take any cards. What if I have a full house? What are the odds of that on a single deal? What if my full house is higher? What if I only have a straight?

"This is when the money flows and stresses the electrical impulses that zip among neurons with every thought. Your noetic prowess awakens. Even if you are excellent at probability math, the thought of riches clouds pure analytics. You rely on your experiences, or you search desperately for a *tell* on my part. Desire cascades and triggers a spike in the neurotransmitter dopamine. The excitement builds with every bet. Higher and higher toward a frenzy. Toward the apogee. Risk and reward. The greater the reward requires the greater risk. Avarice finds the weak spot in an otherwise virtuous heart."

Pepper is the mechanic, Greg realizes. She is the cheat, but before he can suggest as much, she is shuffling the cards again. This time with a wry, cat-like smile while Pancho declares, "It is the not knowing that makes the game worthwhile. How can anyone not love gambling?"

The game and the diversion are over. Greg needed to assert himself.

"Pancho, that was great. Enlightening. Do you have any idea when Mac will be back?"

"Probably."

"Great. When?"

"I don't know."

Greg sighed. The guy thinks he is Abbot and Costello rolled into one, he thought.

"Look, you asked me if I had any idea, and saying *probably* seemed like the most honest answer. I don't like to lie. Don't get me wrong. I am a good liar. I just don't like it. Never did. Did you know that in

France, one may lie at one's trial? It is up to the prosecution to prove that you lied. There is no offense for lying under oath in France. No perjury. I remember once in the fifth grade, I lied to my best friend Bobby Windemere about his bike. I felt awful for the longest time, partly because I could never ride the bike. I had to keep it hidden behind my garage and found myself living precariously on the earth's surface. It was a shame Bobby didn't move away instead of Rae. Do you know who was a great liar? Abraham. He went to Egypt during a famine and told everyone that his beautiful wife Sarai was his sister, and when the Pharaoh took Sarai as one of his wives, diseases came pummeling down on the Pharaoh and his family. Now that was a biblical lie."

Greg realized how tired he was. He hadn't slept much for the past three nights, because of Crissa, and now, for the first time in weeks, he could feel a headache edging its way into existence. He needed something to drink. Water. He looked at Pepper.

"Have you ever seen a dealer as pretty as Pepper is?" Pancho asked.

"I have. Actually, I have."

"I don't believe it. Pepper is beautiful. Untarnished and feral. Eyes like obsidian crystal."

"Believe what you will, but there is a woman in Chiang Mai who wears only white and..."

However, before he could finish, Pancho convulsed backward and almost tumbled to the ground.

"You saw the Lady in White!" he exclaimed.

"Yes. I did."

"NO! Was she as poetic as they say?"

"Yes. Without a doubt. Yes."

"Did she have a white stone on a chain around her neck? An amulet?"

"Yes. She did."

"The myth is that it has a sibylline inscription on it. A biblical reference. A prophecy."

Greg did not answer. He only knew that it had a letter and numbers, and he wasn't sharing that information, but now he knew where to look for R 3:5.

"When were you in Chiang Mai?"

"Just days ago."

"That is so wild. We have heard stories down here about her. Most think she is a fantasy, nothing but an amaranth. An imaginary unfading flower. I can't believe you saw her. You might not be so bad, Egg Thief. Her dealing is immaculate too. That is what they all say. Wow! You said you didn't play poker and here you are playing high-stakes poker with the Lady in White. I said I was a good liar, but you might be better. What else are you lying about? We are not in France."

"I am not lying. I don't play very much poker, but I have played a little, and I am not good at it, mostly because I don't enjoy gambling."

"You don't like the rush of adrenaline, the excitement of a big bet, the dramatic uncertainty. You must have a great emotional cicatrix."

"A what?"

"Scar, amigo. Something has hardened your heart."

"Pancho, can we please have this discussion another time? I must find Mac. Someone he knows is missing and I need his help."

"Who?"

"A British scientist by the name of Sir Albert Saint Clair IV."

"Albie? Albie is missing! When? Why didn't you tell me this in the beginning? Albie is my friend. I have known Albie longer than Mac has known him. Only for a day or two, but that counts. Albie and I spent countless hours discussing the sciences, the intersection of art and mysticism, the retreat of the great Columbia glacier, the incorporeal glow of anchorites, and the incunabula of the most obscure Iranian poet, whose sedulous habits of self-revision and anoetic exploits were an adumbration of his annihilation by the flakes of fire that rained down on his vain parade of arrogance. We shared life experiences. He taught me that well-established science is not always correct, explained the error in the ratio of the size of the universe to the Planck scale, and I taught him the faro. You are sitting here playing cards and Albie is missing. You have some explaining to do, Mr. Egg Thief."

"Fine. Let's start with you dropping the Egg Thief moniker and tell me where Mac is, and I will tell you about Albie. I really could use a drink of water, too."

CHAPTER FORTY-FOUR

Pancho grasped Greg's arm with a firm grip and led him from the bar to a table near the back. Instead of water, Pepper brought them two cold Singha beers. Pancho confessed that he seldom had a beer. He was subdued now. Brooding.

"I don't care for alcohol. Never drank whisky, but I need to be careful. One cold beer a day. Max. No one here will give me another. I was a heroin addict. A companion to the angel of darkness and emissary of the devil. It is a long story."

"Please, Pancho. I want to hear it, but Mac first."

"They dried me out in Leavenworth and after that, Mac brought me back to Thailand. We served together. Had our share of tough patches like everyone else. I hate soda, so occasionally I have a beer. Singha beer is like water, but it slakes one's thirst. People confuse *slake* with *slack*, but when you think about it, they aren't even close, except in spelling. Mac is the same. All beer and no booze. No smack either, but he loves coffee. French press. Did I tell you that Mac saved my life? More than once. He helped to get my release from prison, too."

Greg chugged almost half of his beer in a quiet celebration. He could see Pancho slowly coming around. Finally, he thought, I will find this colonel.

"So, you really were in prison?" he asked Pancho.

"Yep, and the next time you go to prison, make sure you ask for vegetarian meals. But tell me about Albie. I admired that man. He was filled with wisdom. I will never forget asking him about his crusade and he quoted Albert Einstein. *The environment is everything that isn't me.* How great is that?"

"For sure, but you tell me where Mac is first."

"Mac is not here."

"For crying out loud, Pancho," Greg said, raising his voice in frustration. "We just went through all that."

"No. He is nearby, but he is not here at the bar today. We are closed for repairs. The squids and flyboys had a squabble and banged up the joint. Besides, the girls need time off now and then, as well."

"Where is he?"

"About an hour south. He has a boat docked down there and gets away when he can. He will be back in a few days."

"Can't wait."

"Ok. We can go down there, but now tell me what happened to Albie."

Greg drank two beers as he detailed the events of the past few months. Pancho unexpectedly remained quiet throughout, only once sipping his beer and constantly stroking his ragged facial hair with his tobacco-stained fingertips. At one point, Pancho called Pepper for a cigarette, but otherwise, he remained silent. Greg grew uncomfortable with the manner that Pancho stared at him and stopped more than once to collect himself before continuing. He was a different cat, Greg decided. Verbose to the point of annoyance and now withdrawn. His suddenly blank and friendless eyes made Greg nervous, and Greg almost wished Pancho would start talking again. But he was holding his breath. Fixated on every word and detail. Hypnotized by the story. Living it now as much as Greg had in the past.

When Greg had finished, Pancho remained as if in a dream. His vacant gaze was still on Greg. And an air of introspection so forbidding that Greg could see mistiness in his eyes. Disconsolate silence. Greg, now certain that Pancho was deficient, waited for his return.

"And now," Pancho asked, choking for air as if breaking the surface of the water after a deep dive, "now, they want you to find him? Or his remains?"

Greg nodded.

"It all sounds bad. Execrable. Everything. I don't know what Mac will say. He will be angry about Nok, that part is certain. Other people have come looking for Mac, but he always refuses. Not for anything like this, but for other stuff."

Pancho grew quiet again, but the light was returning to his eyes and his breathing seemed less strained.

"It seems like the only thing he does these days is to read books. I've stopped reading books, but it looks like Mac is trying to read all of them. I used to like books, and when I started collecting words in prison, I considered becoming an etymologist but gave that up because you need a substantial library, and the prison library wasn't like that. The best librarian I ever met was in Saigon. We used to play cards with him. His name was Joseph, but we called him *Joey No-shave* because he looked so young. A complete paper jockey. The military is paper on top of paper. Paper to do, to go, to change, to buy anything and everything—and Joseph kept it all in order somehow. Eventually, everyone, regardless of rank, needed him to push something through, sign something, file something. If you had to pick one person to come to your birthday party or to include in any card game, it was *Joey No-shave.*"

"You had birthday parties?"

"Of course not. One night when we were playing cards, and some boys were smoking more than cigarettes, the conversation turned to talk about going home and the next chapter in your life. Someone asked *Joey No-shave* what he wanted to be when he grew up. *Joey No-Shave* thought long and hard about his answer and finally said that he wanted to be a page in a book. Preferably a well-written book. A page. Nondescript but dog-eared because there was a nice sentence or an idea or a word that caught the reader's attention. I was the only one who understood.

"Someone broke the Zen moment, joking that the page might have marginal notes or, better yet, pictures of naked women. Everyone laughed. Laughing is necessary when you play cards with friends because when you really play cards, you can never laugh. Or if you do, you could get hurt. I became friends with *Joey No-shave,* and he started sharing his books with me. He had all sorts. Fiction, non-fiction, biographies, and even books on literary theory. I changed his name to the *Librarian.*

"Shortly after that, I found out that the *Librarian* was writing his own version of the OED. Do you know what that is?"

"Yes. Word derivations. Listen, can we get back to Mac?"

"He had index cards organized in black, four-by-six binders, which he could open easily to add new cards. Each card was filled with his handwritten notes of meaning, history, and usage of any word he chose. And not only seldom-used words like *bedizen* but everyday words like *wheel.* He knew what he knew."

Pancho sat up straight in his chair. "I don't know what Mac will say. He is preoccupied with other projects. Hardly has time for the bar."

"Let's find out."

"Now?"

"Yes. Now."

"We can't go now. I can't. We have a scheduled card game tonight."

"You said the bar was closed."

"It is. Tonight, we have a game for the locals."

"Certainly, you can miss that."

"No. No way. You don't understand. It is for the bigwigs in Pattaya."

While he was still talking, six of the barmaids for the American Bar came walking in from outside. The first four women carried small packages, but the last two were walking arm in arm, carrying only their purses. All appeared to be in their mid-twenties, attractive in short skirts and high spirits, and all seemed to talk at the same time. Greg thought immediately of the sorority sisters in Ann Arbor.

"Ahhh! What a refulgent sight. Have you ever seen such convexities?" Pancho asked Greg. Then addressing the women, "Top of the morning to you, my beautiful gamines."

A chorus of *sawadee ka* came back, but nothing more, and they kept walking toward a door in the back.

"What do you know about Pattaya?"

"Nothing," answered Greg.

"Well, this town is a mob town. Just like Vegas. Only the Thai mob is not as nice. They smile more, but that is it. The Thai Society for the Advancement of Pattaya controls gambling, prostitution, liquor, and dope. A more scrofulous group you've never seen. Even with all the new construction, the Society doesn't miss a beat. Come. Let me show you something."

Greg noticed Pancho limped a bit as he walked to the very back of the bar and unlocked a door, which led to a modest, but more than acceptable, gambling parlor. The room was half the size of the barroom, with ten separate card tables and overhead lamps on the green baize table coverings. A well-stocked bar lined the wall on the right. Two in-wall air conditioners kept the room temperature comfortable. Framed photographs of the barmaids in their red, white, and blue wardrobes were prominently displayed on the other walls. All the girls were wearing hot pants and two-colored halter crop tops. Several girls had USA painted in all three colors on their exposed midriffs. Like Pepper out front, always more skin than clothing.

"It costs two-hundred U.S. dollars to get in. U.S. military only. Best behavior required. *Farangs* must go elsewhere to gamble and no locals. We avoid many issues by restricting entrance. The place sits sixty, and we average a turnover of more than half that number each night, so call it one hundred gamblers times two hundred cash at the door. Twenty grand, easy, before the rake. The Thai Society for the Advancement of Pattaya appreciates it is only U.S. military and leaves us alone for the price of buying all our liquor and beer from them, with a generous carriage fee. The deal is unique to the American Bar, thanks to Mac's negotiation skills."

"How was that?"

"They were heavy-handed in our nascent days when we were getting established, but Mac paid a late-night visit to the local boss. Mac says we can't call him a *don*. I don't have all the details, but I imagined that when *El Jefe* woke up in the middle of the night to take a piss, he found Mac sitting comfortably in a chair in the bedroom. Not quite like the scene in *The Godfather*, but you get the idea. However, when I asked Mac what transpired, he told me he knocked on the door, introduced himself, and the two of them talked. They drank that night, and they reached a mutually satisfying agreement. Mac is like that. He has that muted sangfroid. Not the raconteur that I am, but more of a rapport builder. I watched it for years during the interviews."

Greg understood. He had done the same, not with mob bosses or detainees, but at Elliot's direction with the hill tribe people. *Just sit and listen. Don't ask for anything. Eventually, they will offer you a solution or information.*

"You might find this interesting. Mac was adamant that one stipulation of the agreement required that the Thai Society for the Advancement of Pattaya would keep all the pimps out of the American Bar. *El Jefe* didn't have a problem with that at all. He appreciated the Americans were keeping it in the family and low profile. We are small potatoes compared to all the resorts and bars with sex shows. The gambling joints that cater to *farangs* and Thais make our operation look like Wednesday night church bingo."

"And the local call girls?"

"They are free to come and go as they like, but their handlers are personae non gratae. It is Mac's little piece of conscience. He is strange. Our girls too. Mac treats them like nuns. They can't have a side hustle. Mac pays them well. They make a bundle in tips, but no hooking. Some of them have legitimate boyfriends. Mrs. K. is their caretaker, custodian, and surrogate mother. She is a superwoman. They all live upstairs for free. No rent. No expenses. Everyone chips in for food. A far cry from a convent but equally distant from a seraglio."

Greg gained a small bit of admiration for his soon-to-be bodyguard. He and the assassin both have a disdain for prostitution and human trafficking.

"So, what does all that have to do with this game tonight?"

"The Society hosts a game for the local leaders each month at various locations. As a courtesy, a favor, a show of goodwill, we agree to be part of the rotation. The mayor, the top *carabinieri*—I like the sound of that word—some bankers, and business types like to play poker, and we provide a neutral site. We will only have ten to twelve players. No cover. No rake. Free booze. It is our way of giving back to the community."

"It sounds sick. Corrupt, and more like a B-Movie than *The Godfather*."

"Yea, that is true. 'Tis but a paltry machination. It is not, however, a machicolation, although we could consider that if we ever want to wipe them out."

"A what?"

"A machicolation. A military tactic in ancient times. A hole in the balcony where you dropped rocks on intruders. We are entrepreneurs, and it is a dance with the devil or a fight with the demon. In business, it is better to dance. It is like Mac says, there is evil in the best of us, and just a little more in the worst of us. Mac is a *bel esprit*. He fancies himself an intellectual and has a whole litany of these locutions. He collects them as I collect words. I am certain my compilation has had a macrocephalic effect on me. Either that or my hairline is receding. Mac never looks any different. I think you will like him. Albie did. He called him a gentleman and a scholar. But I need to warn you, don't think because he is soft-spoken and calm in his comportment, that he is a wimp or worse. He is an ardent believer in our first general's mantra. *Be polite, be professional, but always have a plan to kill everyone you meet.*"

When they re-entered the bar, Sasinan shouted from his ladder, and Pancho asked Pepper what he was saying. Greg translated before Pepper could answer.

"He wants you to turn the breaker switch back on."

"You speak gook," Pancho remarked.

"Thai," replied Greg sharply.

"Sorry, my choice of slang there was insensitive and contumelious. Old habits die hard—more often, hardly. Mac, too, speaks a plethora of these oriental tongues. I dabble in romance languages. My French is passable. I have yet to develop the patois of this region. It is a vernacular in which I am woefully deficient. All our dealers and barkeeps speak Thai and English. Sasinan and I are the two outliers. Excuse me, while I address Sasinan's request."

Pancho exited through the same door that the six women had used, but before he could return, the lights came on, the fans spun, and the Beach Boys were booming out *Help Me, Rhonda* from the jukebox.

"We sell nostalgia along with beer," said Pancho as he returned to Greg's side. "I apologize for the infelicitous timing, and I would even invite you to attend the game tonight if that were possible, but your presence could create an imbroglio, and harmony and friendship are our Siamese twins."

The Beatles' *All You Need Is Love* played.

"What time can we leave tomorrow morning to see Mac?" asked Greg.

"At first light, if you so choose. Do you have a hotel for tonight?"

"No. Not yet, but I have the name of one in the car."

"Go to the Royal Cliff. Ask to see the manager, Warong Sirindhorn. He is a bumptious sort, but the hotel is new and easily the best in town, so I suppose he has reason to gloat. He will tell you they have no rooms, but tell him I sent you. Here, give him this."

He scribbled his signature on the back of a white business card that said the American Bar.

"I have a driver. He will need a room, too."

"Just the same. I will be here in the morning at whatever time you arrive. I promise. For Albie, I promise. *Adios. Ciao.*"

Greg placed the card in his pocket.

CHAPTER FORTY-FIVE

According to Charlie, the Royal Cliff was one of two properties that Mr. Geoffrey had recommended to him should they spend the night in Pattaya. It was also Crissa's choice. And despite Pancho's depiction, khun Warong could not have been more gracious. Greg introduced himself and handed him the business card from Pancho. And when Charlie shared the warm greetings from Mr. Geoffrey Hawthorne, the Oriental Hotel's General Manager, khun Warong made a point of upgrading the two of them to adjoining suites on the top floor.

Greg was tired and had no interest in visiting the beach or the town itself. He was content to relax on the balcony and encouraged Charlie to enjoy the rest of the day in whatever fashion he chose. Charlie expressed his immense gratitude and left quickly before Greg could change his mind.

Greg needed to call Crissa at the Raffles in Singapore to update her but decided that he could wait. He missed her, and wanted to hear her voice, but could not determine how much he needed to tell her about Pancho. He showered, slipped on running shorts, opened a cold beer from the mini-bar refrigerator, and stretched out on the lounge chair on the balcony. He smiled at his farmer's tan. A white chest and legs to match contrasted with his dark suntanned arms. He looked like the tourists below at the poolside. Sea breezes from the Gulf of Siam—as the expats liked to call it—retained a hint of coolness as they wafted over the hot, sandy beach to the beachfront hotel. The sky and the sea melded together without a seam in a hazy horizon.

He was worried about tomorrow. Calling Pancho eccentric was being kind. His description of Mac as a permanently primed, prepped, ready-and-waiting assassin did not contradict Rafferty's intel, but the real question was Pancho's dependability and his truthfulness regarding Mac's location. Still, Pancho acted genuinely concerned about Albie, so maybe that carries the day. He emptied half of his beer.

What a life, Greg thought, as he dozed. Surrounded by over a dozen beautiful women daily. Their sexuality on full display. The nymph Pepper at his beck and call. He wondered how Pancho, or any man, could contain himself, and with the images of carnal indulgence replacing his concerns for tomorrow's journey, he fell asleep.

Only when the sun reached around the corner, and the lengthening shadows co-mingled with the evening breeze chilling his naked chest, did he wake.

Crissa was not there, so he left a brief message and the phone number of the Royal Cliff. She called back as he was dressing to go down to the hotel restaurant for dinner.

"The colonel was not at the bar. He has a business partner who promised to take me to meet him tomorrow at a beach about an hour south of Pattaya."

She was quiet. Because she didn't know what to say about the delay or because she didn't know what to say about them.

"The bar is doing well, and this partner manages much of the day-to-day operations, so maybe the colonel will be open to helping. At least, that is what I am hoping."

"How are you?" she asked.

"I am ok. I was tired and took a nap this afternoon. Too much excitement the last few days," and after a pause, "and nights."

He thought he heard her sigh. He wanted to believe that.

"You saw my note, didn't you?" she asked.

That was it, he realized.

"Yes. It was nice."

Another sigh, relief.

"You didn't need to leave money," he added. He heard Gwen's voice in the background.

"I need to go," she said. "Call with an update as soon as you can after you meet with the colonel."

"Will do," and before either of them could say any more, she hung up.

CHAPTER FORTY-SIX

When Charlie and Greg arrived at the American Bar the next morning, they found Pancho waiting for them inside with six bags of groceries. Charlie helped Pancho load them into the boot of the car, and then Pancho, with Greg's permission, sat in the front seat, leaving Greg alone in the rear.

"I can give better directions from up here, and if I sit in the back, I get carsick. It mostly has to do with not being able to see where I am going. I believe that in cars and life, one needs to see where they are going, don't you agree Charlie?"

"Yes, sir. Seeing is important. Sir, where are we going?"

Pancho laughed, asked Charlie to call him by his name instead of *sir*, and gave him directions out of town and onto the southbound highway.

"It is not just seeing, although seeing is important, it is being prepared to see. It allows you the chance not to be surprised. Some people like surprises, but not me. I like the slow, organic discovery process. Discovery is the essence of knowledge. You don't know something inside and out unless you discover it. Discover its meaning, its quiddity, its essence. Aristotle believed you needed to discover its function and form. How something worked was important to him in defining what that something was. That is how he defined what art was and determined the quality of that art. Of course, Longinus set the stage for the Romantics when he thought sublimity in art was the most important factor, so when you reached the Romantics, it was all about beauty. Intense emotion recollected in tranquility. It didn't matter how it worked, only whether the art moved you by its beauty. This disputation of function versus appearance presented a great conflict to the moderns. Is the quality of any piece of art determined by how good it looks or by how well it functions? I mean, you could ask that about almost anything, not only art. What is more important to you, Charlie?"

"I don't know. I never thought about it."

"Well. Take this car. Do you like it because it works well or because it looks nice?"

Greg stopped listening. He opened his window, trying to mute the babble of Pancho's latest discourse. He disappeared behind his sunglasses, and for the next hour, he enjoyed the breeze buffeting his face, much like it did when he rode the motorcycle on an open road, but now steeling himself for the meeting with Mac.

Occasionally, Charlie would slow the car and Pancho's voice would rise like volume on a radio. Words like *aleatory*, *stochasticity*, and *panoply* intermingled with explanations about Elvis, the afterlife, and a lengthy lecture about kinematics.

They stopped at a roadside stand to buy fruit. Pineapples, durians, and cassava. When they returned to the car, Greg asked Pancho how the card game went last night.

"Could not have gone better," Pancho replied.

"How did Pepper do?" asked Greg.

"Pepper?"

"Wasn't she one of the dealers?"

"For heaven's sake, no. Not possible. The girl is ineffably beautiful, but she can barely count to ten using all her fingers. In a year or two, if she keeps practicing. But practicing is tiresome and most give up before they get good. And being good isn't enough. You must be exceptionally good. Excellent. Veritably perfect. It is the work that teaches you how to do it."

Greg had heard similar words before. From his coaches and even Preeya. Good is never enough. Most anyone can be proficient, but greatness requires more. You learn by pain, not age.

"There is a great chasm," Pancho said, "between good and excellent. How do you cross that chasm? For some, it is innate genius, but for others, it is arduous work, and for most, it is impossible. So, they quit.

"I met a dealer once in Bangkok who wanted nothing more than to be the best in the world. She was good. Disciplined. An exceptional memory, too. So, I told her about Ted Williams. I modeled my swing after his. You know all the great hitters were left-handed batters. Anyhow, Ted Williams wanted to be the best hitter that ever lived. He devoted his life to it. Except for those three years in the military. Or take the Beatles. They are the new Elvis, but they spent years in dive bars in Germany developing their sound. Still crossing that chasm is like crossing a Rubicon. Do you know what the Rubicon was, Charlie? It was a river. Not that much of a river, to be honest, but it was a boundary between France and Italy. Back then, France was Gaul, and Italy was

Rome. More name changes, amigo. Caesar was the governor of Gaul, the top dog, and gaining power. So, the Roman Senate told Caesar to disband his legions because he was getting to be too powerful. Caesar scoffed at them. He took a legion of troops and crossed from France into Italy over the irrelevant Rubicon River. It started a civil war. He crossed the line. There was no going back. That's just the way it is, Charlie. Once you cross some lines, you can never go back."

Was Pancho telling Greg something?

"Have you ever crossed a Rubicon, Mr. Pancho?" Charlie asked.

Pancho was quiet for a minute and then answered.

"I have. Several times. The first was when I killed my father."

"You did what?" exclaimed Greg from the back seat.

"Killed my father," he repeated equably.

"Is that why you were in prison?" Greg asked.

"No. I was in prison for heroin, not murder. I never went to prison for patricide. There are several homicide words. You should never confuse patricide with parricide. They are almost the same, but there is a distinction. Then there is filicide. I struggle with anything to do with infanticide. In mythology and religious history, there are countless patricides. One son or another wants to be the next king or emperor. Sometimes, the daughters too.

"Hey, slow down Charlie, the turn is coming up. There aren't any signs. You will see a road on your right just around the next turn. Yep. Right here."

The road was single-lane and all dirt. A handful of houses were on either side, all of them small, only single dwellings. The locals cultivated small patches of land for jackfruit, according to Pancho.

"Mr. Pancho, this road is rough. I am worried it will damage the car."

"It will be fine, Charlie. It is only in the monsoon season when it ruts. Farmers on either side keep it drivable. We only need to go several kilometers. It will be fine. Just go slowly. Everyone down here has trucks and jeeps."

Greg wanted to resume the conversation about Pancho's father and the heroin, but now it had to wait. Dust kicked up from the road, and Greg rolled his window closed.

They drove for fifteen minutes and then Pancho directed Charlie to pull over into a bit of a clearing and to park the car.

"We have to walk the rest of the way. It will be safer for the car. Don't worry, Charlie, no one will bother the car here."

They collected the bags of groceries and fruit from the boot of the car and headed down the path. Pancho used a walking stick, but like the others, carried multiple bags of produce.

"No wisecracks about the shillelagh or I will smack you with it. I am good on flat surfaces, but on these terrains, I need to be careful. There is not much left in this recalcitrant knee."

Greg understood.

"Feel that breeze. The water is not in sight, but you can already feel it. It is cooler here than it is in Pattaya. The Gulf opens and gets wider just south of Pattaya."

After a kilometer, closer to two, the bright blue waters of the Gulf of Thailand came into view, and in the distance, Greg could make out ten small houses and a handful of palm trees. All but two were a hundred yards or more from the beach area. The scene was idyllic.

Two wooden docks, long enough for a boat on each side, ran out into the water. A single boat was along one dock, and a longboat rested on the shore. A snarl of wrack and shells mixed with the seaweed thrown upon the shore or growing there. Well to the south, the sandy beach tapered, and waves beat against a rocky shoreline, casting spindrift into the air.

Greg then caught sight of the colonel. He was playing basketball with three children. The court was a hard dirt surface, and the backboard and rim were lower than the standard ten feet. Greg guessed nine feet. The Thai children appeared to be no older than ten or twelve. One of them was closer to seven or eight. All were playing in bare feet. No one had shirts on.

Mac held the ball when he spotted the three men approaching over the small rise. It was a cue for the children to turn, and recognizing Pancho, they raised their voices in exclamation and ran toward him immediately. Mac stood alone, watching. His shaved head and shirtless torso glistened with sweat. He was of average height. Shorter than Greg was and smaller than the bulky Pancho and his push-up arms.

Pancho bent down to greet the children and shared hugs with them even as they began clamoring for sweets. He introduced them to Greg and Charlie, and the three boys politely unburdened Greg and Charlie of their bags.

"This better be good, Wireless," Mac's deep, bass voice called out as he now approached the group.

As a courtesy, Greg lifted his sunglasses to the top of his head as he shook hands with the colonel and introduced himself. When he introduced Charlie to him, the colonel immediately engaged in a conversation about the car and the trip. Mac's Thai language skills were native, so perfect that Charlie did not speak English. Mac smiled easily. A razor-thin mustache and dark, Asian eyes accentuated his friendly demeanor. The scars on his chest spoke for themselves.

"You are going to want to hear what this *gringo* has to say," said Pancho as he wrestled with the children, rifling the bags for the promised sweets.

"Why don't we go down to the boat where we can have some quiet?"

CHAPTER FORTY-SEVEN

"Do you know much about boats?" Mac asked Greg as he pulled on a plain gray tee.

"Not a thing."

"This is a keelboat. Made with fiberglass. Designed by an American named Stewart. One of the first of its kind. Most all the Thais have traditional longboats, like that one over there, for fishing, but I wanted to sleep on the boat and the cabin space is remarkable for a nineteen-foot monohull. I can dock it or run it up on the sand like the longboats. The sails are easy to use. My only complaint is that the outboard motor is a tad light. I would prefer more juice, but it is what it is. I added this awning. Let me move this air tank. Have a seat on the bench. Slide that gear over. Hand me those books. And that knife."

Greg moved the scuba gear to the side and passed four books and the long blade to him. *Labyrinths* was the book on top. Mac disappeared with the books into the cabin and returned with two cold bottles of sparkling water. He handed the Perrier to Greg and settled across from Greg on the bench, where he trimmed a cigar and lit it.

"How did you get it?" Greg asked.

"The Perrier or the boat?" replied Mac. He drew on the cigar and exhaled heavenward.

"Come to think of it, both."

"A friend bought the boat for me and had it sent here. Remarkable, don't you think?"

"A friend? That friend wouldn't be Lord Albert Saint Clair, would it?"

"How do you know that name?"

Although Greg had told the story so many times already, he knew that this was the most important rendering that he would ever give. And unlike his discretion with others, including Preeya, he knew that the more Mac understood the situation, the better it would be. Not only now in deciding, but even later, should Mac agree to help.

Greg began with his first encounter with Albie in Ban Su, recounted the development of their friendship, and then told Mac about his discovery of a battered and bruised Nok in the abandoned Research Station and all that occurred in its aftermath. Mac interrupted Greg more than once, asking for more detail or clarity, even requesting him to repeat certain details. His interrogation skills operational. Greg gave the timetable of Albie's disappearance, careful never to mention Elliot or the meeting that Albie had with him but detailing the conferences with Fowles and Somsak and all the searches that took place. When he finally arrived at Nok's death, Greg took a break, and Mac joined him in the momentary silence but did not show remorse.

Maybe because it was the only bright spot in the entire mess, Greg digressed from the matter at hand and spoke about Ping's adoption of the baby and even Sister Mary Peyton's help in the matter. Mac, however, made a pejorative comment about nuns and his disdain for cults, and dragged Greg back to the narrative, asking about Fowles—his station at the British Consulate, and whether Greg knew more about the bombastic Thai sergeant. He requested Greg repeat the names of the villages that he visited and even the names of the hill tribe people he questioned.

Greg, despite his training, shared as much detail as he could. He had no hesitation to expand on his own opinion about Fat Boy and Fat Man. Mac confessed he knew them. Protecting Albie from drug lords like Fat Man was the reason they hired him. The only subject that Greg held close to the vest was Wes, but Mac knew him already and wanted to know which locations Wes visited without Greg.

Greg closed his account with a recap of the meeting with the lawyer Blackledge, and finally Lady Saint Clair's request.

Mac arched his head backward and took a long drag on his cigar. The exhaled smoke disappeared above the awning.

"I understand why Lady Saint Clair might want closure. There is no telling how much money they will tie up for the seven years. But what I don't understand is you, why you are doing this?" Mac asked.

Greg explained how Gwen was leveraging his involvement with the financial support Albie promised for Ping, her family, as well as Sister Mary Peyton.

Mac smirked when he heard that.

"You haven't answered the question. Unless you want me to believe that the only reason you are doing this is for those people. That there is nothing in it for you."

"They have been offering me money since Blackledge first showed up in Chiang Mai, and they are offering me more now, but I don't need the money, not like Ping and her family and not like the nun and her clinic."

"A genuine spirit of altruism. Noble," Mac said, but his tone was sarcastic.

Greg bit his tongue. He needed Mac to agree to help. Mac looked nothing like a war veteran, nothing like an assassin or operative behind enemy lines. More like the nightclub owner he was. No stately bearing. Would pass unnoticed in any crowd. A wannabe, a dodgy yachtsman holding court on a dinghy. And yet…possessed of a certain gravitas, not charisma, not puissance, but danger. Menace exuded from his persona, from his deep-toned voice, as if he were free of life's distractions—love, lust. Even fear of death.

"You have spent more time up in the Triangle than most. This information from her bodyguard. Rafferty, right? How credible do you think it is?"

"I haven't seen it. I don't know. I don't know with whom the British talked. Which hill tribe people. Which village."

"But they believe he went into Burma?"

"Yes, but you can cross over to Burma in hundreds of places. There are no barriers."

"Did you talk to the local CIA or DEA?"

"No. It's not a U.S. matter and I don't know those people."

Mac scoffed again. "That's right. You are an academic researcher. A linguist."

Whether or not he believed Greg made no difference at this point. The only thing that mattered was his cooperation.

"Did Albie ever tell you about how he found me or what we did?" Mac asked.

"No. He never mentioned your name to me."

"Yet, you know something."

"Rafferty had a file on you."

"I expect he does. Care for another water?"

"No. Thank you."

Mac stood up, turned his back on Greg, and stared up at the huts. They could see Pancho and Charlie sitting at a small table on the porch of the nearest bungalow playing cards.

"Wireless is a great man," he said and turned back toward Greg. "A war hero. Saved my life and another soldier's life. Carried us to safety single-handedly with a wounded leg, no less."

"He told me you saved his life."

"Not true. Helped him out. That is all. Not the same thing. Now…now he is fractured, but you saw that. It would be easy to blame it all on the war, but I think it has as much to do with his other talents."

Are you kidding me? Greg thought. This is a digression. A blatant misdirection. Greg did not bite. He could wait for stories about Pancho until another time.

Mac sat down, crossed his left leg over the right one, and leaned back, drawing again on the cigar.

"He has a certain mathematical facility. Memory. If you asked him right now, *what is the tenth card from the top of the deck?* He could tell you. *What card is third from the bottom?* No problem."

"So, he is a mechanic. Does that make him a genius?"

"No. Not even close. The cards are something to occupy his mind. For him, they are like meditation. Cards keep him in the present moment. So, he doesn't get lost. It is more complicated than legerdemain, and he is much more than a mechanic."

"He said he was a heroin addict. Is that true?"

"He went from hospital morphine to heroin, but fortunately, he was a lousy addict. They shipped him to Fort Leavenworth to dry out."

"And you brought him back?"

"That's right. We were setting up in Bangkok when Lord Albert arrived on our doorstep. The timing could not have been better. Albie paid us enough to start our business in Pattaya. He also made other arrangements, which leads us to the present question."

Finally, Greg thought.

Mac uncrossed his legs, sat forward a little, and pointed his cigar at Greg.

"These types of searches never go well. We aren't going to find Albie. You and that Wes character went to all the plausible places. The police and army frightened those who might have been reticent with you and got nothing. This British intel will lead somewhere, but it will not be to Albie. You said you spent over two years researching the hill tribe people. You and I both know who lives and doesn't live in the hills. We will go. We will follow the intel and report back. Who knows, we might even get revenge for Nok, if we are lucky, but I want everything up front, in writing and cash, and when we come back empty-handed, there won't be any need for negotiations. At least not with me."

"What is it you want?"

He sat back again.

"I have bribed every government official in Chonburi Province who could sign off on a land purchase near here. By now, you must know just how venal most Thai officials are. It is now stuck in Bangkok in another ludicrous government office there."

"Why do you want the land?"

"Wireless and I are going to build a private resort. A high-end, exclusive, ultra-private, and extremely expensive resort with every amenity imaginable. I have a spot on the Gulf just south of here. The super-rich do not want to rub shoulders with the riffraff, the hoi polloi, and yet they want the exotic. There is a remote cove and everything about it is perfect. I already have backers, but I need the permits and a single-access road built."

Greg could imagine who those backers might be.

"What makes you think Lady Saint Clair could arrange that?"

"Albie did that and more. I know the family is connected. After that, the rest is just money, and I know the family has that too."

"How much? I need to let her know."

Mac chewed on the cigar this time and mused aloud, leaving no doubt that this was his métier.

"This should not take long. We have only one intelligence report to follow. I am not a huge fan of tramping around in Burma. We barely have any diplomatic relations with that group. Just the same, any problem we run into will be with those outside of the government, like the Eastern Shan State rebel army, drug lords like Zhang Qitu, or General Xu's boys in the Fifth Army. If we are lucky, our answers could come in the frontier. We don't want to go too deep into the Shan State territory. Transportation…do you have a motorcycle?"

"Yes."

"And Albie's BMW?"

"It's at the house. Runs fine."

"Ok. So, no expense there. Guns?"

"No. I don't have any guns."

"Can you get weapons?"

Greg considered Wes for a moment. "No."

"Ok. I can take care of that, but it won't be cheap. Tell Lady Saint Clair that after she arranges the government matters, I want one hundred and fifty thousand U.S. dollars in my bank account, fifty thousand in cash, and another ten thousand dollars for immediate expenses. No. Check that. What about a truck or jeep? Albie had a jeep."

"He took the jeep into the mountains, and we never found it." Greg thought for a moment, remembered Mary P's truck, and then said, "I might be able to get a truck in Chiang Rai."

"*Might* won't work. We will need it in Chiang Mai. We won't get too far along the highway on motorcycles with rifles strapped to our backs. See what you can do, but let's add another five grand for immediate expenses, just in case. Got it?"

"One fifty into the bank, and sixty-five thousand in cash. That's a lot of money. Almost a quarter of a million dollars."

"To you, perhaps. Look, money isn't the issue. Wireless and I can make money. It's the principle of the thing. She is asking us to cross the border intentionally. There is no backup. No parachute. No exfiltration plans. No Wireless to radio for help. It is espionage. If you let me think about it some more, two hundred grand might not be enough."

"Ok. I will let her know. Anything else?"

"One more thing. You." He pointed his cigar at Greg yet again.

"What about me?" Greg asked, barely suppressing his annoyance.

"Are you really up to this?"

"I know the area, the people, and speak their language. That qualifies me."

Mac shook his head as if still thinking. Not at all convinced.

"When can you leave?" Greg asked Mac.

"When the papers and money are in order. Wireless can run things here while I am gone."

"Why the name, Wireless?"

"We were in Laos, just three of us, and one local took it upon himself to destroy our radio equipment and inform on us. The informant ripped out all the wiring. To this day, I do not know how Wireless radioed for backup."

"The informant?" Greg asked.

"It didn't end well for him."

Greg didn't ask anything else, and Mac stood, signaling the negotiation was complete.

"I am staying another night here," Mac said. "One more fishing trip tonight. I will be back in Pattaya tomorrow. I assume you are staying in Pattaya."

"Yes."

"Come by the bar after noon. Before it gets too crowded."

It wasn't a request.

CHAPTER FORTY-EIGHT

The meeting had gone well. Greg was relieved that he did not have to stoop to importuning or any wheedling. Greg exchanged places with Pancho on the small porch of the bungalow, and for an hour, Mac and Pancho conversed on the boat. The children had returned to the basketball court, but now were playing takraw. Even without a net, Greg found their skill of kicking the rattan ball back and forth and keeping it airborne throughout extraordinary. Meanwhile, Charlie attempted to teach Greg the card game he had just learned from Pancho.

"It is called piquet. Pancho says it is French. The colonel taught him. It is only for two people, and you don't need all the cards in a normal deck."

Greg listened half-heartedly as he observed the two friends on the boat. Greg considered Pancho defective, but Mac insisted it was just the opposite.

"Pancho said it is his favorite game because of the words like *carte blanche*, *capot*, and *rubicon*. We had another talk about *rubicons*."

When they finally finished and loaded themselves back into the car, an irritable Pancho uttered a single word, *recrudescent*, and quickly fell asleep and began snoring. His all-night card game had finally caught up to him.

Amid the din of Pancho's snoring, a forever-curious Charlie asked Greg what the word meant.

"It means something bad is happening again."

***

And neither man said anything else until they arrived back in Pattaya.

The first thing he did when he returned to the Royal Cliff was to call Crissa and leave the message that he had found Mac. He then put on running shorts and a tank top and went for a run on the beach. He hadn't exercised in days and needed to clear his head. After the run, he swam laps in the hotel pool, until he was no longer hearing Pancho's voice or seeing Mac's cigar pointing at him.

He then settled on a lounge chair at the poolside. The poolside waiter made his way over to him and Greg ordered a Singha. A middle-aged, overweight Dutchman, sporting a speedo, sat across the pool from Greg with his Thai girlfriend, who was rubbing suntan lotion on his pale skin. As the lotion rubbing process became more fulsome, moving beyond excessive to crass, Greg realigned his seat in another direction. A large lizard, easily a foot long, crawled along the far wall that separated the pool from the beach. He wondered how Mac's high-end, luxe resort would keep the *tuk kae* and his reptilian relatives at arm's length.

An hour later, he used the phone at the pool bar to check his messages and, after learning about Crissa's call, he telephoned Singapore again.

Once again, Crissa was all business, so Greg assumed Gwen was nearby.

"He said he would do it."

"Greg, that is fantastic. I knew you could convince him."

"He has a wish list. And is adamant about it."

"Go ahead."

Greg outlined the demands, and he could imagine Crissa taking notes. He wondered which glasses she was wearing. He imagined her in the same white summer dress she wore once in Chiang Mai. The narrow spaghetti straps the only fabric across her sculpted shoulders.

"Where are you now? I hear music in the background."

"I am down at the pool bar."

"Where did you leave it with him?"

"I told him I would submit the requests to Gwen. We are meeting tomorrow afternoon at his bar."

"Ok. I will need to see the papers he referenced. I can't do anything until we understand what is involved. As for the money, I will talk with her ladyship right now."

Both were quiet for a second.

"The beach is nice here. I think you would like it," Greg said, trying to bring the conversation around to them and not just the colonel.

"I am sure that I would if you were there. What was he like? The colonel?"

"Looked like just another guy but seemed supremely confident."

"That is a good thing."

"Maybe."

"Let's plan to talk tomorrow morning at ten. I will call your hotel then."

"Sounds good," and just like the last time on the phone, before he could say anything else, she hung up.

***

When Crissa called at precisely ten o'clock in the morning, she told Greg that he needed to ask Mac for his passport, which contained his permanent residence visa, along with any papers he had requesting the permits for his new project. Foreigners cannot buy land in Thailand, she explained. They can be leaseholders, or own buildings like his bar, or houses like Albie's. She did not know how Mac circumvented the Foreign Business license regulations for the American Bar.

"There is one workaround. We could create a Thai Limited Company, but I don't know how long that will take, and her ladyship is impatient. With every passing day, the hope of finding Lord Albert diminishes. We need his passport and papers. He can have them back the next day, but we must have them."

Just after noon, Greg visited the American Bar, where Mac handed him a manila envelope with the discussed paperwork. He reminded Greg that the land acquisition was a sine qua non for the deal and didn't even bother to mention the money. As far as he was concerned, the negotiation was over, and it was now up to Greg (really Gwen) to deliver. When Greg explained that he also needed Mac's passport, Mac balked. He was not at all pleased with the idea, and shared, in colorfully profane and graphic language, exactly what he would do if Greg did not return the passport.

CHAPTER FORTY-NINE

For the next week, Greg did what he does best—follow directions.

Greg and Charlie drove directly to the address of a law firm in Bangkok. The offices were on the fourteenth and fifteenth floors of a modern high-rise in the same neighborhood as the embassies and consulates. The receptionist, a Thai woman dressed in a white blouse and long, black skirt cut so tightly it made walking look difficult, greeted him as if she were expecting him. She did not offer to take him into the inner sanctum, nor to meet any of the attorneys. She accepted the envelope and asked Greg to wait. Her smile was courteous and no more.

Two hours later, a bespectacled young man, who identified himself proudly as the chief paralegal, entered the reception area and presented Greg with Mac's passport and papers.

By now, it was past seven p.m. and the traffic from the law offices to the Oriental was so brutal that it took Charlie another two hours to reach the hotel. Charlie apologized to Greg more than once for the delay, but there was little he could do to circumvent the traffic.

Greg invited Charlie to have something to eat at the bar with him, but Charlie explained that Mr. Geoffrey would frown on such. They arranged a time to leave for Pattaya the next day.

Despite the luxury of his room at the Oriental Hotel, Greg did not sleep well that night. His headaches returned when they were stuck in Bangkok traffic. He opted not to eat at all after Charlie had passed on dinner, took a shower, and went straight to bed. He slept fitfully until the pain finally woke him completely in the middle of the night. He cursed himself for not bringing any aspirin, as well as not buying any upon their return to the hotel.

Just the same, he dressed and headed down to the lobby in search of relief from the front desk or a nearby all-night market.

As luck would have it, the night manager had medicines in the office and then insisted that Greg have a seat in the lounge while they prepared him a cup of tea. Greg declined at first, but the night manager was so accommodating, Greg felt it would be an insult not to oblige him.

The lounge area was empty, but the air was still thick with cigarette smoke, so Greg made his way to one of the six tables on the adjacent garden terrace. It seemed like the first quiet moment he had in weeks. He couldn't stop thinking about Mac. There was an energy about him, and yet a quietness in his eyes. *Mostly you do what you are good at* was one of Elliot's favorite expressions. An older Thai woman brought him a tray with tea and English biscuits, and after fifteen minutes, his headache subsided.

As daylight broke the Bangkok sky, he made his way back through the lobby, where he grabbed a copy of the *Bangkok Post* newspaper. He thanked the night manager yet again and asked him about breakfast hours. Although the restaurant was not yet open, the night manager assured Greg that he could have a full American breakfast with room service, if he could but wait thirty minutes.

Breakfast arrived by the time Greg had finished shaving and showering, and while he ate, he read the *Bangkok Post*. The back page featured international sports, so he started there. The headline story was about Bobby Fischer and Boris Spassky and the speculation of a rematch. He read the article more out of boredom than interest and then flipped past interior pages filled with advertisements for the current movies in Bangkok, including *Enter the Dragon* with Bruce Lee and Marlon Brando's *The Godfather*. On the next page, he noticed a terse report about an explosion in the Gulf. Police had reason to believe that a houseboat, which contained a heroin lab, caught fire, and exploded. Longboats with high-powered motors were spotted in the area, and speculation was that they were ferrying product for processing to the boat. This was not the first incident of this kind, and the investigation was ongoing.

When Crissa called later that morning, she echoed what Mac had originally said—none of this is much out of line, and certainly not preposterous. The problem was, as she expected, land ownership itself.

"We have a good contact, and a Thai Limited Company is possible, but the process is painfully slow and complicated. I won't say it is off the table, but he needs to prepare for a lengthy lease in its place. We might manage a fifty-year guaranteed lease. A term that will outlast his life. I am confident that we could arrange that quickly."

"All right. I will let him know and see if there is pushback."

"Also," she asked, "who is Stephen Joyce?"

"I don't know. Why?"

"One provision Mac included with this request was that this was a partnership and if anything happens to him, then the money and property rights are bequeathed to one Stephen Joyce. On the surface, it is not an impediment, but we don't know who this person is. I assume that like Mac, he has residency status, but if not, then we, he, will have another hurdle. Ask Mac."

Before ringing off, she suggested Greg remain in Pattaya at the Royal Cliff until she had something concrete from Bangkok.

CHAPTER FIFTY

By late afternoon, the bacchanalian atmosphere of the American Bar was on full display. A handful of GIs were singing along with the Rolling Stones, and escorts abounded, leaving very few without companionship.

As entertaining as that might have been for some, the chief attraction remained the bar itself. Greg did not realize until now that the nubile barmaids, clad in their red, white, and blue hot pants and halter crop tops, worked on an elevated platform behind the bar. Thus, the legions of soldiers, sailors, and flyboys standing at the bar were eye-level with the girls' chests and bare midriffs, while those fortunate enough to secure a seat on a bar stool, stared straight ahead at winsome territories slightly south of the equator.

For all its suggestiveness, the elevated position made serving drinks easier for the girls, while creating a shrewd position of control, if not authority. The bar's countertop was just deep enough to distance the patrons as harmless supplicants, furthering the house's first commandment. *Hands off the employees—always.*

Greg spotted Pancho sitting at a table with a group of soldiers, and Pancho waved him over.

"My boys here are celebrating the drawdown. They will head home soon. Come join us. You should head home soon, too."

"Thanks. I am looking for Mac."

"You said that the first time we met. It seems like you are always looking for Mac. How do you keep losing him? Do you lose others as easily as you lose Mac?"

"Who is your friend, Pancho?" asked a soldier with a baseball cap on backward.

"Everyone, this gentleperson is Greg. Sounds like egg, but he is a yegg."

"Pancho, what the hell is a yegg?" another soldier asked.

"A yegg, *compadres,* is a robber. More precisely, a safecracker, but for our discussion, a robber will suffice."

"What has he stolen?"

"He is about to steal, my friend. Should I tell him where to find him?"

Another inebriated soldier jumped into the discussion. "If your friend is locked in a safe, then maybe the yegg here can get him out." They all laughed, despite the absurdity. Or maybe because of it.

And with that, Pancho pointed Greg toward the private back room.

Two attendants scantily garbed in their red, white, and blue stood guard at the door, collecting the entrance fees. Greg made his case and pointed back at Pancho, who nodded his head. Both girls smiled nicely as they unlocked the door and allowed him to enter, escaping the ceaseless din of the American Bar.

The cool quietude of the private parlor welcomed Greg. No daylight and no loud music. Only a dim light at the bar and overhead lamps at two round tables with players. A mournful jazz saxophone wept from the speakers in the upper corners just loud enough to cover the whirr of the air conditioners. Mac, his back to the door, sat at the small bar reading a book, while Pepper sat at his side watching the card games. She appeared more provocative and striking today and reminded Greg of Preeya. He realized she had the same Chiang Mai eyes.

Pepper whispered to Mac when Greg entered and vacated her seat.

Greg placed the passport and papers on the bar next to Mac's half-filled coffee cup.

"No problems, I take it," Mac said as he set down his book and lifted his cigar from the ashtray. He motioned to Greg to sit as he relit the cigar.

"None to speak of," Greg replied. "The lawyers, however, believe it would take quite some time to complete ownership of the land. Something about establishing a separate Thai commercial entity. They are recommending an extended lease. Like you have with the bar."

"How long?"

"That is open to discussion. Twenty, thirty years. What would your preference be?"

Mac pulled at his cigar in thought. Both men knew Mac was getting what he wanted.

"Tell them, forty years. And make sure this place has the same length, too."

"Will do."

"Anything else?" Mac asked.

"Yes. They had a question."

Mac had his cigar going by now. The smoke wafting between the two men.

"Who is Stephen Joyce?" asked Greg.

Mac set his cigar back in the ashtray and rubbed his perfectly shaved head with his left hand.

"Stephen Joyce is the name on Wireless' passport. Despite his attempts to alter his name before he returned to Thailand, his passport and visa papers still read Stephen Joyce."

"That makes sense. At least the identity of Stephen Joyce is now making sense. I am not so certain about the other."

"What exactly is the other?"

"His behavior. He seems…erratic."

"That is a kind way to put it. He saw barbarity, savage cruelty. Death is a phenomenon to which all men react differently. And killing—especially too much killing—a horror. In Stephen's case, he cannot forget any of it. For him, the past is never far behind. It flickers and glows, becomes unstable, shifts, and rearranges back there. He relives elements of the past when his mind gets too quiet. His guilt does not diminish with time. His rage, an impotent fury of denial."

"Is that why he became a heroin addict? An escape?"

"Maybe, but his draconian treatment was worse than the disease."

"What do you mean?"

"He was part of a study when he landed in the prison. One group was callous, cold turkey. Another was methadone. And his group was cyclazocine. Both methadone and cyclazocine negate the effects of heroin. It was effective. However, the side effects of cyclazocine include uncontrollable thoughts and delusions. What he thought were flashes of imaginative genius were hallucinations."

"Holy shit."

Mac began smoking his cigar again.

"Do you want a drink?" he asked Greg.

"A beer."

Mac nodded to Pepper to come over and asked for a beer and water.

"Have you ever heard of synesthesia?"

Greg shook his head. "Is it a disease?"

"Hardly. It is a rare trait. Like genius, a gift. It involves the merging of senses. A smell or a musical sound can produce a color. So can pain. Others see moods, dispositions, or propensities in ethereal airborne colors. A luminous radiation of deep blue surrounds a thinker. A halo of canary yellow for a disingenuous person teeming with ill will. Black. Pure Evil. The list goes on with hundreds of forms of synesthesia. In Stephen's case, it involves his sight and memory. Colors are associated with letters and numbers."

"The card mechanic."

"That's just a distraction. A hobby for him.

"Stephen told me as a child he became confused on math tests because the numbers all had colors and it took him time to sort out simple math problems. One teacher called him stupid. His memory is beyond remarkable.

"He was not the same after the cyclazocine. He struggles with what he cannot see, and fixates on tangibles, like cards. Knows where every card is in the deck, all the time, not just on a faro or a perfect riffle shuffle. Not for any reason, other than to know, like you know where your beer is right now, and I know where my cigar is. Seeing is like gravity for him. How did he react when you told him about Albie's disappearance the first time?"

"He was attentive."

"Transfixed?"

"Maybe, yea."

"He becomes a real-time observer and occasionally attempts to become a real-time participant. Fails, of course, and then spirals into delusions. The delusions take him halfway to divinity and then dissolve into a sea of grief. He tried to throw away all his books. I have them now. Fiction is unbearable for him. Nonfiction boring. He is tired of past truths. He is the laureate of mistrust."

Greg scolded himself for his monumental poor judgment of Pancho. *Light travels faster than sound. Better to appear bright than to open your mouth and prove otherwise.*

Mac continued. "Stephen's synesthesia and his eidetic-like memory hurt him now, but only because the heroin and cyclazocine scrambled his psyche."

"You don't think it was the killing, then?"

"Everyone reacts differently to killing, but like everything in this world, killing has a time and place. Let me tell you something. Do you see those guys over there? All of them GIs. One or two enlisted and the others drafted. Trained in a matter of weeks, months at best, and fighting in a war that they don't understand. They are barely high school graduates. Plumbers, mechanics, not proper soldiers. Like Stephen, they had no business being in 'Nam. Ill-prepared for the heat, the exhaustion, and the filth, let alone the enemy. That they are still alive is just total chance or the providence of God if you believe that stuff. It is no wonder that this was a shit show.

"You read my dossier. I am a professional. Educated and trained at West Point. Schooled as an Army Ranger in Fort Benning, in the mountains at Camp Merrill, and in the Florida swamps at Eglin Air Force Base. I am an expert at war—which means an expert at killing. Training in SOCOM with Delta Force and SEALs. Infiltration and exfiltration. Skilled at debriefing and interrogation. More acquired tactics in country. Years, not months, in battles, firefights, and clandestine ops. I have lived in a hole in the ground filled with mud, with shells flying overhead. I've prowled through the jungle with men who did not know what moment might be their last. And I have seen men die beside me. This mess is finally ending, but let me tell you, the day is coming with the next wave of generals and officers, not me that is for sure, but the ones who survived this cock-up, when they will create a professional army. None of this draft idiocy and blancmange. Those who enlist will think hard and long before they sign up because they, too, will be educated and trained. Proud to defend their country, yes, but more importantly, skilled in multiple areas and trained to kill—to kill without question, without remorse, and always without hesitation."

Just then, the door opened, and four more gamblers entered the room.

"Welcome, gentlemen," Mac said. His baritone greeting was warm and sonorous, almost musical. "Please have a drink while Pepper gets you set up at a table." And turning to Greg. "You will have to excuse me as we get these guys settled. I will be here. Let me know when you have something."

CHAPTER FIFTY-ONE

Crissa called again that night when Greg was in his hotel room at the Royal Cliff. He had been thinking about Mac's axiom, that *with a great memory, the past is never far behind.* It reminded Greg of Mei Li and her thought-provoking Chinese maxims, which her loving father feared were clichés. He wondered how much of his past he purposely forgot and how he still clung to other memories, including Preeya and Crissa.

She was alone. Lady Guinevere and Rafferty were at a function. Greg went over the conversation with Mac but kept the information about Stephen, aka Pancho, aka Wireless, to a bare minimum. He felt he had done Pancho a disservice already with his uninformed opinion. It served no purpose to share more than was necessary.

The most important development was Mac's willingness to accept the guaranteed lease in place of land ownership. Crissa said it would make all the difference.

"You were so clever to get the forty-year term," she said.

"Lucky. It just happened as I explained the issue. It was a win as soon as you placed that on the table. I served it in little pieces, and it worked."

"Do you think you, we, can trust Mac?" she asked.

"I don't think we have a choice. Albie trusted him and even rewarded him after their time together."

"Lord Saint Clair gave everyone treats."

They both laughed.

"How much longer are you in Singapore?" he asked.

"One more night. Then it is a long flight to Sydney. Have you ever been to Australia?"

"No."

"Neither have I. I hear nothing but wonderful things about it. We will be in Sydney and then Melbourne for two days as well. I am looking forward to it. Have you thought at all about what you might do after this exploration for us?"

Greg thought it was curious how she used the words *exploration* as well as *us*.

"No. I have been on autopilot since Albie disappeared. First the searches, then Blackledge's request to remain in Chiang Mai, and now this."

"I miss you," she said. "More than I thought I would."

"There is not much either of us can do about that now unless you want to join *us* on our *exploration* of the Golden Triangle."

"What about after?"

"I don't know."

"You could come to England."

"Why would I go to England if you are in Australia?"

"You know what I mean."

"Is that an invitation?"

"Yes. My time in Thailand was…special. You can't stay in Thailand forever."

"You don't know me," Greg said.

"That is true, and it is why I am asking. Do you have a secret past that should worry me? Maybe I have a secret past."

"Do you?"

"Come to England and find out. I would never share such secrets on a long-distance call."

They both laughed.

"Will you at least think about it?" she said.

And with a certainty that surprised him, he said that he would.

CHAPTER FIFTY-TWO

A moonless night. Darkness over the seascape. Dawn was still an hour away, and the stars still held their light so he could just make out the water's edge. Soundless lapping. That's when he saw the shadow on the beach. A dark figure running. And running fast.

The restive nights roused him from his sleep and drove him to the balcony. He hated waiting. Always had. But Greg had no alternative other than to wait. He spent the passing days at the pool, entertained by the banal and recurrent mating rituals of *farangs* and their respective Thai girlfriends. A skinny German replaced the fat-pouched Dutchman. Soon a muscle-bound Swede appeared, followed by a middle-aged Australian, who insisted on demonstrating his machismo using his diving skills. The laid-back atmosphere of the pool was finally shattered by a loud-mouthed Canadian, who, unlike his predecessors, required not one, but two fawning female attendants.

This last invader drove Greg to the hotel's lounge chairs and umbrellas on the beach, where his only distractions came from the local children selling sweets, or slightly older natives proffering hashish, Thai weed, and companionship—with either sex. After failed attempts by all of them, and recognition of Greg's fluency and cultural familiarity, the hawkers sidestepped Greg. All, except for one teenager, who, taking breaks from his sales activities up and down the beach, settled in the sand next to Greg's chair once or twice a day, and even on one occasion, adjusted the large blue umbrella to give himself shade.

He called himself Lucky, and Greg, in his most cynical attitude, registered him as a spy sent by Mac to report on Greg's activities. Lucky said that he wanted nothing more than to practice speaking English with Greg and to ask him questions in Thai about certain English words or sentences. His dream was to one day work in an opulent hotel like the Royal Cliff. He believed speaking English was his ticket to success.

***

Once Mac agreed to the leaseholder strategy, the process moved incrementally, and Greg—along with his trusted driver, Charlie—made multiple trips to and from Bangkok collecting papers and signatures. Greg's suggestion that Mac might make a single trip up to Bangkok and expedite all this paperwork in one sitting met with instant refusal. The law office rejected the idea even more stridently. Plausible deniability was the order of the day.

All went smoothly, except for the incessant traffic delays in and around Bangkok, and a confrontation with Pancho, when it was determined that the lawyers required his passport and signatures, too.

Mornings are tranquil at the American Bar. A brief respite from the challenges of personalities, mishaps, drunks, and fights that come with bars and late-working nights. The cleaning crew was leaving as Greg arrived, and a girl by the name of Destiny was helping Sasinan and Pancho restock the bar.

"No. You cannot have my passport, and I am not signing anything."

"I will give the passport back to you tomorrow. I promise. I did the same with Mac's on two separate occasions. Ask him?"

"I don't care. I have to go."

"Where are you going?"

"To the movies. There is a new, Chinese kung fu movie playing at eleven. I never miss them. They are the best. Goodbye."

"Pancho, what's wrong? Have I offended you? I am only trying to help."

"The only one you are helping is yourself. Your tricks and *tromp l'oeils* do not deceive me. You are the Jabberwock."

And without another word, he was gone, leaving Greg no alternative other than to wait for Mac, who arrived within the hour.

Mac assured Greg that he would get the papers signed and have the passport for him later that day.

"He said he went to the movies," remarked Greg. "I thought fiction set him off."

"Books, words, images he cannot see, yes. Pancho finds fiction too filled with emotionally plangent scenes. He can't manage emotion anymore. He gravitates toward the physical, the tangible, the tactile. The ephemeral is exactly what it is—a ghost. And it haunts him. Words leave too much to his imagination, but actual pictures and visual phenomena are not a problem.

"These movies are good for him. They are all in one dialect or another of Chinese, which he cannot understand, and the subtitles are in Thai, which he cannot read. Simply perfect. Hyperbolic with flying, kung fu experts, and bad types who always lose. Think silent, American westerns without horses. Toss in an old and cachexic Roy Rogers with mystical powers. After he saw the most recent one, he couldn't stop talking about the ancient master who never looked up while eating his rice but caught a deadly Chinese throwing star—you know, a metal ninja star, a shuriken—with his chopsticks! He said it was like catching an arrow with your thumb and finger!

"Just leave the papers. I will send them over to the hotel, so you don't have to fight the afternoon crowd."

"Why is he so upset with me?"

"He doesn't like this idea. He thinks it's futile and not worth the danger. A bad bet."

"And you?"

"I already told you. We are tilting at windmills."

CHAPTER FIFTY-THREE

The last time that he would speak to Crissa, she was in Australia. Gwen was once again in the room, so the conversation was all business. Greg had collected the cash from the attorney's office earlier that day. Sixty-five thousand dollars. He planned to spend the night at the Oriental—the money tucked away in the hotel safe—and deliver the cash to Mac the following day. With a little luck, he could get to Pattaya and then go back to Bangkok and catch the evening flight to Chiang Mai. He felt like he was finally going home.

Crissa said she would make the flight reservations, but her ladyship wanted to talk with Greg.

"Do you think we can trust this colonel?" She didn't start with any chit-chat. "I am not comfortable giving him the entire amount before he even leaves his hovel."

Greg dropped his head backward and stared at the ceiling.

"Lady Saint Clair. We have been through this. This is your guy, remember? These were the terms, and you agreed to them. I don't think this is the time to negotiate."

"It is always the time to negotiate, young man. One day, you will learn everything is negotiable. Everything." She could not have been more condescending.

"It's your money, and your decision, but knowing Mac, the little that I do, I think it is a deal breaker."

"What if we hold off on the bank transfer until he reaches Chiang Mai? At least that is a modest show of faith on his part."

"I will ask, but I think it is silly."

"Why?"

"We either trust him or we don't. Either we are on the same side, and we are all in, or we are not. It is that simple to him and it should be to us. Remember what you are asking him to do?" *Asking me to do*, he said to himself.

She was quiet. Thinking. Perhaps weighing the reality that they would be arrested as spies if caught by the Burmese authorities or, worse if by a drug lord. Or maybe she was just processing his impudence.

"I don't care about the money. This was Rafferty's idea. I've never enjoyed having partners like this. My father did, and I have spent a lifetime disengaging and distancing myself from them. It's one thing to dance or to endure a slap and a tickle with this type of lowlife, but quite another to be a scrubber and pay a rotter for a boffing. Or bang-up, as you Americans call it."

She gathered herself. Maybe even remembering that Greg was already on her side.

"We spent more manipulating the land lease than we will on transferring these funds. Very well. Crissa will make the arrangements. I pray to God we are all doing the right thing."

Greg couldn't understand the last statement. Wasn't this all her doing? Like Mac, Greg believed Gwen's interests centered on the financial implications of the seven-year wait period more than anything else. This search was for proof of Albie's remains, more so than it was for Albie himself. Why the sudden attack of conscience? What secret was she holding back? He wanted to ask Crissa, but she was already talking about the wire transfer and another envelope that the hotel manager had for Greg. She, too, was wrapping up quickly.

"Call me if you need anything, but be careful, please." Her voice was no longer strong and confident but tinged with uncertainty, even apprehension. Was she suddenly realizing how dangerous this expedition could be? And her angst, an implicit profession that she cared for Greg now, far more than she did on that first day in Chiang Mai?

He sat on the balcony of his Oriental Hotel suite, looking across the brown and turbid waters of the Chao Phraya River at the lights in Thonburi. He remembered a meeting he had with Elliot as they walked along the busy road next to the river. *The Agency is perfect for Asia. Like the Thai and the Chinese, we keep secrets and seldom tell the truth. We are more eastern than western. No black and white, here. Just gray oceans of vagueness.*

Not so with Crissa. He had lived long enough in the gray. He imagined returning to England and being with her. Wondered for a moment what he might do there but knew that he had money and time to find something he might enjoy. Being with her that was the first step. He smiled to himself, thinking maybe this time he had found someone he could genuinely love.

He began packing his bag for an early morning departure for one last trip to Pattaya with Charlie, and then back to Bangkok for his flight to Chiang Mai.

Yes, he would be careful, if for no other reason than the prospect of seeing Crissa sometime soon. But despite his every intention, how was he to know that so many others were of a different disposition?

CHAPTER FIFTY-FOUR

Always sweat the details. If Greg heard that once, he heard it a hundred times while in Ann Arbor. Success, victory, excellence, genius—the list goes on—were all fruits of such attention. Those thoughts ran through his mind, yet again, as he sat talking with the Oriental Hotel's Mr. Geoffrey Hawthorne, who expounded on the same theme, crediting his staff's unrelenting commitment to such detail for the hotel's international fame.

"It is a complete and total buy-in. Listen carefully, the next time that you visit us, which I hope will be soon. Everyone on staff uses collective pronouns. *Our hotel, our restaurant, our pool. Don't you just love our flowers in our lobby*? They genuinely believe it is their property and their success. No task is too menial for anyone. I have cleaned toilets in moments of crisis. One person's calamity should not ruin another guest's experience. We are all united in our mission."

Greg said that he could not disagree. He had never stayed in a nicer hotel, and the royal suite, which he saw when he visited with Lady Saint Clair, was unrivaled.

"Yet, I did not detain you, Mr. Robber, merely to deliver your briefcase from the safe and to give you these additional envelopes, per Miss Crissa's instructions. No indeed, but before I explain, please let us complete the task."

At that point, Geoffrey transferred to Greg the brown leather attaché case, still locked, with the combination codes taped over and untouched, and two large, bulky manila envelopes, also sealed with tape.

"If you would, please sign this receipt," and Geoffrey, with his small and manicured hands, passed him a pen. "I can leave the room if you need to inspect the contents."

"No, that will not be necessary. I have no doubt everything is in order."

Geoffrey smiled proudly. He appeared a little older than Greg was, mid to late thirties, smallish, with a fresh complexion, and a bit of a dandy despite his attempt at dapper in a hand-tailored, pinstripe suit.

Knockoffs are a Thai specialty. A violet-colored shirt and a well-matched floral design tie, along with a fresh boutonnière, which he touched repeatedly as if to remind himself—or others—that it was there, all added to his barely suppressed supercilious demeanor.

"Very well. If I may, I wanted to express to you my deepest thanks, Mr. Robber."

"Why is that? I should be the one thanking you. Your willingness to share Charlie with me for such an extended period was beyond gracious," Greg said, politely omitting any comment about how Gwen must have paid enormous sums to the Oriental for Charlie's time.

"Thank you for saying that, but that is part of my gratitude. I have talked with him at length about his service with you and must tell you that never in my time here, or at any other establishment, has someone been so thoughtful toward one of *our* staff."

"Charlie was great. I would hope he considers me a friend."

"Indeed. He admires you to no end."

"That is kind, but he is incredibly bright, gifted, and given the right opportunity, will be successful. I think he could do a great deal more for the Oriental than driving lost souls like me around Bangkok."

"You are quite modest. You remind me of a friend that I had when I was in the Peace Corps, which I must confess seems like eons ago. I envied his language skills, his easygoing nature, and his cultural astuteness. He was a graduate of Yale and could have been making sizeable sums of money, and much like you was humble and self-deprecating. I liked him because, far more than the rest of us, he genuinely thought he could make a difference. Alas, dare I say, save the world."

With that said, Mr. Geoffrey stood, adjusted his boutonnière yet again, and with a grandiose exaggeration, extended his hand to Greg.

"I appreciate your robust recommendation for Charlie, and I will take it into thoughtful consideration. I know you must run, but let me offer you an open invitation to visit us again. You will be my guest as long as I am the General Manager here."

***

Greg opened both envelopes while Charlie drove to Pattaya. The first contained more cash. U.S. dollars, and a note on the law office stationery with Crissa's typed name on the bottom.

Here is an additional 10K for your immediate expenses, whatever they might be. I have already transferred funds to Ping's account in Chiang Mai, but I need an account and routing information for the nun to complete that transaction. I do not know why Blackledge did not manage this as he did with you and Ping. When you have that information, contact the number on this letterhead and ask for the senior accountant.

To be clear: his lordship's last will and testaments remain sealed, and these are not bequests nor legacies, but directed payments as previously outlined by Lord Saint Clair. They, along with deposits into your account, will continue monthly until all is resolved.

Crissa Bradley

cc: GSC

Greg laughed to himself. He had never seen so much money tossed around so easily. Gwen was emulating U.S. foreign policy. *If you can't solve a problem, throw money at it.*

The second envelope was the intelligence report from Rafferty's friends. Greg recognized all the village names. A map was also included. The topographical detail seemed accurate but no lines or marks for the borders.

One map, more of a drawing, had the Research Station at the center of the page with roads and the often-questionable footpaths stretching out like a spider web. The road down to Chiang Rai, the narrow road to Ban Su, and every conceivable pathway from or nearby the Research Station.

Copies of interviews and two separate accounts from local friendlies pointed to areas where Albie may have explored. More hand drawings. Two routes that might be used for border crossing. Question marks scribbled in red ink next to each. The most intriguing pages were at the end and included detailed accounts of the construction of the Research Station, a timetable of its progress, and even an inventory of equipment.

Why are they surveilling Albie? Who is surveilling him?

Then came shoddy photos—nothing close to the quality of Greg's work—of Albie in the village at Ban Su, walking with Nok, talking to T'ang. Pictures of crates, as villagers unloaded them from Albie's Land Rover, as well as from open-bed trucks. Farm equipment, hand tools.

Photos of the Thai army while stationed up there. Dates on the back of only a handful of the photos.

Greg must have uttered something under his breath because Charlie was asking him if everything was all right. Greg ignored him as he looked at photos of himself alone and others of him with Nok and with Albie. A snap of Wes and Albie sitting on two chairs in front of the Research Station drinking beers. Finally, shots of Fat Man and T'ang together in front of T'ang's hut. Fat Boy and his cronies, standing by their motorcycles and smoking.

Even more interesting, however, were photos of the inside of the Research Station. Photos taken surreptitiously in Albie's absence. The desks, file cabinets, and the storage area, filled with seeds, fertilizers, and other large sacks. The bedroom area. Even the closets.

These were all the types of photos Greg had taken in villages from the beginning, although he had never broken into anyone's house or property. Anything and everything to capture the gestalt of the village. Pictures, not words. *You can never take too many photos.* Elliot's constant reminder.

Words, in this case, followed. A chronological report with a record, a timetable of Albie's coming and going.

He works in the orchards side by side with the villagers. No task is beneath him. He amuses himself by walking in all directions. He is quite fit. Often venturing for short distances down unpassable lanes. Sometimes, he uses the jeep to explore the same.

Greg recalled doing as much when they ran into the tiger.

The last page had only two brief paragraphs.

Some areas are too remote, making it impossible to track him without detection. Tried once but spooked him. Wanders as if bored. Demonstrates no tradecraft but shows discretion just the same.

Despite reports that Xu was close to the border while the subject was in Ban Su, cannot confirm rumors he has met (or continues to meet) with Xu.

"What the hell?" Greg exclaimed loudly, "Who the hell makes up this garbage?"

"Mr. Greg, what is the matter?"

"Nothing, Charlie, just some idiot peddling drivel."

He stuffed the papers back into the envelope. *Why the hell would Albie meet Xu?* He wondered if he should even share the last page with Mac. It was so offensive and denigrating. Not even speculative. As if someone were trying to cast a shadow on Albie. A smear job.

He stared out the window. Incensed at the thought of Crissa and Gwen reading this rot and believing this nonsense.

He was still running hot when they reached Pattaya and the American Bar. Once again late morning, once again quiet, and again Pancho at the bar with Pepper, playing cards.

Pancho dismissed Pepper as Greg approached.

"Beguiling is but one of the countless words to describe her. Recherché. Lethal delectation. I see the way you look at her. A belgard. A libidinous stare. Each time more shameless. Delightfully lubricious in any wardrobe. Her mouth just a little petulant. Sullenly beautiful. Is she my *inamorata*, you wonder? Or she reminds you of someone? I think that might be it. You are not the lecherous type. Do not disturb the waters of your Zen calm. She is taken. Betrothed, in a manner of speaking, to Mac."

Greg scowled as he said, "Good morning."

"Ichthyology," said Pancho. "The study of fish, as you know. Ologies fill our world. The study of everything. Philology—language. Deontology—ethics. Eschatology—the end of time. Epistemology—knowledge. Pepper's favorite. Numismatology—money and the collection thereof. And then, of course, your favorite—cryptology, which is ever so slightly different from cryptography."

"Thank you for the lesson, Pancho. Where is Mac?"

"Yet again with the search. You appear irascible today. What, pray tell, has you distraught? Immersed in a new imbroglio, are you?"

"Nothing."

"Come now. Something pestiferous has unsettled you. As you know, I am a great reader of *tells*. And your saturnine mood is on full display."

"Nothing more than the predictability of this delay."

"Humph. A shivery *froideur* has become manifest. You are very much a seagull. I regret not recognizing it from the beginning. I was close. Ever so close. Had we played only two more hands, I would have nailed it."

"What is your point?"

"A seagull. You swoop in, make screeching noises, shit on everything, and fly away. Tell me, which part of that is not accurate?"

Greg's feelings were effectively bruised, but he refused to show it.

"The last time you said I was a Jabberwock, now I am the seagull."

"Names change all the time. It's an organic process."

"Is that what happened to you and your name, Stephen?"

Pancho's face became hostile. He glowered at Greg.

"How quickly you have become a *bête noire*. You know nothing about Stephen. Not how he lived and not how he died."

"I never said that I did. Why don't you enlighten me?"

"There is always someone who remembers things nobody else remembers, notices things everyone else seems to have missed. Does things that nobody would ever do."

"Is that you?"

"No. It is Mac. No one is like him."

"I didn't ask about Mac. I asked about you."

"I don't matter. Mac is the one you are dragging back into the jungle, not me. Do you know the number one rule of the jungle? Any jungle? Every jungle? Do you?"

"No idea."

"Of course not. How could you? Why would you?"

"Tell me."

Pancho looked down. A long time. Was he thinking? Seething? He lifted the cards and began shuffling. Two hands, sometimes with one. He passed the cards back and forth and never once looked at them. His gaze was only on Greg. Pancho finally broke the brooding silence. Abandoning his trenchant tone and manner, he adopted a tranquil voice.

"In between our various excursions—*missions* in army-speak—we interviewed prisoners of war. I am not talking about Phoenix or the interrogations with the nationals who ingratiated themselves to us and then spied on us. Those were different, not so pretty, and resolved with impunity. Mac did all the heavy lifting.

"He was masterful with the enemy POWs. No torture, nothing heavy-handed, nothing brutal. As Mac liked to say, they were soldiers just like us doing their job. He would learn what he could and determine whether this person should be part of a prisoner swap.

"We also managed debriefs of our people who came back to us by the same swaps. I handled these, and after every debrief, wished I hadn't. Most of these interviews took place in hospitals, as the men recovered before reassignment or discharge. Doctors were aggressive with sedation drugs, so catching the returnees when they were lucid, even if uncomfortable, was important.

"They always thought that they had failed. They had broken under torture, alive now, but filled with self-loathing, even self-hatred. I was not a shrink. I couldn't help them. I was just looking for intel—where they were captured, where they were held, who else was captured, anything along that line. With less battered and forsaken souls, we reviewed what types of questions the interrogators asked of them.

"Eventually, the intrepid Mac and I went back up country, as we always seemed to do.

"A year later, maybe two, I was back in the same hospital, only this time I was the one in a bed recovering from ill-placed bullets, and as luck would have it, a recently swapped POW was nearby. I couldn't help but listen as he shared his responses with the officer who had inherited my old job.

"Later that night, when both of us were morphed up pretty good, we talked. His name was Stefano. The irony was palpable.

"The VC put him in a ten-by-ten cell, but it had a ceiling of only four feet. He could never stand up. He could stretch out on the ground, but never stand up. He said he cracked in a matter of hours. Not even days. He said he tried. He knelt like an altar server, stretched on the ground, and rolled around, but lost it—just lost it. He cried and collapsed, realizing that they could keep him boxed up like this forever. He could not endure a march to death like this. He lacked the requisite courage. Told them anything and everything that he could. Betrayed everyone. He did what he had to do to save himself.

"I saw Stefano again months later. By then, I was easing into measured quantities of smack, thinking of course that I had it all under control, even cutting my stash with sugar or quinine, but by that time, he was horsing into the China White full tilt. He didn't recognize me. Why should he?

"When I was at Leavenworth, in my cell, I danced and jumped up and down, pranced and kicked. Did jumping jacks. Tried to leap and touch the ceiling. Anything I could do while on my feet. The doctors thought I had gone crazy, but I hadn't. I was paying homage to Stefano and reminding myself of the only rule that ever matters, even while I was incarcerated. *Never get caught.*"

In all their previous exchanges, Greg had never heard Pancho speak so plainly and with such self-assurance. He had been shuffling the cards for the entire time that he spoke, and with his last words, set the deck of cards down on the bar.

"Listen carefully, *amigo*, you are jumping into an oubliette of your own making, and were you not taking Mac with you, I would nary say a word. Just stop would you, pretend for a moment you are a gambler, and ask what the probable outcomes are?"

Greg remained silent. He did not know what an oubliette was and remained unsettled by the image of the low-ceiling prison cell.

"Mac has told you already. You will never find Sir Albie. He is dead, captured, or has absconded. There are no other possibilities. You are chasing a chimera. You are chasing smoke."

"Mac does not agree with you," Greg heard himself lie, still off-balance, as Pancho's polemic veered from the rational, inexplicably quoting T'ang of all people!

"Mac is trying to preserve himself from the atrophy of retirement. He is quixotic. Has a hero complex. A nonpareil warrior-saint. Daedalian by nature. He has read too much Kierkegaard. He was the apotheotic warrior whose apodictic loyalty knows no limits. Mac could not refuse you. He would see it as an abnegation of his responsibility to Albie. Loyalty and honor mean everything to him. Perfidy is a sin second only to subjugation. He is not afraid of death; he is afraid of a life of oppression. Considers heroin addiction as a slave master. Who do you think sabotaged that boat in the gulf? The floating heroin lab. And why? Because it was a source of evil. We did the same in Bangkok years ago. He called it cathartic. A purgation of sins. He is bored. He embraces the merit of extrajudicial execution. Endorses moral relativism with a scythe. Vigilante justice is justice served. He believes that everyone he has killed has deserved it. When a bullet goes through you, it leaves something behind. Vengeance is unnecessary if you believe in heaven, but he has no such belief. He is a nihilist. He does not believe in hell, but I do. The entrance to hell is the jungle. No one descends into hell, crosses the profound abyss, and comes back. Only that Jew prevailed in the Harrowing of Hell, but you are no Christ."

"You are exaggerating the danger of the hill country," said Greg.

"Am I? The jungle, the hills, and the caves have no laws. Do you think there is one entrance to hell? I went to the highest mountain and found an entrance. Charon took me halfway across the River of Death, but I spit out the coin and swam back before I saw the devil. His dark angels chased me. They roam the earth with other revenants. All you need to do is open your eyes. There is evil in this world, and it frightens my soul. It should frighten you. You can pretend to have courage, but if you see the devil, you will never come back. You are not the *beamish boy*. The *frumious Bandersnatch* will devour you. Don't be stupid.

Absquatulate. Flee. You are not pusillanimous for refusing. No one can see in the darkness. Only the fanatical zealot descends of his own volition.

"I am not the one who is crazy. Mac is. You should take me with you into this inferno. I should be your Virgil. Not Mac. Mac will walk into the tiger's den. He will walk into the darkness. You don't want to do that. You want me. You want someone to keep you out of the den and to keep you in the light—even out of the shadows."

Mac walked in just as Pancho finished.

"Right on cue, out of the shadows," said Pancho mordantly. "Come join us, Mac. We were discussing tigers."

"Nothing like the ones we saw in Laos, I hope."

"That was amazing. Tigers do not gather in groups in the wild very often. A hundred baht, no, a thousand baht, if our academic here can tell us the name for a group of tigers," Pancho queried.

"I am still trying to figure out what an oubliette is," Greg said.

Mac laughed. "An oubliette is a type of medieval prison cell whose charm rests with its single method of egress—a trapdoor in the ceiling, often twenty or thirty feet above the ground. A cruel and barbaric place. Knowing Wireless, I will not ask what discourse led to an oubliette."

"Fiddlesticks," said Pancho, irritability in his tone. "We are discussing tigers. Not a puzzling quodlibet. Come, the wager. A group of tigers. A thousand baht, *amigo*."

Greg shook his head.

"Alas. It pains me that one so educated in the university system cannot identify an *ambush*. How about a *fiddlestick*? You know what that is, don't you?"

"Enough," said Mac. "Stop the palavering. No one can keep up with you." He turned to Greg. "I assume you have something for me."

"I do."

Pancho excused himself. Mac told him he was more than welcome to stay.

"Thanks, but Pepper and I will withdraw to the back room where we can resume our daily tutorial, although it has tutelary purposes too. Alas, those who cannot are condemned."

CHAPTER FIFTY-FIVE

Greg gave Mac the briefcase and the combination numbers. He opened it, set aside the leaseholder papers for the moment, and surprised Greg when he took the time to count the money, flipping through each of the banded bundles of one-hundred-dollar bills, and then counting the packs themselves. Only then did he review the land permits.

"The other money should be in your account before the end of the day," Greg said. He had not yet decided what to do with the intelligence report.

Mac closed the case.

"Are you sure you want to do this?" Mac asked Greg. "A thousand baht says Wireless did all that he could to talk you out of it."

"You are right. He doesn't like the idea, but I am not afraid if that is what you are asking me."

"I am not suggesting that you are. I appreciate all the trouble you went through to get the leaseholder agreement, but I can pay for that, and Lady Saint Clair can have this money back."

"Are you backing out?"

"No. I am giving you the chance to back out. We can scrap the entire mission."

"No," Greg snapped. His patience was exhausted. First the denigrating intelligence report, then Pancho's harangue, and now Mac's demeaning invitation. Enough already, he thought.

"The other option would be to let me do this by myself," proffered Mac.

"That won't work. Lady Saint Clair would not have the assurance that you followed the intel to its fullest. She is counting on me."

"Are you saying that she doesn't trust me?"

"Yes, but I don't think she trusts me, either. She just knows that I have Ping's and Mary P's interests at heart. She is as distrusting as anyone could be and equally uncompromising," replied Greg.

"Wireless is the most distrusting person I know. He is skeptical in the best of times. I think he will miss the paranoia if it ever wears off."

Greg feigned a smile.

"Ok. Have it your way," said Mac. "Do you have the intel report from Rafferty?"

"I will have it for you in Chiang Mai." Greg still had much to consider, wrangling with a nagging fear he refused to define. "What are your travel plans?" he asked Mac.

"We need a business in Chiang Mai that can receive a shipment from Bangkok. A crate that will have our weapons. I have someone who can manage the delivery. It is better if I travel as light as possible."

"Why not just send it to the house?"

"No, for a dozen reasons. You must know someone who runs or works in a shop or business in Chiang Mai."

Greg considered the scarcity of options and settled on Jack.

"There is a Thai who runs a gaming house. A bit more than just the card game that you have in the back. A small casino. I might convince him."

"Someone like that would be good. We can pack items like drinking glasses into the cases as cover. Even chairs or office furniture. Call me as soon as you talk to him. I will need the name of the store and the address. I will travel to Chiang Mai after the shipment arrives."

Greg stood, but before he departed, Mac had one more comment.

"I know you are discreet. You've said little to nothing about yourself—only that which is linked with Albie. I respect that. My recommendation is that you say as little about our expedition as possible. Categorize it as *need to know*. Even for those with whom you are the closest. It will be better for them, and better for us, especially if we have any hiccups. Understood?"

"I understand," Greg said, and he suddenly understood the nagging fear he had about Rafferty's report. Elliot himself could have been sitting there. *We don't have answers. We only have secrets.*

"Good. I will wait for your call."

***

At the airport, Charlie gave him a gift. *The Dhammapada* (The Path of Dharma). A book about the Buddha written in English. Charlie admitted he had not read it but explained that Mr. Geoffrey recommended it.

Greg thought Charlie was going to cry when he looked at the money that Greg had given him.

"This is a thousand U.S. dollars," Charlie exclaimed.

"It is. You've earned every bit. Thank you for all you have done."

"I did nothing but drive the car. It was my job."

"You showed great patience and discretion. You never crashed in all that crazy traffic and that alone should be rewarded."

"I don't know what to say, Mr. Greg. Thank you so much."

"No need to say anything more than that. You are welcome. If I ever get back to Bangkok and the Oriental, I hope to see you again."

Greg shook his hand, grabbed his bag from the back seat, and said goodbye.

When Greg looked back through the glass windows of the air terminal, he could see Charlie still sitting in the front seat. His head rested on the steering wheel as if bowed in prayer. The money might not have been life-changing, but it certainly was impactful and underscored just how important Albie's money for Ping and Mary P was and would be.

The Thai Air flight to Chiang Mai was crowded. Single seats on one side and doubles on the other. Greg settled into his assigned seat, a single, near the front and by the window. He opened a copy of the *Bangkok Post* and read about Bobby Fischer and then a story about Muhammed Ali. Greg wondered whether Pancho was telling the truth about the explosions at the heroin labs, which Greg, along with everyone else, had read about last week in this same newspaper. Pancho's frenzied speech about Mac was not typical of Pancho. It lacked the whimsy and capriciousness of his previous lectures. Today was grim, more like a howling. No doubt a scintilla of truth buried in the hyperbole of his distress. But even his assertion about Pepper and Mac begged the truth. That Pepper reminded Greg about Preeya. Yes. That part he got right.

He stared out the window as the plane took off. You forget how bad the smog is until you rise above it. *You will learn to adjust to the food, the language, and the culture. It won't take long until you think in Thai. And once you know the local names and how to spell them, you'll feel attached, or less detached…still, only report what you see. Let the analysts in Langley connect the dots—yours and others. No conjectures. No speculations. They will only muddy the picture. Your pictures.*

When the plane had leveled, he reached under the seat for his bag and took out the envelope with the report. He fingered the pages, removed the last one, and set it face down on his lap while he returned the bag to its spot under the seat.

The document stayed there—face down—while he drank a beer and replayed the last few weeks. For a moment, he imagined he was returning to Preeya.

As the flight attendant announced preparations for their landing in Chiang Mai, he flipped over the page and read it yet again.

Some areas are too remote, making it impossible to track him without detection. Tried once but spooked him. Wanders as if bored. Demonstrates no tradecraft but shows discretion just the same.

Despite reports that Xu was close to the border while the subject was in Ban Su, cannot confirm rumors he has met (or continues to meet) with Xu.

He ripped the page into strips, and then the strips into shreds, and when the flight attendant passed by with a garbage bag to collect bottles, cups and refuse, Greg discarded the remnants into the bag—feeling for the first time that he was now in charge.

CHAPTER FIFTY-SIX

Known only as *Jack's*, the casino sits in a sketchy quarter of Chiang Mai, bearing all the similarities of Bangkok's Phetchaburi Road district. Unlike Fat Man's garish exterior announcing its location and business, Jack's was far more discreet, and one needed to know, or be told, that the narrow doorway, sandwiched between the Paradise Massage Parlor and the Seven Heavens Go-Go Bar, was the primary entrance to Jack's. *Samlor* and *tuk* drivers, of course, knew, as did most taxi owners, but first-time visitors to the area, especially *farangs*, often struggled to find it.

None of this bothered Jack. He had little interest in attracting anyone but serious gamblers—and serious money, and his reputation now, especially in the wake of the Lady in White, did just that. Make no mistake, there were dozens of shady gambling dens in the area and throughout Chiang Mai, but Jack's—and the House of Fat Man—were for pros and high-stakes wagers.

Everyone in the industry knew where the Lady in White now worked, but Jack's was the creation story. Whispers of her conception circled the gambling world even beyond Chiang Mai. Jack found her. Jack fashioned her. Jack formed her. Take your pick of narratives. Even her departure, his loss, seen as tragic, took on a life of its own with one fable or another. Most were convinced that the nefarious Fat Man had stolen her in a foul and fetid manner. The most recent tale was that Jack himself lost her in a card game. No one knew the truth. And Jack's adamantine refusal to discuss it fueled the speculation and contributed to the mythic legend of the Lady in White, and as a byproduct, to the popularity of both eponymous casinos as well.

Jack, affable as ever, recognized Greg immediately when he entered the large casino area, and with a well-practiced smile, approached him from across a crowded room, stopping for a moment at a busy blackjack table where he whispered to the female dealer. It was only when she turned her head that Greg recognized Jaz. Her hair was longer, and her sleeveless black dress resembled the type of fashionable design Preeya would wear—in white.

Greg and Jack's first meeting had been little more than a handshake on that night when Greg first laid eyes on Preeya, but the two spoke in the early times of Greg's romance with Preeya, once at length, when he came to the casino to pick her up after work. It was shortly thereafter that Jack asked Preeya to be circumspect, if not completely secretive, about having a *fan.* A serious male companion can only sully the illusion.

None of which bothered Greg. Until she moved to Fat Man's, and shortly thereafter, Fat Boy's inexplicable savagery to Mary P propelled Greg to break his promise. The failure had been completely his own, and he never pretended otherwise.

Both men greeted each other with a respectful *wai* and then shook hands.

"Looks like business is going well," said Greg.

"It is. Gambling is like air for some. They cannot live without it."

"I see Jaz has a crowded table."

"Jaz is a favorite of many. She has an empathetic charm for the losers, so they go away with a smile and look forward to a return engagement. She can also spot card counters quickly and is polite, interrupting their strategies with additional shuffles of the shoe. They appreciate her artfulness and discretion and then look elsewhere for a game of blackjack. Her following is not as legendary, but it is growing."

Greg read the reference to the legendary as a subtle message to tread carefully.

"Can we speak in private somewhere?" Greg asked.

"Certainly. Walk with me as if I am giving you a tour of our new renovations, and we can sit in my office."

They took a circuitous route away from Jaz and the blackjack tables and walked near the poker tables and then the roulette table. Thais, Chinese, and *farangs* engaged in equal interest at all the venues.

Just before reaching Jack's office, a Frenchman hit big on the roulette table.

"*Mon Dieu! Enfin*!" he shouted so loudly that even the most discarnate gamblers looked up. Jack smiled half-heartedly.

Jack's well-lit office was neat, uncluttered, and underscored the character of its owner. A statue of the Buddha rested high on a shelf behind his desk.

Greg got right to the point.

"I need a favor."

"Yes?"

"Elliot told me to see you if I needed something."

Jack smiled ruefully and asked, "Are you in trouble, khun Greg?"

"No. Not actually in any trouble."

"What is it then?"

"I have a crate arriving in Chiang Mai, and I need a business to receive it."

"Drugs?"

"No."

"Contraband?"

"Closer. Yes."

"Weapons?"

Greg did not answer.

"It is one thing to be in trouble, khun Greg, but it is quite another to invite it."

"I am not looking for trouble. I simply need a discreet receiving agent. I can pay."

Jack lit a cigarette and offered one to Greg, who declined.

"How large is this shipment?"

"A single crate, but we can disguise it with others if you prefer. Add furniture, glassware, and items for your casino."

"You have put some thought into your scheme," Jack said.

Greg had indeed done just that, though *worry* was a better description. He was not an experienced smuggler, his capacity for subterfuge was limited, and he had agonized about transferring the crate since he left Mac. He did not know Jack, but he knew Elliot trusted him and so did Preeya. He was hoping he could trust him as well because the penalty for trafficking in firearms in Thailand was jail, clear and simple.

"I hate to involve you," said Greg after a moment of silence.

"And yet here you are." Jack crushed his cigarette in the ashtray. "Elliot told me you might one day need help. I thought a passport or something less perilous. Just the same, for Elliot, I am at your service. I receive shipments of one sort or another every week. It will not be an issue. Multiple crates would be a better idea. A little duplicity goes a long way. However, there cannot be any type of alcohol. I have a special supplier for that. Do you understand?"

"I do."

"Good. I don't understand why you are mixed up in something like this. It does not suit you. I thought you were an academic. This is dangerous, if not foolhardy."

"I am only trying to help a friend. I am not mixed up in anything."

"Hmm. A friend. The Buddha encourages us to have four types of friends. One type is *the helper*, but I don't believe he meant this type of help."

The Buddha has all the answers, thought Greg irreverently.

"I need an address," said Greg.

Jack wrote out the details on a small index card and handed it to Greg.

"All the deliveries are in the building's rear. Early in the morning is the best time."

"Ok. That is good. I will give you the details as soon as I receive them."

"May I suggest a phone call with the delivery date, a driver's name, and nothing more. Your presence here once was of little consequence. Call it curiosity. I fear a second visit will draw attention. Not everyone in Chiang Mai thinks as fondly of you as I do."

Greg dismissed the criticism of his reputation.

"I will need to collect the crates when they arrive," Greg said.

"We can arrange that with a second phone call. Let's keep it simple."

"I understand. That makes sense. I have one last request. I would like to speak to Jaz, if possible."

Jack's face darkened.

"I don't think that would be wise. She is busy and very much in public eyes."

"I want to send Preeya a message," explained Greg.

"That is even less wise. Everyone knows what happened with you and Fat Boy."

"I just need a minute," Greg implored.

"Khun Greg, you and I are the only ones who understand the relationship between the two women. It remains for them a great secret. I cannot allow you to threaten that secret for any reason. You can understand that."

"I do. Maybe you can tell her then." Greg paused for a second. "Just ask Jaz to tell Preeya that I am sorry."

Jack, recreating his well-practiced smile, nodded, but Greg understood Jack would say nothing to either woman. For everyone's well-being, this was but a social call.

CHAPTER FIFTY-SEVEN

Ping sat across the table from him in the bungalow's kitchen. She clutched Albie's notebooks across her chest with both arms. She might just as well have been hugging Albie himself. Her eyes welled with tears. Greg no longer cared. He had rifled through every drawer and book in Albie's office for a second time, looking for anything to incriminate him of an association with Xu or anyone else. He found nothing, but he knew he was not finished. He refused to accept that it was meanness in his nature to press Ping for the notebooks, but he was chasing both truth and secrets, despite Elliot's dictums.

Her joy at Greg's return and his good news that the checks would continue to arrive were short-lived. He told her he had added information. He would return once more to the Golden Triangle based on that information, but that someone has said evil things about Albie. He didn't know the Thai words for calumny or vilify so repeated evil more than once. He needed to be sure.

"We have discussed this long enough. The notebooks are the last place that I need to look."

She was no longer protecting Albie's secrets. She was protecting his goodness. His kindness. She could not speak. She kept closing her eyes, fighting back the tears. Greg had tried kindness for the last two days to no avail, but enough was enough.

The crates arrive tomorrow morning. He still needed to get Mary P's truck from Chiang Rai and arrange a time to pick up the shipment from Jack's. His was a delivery destination, not a storage facility. The clock was ticking. Mac would be here the day after that. It was all happening fast, and he needed the notebook question resolved immediately. No more patience.

"If I don't see those notebooks, then I don't go to the Golden Triangle. I leave. I go away and the money and the house and everything dries up."

Maybe he was mean.

It struck Greg that if Preeya had these notebooks, then in fact he would go away because no one would ever see them. Thank God that Ping was not Preeya.

***

A little more than an hour later, he was driving his motorcycle too fast on Highway 1 and did not slow down until he cambered into a bend and came up quickly to an off-balanced and overloaded ox cart juddering down the middle of the road. For a flash, he thought he was back in the Oxford countryside running up on a lorry. He missed this feeling of speed on the open road.

His first motorcycle had been in England. He would drive out from Oxford on A 44 past the airport and toward Blenheim Palace. Maybe stop in Woodstock at the Black Prince to have a pint, where he would flip a coin to decide if he should explore the country roads to the east or the west. He wasn't directionless; he was bored and without purpose.

Sometimes he would take a girl. And why not? It was the heyday of his rampant self-indulgence and unabashed promiscuity. At first, he blamed it on his breakup with Heather and her betrayal. He berated his naiveté by visiting her unannounced in Germany and discovering her with another. But that was a poor excuse. He had cheated on her more than once and would have continued even with an engagement. No, he ran out to the Oxford countryside and into bed with women because he liked it, and they liked it. No hard sells, no guile, no cajoling, no bloviated appeals. Polite invitations, and if not this one, then another.

He had been driving too fast on the road long before he ever landed in Oxford.

He doubted Ping would ever forgive him. It meant that much to her. He had yet to raise his voice, but that moment too was passing, and then unexpectedly and in the spur-of-the-moment, he promised her that whatever he discovered in the notebooks would stay at the same kitchen table. *What we see here and read here will stay here.* Why did it take him so long to think of that?

So, with that promise, or at least the faint belief of that promise, she slid the three notebooks across to him and waited silently while he read.

Albie's penmanship was neat, tiny, and tiring to the eye of the reader, but Greg knew what he was looking for.

The first notebook contained commentary on deforestation and references and quotations from journals, scientific articles, books, and magazines, which Greg had observed on Albie's bookshelves. Long passages about responsibility. *Environmental degradation has a catastrophic impact on the diversity of life on the planet. The two environmental imperatives are ecosystem protection and renewable energy, and yet there is no plan for the latter and no interest in the first.* Notes for his speeches at colloquiums. *If we cannot make changes, minor changes on the granular level, then all the discourse on the global level is useless. How to stop slash and burn? A simple fundamental question.* Pages of notes seething with frustration, even questioning his own decision to come here rather than to study the decline of phytoplankton in the Southern Ocean with someone named Bailey.

Notebook two contained details about the Research Station and Greg was certain, that like Rafferty's map, which plotted the station as the epicenter of their surveillance reports, the secret would be here, but the notes were about coffee beans as an alternate crop, and the challenges of transporting buckwheat and sugarcane once harvested. Opium packaging and its conveyance were more efficient. Advantages and disadvantages of olive trees. Water tables for orange and apple orchards. A resignation of sorts. *It's fine to say we should do something, but only when you try, do you realize how hard change is. Processes are organic, and we have grown into them, and growing out of them is not always simple.*

Notebook three might well have been the most interesting if someone were writing a biography of Albie. The cloistered door to the chamber of ideas and secrets that we all have and guard. Reflections on science. *It has taught us more about relationships than objects.* Musings about his father, *a charlatan, a cheat,* and worse. The patriarch's sprawling underworld of antiquities, traffickers, and money launderers. His father's *only redeeming action was his unearthing of a collaborator with the Germans, a Greek quisling*—tainted as his father profited after WW II, by acquiring the traitor's art collection. Reproaches of his sister. *A high-society schemer and Svengali. A termagant.*

Pages of reflections about religion and the love of God, Buddha, and Mohammed. *If you pray to God and ask him what to do, and he answers you, can you do it? Will you do it?*

The section on Caterina was heartbreaking, the word *why* scrawled throughout—sometimes in caps, oversized, underlined, written again and again, blotted, and smeared by tears. Greg refused to read it. He was looking for one thing and one thing only. He held his breath when he saw an underlined passage. *We are coming to an end, the end of the world.*

Comments about Thailand. *Everyone has the answer... but no one asks the Thais... Ping alone knows more than all of us put together... she knows what love means.* Rambling observations about the hill tribe people comparing them to the Hebrews in the desert—*a lost nation.*

With that, he looked up at Ping, clutching the first two notebooks and holding her breath as she waited for the final one.

"Nothing," he said and watched her shoulders relax, even as she extended her hand requesting the last journal.

That was it. Nothing else. Nothing more until he started to close the last notebook and saw an inscription on the back of the last page.

What is more deplorable: a good man doing something evil, or an evil man doing the same?

"Nothing," he repeated to her. "Keep them all. Someday, when you can read English, his words will help you understand him a bit more and you will see even deeper into his love for you."

He lied so she might forgive him. Lied so she might feel less like a traitor or Judas. The notebooks held something only she imagined, and Greg left her with that illusion. Left her clutching the notebooks and telling him with a voice weak from the suffering silence. *I told you so.*

Now, convinced of his mission, filled with purpose, and his mind animated with the prospect of felony, he sped on Highway 1 toward Mary P's clinic, where he would trade his motorcycle for her truck and return to Chiang Mai.

He was lighthearted. Energized. This was all going to work. *Hell, we might even find Albie*, he said to the rice paddies. Just because Rafferty's file was wrong about Xu doesn't mean Albie's footprints into Burma were erroneous. No. It is a solid lead and worthy of investigation. We can do that. How many times before did he wander across at Elliot's urging? Perhaps not as blatantly, but they would be discreet. Mac was without equal. *Nonpareil*, Pancho called him.

Tomorrow morning, well before dawn, he would wait by the phone for a single ring, signaling the shipment. At that point, he would go immediately to Jack's to collect the crates and carry them directly to Chiang Rai and Mary P's storeroom. He would keep her in the dark. She disliked secrets, but as Mac said, everything was *need to know.*

Keep it simple. Jack was right. He sounded like Elliot. Except Elliot would not have said *simple,* Greg thought. He would have used a different word. A different expression. Spook-speak like *leave no trace, leave no footprints.*

Greg had been good at that. No left-over photographs or negatives. Every word he wrote in his journals went into the drop boxes. Never a stray message. Never carried a matchbook from a Bangkok bar or a souvenir gift from a new hill tribe friend. No trace. No footprints. He was just a lusterless academic.

CHAPTER FIFTY-EIGHT

The fact of the matter was that expats don't like their own and don't gravitate toward their own in foreign lands. An American expat would rather talk with a stranger from Canada rather than a recognized Ohioan. As a Michigan man, Greg could relate to that, but what Greg continued to forget was that not all expats are Americans, either. *Farangs*—especially from all over Europe—populated Chiang Mai and, like most foreign men sought, and even married the native females. Sometimes more than one.

Michel Corsair was one such expat. The prevailing rumor was that the Belgian—frequently mistaken for a Frenchman—was a former Catholic priest who, unlike St. Augustine, did not pray fervently enough for relief from his concupiscence. Rather, the former man of the cloth had multiple wives (and families) in Thailand but was sufficiently judicious to have them in separate cities.

Michel and his most recent wife, Suchada, owned and operated a café down the street from the train station, where Greg waited anxiously for Mac.

At first, it surprised him that Mac had decided on the train because of the twelve to fifteen hours of travel, but Greg also knew that with extra *baht*—both over the counter and under—one could secure a private, first-class sleeper and considerable privacy.

The train ride could be scenic and given all the hazards involved with a bus or a car on Thai highways, and even the frequent delays of Thai Air flights, perhaps the train made sense. Until today, when the ETA of nine a.m. passed by more than an hour and the gathering crowd of passengers for the eleven-a.m. return trip to Bangkok now backed up into the street.

Michel pulled up a chair and sat with Greg. They had shared drinks at Mama's and even once down by the river at the Night Market. Both men spoke Thai, but Michel's English was much better than anything Greg could say in French, so they defaulted to English.

"The train has hit a cow," Michel explained. "Suchada just came back from the station. The cow wandered onto the tracks and the train hit it, damaging part of the engine. They are sending another train to collect the passengers."

Only in Thailand, Greg thought.

"You are expecting someone?" he asked.

"Yes. A friend of sorts," replied Greg.

"An *amoureuse*, perhaps?"

"No. Not at all. A mutual acquaintance. A world traveler," he answered with a gentle lie.

"Ahhh. Yes. The WTs are always visiting Chiang Mai. We get our fair share here. They like our fruit smoothie drinks the best."

Greg nodded knowingly.

"Monsieur Greg, I am so glad you stopped in. We have not spoken in a great while, although I was at the Chinese casino the day you accosted the Fat Boy. It was quite pleasant for many of us. So many desire your courage. What I wanted to tell you, however, was that I was sad to hear about your friend Monsieur Albie. He, too, was a favorite of many. His noble work to save the hill tribe people. *Magnifique*! I understand you are now living with his two women. *Bravo!* I must confess that I lack the courage to keep two women in the same house, so there too, I am an admirer."

"Michel, I am not living with Albie's two women," replied Greg. "I have a separate bungalow in the back. Furthermore,..."

Michel interrupted him. "*C'est la vie.* It is of no importance to me, *mon ami.* I am happy for you and happy you remain in Chiang Mai, as I need your opinion on a very secretive matter."

"What is it?" Greg asked curtly, peeved by the insinuations.

"Coffee! Our Chiang Mai is growing so quickly. So many more Europeans and North Americans visiting here and even living here. There are no quality coffee shops. Nowhere to have good espresso. What would you think of opening a coffee shop?"

"I don't know. I never really thought about it."

"I know a secret, but you cannot share it."

"Ok," replied Greg.

"My first wife has a close friend in Bangkok's agricultural ministry, and King Bhumibol Adulyadej himself is going to announce a great coffee-growing initiative for northern Thailand. Chiang Mai will soon have the freshest coffee beans imaginable."

Greg laughed mournfully inside his mind. The coffee initiative was hardly a secret.

"It is a great idea. Toss in baked goods like Mama's and you could have a hit," replied Greg with an encouraging smile.

"I think so too. Suchada does not agree, but that is of little importance. Despite her youthful age, she is old-fashioned. Traditional, if you would. She loves her teas, but we can have both.

"Now, let me ask you a second question. How would you like to be partners in a new coffee café?"

"I don't know about that. I don't know anything about restaurants or cafés except how to order from the menu. I don't have that type of money either."

"It doesn't matter. I am an expert at such. I just need a partner, a collaborator. A modest investment to help me start another place. Everyone knows you have the wealth of Albie now. This place has been a gold mine, but I need a cosigner for another bank loan. The return on your investment will be great. I can assure you of that. The café in Lampang, which my second wife runs, is additional proof. I have the Midas touch."

Suchada called to Michel, imploring Midas to help with the rush of additional customers, so Michel excused himself hurriedly before Greg could answer, but not before collecting Greg's unpaid bill and beseeching him to guard the secret.

"Please think about the plan and please not say a word to anyone. One key to success is to get there first."

He left the café, embarrassed and irritated. So, this is what people thought about him? *Here comes the rich American with two Thai wives. The interloper, who pirated both the women and the wealth of his now missing friend.*

He stood for a few minutes with the crowds outside the train station. Eventually, a booming loudspeaker announced that the passengers from the overnight train from Bangkok would arrive at approximately four p.m.

Their original plan, predicated on the mid-morning train arrival, had been to collect Albie's motorcycle at the house and then leave immediately for Chiang Rai. At least that was the message Greg left yesterday for Crissa, who was somewhere with Gwen and Rafferty in Australia or New Zealand. All of Greg's updates were going to London and contained only the most basic information.

An arrival after four p.m. would mean driving a fair portion of the trip to Chiang Rai in the dark on Highway 1. The more prudent option would be an early start tomorrow morning. There would be more ox carts, but less overall traffic in the early hours. Mac could bunk up in the extra bedroom at the house and keep the low profile he preferred.

Greg squinted as he returned to collect his motorcycle parked near the Café de Michel. Headaches again. More frequently since his return to Chiang Mai, and he wondered if there was a connection.

Dr. Q's place was nearby, and with time to spare, he decided to replenish his supply of teas, thinking they would be good to have on the trip to the Golden Triangle area. Perhaps the good doctor has an opening and can even do a treatment.

CHAPTER FIFTY-NINE

When he arrived at Dr. Q's office, Greg could see Mei Li working behind the counter and was surprised to find the door locked. He knocked, but Mei Li did not appear to hear him. He looked through the glass again and rapped on the window with a little more energy until he caught her eye. She hurried to the door and let him in.

"I am sorry, I did not hear you. I had music playing while I was working."

She was not dressed in her usual Chinese fashion, but today wore jeans and a stylish white blouse with a plunging décolletage. Adorned with a gold chain and loop earrings, she looked very much unlike the prim shopkeeper Greg knew. Her black hair was in a braided bun at the back of her head, with tendrils falling loose on both sides, framing and flattering her face. She had just the right amount of makeup and pink lipstick applied. Greg, speaking in Mandarin, could not help but comment.

"Mei Li, you look very pretty today."

"Just today?" she replied teasingly.

"No. That is not what I meant. Just that…"

"Thank you. You don't need to explain," she said, smiling. "How can I help you today?"

"I don't have an appointment, but I wondered if I could see the doctor."

"He is not here today. He had to return to China for a personal matter."

"I hope everything is all right."

"Thank you," she replied and offered no other detail. "Would you care to buy some tea?"

"Yes. My supply is low."

"Great. Let's check to see which teas you have been using, unless, of course, you want to try something different. I have pu-erh tea right here. Would that interest you?"

"I don't know what that is."

She showed him a small box, which looked very much like a cigarette case. Inside were four tiles of tea connected like a chocolate bar. The tea was completely black except for a green line that coiled around the tea.

"Pu-erh tea is from Menghai in the province of Yunnan near the Burmese border. Are you familiar with the Kunlu Mountains?" she asked, feigning seriousness.

"No. One of the many places I have never visited," he answered, interpreting her joke.

"This is the type of tea that the Chairman gave to your President Nixon as a gift. This package is worth thousands of American dollars. The longer it ages, the more valuable it becomes, and the more coveted it becomes. Should I wrap it for you?"

Greg raised his hand to his chin in mock consideration.

"Next time. For now, I prefer the teas that you and the doctor initially recommended. They helped with my occasional headaches."

"I assumed you were not inexperienced in the labors of love. Ancient Chinese wisdom suggests that headaches in young men occur from insufficient sexual activity. Have you considered that possibility?"

Who was this woman? He asked himself. Was she offering more than tea to cure his headaches? The only Chinese wisdom he could think of right now was that *beauty and danger go together.*

"I was not aware of that teaching," Greg said.

"Come. Let's look at your file."

Mei Li kept index cards on all the customers with a history of their purchases. She found Greg's card easily, and she invited Greg to follow her into the tearoom.

"Please have a seat. I will move these items."

Greg settled cross-legged at the small table that he and Dr. Q had used on his earlier visits. Books and cards were currently splayed across the surface. The room was as Greg remembered it from his previous visits. Muted lighting to protect the tea, and a cool, dry temperature. A calming vibe.

"Are these your *I Ching* postcards for customers?" Greg asked.

"Yes," she replied as she knelt across from him to gather up the loose items and three different translations of the *I Ching*. "Have you read the *I Ching*?" she asked.

"Only the cards you gave me."

"The *I Ching* is a guide to self-realization while living an ordinary life. I never paid attention to it while I was growing up. Not that I had any aversion to such. I was much too concerned about my studies. I had little patience for anything else.

"Sometimes in a room with older people, such as my grandfather and his friends, they would talk about something one of them had read in the *I Ching*. It was very boring for a young girl. And despite my every intention to stay alert and be respectful, my grandfather would notice my inattention. He would then make a speech to the entire room for my benefit. *The fundamental principles of life are in this book. For over two thousand years, philosophers, politicians, mystics, and even sorcerers, have studied its meaning. You say you want to study medicine and you do not care that scientists and mathematicians continue to search for the meanings in the I Ching.*

"The others would nod wisely, and eventually one of them would start talking about the scholar Confucius and his commentaries on the *I Ching*. Then someone would start on about Lu Tung-pin and the Tao of immortals and the secrets of the workings of Heaven in Taoist thought. On and on it would go. I never cared and I don't care now."

"I don't get it. Why do you include the messages?"

"Marketing. People like it. It costs nothing but a bit of my time."

She leaned forward to collect the last remaining cards, and Greg's eyes drifted toward the low decolletage. She looked up at him with her almond-shaped, brown eyes and smiled just a little.

"My father finds the practice bothersome, but almost every Chinese family knows the *I Ching*, and whether or not they follow the teachings of the Tao, almost everyone has their favorite aphorism. Sometimes, if I know a person, even a little, anything about someone, like someone in the family recently had a child, or someone had an accident, I will try to find an appropriate section.

"People love special notes—women especially. You should try it with your girlfriends."

She turned the heat on for the kettle at the small stove and walked to the far wall where all the canisters of tea were located. She needed a small wooden stool to reach one canister. Her jeans hugged tight at her girlish hips and Greg took notice of her narrow waist, now exposed as she reached high to grab the canister. He thought he glimpsed a tattoo on the small of her back. Greg had the impression that she, too, was aware of his stare.

"I would like you to try this tea. I also have something else that I think you will like.

Give me a minute. I forgot to check the front door. I will be right back."

She returned almost immediately, carrying a pint-sized bottle of a liquid, which she set on the table next to the teapot.

"Most of Father's patients suffer from the same type of maladies, but lately I have noticed that many struggle with exhaustion and lethargy. It is as if they have a weariness of life itself. I find that sad. It is so refreshing to meet with others like you who show great energy."

Unlike her father, who sat across the table from Greg, Mei Li sat next to him while she sprinkled the tea leaves into the small pot. Her hands, deft and delicate, never touching the leaves themselves. Greg had not sat with her this closely and never realized just how attractive she was.

"I prefer to drink tea the old-fashioned way, with the loose tea in the pot and even in your cup, and let your teeth serve as the natural filter. You can experience full penetration without extra filters. Whatever you do, don't tell my father I treated you in this manner."

"Don't worry. I am good with secrets."

"Good," she said, touching his arm with the shy weight of her hand. "Let me get the water."

She traveled with the teapot to the kettle, poured the steaming water into it in a slow, deliberate manner, and returned with it to her place next to Greg.

"Where did you learn to speak Mandarin?" she asked Greg.

"At university. I have a feeling you speak English."

"Why would you say that?"

"Your notes in the packages. Your *I Ching* messages were written in English."

"Not all my postcard messages are from the *I Ching*. I use other sources. Our culture is abundant with maxims. But to answer your question, yes, in your case, I have some that I have transcribed into English. I use Thai for my local customers and, of course, Mandarin for the ethnic Chinese. I can read English and write a little, but do not speak the language with any competency. You have a good tongue. Perhaps you can give me lessons."

Greg could not tell if she was serious. He was having a tough time reading the room. He misjudged her devotion to the *I Ching* and wondered what else he had wrong.

"So, tell me, what is your favorite maxim?" Greg asked, trying to get his bearings.

"I am afraid it is shallow. A cliché."

"I very much doubt that."

"*Qí hŭ nán xià.*"

"Really?" Greg was genuinely surprised.

"Have you heard this expression before?"

"Yes. A friend of mine shared it with me recently."

She smiled happily. "You must have some clever friends."

Both laughed.

"The tea is ready, but before we drink it, I would like you to try this drink for your headaches. It is a perfect accompaniment with this tea."

"What is it?" he asked as she poured a clear-colored liquid into a third teacup.

"It is a twelve-year-old rice spirit in which powdered tiger bones have been steeped for more than half that time. It has untold benefits. It stimulates the spirit. It fortifies the nerves and lends tiger courage. It is said to render the childless prolific. If you believe that type of thing. Shamanists even consider it a substitute for a rare aphrodisiac found only in the remote mountains of the Tibetan region."

She filled the teacup, quivering to the brim.

"We can share this. I like to hold it in my mouth for a little before swallowing."

She took the first drink as if to tell him it was safe. He drained the rest, and she then poured the tea for both.

The tiger bone dram had a bitter taste, but with the first sip of tea, a friendly warmth, unlike the heat of alcohol, eased into his chest, and he reached greedily for another sip of tea. A hint of euphoria and relaxation waved through his brain, and for a moment he sat still, staring at the dregs and remnants of the pale brown decoction in his empty teacup.

"What do you think?" she asked. Her voice was musical, light.

"It tastes nice."

"Let me try one more thing to help with the headache."

She moved over, knelt behind him, placed her hands on his head, and used her fingers to massage his temples in a small circular pattern.

She would stop every so often and press firmly with her thumbs on the back of his neck, again using a circular motion on those taut muscles.

Time slipped out from under him. She didn't have to murmur to him to close his eyes and to relax, as he leaned back into her tender touch and soft voice. He could feel the heat of her body and her muffled breath on the back of his neck. His mouth was dry, and he wanted another drink, but he couldn't move.

He swallowed hard and thought he sighed aloud when she leaned forward, pressing her stomach against his lower back and her small breasts against him.

She squeezed his shoulders with her arms as she continued to work her fingers on his head. Her voice, now a reverential whisper, continued sweetly.

His jeans were too tight for the flood of warmth in his lower body. He wanted to uncurl his legs. A sense of urgency was building. His hands, damp with anticipation, felt trapped on his hips by her bonded grasp. Her hands and her voice never stopping, never rushing.

He knew his breath was longer, deeper, even louder, and she controlled him. He leaned back into her, and her hands worked their way across his chest, still trapping his arms in her grasp, her fingers spread, pressing, and again working in circles slower and lower toward his abdomen.

Her body fully pressed against his back with indistinct trembling whispers on the nape of his neck. Her mouth touched his skin. Her tongue was moving against him. He was trying to move but couldn't. His legs were leaden, locked in the twist of his cross-legged posture. And all the while, her hands kept moving lower and lower until she was on him, pressing through his jeans. One hand, then another, slowly and rhythmically. He heard himself moan as she unbuckled his belt, then the snaps, and slid her hands deeper. Her voice now pleading, desperate, calling for the power of the tiger, and with a burst, he raised his arms free and reached around to pull her forward, kissing her hard as she slid first to his side and then onto his lap. He could taste the bitter drink in her mouth and wanted more. A loose tea leaf passed between them carried by her darting tongue.

Her hands released him, and she slid around to hug him, her arms around him as if she would bind herself to him, rocking on him, pulling off his shirt and then hers, until they both finally fell backward where she finished undressing him and knelt over him holding him in place, quivering, trembling, and calling him, again and again, *my tiger, my dearest tiger, my tiger.*

When he opened his eyes again, he found her cuddled next to him, with her right arm across his midsection. She was silent—finally. Her mewling, unrelenting, and volcanic lovemaking spent. Her face nestled against his shoulder and her post-coital breathing was so quiet it was almost inaudible. He stared at the ceiling and lay as if paralyzed by what they had done. Gradually, he gathered himself. He did not know what time it was, and panic suddenly hit him, worried he had missed Mac's arrival.

He slid out of her grasp, looking one last time at the blush around her nipples, and looked for his clothing, stepping over her to collect his shirt on the other side. She remained curled up like a cat, the back of her shoulders barely moving with her gentle breathing.

She called him as made his way toward the door.

"Wait. Please."

She slipped on her shirt, grabbed the small package of tea leaves from the table, and went to him.

"Don't forget your tea. When you drink this tea, think of me."

She then reached upwards to kiss him, and taking his free hand, placed it between her legs. Her soft, small bush was still damp, and warm, as she told him, "We will wait for you."

Before he could speak, she placed her other hand between his legs, whispering about keeping the tiger bone elixir safe until the next time he had a headache. He wondered why he was leaving, the urge to stay pulsating yet again, but she released him, and he regained his freedom.

CHAPTER SIXTY

It was closer to six p.m. when Mac finally arrived. He wore dark sunglasses, a blue L.A. Dodgers hat on his shaved head, and carried nothing more than a green rucksack over one shoulder as he walked out of the station toward Greg. Despite the inordinate delay, he did not act the least bit upset. He took it all in stride.

They shook hands, more for the benefit of anyone watching than the exchange of friendship, and he climbed on the motorcycle behind Greg.

"You smell like a whorehouse," he said candidly to Greg. "I'm glad you weren't bored waiting so long."

Greg considered he felt like one and mumbled something incoherent about the crowds of people and with a clearer voice explained that he had called Ping and she would have dinner for them. Greg thought it was better than going out, and Mac agreed.

Greg thought Ping would be more comfortable with Mac in the bungalow and Greg in the extra bedroom down the hall from Ping, but Ping would not hear it. Mac had been Albie's friend. He could stay in Albie's house.

Greg showered in his bungalow while Ping showed Mac the extra bedroom and adjoining bathroom.

Mac insisted Ping join them at the table, even though she had shared dinner with her sister and the children earlier. The northern Thai specialty of sticky rice and chicken was, as usual, delicious, and Mac declared it was the best he had ever had. He and Ping had never met but talked as if they were old friends, catching up on the latest developments in Ping's life and the changes in Chiang Mai over the past few years. If Ping were still upset with Greg about the notebooks, she didn't show it, but Greg was eager to complete their planning, and as soon as the dinner was over, he made the unusual gesture to help clear the table, which Ping categorically refused. He and Mac retreated to the next room, the same room Greg and Crissa had used for their first meeting.

Mac quizzed Greg on the crates and seemed pleased by his competence to manage their transfer with no issue. Greg then gave Mac the intel report from Rafferty.

Mac was not at all impressed with the overall information, which started a discussion about the reason Albie went up there alone with Greg's camera equipment.

"It stands to reason," said Mac, "that Albie believed he knew where the opium cooking was taking place, and it is not too far-fetched to think that locale was across the border or in the frontier region. Their report gives what they think are at least two corridors.

"Looking at it overall, you could surmise that Ban Su served as a drop-off zone for other crop growers. Farmers in the area harvested their crop, loaded up a backpack or two, and moved it to Ban Su.

"Whoever was running the dope, Fat Man, Fat Boy, or another drug lord would collect it there, weigh and pay the farmers, and move it to the kitchen, cook the opium, and transport the morphine. Standard procedure. Albie was likely hoping to photograph that activity. Who knows? Maybe he was even crazy enough to follow them and detail the subsequent route to Bangkok. What do you think? You knew him better than I did."

"Something doesn't make sense," replied Greg. "I don't know what it is. It's hard to believe he would take such a chance. Even if he photographed them mixing barrels of raw opium, distilling it to morphine, loading pack horses, so what? Was this a revelation? A front-page story in the *Bangkok Post*? There must be something else, something we aren't seeing."

"What if it is more than just cooking the raw opium?"

"What do you mean?

"When I was first up there, Xu was setting up heroin labs along the northern border trail in Tam Ngop, Tachileik, and Mae Salong, even after the Border Patrol arrived there. He would then get it across to Pakse in Laos."

"How do you know this?"

"I was in Saigon, and as you already know, handled sensitive intelligence. Intelligence, which came from various sources, including the CIA and DEA. I also visited Laos once or twice," he said.

Greg thought he made it sound like he was vacationing there.

"Pakse had more air traffic than Chicago O'Hare. The Vietnamese National Air Force, the Royal Air Lao, hell even private contractors working for the Corsican Mob, flew product out of Pakse. Most all those routes went to Saigon, Phnom Penh, or Pleiku, which was just across the border from Cambodia in central Vietnam.

"Initially, Xu was refining the opium into no. 3 heroin—the cheap and low-grade product like Curved Dragon, which is sold throughout Asia, China, and Nam. He no doubt has upped that process by now and is making no. 4 heroin—98% pure heroin.

"Xu and his army owned that route and so the local drug lords—ethnic Chinese and Thai, transported their morphine to Bangkok, where the labs there make no. 4 for shipment to Europe or even Saigon, where it then heads to the States."

"So, what is your point?"

"What if Albie wasn't looking for the kitchen where opium is cooked into morphine? What if Fat Man had a fully operational heroin lab nearby and was making no. 4 heroin? For starters, it would be easier to transport than morphine. No. 4 heroin, like packaged *Tiger and the Globe* and *Double U-O Globe* at 99% pure, is worth fifteen to twenty times more per gram than any no. 3 heroin."

Greg was dumbfounded. He had never considered such a possibility, and Mac's knowledge of the finer points of trafficking was an unexpected revelation.

Mac tossed the papers on the teak table between the engraved elephants and tigers.

"There has been a cultural acceptance of opium use forever in Asia. The seeds, for example, are edible and are used for preparing pastries, and they provide a quality oil fit for human consumption. The Chinese use the first juice extracted from the plant to make oil varnishes, soaps, and perfume. Opium is medicinal. Less so in the cities, but prevalent in rural and mountainous areas. Headaches, toothaches, you name it, are all treated with opium patches, mixtures, and tinctures. Look at morphine. A direct derivative of opium is our chosen pain relief in Western medicine.

"Heroin is another story. No one questions its iniquity anymore. If Albie showed how blatant the heroin production was and showed that his Research Station and teak preservation project were sacrificed to make room for not just opium flowers, but for the actual production of smack, then it might be enough of an embarrassment to spark a stronger drug interdiction program by the DEA or Thai Government. The story is no longer just opium from Thailand, but skag from the Land of Smiles."

Everyone knows what is going on, thought Greg. It is too lucrative, and no one wants to stop it. Except for Mac.

"Enough speculation for tonight. Let's stay on the plan. Go up and have a look at the points of ingress into Burma from the Rafferty report. We need to talk with T'ang. He knows more than he has shared, but he no doubt has his reasons, too. We leave at dawn."

Greg's head was spinning as he brushed his teeth and crawled into bed. Both his thighs ached from the pounding of Mei Li when she was on top. He expected they would show bruises tomorrow. He was nearly asleep when the irony of the situation crossed his mind. If they crossed into Burma and discovered that Albie and Mac were correct about Fat Man's heroin lab, then it would make no difference. It was all in Burma, not Thailand. It was a fool's errand for Albie, and it would be the same for them. But then he realized as he fell asleep that it was the transport to Bangkok that mattered.

CHAPTER SIXTY-ONE

When the alarm clock rang, Greg was convinced that he had not slept at all. He attributed his restlessness to his trepidation about this trip, refusing to acknowledge any hangover effects from the tiger bone philter. Recognizing that this would be his last shower for the next week or two, he remained under the flowing water for longer than usual. He was comfortable with the good life. For the past months, he had been enjoying hot showers, cool, air-conditioned bedrooms, and well-prepared meals. More recently, luxurious hotels and chauffeured cars. He thought of Crissa. How easily she moved in the wealth, and he wondered if he could do the same. He missed her, missed her mesmeric ice-blue eyes, wondered if he would ever see her again, and then remembered that he needed to call and leave her a message in London before he and Mac departed for Chiang Rai.

Ping skipped her early morning practice of making merit with donations to the begging monks and prepared breakfast for Mac. The two of them were at the table talking when Greg entered the main house. Their immediate affinity astonished Greg, but he had already seen Mac in action with Charlie. The school of Elliot. *Easy rapport is the best asset in your tool kit. Charm is indispensable.*

Ping loved to talk and finding a *farang* who not only knew Albie but also spoke perfect Thai, made for an easy connection. She offered Greg something, which he refused, anxious more than ever to get started.

Ping hugged Greg before he went out, signaling her forgiveness, and she cautioned him to be careful. He waited a second for her to tell him to take care of Mac, but both knew that it was the other way around.

Albie's helmet was too large for Mac, so he decided not to wear one. However, Greg tossed him his second helmet and reminded him that Highway 1 had had more than its fair share of accidents. It was Mac's idea to walk the motorcycles down the driveway to the gate before starting them so as not to wake the children.

Albie's BMW motorcycle was sleeker, heavier, and more powerful than Greg's Honda, but despite its heft, Mac had no difficulty managing it. Daylight broke completely when they were twenty minutes out of Chiang Mai. The early sunlight sparkled through scattered clouds.

It had been a wise decision to leave early. The traffic was even lighter than Greg expected. They rode beside each other, but often one of them dropped back to make room for oncoming traffic or to facilitate as they passed slower vehicles, mopes, and even bicyclists.

Greg was overly reflective. He told himself that this would be his last trip to the Golden Triangle. Even to Chiang Rai. Elliot was right. It was time to move on. Then he asked himself how many other times he had professed, even promised, that something would be his last time. A night of debauchery. An affair. A loss of composure. He shook his head in dismay, recognizing he lacked the self-discipline, even toughness, of someone like Mac. Or Preeya and her strong-mindedness. Even Pancho, with his mental acuity and mastery of cards. They had a purpose in their lives. What did he have?

About thirty miles south of Chiang Rai, Greg caught sight of a speeding, black pickup truck gaining on them quickly. Mac must have seen it as well and dropped behind Greg to make room for the truck to pass. Both men eased a little closer to the side of the road, even though there was little to no pavement outside the driving lane itself. Greg thought he recognized the truck from one that they had passed a few miles back, but such vehicles were ubiquitous in Thailand, and one looked very much like another.

There was no one around and no on-coming traffic, but the speeding truck was making no effort to create a wide pass of them. Instead, Greg could see by glancing in his mirror that the truck pulled dangerously close behind Mac.

Greg and Mac, both sensing something unusual, slowed, but the truck driver did just the opposite, gunning his engine and slamming into the back of Mac's motorcycle, sending him tumbling off the side of the road and down toward the drainage ditch. Greg was horrified, and as he pulled over to stop, the truck attempted to hit him as well, but fortunately only brushed him off the road, forcing him to lose control and dump the bike, which slid away from him as he hit the ground on his side. His shoulder and hip endured the brunt of the fall. Somehow, he kept his head from bouncing on the ground.

As he struggled to his feet, Greg noticed the blood covering his hand and then the gash. He pulled off his shirt and wrapped his hand even as he was hurrying over to Mac. Looking over his shoulder, he saw the truck racing toward Chiang Rai.

Mac was unconscious but appeared to be breathing. He had been thrown off the motorcycle into a clearing and had landed almost twenty yards from the bike. The soft run-off from the nearby rice paddy saved his life. Greg went over to the mangled BMW, unfastened Mac's green rucksack, and placed it under Mac's head as a pillow after removing Mac's helmet. His dark sunglasses, held tight to his head by the helmet, were unbroken and still on his face. He examined Mac for bleeding, but miraculously, there was none. Greg's hand was quivering as he checked Mac's carotid artery on his neck. He wanted to make sure he was alive. Greg's chest was heaving. The bitter taste in his mouth, he recognized as adrenaline, and suddenly he felt like he was going to be sick. He stood up too quickly and almost fainted. Gathering himself, he leaned forward, placing his hands on his knees, and took a deep breath, once, and then again, and then a third time. He felt his heart slow a bit and the nausea pass.

Strangely, he remembered doing the same thing during summer football workouts, when they were running sprints in the oppressive heat. He shook his head and stood up straight. Football?! What the hell was he thinking?

He thought of Nok. Finding her unconscious. Never waking again. He was terrified and angry at the same time.

It didn't take long for passing vehicles to stop and for various locals to offer help. Mac's condition was the most important thing and getting to the Chiang Rai clinic as soon as possible made the most sense. Let Mary P examine him. She was the closest medical help. They could decide what to do after that.

Several good Samaritans helped to lift Mac into the back of a truck. An elderly woman had spread blankets and clothing on the truck bed. She insisted on riding in the back with him and keeping his head on her lap. More than once, she shouted directions of one sort or another to the young driver.

Greg's motorcycle still worked, and although the steering was wonky, he knew he could manage the short distance. Someone brought him duct tape, ripped his shirt into a smaller bandage, and re-wrapped his hand for him. He told the others to take the banged-up BMW to Prawaite's shop next to the clinic. He promised to pay everyone for their help, but no one expressed any interest in taking his money. Sometimes the good in people wins the day.

He struggled to use his right hand while driving, but the driver carrying Mac did an excellent job of maintaining a steady speed, and Greg did not have to brake and change gears too often. His right shoulder and hip ached, but it was his hand that hurt the most.

As they entered Chiang Rai, Greg saw Mac raise his head. The would-be nurse settled him back into her lap, and Greg felt a small sense of relief.

Greg pulled past the truck to guide it to the clinic, and in less than ten minutes, they were helping Mac off the truck and into Sister Mary Peyton's examination room.

CHAPTER SIXTY-TWO

"He's resting in my bed. I will need to check on him regularly. I don't want him to sleep too soundly just yet. It's not safe with a concussion. At least not for the first four or five hours. His eyes are still glassy, and the pupils remain dilated."

"Is that serious?"

"It is all serious. Pupil dilation is not limited to concussions. It can also occur as part of the autonomic nervous system's fight-or-flight response, but it is an important concussion indicator."

"And the shoulder?" Greg asked. "I didn't know anything was wrong at first. We just loaded him into the back of the truck."

"It was a subluxation. A partial dislocation of the shoulder. As soon as we got it back into place, he relaxed. Most people could hardly stand the pain, but he barely grunted. I have the impression that he might have reduced the shoulder himself on previous occasions. I offered him something for the pain, but he refused. I don't think he knew who I was or where he was. Now, can we look at your hand while you tell me just what the dickens happened?"

Greg placed his hand on the examination table between them, and as she unwrapped the cloth and cleaned the wound, Greg detailed their accident. Mary P interrupted him once to quiz him about his most recent tetanus shot and encouraged him to keep talking as she stitched the wound.

"Do you think it was purposeful?"

"No doubt. Zero question about it. Ouch."

"Be still. But why? Who would do something like that?"

"I think we all know the answer to that."

She finished the stitches and bandaged the hand without further comment. A brutal and unbalanced Fat Boy had attacked her once, and now someone had tried to kill Greg and Mac. Greg could tell she was as frightened as he was. She was the kindest person he had ever met. Never a harsh word for anyone, let alone about anyone. Never dissembled her true feelings or beliefs. And now, here was evil knocking not once but repeatedly at her humble door, and the virulent darkness she had spent her young life fighting against was becoming an implacable threat, picking them off one by one.

"How does that feel?" she asked.

"It hurts."

"Of course, it hurts. You had a gash the size of the Grand Canyon. You are lucky that you didn't sever any nerves. Wiggle your fingers. Good. Now flex them and close your hand a little. Good. Now stop and don't do anything and let it heal. I want to check you for concussion and look at your shoulder and leg where you landed. You were limping badly when you walked in. It's time to see what the full extent of the damage is to you."

"Has anyone ever told you that you were bossy?"

"Yes. You, on multiple occasions. Now sit on the exam table and let's have a look."

After the checkup, the two friends sat in the kitchen and Greg told her what he knew about the partnership between Mac and Albie. He was careful to characterize Mac only as a war veteran and refrained from any of the disagreeable details which he gleaned from the Rafferty dossier or even from Mac himself. He told her about meeting Lady Saint Clair—once again, the abridged and laundered version—and the tedium of the back and forth from Pattaya to Bangkok as negotiations continued.

"Was she as nice as Albie?"

"No. Not really. She was gracious in the beginning, but when I hesitated to search for him again, she became…callous, manipulative."

"How so?"

"Albie made arrangements for Ping, and Lady Saint Clair threatened to withhold the allowance unless I agreed."

"That wasn't very nice."

"No. It was unscrupulous. It threw me for a loop, to be honest."

"And your new friend, Mac?"

"He's being paid, much as he was the first time that he and Albie reconnoitered the area around Ban Su."

"That's quite a military term."

"He is a military man. I have the impression that he is very detail driven. Speaking of details. I just remembered that I need something from you."

"What's that?"

"I need a bank account and a routing number. Albie has also made a provision for you, and Crissa needs that information."

"Crissa? Who is Crissa?"

What a question, he thought. *Who is Crissa?* He was still trying to get his mind clear on that.

"She is Lady Saint Clair's lawyer, one of many, if I understand it correctly, and she is managing the financial transactions for her ladyship. Albie was clear that an allowance was to go to you to help with the clinic."

"I didn't know anything about it. He said nothing to me. He gave me money in the past, but I have no expectation or even the right to continue to receive such."

"Expectation or not, it is what Albie has directed his lawyers to do, and Crissa is following those directives. Knowing you, I am sure you will figure out how to help others with it. I just need the banking information to complete my responsibility."

Mary P did not need Greg to connect the dots for her. She was smart enough to know that along with Ping, she too had been part of the leverage, and the nervous tapping of her fingers on the table expressed her uneasiness with the entire arrangement. Greg waited for the next question, preparing his lie. He was certain Mary P would ask him what Gwen was requesting Greg to do that demanded so much inducement. She zigged.

"Are you going to tell me what is in those crates you left here?"

"Have you told anyone about it?" he asked too quickly.

"Certainly not. You know I dislike secrets, but you asked me to keep it a secret, and so I did. I almost told Wes when he asked me if I had seen you."

"Wes? When did you see him?"

"He has been here several times while you were busy in Bangkok. When he brought me back here after my stay at the hospital and then at Albie's house, he offered to accompany me on future trips to the hill tribe villages. I told him it wasn't necessary, but he said he was bored and would love to do something useful. He has gone with me twice already. He and I were just up there two days ago. He has been ever so helpful. He drives. Helps translate. We get up and back in a single day and often get to two or three villages each trip. You just missed him. He left yesterday to go back to Chiang Mai. I told him you were coming up here this morning, but he said he had to get back to see Mama at the café to help with restocking or something like that."

"You told him yesterday that I was coming here today. Did you tell him anything else?"

"I don't know. What would I tell him?"

"Nothing about Mac or me going back to Ban Su?"

"Greg, I don't remember. Wes and I were together for almost two days and talked about dozens of things. I don't think I said anything about Mac, because you never told me you were arriving with another person. Why are you asking me this? What does Wes have to do with anything?"

"No reason. Nothing. Just thinking."

"Except for Albie," Mary P continued, "no one has done more to help me than Wes. He has been a godsend in so many ways. I don't know what happened between the two of you, but I am telling you his heart is in the right place. Sometimes he comes across as bitter and beaten down, but he is still mourning. Albie was the only devoted friend he had here in Chiang Mai."

"I'm sure you are right. I just didn't know that he had been here so recently. I am a bit confused about everything. I think it's the crash."

"We were talking about the large cases, remember?"

"Camping gear. The crates have camping gear in them, so we can stay outside a village if it gets too late. I wanted to ask you if we could use your truck to get up the mountain. It looks like the motorcycles are too banged up to be an option."

"You can't consider still going. You said that someone knocked you off the road on purpose. What do you think might happen in the hills?"

"I don't know. I just know we must get this over with."

"Greg, you are still in a state of shock. I know Mac is. You both were run off the road and nearly killed. This is classic machismo denial. What are you trying to prove? I am frightened by all this violence, and you should be too."

Before Greg could offer another lie or excuse, Mac's deep-toned voice reached them.

"Robber. Robber, are you out there?"

Mary P and Greg entered the room to find Mac trying to sit up in the bed. He struggled to push himself up with the bad shoulder and rebuffed Mary P's efforts to assist. Undeterred, Mary P grabbed him around the waist and set him aright. His breathing was labored, and he squinted derisively with his coal-black eyes at the small woman at his side.

"I would like to check your vitals, Mr. Mac," Mary P requested.

"Who are you?" he asked sternly, with a gruff voice.

It was Greg who interjected himself before she could answer.

"Mac, this is Sister Mary Peyton. The person I told you about in Chiang Rai. Where I sent the crates, remember? She runs this clinic."

Mac collected himself. "You were the one who put my shoulder back in place," he said.

"It was mostly you. I only helped a little. Do you mind if I check your heart and your breathing?"

"No. I need to talk to Robber here. You can check it later. Please. Thank you for your help, but give us five minutes, please?" His tone softened.

Mary P made a face at Greg as she rose and left the two of them. Mac waited for her to close the door behind herself, before talking again.

"How are you? Are you hurt?" he asked Greg.

"No. Not really. I dumped the bike when he hit me. I slid onto my side."

"What's with your hand?"

"A slice. Not a big deal. A few stitches. How do you feel?"

"Like I got hit by a truck. Did you recognize anyone or anything?"

"No."

"Thoughts?"

"It had to be Fat Man. Likely Fat Boy himself or one of his claques."

"How the hell did they know we were driving up here?"

"I don't know. That's all I have been trying to figure out. I didn't tell a soul."

"There is poison in the water. Someone is watching you—that part is for certain."

"What do you think we should do? Do you want to call it off?"

"Hell no! No one is going to run me into a ditch and scare me off. So much for your walk in the park."

Mac's mettle assuaged Greg's most immediate fears and his resolve to continue bolstered Greg's weakened confidence.

"Where is my rucksack?" Mac wanted to know.

"It's over there. Against the wall. Do you want it now?"

"Please."

Greg retrieved the green bag and placed it next to Mac. He pulled out two clean shirts and, setting them aside, dug deeper into the pack, before finally extracting a cloth-covered item. It was a handgun. Greg recognized it as the same type that Wes had. The .45 caliber Colt 1911. Mac checked it quickly, dropping the clip, clearing the chamber, and reinserting the ammo. He then wrapped it in the cloth and replaced it with the shirts on top.

Greg held his breath. He knew they were going to carry rifles, but he naively thought of them as decorations, adornments to look the part, just as they were when he traipsed about with Wes the last time. Now, in the aftermath of today's treachery, seeing the gun and the supreme ease with which Mac handled it confirmed for Greg that this was just the start of the violence.

Mac grimaced as he tried to stand up.

"Help me get up," he directed Greg. "I need to take a leak. This shoulder is going to take a day or two. Do you trust this nurse? This nun?"

"Yes. Completely."

"All right. Where is the latrine?"

"Do you need any help?" Greg asked as he pointed toward the adjoining bathroom area.

Mac smirked but refrained from the obvious foul-mouthed response.

"Just give me a few and then tell her she can come back in and do her checkup. We are going to have to give this some more thought. Whoever you have pissed off isn't likely to stop now. You and the Brit have made some great friends, that's for sure."

CHAPTER SIXTY-THREE

Greg slept poorly. He had pushed the two examination tables close together so he could roll over a bit each way, but they were too short, and he was forever readjusting himself throughout the night. His hip ached, as did his shoulder, and he wanted to stretch out on his back, but his legs hanging over the end made such an arrangement impossible. Once he woke, believing the truck was about to hit him again. He got up and changed his sweat-soaked shirt. At four-thirty a.m., he heard the gongs from the nearby temple calling the monks to morning meditation, and after that, any movement in the street—a car, a mope, even the rattle of a passing bicycle—caught his attention. He soon abandoned the makeshift bed and sat in a nearby chair, recreating the attack, convinced he saw Mac airborne over his motorcycle. He reviewed all his encounters with everyone he had seen since he arrived back in Chiang Mai in a hopeless search for his betrayers.

He wanted to settle on Wes, but in his heart, he agreed with Mary P. However scurrilous and jaundiced Wes might be, there was a part of him that was generous. He might be a knave and a rascal, but Greg attributed Wes' duplicity to his training and his survival skills. Lying had become second nature to Greg. How much more for someone like Wes? There was no telling what lengths Wes went to during his forays into China. There is always debris left behind, especially the detritus of death. A look at Mac and Pancho will tell you that killing someone, even an enemy, scars your soul and changes your DNA forever.

No. It had to be someone else. Michel at the café? He frequented Fat Man's casino. He knew Greg was waiting for someone. He could have even witnessed Mac's arrival. For much-needed capital, Michel might have shared intelligence. Fat Boy only needed a single lead. Wasn't he already watching Albie's house?

Daylight slithered under the framework of the front door. Would the sun reveal him today for the fraud that he was? Passing himself off as an academic. What a charade. He closed his eyes to the encroaching light, trying to imagine halcyon days of the not-too-distant past, happier days at Ann Arbor like waking to the first snowfall blanketing the quad, but all he could summon was a vision of dirty snow sinking into itself.

Mac jarred him from his trance. Mac had moved into the spare room as soon as he realized he had been recovering in Mary P's bed. She tried to convince him otherwise, but he would have no part of it. Now he was standing in his boxer briefs, shirtless in the doorway to the back rooms, the sling for his arm hanging empty around his neck.

"You look comfortable," he said with more than a hint of sarcasm.

"Could be worse."

"Wait a day or two and we will find out. We should talk."

Mac pulled up a chair next to Greg, who shared Mary P's willingness to allow them to use her truck. Mac was pleased and walked Greg through a list of items that Greg should buy at the market. Mary P had told Mac about her neighbor, Prawaite, and Mac suggested Greg get Prawaite to do a once-over on the truck. Just to make sure something simple doesn't bite them in the ass.

"The first rule is to look after your person and your safety. That needs to be at the forefront of your thoughts and decisions. You're no good to anyone else if you are dead. After that, we look after each other. Got it? No exceptions. No hero stuff. Do you understand?"

"Yep. I get it."

"Someone out there is playing for keeps. You will have a gun. Two guns. A rifle and a handgun. If you have to think or ask, it is already too late. If someone comes at you, you shoot. You don't think. You don't talk, you don't hesitate. Got it?"

"I got it."

"Will your hand be ok to grip the gun?"

"It should be."

"We will test it out up there. Listen, I know you are not a soldier. Not a killer. You might never have been in a fistfight. But there are no rules where we are going. No innocents. You shoot or you die."

Noise and lights in the back. Mary P was moving in her area.

"How is your shoulder? When do you want to leave?" Greg asked.

"My arm will be fine. We will go tomorrow. Get the items organized. Take her with you today. Keep her busy. I will go through the crates and get our gear organized while you are gone. It shouldn't be difficult to get everything into a single crate. She will spend the day trying to talk you out of going. Better you than me."

***

"How did you sleep last night?" Mary P asked as they were driving to the market.

"Just fine," Greg said, lying without conviction. The restless night and his failure to identify the *poison in the water* had him irritated.

"Your headaches? How have they been?"

"Are we going to have a medical review all day?" he asked, a little too harshly.

"No. Just the *introit*," she answered, deflecting his brevity.

"What?"

"The entrance psalm. The start of our day."

"Ok. Better medical than religious. My headaches have not been an issue for the last few weeks. Did I tell you I saw an acupuncturist?"

"No. I don't recall that nugget of information," she said, nurturing their usual banter.

"A Chinese doctor. Stuck me with a bunch of needles and sold me tea."

"Sounds like a good business model."

"He was nice. I liked him. He explained my meridians were out of balance."

"Your *yin* and your *yang*?"

"Something like that. It was effective, and I have been feeling better."

"Maybe you have been too rough on your body," she suggested.

"I expect that is partially true."

"Your patron saint, Saint Gregory of Narek, is famous for saying that he indulged his body and wore out his soul."

"I don't have an answer for that. Is there more that you want to say?" Greg asked.

"No. Just wanted to get that off my chest," she said, and her saintly spirit garnered a smile from him, releasing him, at least for the moment, from his self-recrimination.

"Noted. Now, where should we start?" he asked.

"Albie would get plastic jugs of purified water from the small shop across from the White Temple. We can park there and walk down the street to the open-air market for the food items."

"What do you think the chances are that the water from there is actually purified?" Greg asked.

"Albie and Wes always get their water from there, so I am guessing better than fifty-fifty," she said.

"I guess we will take those odds."

The market was aswarm with vendors, and unlike Chinatown's lengthy, dour stretches of similar products side by side, these open-air market merchants displayed their mangos, rice, cabbage, and pickles as easily beside fermented fish as they did laundry soap. The jostling and bargaining were nonstop, but so were the greetings and the compliments. There was no shortage of laughter.

Everywhere that they went in the market area, someone knew Sister Mary Peyton. She talked to everyone in her broken Thai, and they loved it. More than one vendor did not want to charge her for the goods, but Greg insisted on paying, knowing full well that the items were not for her but for him and Mac.

At one point, a red-mouthed, elderly, Siamese woman chewing betel nut boorishly blocked their path hawking monkey paws. Mary P sidestepped the aged and overly solicitous woman and explained to Greg that any type of divination is a sin, even as the woman's clamorous, importuning voice pursued them down the aisle toward the sticky rice. The young girl at that food stall wanted to know if Greg was Mary P's brother. At first Mary P didn't know what she meant, but after Greg translated, she gave out a loud laugh.

"Tell her I wish that I could have someone like you for a brother," she told Greg.

Greg adjusted the translation and told her they were simply good friends.

As the Thai woman prepared a package for them, Mary P reminded Greg to get extra for the *camoys*.

"You should remember to get cigarettes and whisky too," she said.

"When you think about it, it's extortion," Greg said. "Don't get me wrong, it is far better than arguing or confronting them."

"I don't know. Albie and I saw it as charity. The robbers have a need, and we have the resources, so why shouldn't we share? Charity can change a person's heart."

Greg wondered if Mac would have any charity or patience for bandits.

"One more reason to pray to Saint Dismas for them," she continued.

"Another saint? Who is this one?" Greg asked.

"The patron saints of thieves, of course. I thought with your last name you would surely know him," she said, smiling.

What should have been only an hour at the market took close to two, and when they had finally collected all their supplies and loaded them onto the truck, Mary P asked him to drive out the road toward the Mai Sai waterfall. She wanted to visit a young woman who lived near there, and without the truck for the next couple of days, today made the most sense.

The road out of the city center became hilly and rural almost immediately. Trees and verdant shrubbery lined the two-lane road, which, after five or six kilometers, gave way to hard-packed dirt. The truck labored, climbing one steep incline and then juddered noisily down another, reminding Greg to have Prawaite do a once-over. Mary P, always affable and lighthearted, was especially sunny as they drove, and without prompting, talked about her childhood.

She said that when she was still just a child, her father would take her and her brother to a nearby lake to go fishing. Back then, it seemed like the drive was for two or three hours, but in fact, it was barely even one hour. Somewhere along the way, they would stop at a small store that sold bait and tackle. Everyone had a job on the trip. Her younger brother had to pick out the worms and sometimes another bait, and her task was to load the ice into two ice chests. One chest was for the fish they would catch, and the other was for the soft drinks. She would have to lug ice bags from the outside cooler in front of the store, set them on the edge of the trailer, and then climb up onto the boat. The bags were heavy, but she could manage, and she refused to let anyone help.

Her father would ask her what she wanted to drink, and she always asked for ginger beer. She said she loved the burning taste in her throat. She and her brother could each have two drinks, and only two drinks for the day, so you had to strategize on when you drank them. One for sure with the peanut butter sandwiches while on the boat, and the other for the drive up or later in the day. Her brother always drank one immediately, while she saved hers for later.

"We would stay out on the lake all day and catch loads of fish, and when we were a little older, my father would let us jump in the lake and swim, but only after all the fishing was done for the day. It was so much fun. But what I remember the most, what I still think about when I am driving up country roads like this, is my favorite memory."

"Which is?"

"Bare feet out the window! Sitting back in that front seat with my dad driving and hanging my bare feet out the window and wiggling my toes and the wind sailing over them. I don't think I was ever happier as a young girl. Just thinking about it makes me smile."

Greg remembered Crissa's wiggling feet from the first day that they spoke in Albie's front parlor.

"Do you want to stick them out the window now?" Greg asked.

"I do, but just thinking about it is good enough."

***

The house they visited was off the main road and up a steep hill. It was one of a dozen spread along the hillside area. Stone slabs, fastidiously placed on the slopes, formed the steps to the houses. Vegetable gardens and fruit trees bordered the homes. Greg sat outside on a wooden stool talking with the husband, while Mary P met with her patient inside. The couple's first child, a boy of three, was playing with a soccer ball, kicking it toward the father, who sent it flying in various directions, to the delight of the youngster.

The father made a living as a carpenter. He told Greg that he started in one of the woodworking shops as a young teenager, crafting wooden elephants, windpipes, and knick-knacks for the tourists. When he was sixteen, he became an apprentice to a master carpenter and learned the craft and trade. He later worked in construction for five years, framing houses, but on weekends, he started doing renovations and remodeling for the richer families in Chiang Rai. It became lucrative enough to leave the construction business. He would never be wealthy, but he had more time with his family and still made a decent wage, so much so that he now owned a truck. His neighbors drove motorbikes and mopes into the city to work and, as of late, relied on him to carry larger items back to the neighborhood when needed.

They were only out there for ten minutes when Mary P came out and asked Greg if he would come inside and translate. The father and son followed him in.

The inside of the house looked like a carpenter lived there. It was modest, but the tables, chairs, and shelves, all simple in design, had been meticulously crafted. The young mother stood and bowed respectfully to Greg when introduced. Mary P waited for everyone to take a seat.

"Greg, she has gestational diabetes. She understands this and has been careful with her diet as directed. She is healthy, and all signs are that the baby is doing well. I am not sure she understands how important it is that I need to check her blood sugar regularly over this last trimester. We need her to come into the clinic on schedule."

Greg repeated Mary P's prescriptive advice.

The young father joined in immediately and said it would not be a problem. His truck would be back within a week. His father and brother had borrowed it, but once returned, he would make sure that she came into the city as required. They made an appointment and then invited Mary P and Greg to stay for a meal.

Greg did not wait for Mary P to answer but declined, saying he had much to do in Chiang Rai. The idyllic family scene had, for an unknown reason to Greg, agitated him. He started the truck, and as they headed back toward Chiang Rai, he watched the tiny neighborhood disappear in his rearview mirror. Could life be this simple and serene? Sure. But not for him. It was all too sedentary. Tranquil, yes, but boring. He preferred—no, *needed*—more. Needed all the distractions, even the disruptions—certainly not the most harmful ones, but all the chaos of life's unpredictability. Already, he felt the residuum of the frightful attack on the highway evaporating. Fading. A memory gaining distance. No different from hundreds of the other close calls we all have in life—stumbles, near falls, mishaps, wrong turns, and misadventures. Accidents amid the endless vicissitudes of life. Even friendships. The close calls that come with living life to its fullest. You can't hide and you can't divide your life into compartments. No calculated half-measures. You must throw everything into every game. Accept the risks. Accept that every roll of the dice is aleatory, and as Pancho said, it is the randomness that makes it exciting, the not-knowing.

As predicted, Mary P cautioned Greg about returning to Ban Su. Echoing the same arguments that he had made to her about too much physical exertion after her cracked ribs episode. In her heart, she knew that nothing she said was going to persuade him, and she said as much. But she also reminded Greg how she regretted not stopping Albie when he last returned there.

"I know I should not feel guilty, but I do. You were the one who said to me that if someone is driving on the wrong side of the road, we have a responsibility to stop them and alter their path. Are you listening to me?"

"I am, but I don't agree with you. I don't believe we are on the wrong side of the road. It is just the opposite. What we are doing is the right thing to do."

His tone was sharp, and for a moment, he worried he had hurt her feelings, then decided it didn't matter. Nothing was going to stop him. This would be his opportunity to make a difference. Finally, he was doing *something.* Not just watching. Not sitting on the sidelines. He was in the game and could impact the outcome. This was his chance, and if a truck running him off the road couldn't stop him, then what chance did words from Mary P have?

"I just don't know what it is you are hoping to find," she continued doing all that she could not to sound offended.

Greg knew better than to say *the truth,* so he did not answer, and they were both quiet.

"I talked with Mac last night," she said, resuming the dialogue. "After you fell asleep, he moved into the other bedroom. He was dismissive, too, not as adamant as you seem to be, but unconcerned. Did you know his mother was French Laotian?"

"I did."

"His father was a missionary, so you know we talked about that."

"What did Mac have to say?"

"Not much. He asked most of the questions and I did most of the talking."

"Surprise."

"Don't be mean."

"I am sorry. It is only that I had the impression that Mac wasn't the talkative sort. What type of questions did he ask you?"

Elliot taught the questions reveal as much about the person as the answers, but he doubted that Mary P decoded conversations in that manner.

"When I arrived here? How did I meet Albie? Those types of questions. Do you know I missed meeting Mac by only a month or two? He wrapped up his work with Albie just before I arrived in Chiang Rai. I told him about the type of work I do at the clinic."

"That's it? That is all you talked about?" Greg asked.

"He asked me why I was a nun?"

"What did you say?"

"I told him it was, for me, the best way to serve God. And then he said, *so you live this way for the love of God.* And I said, *yes. That is a wonderful way to say it.* And then he completely surprised me when he paraphrased Saint Augustine. *Everyone falls in love…it is only a question of what or whom one loves.*"

"Mac quoted Saint Augustine?" Greg asked incredulously.

"Mac said that when he was young, a day didn't go by that his father wasn't reciting to him one biblical passage or another. Quoting Old Testament prophets or New Testament evangelists. Philosophers and poets. Mystics and saints."

"I bet you loved that."

"I did, but then when I asked him more about his father, he said when he was away at college, his father was arrested and died in prison."

"Really?"

'Mac said that *one day, he spoke full-throated against all injustices. Consistently and publicly against racism, abortion, human trafficking, prostitution, addiction, and rampant materialism. All social, moral, and spiritual failings. They couldn't decide if my father was crazy or dangerous. In the end, it didn't matter.*"

CHAPTER SIXTY-FOUR

Despite dozens of trips up the mountain to Ban Su, Greg had never once come face to face with the *camoys* about whom everyone spoke. Perhaps the bandits saw the lone motorcyclist as a wasted effort, their experience teaching them that a single backpack had little value, or maybe they recognized him as a regular visitor, servicing the villagers or even the larger communities like Mae Salong, carrying mail, messages, even medicine like the nun.

Greg speculated about the reasons aloud as he drove, but Mac had little interest in the hypotheticals.

"My guess is that they will recognize the truck as the nun's and stop us, knowing she brings them food, drink, and even medicine," Mac said. "It is not a good look, no matter how you characterize it. I am not a fan of thieves. And Sister Mary Holy Water is playing with fire."

"Mary Peyton. Her name is Mary Peyton," said Greg icily.

"Yea."

"Peyton is Gaelic for Patrick. Did you know that?" Greg continued, driving home his connection and even fondness for Mary P.

"No. Hey, I am sorry if I insulted you or her in her absence. My bad. She is a nice person. No doubt about that. A good medic, too. Put us both back together. I am even using the sling, which she suggested. And the wrap on your hand looks tight. No excessive bandage. Let's just drop it."

"Ok. Thank you."

Sunlight rose above the hills, casting a glare on the windshield, and both men put on their sunglasses. They passed the first cut-off to the right, which led to the hill tribe communities popular with tourists for the hand-crafted clothing and crafts sold by the villagers. The track was wide and firm up to this point, and the vans carrying *farangs* easily managed this section of the climb.

After the split, the road upwards toward Mae Salong and Ban Su became narrower with sharper, twisting turns and steep inclines. The truck labored a bit as Greg shifted gears and items in the truck bed jostled and shifted.

Mac began outlining their first steps. His voice was steady and serious. He wanted to start at the Research Station and check the accuracy of the map provided by Rafferty around that section. Establish the credibility of the most basic and well-known intel. Something about the detail bothered him, but he couldn't put his finger on it.

"After that, we should head over to Ban Su and talk with T'ang. We do that together in the beginning, but if he is not forthcoming, then I want you to excuse yourself and leave me alone with him."

"You will not hurt him, will you?"

"For God's sake, no. Trust me, we aren't here to hurt anyone. We get nothing by harming any of the villagers…"

Mac was still talking when Greg made a sharp left turn on a flat area and came upon the much-discussed *camoys.*

A more hapless bunch of hoodlums would have been difficult to find. The shabby group of four men standing astride a large tree limb, which they had placed across the road, formed the pitiable phalanx. One old, gray man, so aged, he supported his worn-down self with a long stick, stood next to a teenage boy clothed in a dirty, white, sleeveless shirt and weathered jeans with holes in both knees. The pock-faced boy, lanky and skinny as the stick which held up the old man, could not have been over fifteen or sixteen years old. The kid held what looked like a rusty hammer in his hand.

The man standing directly in front of the truck was the alpha dog, brandishing a rifle, held in a faux military posture across his chest. Greg guessed mid-thirties, with bloodshot eyes and wild sprouts of facial hair on his chin and upper lip, complementing his long, greasy, black hair. Shirt and pants dirt brown, more from dirt than dye.

The final gang member, dressed in a faded flowered shirt, approached the driver's side of the truck. He smiled widely, if not perversely, revealing more missing teeth than not. Declaring himself the spokesperson for the group, he pretended to greet Greg with deference and respect, using a combination of English words and hand signals beckoning him to exit the truck. He, too, displayed a weapon. A machete.

As Greg opened the truck door, he heard Mac murmur *play nicely.*

Thinking about it all in hindsight, Greg wondered if he should have ever said anything in Thai. Would it all have gone differently had he feigned ignorance? Passed over the whisky, rice, and cigarettes and been done with it. Instead, he broke the first rule Elliot had ever taught him. *Talk as little as possible.*

He chatted with the machete man like they were old friends. Told him how the good nun was his friend and had helped him pack the food and drink just for these good fellows. Told him he traveled this way often to see his friends in Ban Su, lying about the number of people he knew in Mae Salong. He asked how many jugs of water they would like, even as he lugged the containers from the truck and set them on the ground behind the vehicle. Later, he realized how nervous he was and understood that no amount of charm or goodwill could offset the terror of the blade and rifle.

Just the same, he thought they were home free after the last bottles of whisky had been set on the ground. That is until the machete man nudged Greg on the shoulder with his free hand and, flaunting the machete, pointed it towards the rear of the truck bed.

"What is in the large case?" he asked.

"Nothing," said Greg stupidly.

"Nothing?" asked the overly inquisitive and ever so perceptive spokesperson. "Why have a big case and nothing in it? Let's have a look."

"I gave you rice, water, whisky, and American cigarettes. Let's call it a day. Most people would say thank you after receiving such a bounty."

The alpha dog was the one who spoke next. He adjusted his rifle from his modeling pose and directed it at Greg.

"Open the case," he said. "Do as the man says."

It was then that Mac opened his door, and with a great, slow flourish eased out of the truck, demonstrating to all his wounded arm in the sling. He closed his door and looked past Alpha to the old man.

"Khun Pa," he said. "We have been generous and gracious. My friend has been kind and polite, has he not?"

The old man, surprised to be addressed with such respect, nodded in agreement.

"Ask your sons to please move the log, take the gifts, and let us proceed," said Mac meekly in a voice as courteous as he could.

Alpha would have none of it. He was suddenly enraged.

"Shut up, you black cripple, you," he growled. "The old man is not my father, and no one like you will decide what happens."

He then raised the rifle and pointed it straight at Greg.

"Open the case. Now!"

No one, least of all Alpha, saw what happened next. But all—except Alpha—heard the three loud shots. Three to center mass. Textbook. And Alpha dropped his rifle and slumped to the ground, dead.

"Robber," Mac was calling him through the echo, speaking now in English. "Robber, listen to me. Take two steps away from your new friend. Slowly, but move now."

In a trance, Greg did as he was told, and now watched as Mac pointed his gun towards the machete man.

"Drop the sword," Mac ordered.

Machete man didn't move. Either he was frozen in shock or else contemplating his next move.

"Drop it or die. I won't say it again."

The machete fell to the ground.

"Move," Mac said to him. "Move over by the other two. Let's go."

Machete man hurried toward his compatriots.

"The simplest thing would be to kill all three of you right now," Mac said. "There isn't a soul in the world who cares whether you live or die. No one will even know you are dead because no one even knows you are alive. Living like animals, preying on innocents."

Greg could see the fear in all three bandits. The young boy was crying. He had dropped his hammer and his hands were crossed and shaking across his lower belly near his crotch.

"Move the tree limb and throw it over the ledge."

The old man could barely stand. He was shaking uncontrollably, but he stepped back, and the two others did as commanded.

"Now go over there and lie down. All of you. Face down." And turning to Greg, Mac told him to throw the rifle and machete over the ledge and then get back into the truck.

Everyone did as directed.

Mac walked over to where the three men were positioned on the ground. Greg was certain that this was how executions took place.

"If I ever see you again on this road, if I ever hear from anyone, anytime about you animals robbing, harassing, even talking to anyone ever again, I will hunt you down and kill you. Do you understand?"

All three nodded, rubbing their faces in the dirt.

"Go somewhere far away from here. So far, I can never find you. Leave these hills. Leave this province. Leave this country if needed, but don't ever let me find you near here again. Do you understand?"

The three were still nodding as Mac got into the truck.

"Drive."

Greg started forward as ordered and tried to avoid running over the dead body, but from the crunch of the tires, he believed he ran over at least one leg of the dead man. Greg's hands were shaking on the steering wheel, and he gripped the wheel as tight as he could to stop his trembling. He had never seen a killing before. Never seen someone shot at close range. Never seen someone die as Alpha did. He didn't know what to think. It had happened so fast. One minute the man was alive and then he wasn't.

"Drink some water," Mac said as he handed him the canteen. "First time. It's always a shock. No one points a gun at someone unless they are prepared to use it. Are you ok?"

Greg didn't answer.

"Are you ok?" Mac repeated, raising his voice.

Greg looked at him and nodded. He could barely swallow the water, let alone talk, so he drove in silence. His gaze fixed firmly on the winding road. His heart and mind were racing. Wordless damnations. Not at Mac, but at the absurdity of the altercation. His inner voice kept screaming *stupid, stupid* at himself. He replayed the scene and wondered if Alpha's racist insult was the provocation that sealed his doom.

He did not know how long he scowled at the windshield, but eventually, he relaxed his furrowed brow, turned his head, and looked again at Mac. Like Alpha, Greg never saw the gun. One minute they were talking and the next…Mac had surreptitiously removed the gun from the sling of all places and acted precisely as he said he would, and as Greg should under such circumstances.

It was that realization that shook Greg from his regret and whimpering. Alpha could have shot Greg just as easily as Mac shot Alpha. They could have left Greg for dead in the same spot. Why not? One more word from Greg. One more refusal to open the case…no telling if Alpha would have pulled the trigger.

"What the hell were those guys thinking?" Greg declared more than asked.

"They didn't know," Mac replied. "And they didn't know that they didn't know."

"You're right. So much for playing nice."

"Hey man, we tried. You did an excellent job. Talked politely and kept them at ease. Gave them everything as planned. Greed destroys you every time. The vice of violence."

He was right, Greg thought. Avarice. Avarice and pride. The missionary's son could likely name all seven of the deadly sins. But the question formulating in the back of Greg's mind was not the list, but whether this angel of death was finished wielding retribution or had the killer angel just started.

CHAPTER SIXTY-FIVE

Mac lit a cigar and remained in his thoughts as the drive continued. Albie liked an occasional cigar, Greg remembered. He would light one when they were in these mountains together. He said the smoke chased away the mosquitoes. Elliot joked he disliked cigar smokers. *Difficult to know what they are think*ing. It was Greg who broke the silence.

"Does it ever bother you? Killing someone?"

Mac didn't turn. He kept staring at the hillsides growing ever more rugged as they climbed toward the Research Station.

"No," he finally said. "You don't fight evil with tolerance and understanding. Besides, it's a good feeling to shoot a bad guy. America was founded on shooting bad guys. The biggest mistake civilians make is to confuse *the war* with *the warrior*."

Greg slowed the truck as they crossed a dangerous section of the road pitched beside deep ravines. *Is that what this was? A war?* Greg's grip tightened on the steering wheel, guessing that this was Mac's attempt at encouragement. His pep talk for the challenges ahead.

***

They unloaded the truck and carried the bags and the wooden crate into the abandoned Research Station. Mac struggled a bit with his damaged arm but shifted sufficient weight and balance to his good one so that it wasn't an issue. Greg commented and marveled that the local hill tribe people never once vandalized, damaged, or removed anything from the building. Mac was not interested.

Mac directed his efforts to opening and unloading the crate. The extraneous cover items remained at the clinic with the second crate. He first removed an army-issued green blanket from the top and then laid the weaponry methodically on the same blanket. Two M-16 rifles, each wrapped carefully in its own blanket, and cardboard cases of ammo for the rifles. Two more .45 caliber handguns, both Colt 1991 and identical to the one Mac had carried in his sling and used only an hour ago and now safely tucked in his belt against his lower back. Mac unwrapped the towels from the handguns and set them next to their extra ammo clips. Two long knives in leather sheeves were next, followed by a wooden box, which he opened to reveal a half dozen hand grenades inside. Then a metal case with cleaning supplies for the weapons. Binoculars. A long stretch of rope. Extra canteens for water. Two sleeveless vests with extra pockets for ammo. And finally, a large, green rucksack, not unlike the one Mac had been carrying with him since he first arrived in Chiang Mai.

"Some guys moaned that the M-16 jammed, but I never had a problem. These are not long-range rifles. A hundred meters max, understand? Closer is always better. Let's start with the basics, and then we can fire a few rounds and see if you can hit the side of the mountain."

***

T'ang and Arthit sat on small wooden stools outside the huts, smoking cheroots and sharpening their tools. T'ang had cut his hand and was trying to file with just one hand, holding the hoe between his knees. Both men recognized Mac immediately and stood to greet him. After the customary bowing, they all hugged like old friends. Greg took T'ang aside and re-bandaged his wound, explaining that he had a similar gash and, fortunately, had extra gauze, tape, and ointment. Recommending a precautionary tetanus shot was laughable. He might just as well have suggested a dental cleaning or a vision exam.

Mac, meanwhile, placed his rifle and both rucksacks on the ground and sat on T'ang's stool next to Arthit. He showed him the two maps Rafferty had provided. Greg learned as they walked over to Ban Su that it was Arthit, along with Nok, who guided Mac and Albie when they first surveyed the area years ago. Arthit had walked an untold number of miles in every direction during his life here, and he shared his knowledge with Albie and Mac to help them. He detailed where the borders *might* be, or where the Thai National Army *believed* them to be, and it was Arthit and Nok who kept them at a safe distance from Burmese drug lords like Zhang Qitu. Ironically, it was Mac who one day saved Arthit's life. The two were making their way back to Ban Su as night was falling and a tiger crossed their path. Mac shot and killed the tiger as he raced toward them both. Arthit stills wears a tiger tooth on a leather string around his neck for good luck.

Arthit looked at the first drawing around the Research Station and commented immediately that it was accurate but incomplete.

"What do you mean?" asked Mac.

"There are more paths now than when you first came here years ago. They are very narrow and thick with brush. Here, look at the area north of the station and on the far side of the orchard. Your drawing has nothing, but that is exactly the route that we used to transfer the opium to the General. It is a long way through the jungle but goes to the road Xu built to cross eastward in Burma with his troops. And here," he said, pointing to another area on the drawing, "are two more routes that we used to cross over to a hillside where we grow. It is a long way from the village, but the mountainside there is fertile. These are all footpaths. Narrow trails."

T'ang sat in silence, listening to Arthit, but Greg interrupted the narrative.

"Did Albie go in that direction?"

"I don't know why he would," said Arthit. "There is nothing there but jungle and a path to Burma and the General."

Mac took out the second drawing with the two routes that Rafferty's intel suggested Albie used, but Arthit dismissed them as well.

"They go across the border, in that direction," he said and pointed over the hut, "but only to another hillside. We tried to grow there on two occasions, but the ground was far too rocky. Not enough area for even small plots. Just rocky hills for miles."

"It doesn't make sense," Greg said.

Mac, using his good arm, rubbed his hand across his shaved head and then settled his chin into the palm of that same hand. He looked across to his right at the silent T'ang who had been sitting on the ground next to Greg and then looked back at Arthit.

"Arthit, my friend. I need to talk with T'ang alone."

"No," said Arthit. "He is fragile. Talk to me."

"No," said Mac. "Because you will lie to save your family. You always do the right thing. Take Robber and go for a walk."

Arthit sat up as straight as he could. His taut muscles and leathery skin from decades-long in the hills stiffened his resolve, and he refused yet again.

"All right," said Mac. "We do it your way. Who bought your last harvest?"

"I can't tell you," Arthit replied.

"How large was your last harvest?"

"I don't remember."

"How much did they pay per kilo?"

"I don't know."

"Did they have horses or mules?"

Arthit shook his head, refusing to be anything but circumspect.

"Good. Now we have that out of the way," said Mac. "No need to waste more time with the inane."

Arthit looked confused, and T'ang even more so. Greg the most.

"I don't care about any of that," said Mac. "We don't care who, how much, or where. No one ever asks why. You have your arrangements. You are a loyal business partner. A good friend, even. So, everyone can relax. Business as usual. You can tell your partners that you revealed nothing. Everyone is safe. Promises kept."

It was then that Mac pulled over the second rucksack, the one which had been in the crate. He opened it and removed the Colt from it. Greg held his breath. Mac had promised not to hurt anyone. Mac then pushed the rucksack past Greg and in front of T'ang. Arthit started to talk, but Mac held up in hand, silencing him.

"Look," said Mac to T'ang. "Look inside at the contents."

T'ang didn't move but looked at Arthit, who soon nodded his consent. T'ang opened the sack fully.

Greg could see as easily as T'ang that Mac stuffed the rucksack with money. Thai baht. Thousands of dollars' worth of Thai baht.

Mac tipped the bag so Arthit could see.

"There is more money in that bag than twenty times your last harvest. More there than you have ever had at one time in your life. It is yours. All of it. You will spend all night counting it."

T'ang and Arthit looked at each other. T'ang's sad eyes kept his promise to Arthit not to say a word.

Mac let it settle for a full minute. He reached into his pocket and pulled out a cigar. Offered one to T'ang and Arthit, who shook their heads declining, and then lit it.

"I want to know one thing, and that is it. One question. One answer. You keep the money and Robber and I go and never come back."

Everyone waited as he puffed yet again on his cigar.

"Albie came here and then walked back toward his Research Station. Those were T'ang's exact words to Robber. The last time T'ang saw him, *he was walking back toward his building*. But he never went to the

Research Station, did he? He crossed over to Burma. And you know where. These maps are shams. I am guessing you might have even been the one who drew them. But it doesn't matter. I don't care. Tell me where he crossed, and we leave, and no one ever knows that you told us. You keep this money."

It was Arthit now, rubbing his hand across his head and through his thick, black hair, and everyone sitting in complete silence. Greg was mystified but knew better than to be the first to speak. Mac tugged at his cigar and waited. Greg figured Mac could wait all day. This is what poker was all about. He finally understood. The next bet belonged to T'ang and Arthit.

They waited and waited, and then Greg figured it out. It was so obvious. It was quintessential Albie. Every part.

"Albie!" Greg shouted his name. "Albie made you promise not to tell anyone, didn't he? Albie was always making others promise one thing or another. Nok. Mary P. Me."

Arthit shrugged his shoulders, but Greg was on a roll.

"He paid you, too! Of course, he did. *If you can't solve a problem, throw money at it.* But…but…there's more, isn't there? He promised you more, even more than all this. Said he would bring you more money. Just be quiet. Keep a secret."

Mac was nodding his head, almost smiling. He would take it from here. He could make promises, too. Greg, for the first time, had connected the dots. Elliot would have been proud.

CHAPTER SIXTY-SIX

"What I don't understand is why or even who created the false narrative for Rafferty's report?" Greg said as they trudged along through thick brush.

"Shhh," said Mac in a hushed voice. "Look. Horse shit. Still warm, too. Listen to me. None of that is our concern right now. Understand. We need to stay focused on the present moment. Keep your mouth shut and your eyes open."

They had crossed over into Burma and the eastern Shan state almost immediately after they cleared one of T'ang's old opium fields. Without Arthit's help, they would never have found the trail. For the first hour, they climbed easily up two hills on the other side of the harvested plot, walking along dry creek beds that ran between two towering peaks before coming to a deep swell and the onset of thick jungle. A rugged, dense forest of bamboo and teak. A second path from the north merged with theirs at this point. The trail into the jungle was obvious only because of the recent traffic. Someone had hacked the encroaching vegetation just enough to make passage sufficiently wide for Greg and Mac to walk single file. Flies buzzed near the random dung piles, and they stepped around them carefully. Each stride now taking on a new sense of danger.

Arthit knew whom they were hunting for but reminded Mac and Greg that they would enter the eastern part of the Shan State, where the notorious drug lord Zhang Qitu and his growing faction of rebels operated with impunity. It was a land of guns and mayhem. No villages. No opium fields. No innocents. General Xu had long been offering the ruthless Zhang Qitu and his gang of resistance fighters support in their insurgency against the Burmese government and the infamously brutal Burmese National Army. Xu gave Zhang Qitu free rein over the illicit opium trafficking in this eastern part of the Shan state, leaving the northeast section for Xu. Arthit's parting advice to Mac and Greg was *don't cross the river.*

Mac led, carrying his stuffed backpack, his rifle, and the rope. Greg had only the extra water canteens and his weapons. Back at the Research Station, Mac had instructed Greg on how to walk with his weapon, carrying it over his back shoulder or in a ready position across his chest with his hands fixed in the correct position. Both men stepped watchfully now with the rifles in that latter position. Greg's heart raced as soon as they entered the dark, damp vegetation, and his mouth was exceedingly dry in anxious anticipation. His eyes remained fixed on the back of Mac's head while watching for any hand signal Mac might give.

They marched for more than an hour in the thick forest, climbing and descending more frequently than Greg could imagine possible. It was amazing how quickly the jungle swallowed them up. The forest blocking out much of the sky and turning the light green. Greg had never been claustrophobic, but the endlessness of this wilderness was distressing him. He finally tapped Mac's shoulder. He needed to pause and have a drink of water. Greg handed the second canteen to Mac.

"Are you ok?" Mac asked.

"Sure. Just needed a drink. What do you think?"

"At least two horses, most likely three. And two men, for sure. You can see the footprints. No one is in a hurry. The stride lengths are all shorter than ours. I am thinking they are tired."

"More than one trip through here?"

"Exactly. Collecting their bounty from Ban Su and the other villages. Are you certain that you are all right?"

"A walk in the park."

"Let's push on."

Greg's mind wandered over the next hour as they trudged along with no break in the density of the verdant flora. Nettlesome branches scratched at his arms and face. A steady incline of the trail made each step now more difficult than the last. Greg was breathing hard and remembering how easy it seemed when he walked in the open hills of other villages. *He was younger then,* he said to himself wryly. Sweat dripped across his forehead and nose. His back was damp. Reluctant to change his grip on the rifle, he wiped away what he could on his face with his forearm. Mac's pace never altered. It was painstakingly vigilant. Measured. Dogged. Strangely, Greg thought of Heather. His very first love. What would she think if she saw him now? She had called him erratic. His restlessness made him unpredictable. They were so naïve. He certainly was. A faithless woman. Why are there things we never forget, and worse, never forgive? They would never have made it. It was only a matter of time. They had lost all calmness in each other's company. The most banal conversations went sideways. What held them together for so long was that they lived apart. The absence created the mystery. But now all the mysteries and the varieties of human desires were being suffocated in this wilderness. The most beautiful women in the world would decay here. And he was slowly rotting to death with them. Everyone was. Except for Mac. Mac was implacable. Inured to conflict. Hardened to pain.

Greg stumbled forward but caught himself without embarrassment. Thankfully, Mac did not see his weakness. His fatigue.

"Son of a bitch!" Mac growled as he put up the stop sign with his hand.

"What is it?" inquired Greg.

"Walk back slowly, Robber. Slowly."

Mac did the same.

"What is it?" Greg repeated.

"A cobra. A king cobra. Right in the middle of the frigging path."

Greg strained to look around Mac and over his shoulder. The coiled, venomous reptile was not poised to strike but raised its head when it heard them.

"What are we going to do?"

Mac took out his .45 caliber handgun.

"Can we risk a single shot?" asked Greg.

"No. We just wait it out. We are out of range from him. He shouldn't perceive us as a threat."

Both men kept their eyes fixed on the snake and Mac held his gun ready, just in case. He told Greg that snakes are more frightened than we are, but Greg refused to believe that. He wanted to run in the other direction. Five minutes passed, and the snake slipped into the undergrowth to their left.

"Now what?" asked Greg.

"We wait five or ten minutes and then start again."

"How do we know it is deep enough into the brush?"

"We don't."

Mac picked up a rock about the size of a baseball and handed it to Greg.

"You can throw it into the trees if you think that will scare him farther away."

Greg threw his best fastball into the area where the snake disappeared.

"Feel better? Still think this is a walk in the park?"

Greg was certain Mac picked up the pace as they passed the cobra's location, and shortly after that, the path descended steeply, so much so that Mac commented on the horses and the footprints of their associates, speculating that they stopped the tired animals more than once to keep them under control.

It also became obvious that the jungle was ending, and more daylight was ahead of them, but as they approached the last steps into an opening, Mac put up his stop-sign hand yet again.

"Not good." And another, "Son of a bitch."

Stretching out in front of them was a wide, flat, open area, patchy with occasional bushes. A landscape covered with rocks and boulders, which was not an issue. The problem was that across this rock-filled plateau was another rocky hill, also clear of vegetation.

"What's the issue?" Greg asked.

"Look," said Mac.

"I don't see anything, but rocks scattered around."

"And past the rocks?"

"A hill. A side of a mountain. Not much different from any other hill that we've already climbed."

"And if someone is on top of that hill over there…"

Greg finished Mac's sentence.

"Then they could spot us immediately."

"We must wait until it is dark. I have to believe we are getting close. We can't chance crossing that opening in the daylight."

Greg sighed and sat on the ground.

Mac took out his binoculars. He scanned the range in front of them. He told Greg that they would wait until it was dark and then make their way along a route to their right.

"We can climb over there just as easily as the path in front of us. Keep us from bumping into anyone unexpectedly. Look with the glasses, so you know what we are in for."

Mac was right, of course. Going up where he showed didn't look much different from any other way over this barren mountainside. The slope was the same.

"It looks rockier," said Greg, handing the binoculars back to Mac.

"Not a bad thing," answered Mac. "More cover, just in case."

With two or three hours to kill, Mac suggested they remain in the forest's shadow and catch their breath. Walking across this plateau in the dark, and then climbing on uneven ground and navigating around the boulders will be dangerous and tiring. Greg tried to relax on the ground, but the thought of the cobra kept him on edge, and he never stopped looking around.

Mac said that they needed to keep an ear out for anyone approaching from behind, and while saying as much, decided on an alarm system.

"Sit tight. I will be right back."

"Where are you going?"

"Just sit."

He left and retraced their steps into the jungle. He was only gone ten minutes at the most.

"What did you do?"

"Placed broken limbs and debris across the path. Enough for us to hear someone kicking them aside. It's not much but will give us an edge."

Greg's nervousness did not abate with thoughts of a firefight on this trail. He sat with his rifle across his lap, wondering what he would do if others approached from behind. Would we open fire on them?

"Did you ever do anything like this with Albie?" Greg asked, unable to control the anxiety in his voice.

"Hell no. Are you kidding? We wandered for sure, but mostly from one village to another."

"What did you think of him? Albie. What was your opinion?" Greg pressed, seeking a calming voice as much as learning Mac's view.

"In the beginning, I thought he reeked of inherited wealth and reveled in his eccentricities, but I came to believe that he genuinely cared about his project. On one of our earliest recons, we were in a Meo village, but it could have been Yao or Kachin or any other tribe as they all do the same thing with the land. The men spent weeks cutting down the trees, all the forestry, and any jungle woodland, slashing smaller growths with ancient handmade axes. Albie watched—heartbroken, I thought. He talked about atmospheric conditions and global warming as if this speck on the earth made all the difference.

"And then one day, at the end of the dry season, we were down in a swell below a rocky hillside covered with all these fallen trees and brush, which by now were as dry as could be. Ideal kindling, to be sure. And we watched as the younger tribe members raced down the mountainside, tossing torches into the dried timber. Clouds of smoke billowed skyward as the fire cascaded down the hill. It was majestic, to be honest, and I thought Albie would cry. He gathered himself, and like the scientist he was, explained that the wood ash would eventually cool and nourish the soil and trap the moisture beneath the fire-hardened surface. After that, it was planting season.

"He was shrewd. As we spent more time together, I realized he was lonely, and I wondered if he was trying to save the world or find a friend."

"Was that you? The friend."

"No. Not even close. But I came to respect him and like him. He was tougher than I thought. The one thing that surprised me the most was that he never complained. Never bitched. I respected that."

Unlike me, Greg said to himself.

***

They crept in the dark across the flat, ossified landscape. A cloudless sky and gibbous moon provided helpful light. Neither man commented on the stunning starscape. Mac was pleased not to have a full moon tracking them. The climbing, however, proved difficult, and both men tired quickly.

"We are trying to go straight up. We need to crisscross more," explained Mac. "Work laterally as much as vertically."

"I agree," said Greg. "Let's take a break, just the same." His aching hip from the crash on Highway 1 had him compensating with his other leg and now his left knee was barking at him.

"No problem. We have time. We are only going to wait once we get to the top."

It irritated Greg to be a wimp, but he knew they would both be in trouble if he fell lame, so the rests were a precaution he knew they had to take. Mac's resilience astonished Greg. The man was unflagging.

When they finally reached the summit, Greg collapsed in a heap. Any reservation he had about sleeping was gone. Mac told him he would take the first shift and wake Greg in four or five hours. Mac tossed Greg a blanket from his bag as he, too, finally sat down.

***

Daylight, the rock-hard ground, and the morning chill, not Mac, stirred Greg from his sleep. His body ached all over. He sat up slowly and discovered Mac was not in sight, but his rucksack was there, so he figured he couldn't have gone far. He struggled to his feet, stretching slowly, trying to work out the stiffness. He looked around again for Mac and then headed behind nearby boulders to relieve himself.

Mac reappeared ten minutes later.

"I thought you were going to wake me after the first shift," Greg said.

"You were out cold, and it would have only been another couple of hours, so I popped two bennies and did some recon in the pre-dawn light."

"Amphetamines?"

"Yea. Benzedrine. Not the same kick as Dexedrine, but it works. You gotta do what you gotta do. Come, look at this. You can walk now, but then we will have to get down."

They crawled to the edge of the cliff, remaining partially shielded by a large boulder, and peered down from this high vantage point at a magnificent vista. A winding, brown river twisted and sliced through a narrow gorge amid the steep mountains. Mac handed Greg the binoculars, telling him to look right below them. A wide clearing near the edge of the deep ravine was home to a campground with three tents, a lean-to shed protecting bags and plastic jugs of chemicals—most likely the lime fertilizer and the concentrated ammonia—and at least six, large drums, no doubt to cook the opium. Mac said the two other large mounds looked like raw opium and bagged morphine. Two men were sitting around a small fire and a third man was tending to five horses on the far side of the clearing.

Mac said it was a northern tributary of the Salween River. Further south, the river formed the Thai-Burmese border, but up here it runs through the rebellious Shan state. No authority from Burma or Thailand comes here.

"It's brilliant when you think about it," Mac said. "Zhang Qitu and his army on the other side of the river. Who knows how mountainous and impassable that area is? The treacherous ridge drops straight down into the gorge, providing added protection from that side. And this side of the river is equally desolate, so Xu has no interest in traversing here. Genius."

"It's Fat Boy," said Greg, surprising himself with what should have been obvious. "Here, look."

"Yep. Sure is. Dumbo has gained weight since the last time I saw him. He is leaving. He is taking one horse and heading back. Likely making one of the final opium collections from a village or two."

"I didn't know you knew him by sight. When did you last see Fat Boy?" Greg asked.

"Years ago. When Wireless and I were with Albie. Wireless and I went to Fat Man's casino. Albie, too. Wireless called it a scouting trip. Wireless went to every gaming house in every city, regardless of size. He used to joke that Bangkok had more casinos than spirit houses."

"Pancho was with you up here?" Greg asked, discovering more with each conversation.

"He wasn't. It would have been too much for him. He waited for us in Chiang Rai. After a day or two, we would come down from the hills and we would give him a list of things we needed or wanted from Chiang Mai. Albie wasn't built for long stays in the mountains. We would take a night to recover, and get something decent to eat, and when we went back up, Wireless would run down to Chiang Mai to collect the supplies and have them ready for us when next we came down. He put more miles on Albie's jeep than Albie ever did."

Mac looked back at Fat Boy climbing the hill.

"He is hurrying. It isn't that strenuous of a trip if you weren't walking on eggshells like we were. He looks like an idiot with that Manchurian queue hair. A rat's tail. It suits him. You know, his real name is Shu, but the pronunciation and even the Chinese character are close to the word *rat*. Dumbo and Jumbo. That was my take on him and his old man. Come with me. Stay low. I want to show you something else."

They crawled on all fours around the rocks to another ledge that blocked their view of the opium kitchen but gave them a better angle to scrutinize the ravine and the side of the mountain leading up to the kitchen.

"It was foggy early this morning when I was looking, but you can see the river now."

Again, they traded the binoculars.

"Look as close to the river's edge as you can," Mac explained.

"Boats," said Greg. "Five of them. Longboats, like the one next to yours in Pattaya. There are two men dressed in light-colored clothing sitting on the boats. They are smoking. They have something hanging down around their necks."

"Gas masks," said Mac. "The fumes during the process are so toxic that they could knock out an elephant. Now look even closer past the edge of the hill. Right where the jungle starts."

"I don't see anything but jungle," answered Greg.

"Let me have the glasses."

Mac surveyed the situation again and gave the lenses back to Greg.

"Look a hundred meters downriver from the boats and then look thirty to forty more into the jungle. See the roof."

He did. It was a building. Hidden in the jungle but only a stone's throw from the water.

"What is it, do you think?"

"A lab. It must be. Sophisticated has advantages, but rudimentary is sufficient. Fat Boy cooks the opium on the ridge. His goons transfer the morphine down the hill. It's tricky because it is so steep, but once there, the techs in the lab go to work. The best process requires at least three techs, and in about twenty-four hours, they can produce twenty pounds of pure heroin. They take their time. They must be precise because it is hazardous. The key is temperature control. One mistake and the lab will explode. Meanwhile, his boys load up the bags of chemicals that Fat Boy needs for the kitchen, and they climb back up. Wash, rinse, and repeat. Once they finish, they load up all the smack on the boats and down the river they go."

"Where?"

"Who knows? Mae Hong Son is my guess, but there must be dozens of options for them."

"Well, I guess that's it. We head back."

"Head back?" replied Mac, laughing scornfully.

"We aren't going to find Albie down there with them," said Greg.

"We might find his body," Mac said grimly.

"What are we going to do?" Greg asked yet again.

"I am not sure yet." He was looking through the binoculars.

"Got 'em!" Mac exclaimed. "Three more men. They have three more horses and are climbing back up. It is steep, that's for sure.

"Look again. Look another one hundred or two hundred meters even farther down the river, past the lab, and you will see openings in the jungle's roof. Watch. They will pass by."

Mac was dead on. Three more men, carrying rifles slung over their shoulders and three horses packed with bags. The chemicals needed for the kitchen.

"Here is what I think we do," Mac began. And all Greg could think about was Pancho's prophecy while sitting in the American Bar. *Mac will walk into hell.*

CHAPTER SIXTY-SEVEN

Mac would have preferred the cover of darkness, but the window of opportunity called for immediate action. The same perch that afforded them the view of the lab near the river, the beached boats, and parts of the steep trail that led up from the heroin lab to the kitchen, also shielded them from the view of the two men still working in the kitchen clearing. Mac and Greg climbed down the craggy slope to a ledge halfway to the flat, where Mac affixed the rope around what he hoped was a sufficiently heavy and secure rock. Greg, despite his wounded hand, provided an additional anchor, and Mac, grimacing as he struggled to keep his grip with his dislocated shoulder, kept his damaged arm low and close to his chest as he rappelled to the ground.

From there, his plan was simple enough. Dispatch the two in the kitchen, ambush the three on the trail, and blow up the lab. What could possibly go wrong?

Greg was to sit tight and wait for a signal until the kitchen was secured. If anything went sideways, then he was in Mac's words, *to get the hell out.* Greg climbed back up the slope, and returning to their first vantage point, repositioned himself on his stomach and chest, and watched the scene with binoculars. Mac said that for this to work, he couldn't use a gun. It had to be done with the knife. Otherwise, he had little chance of surprising the other three. The shroud of darkness would have been an immense help, as would some good luck.

The two men, assiduous worker bees, were connected by the hip in everything that they were doing. Smoking by their tents, shifting heavy bags of fertilizer and jugs of ammonia solution from the covered lean-to closer to the drums and fire pits, as well as prepping the fire pits themselves with new kindling and logs. It must have taken them days if not weeks to cut down as many trees as they did to form this clearing, as well as to cut the trees themselves into manageable sprags. Backbreaking work with axes and saws. These were hard workers, Greg thought with a hint of admiration. As were the three smugglers hiking up the steep mountainside.

Greg wondered if Mac would try to close ground by using the remaining trees and the large boulders as cover but realized what he needed was a diversion. Something to separate the two workers, isolate them, and not drive them to their weapons. An element of surprise would help too. His damaged arm would handicap him in any hand-to-hand combat, so maybe Mac changes the plan and just comes out shooting.

Greg felt helpless. He was frightened, but this felt like being sidelined, and that irritated him. There must be something he could do.

Finally, one worker headed away from the fire pits and walked over to the tents on the far side. Greg could not see where Number One went, but he was heading toward Mac. Greg repositioned himself and found a clear line of vision and a view of the tents. He wished he hadn't. Number One entered his tent and when he stepped out of it, Mac grabbed him from behind, covered the target's mouth with one hand, and with his injured arm, drove the knife blade into his lower back. Number One slumped backward immediately, and Mac pulled the body away from the tent and made sure he was dead.

Greg shifted spots and went back to watching Number Two work near the fire pit. Five minutes, ten minutes passed, and Number Two began looking around for his associate. He called out to him once and, hearing nothing, called again. The silence drove him to his rifle. Slowly, he marched below Greg's vision across the clearing toward the tents. Greg slid over to his view of the tents. Mac must have pretended to be Number One, imitating him with a muffled voice and calling from inside the tent, which prompted Number Two to lower his rifle and enter. Greg could only imagine what had transpired.

***

After receiving Mac's signal, Greg gathered his and Mac's things and traversed across the top ridge to the same worn path that Fat Boy had recently used. From there, it was an easy descent down a winding trail to the kitchen clearing.

"Have a look around," Mac told Greg. "Toss any weapons you find over the ledge down toward the river. Same with any ammo. Scatter that over the ridge."

"What are you going to do?"

"I want to get down that steep trail and find an advantageous location."

"To ambush them?" Greg asked.

"Yes. Unless you think they will just surrender if I ask them nicely."

Greg remained quiet. Mac's cold indifference to taking more human lives was unsettling. And yet, this is why they were here.

"And then what?" Greg asked.

"If it goes well, then more of the same at the lab."

Mac looked through his backpack and removed two of the six hand grenades and gave them to Greg.

"Here, hang on to these," he said. "The lab is combustible. A well-placed grenade should send the entire place up in smoke. I don't know how much protection those techs have. I didn't see any extra guards, but someone with a weapon must be down there, too. Now listen, take fifteen to twenty minutes to clean this area up and then I want you to position yourself over here by this tree. Come here, I will show you."

They walked over to a large tree that gave cover to Greg against anyone coming up the trail. Greg set the hand grenades and his rifle on the ground next to the tree.

"You stay here and wait for the gunfire. If it goes as I hope, I will signal you with two double rounds," Mac explained.

"Double rounds?"

"Bang, bang. A pause. Bang, bang."

"Got it."

"That means I am heading down to the lab. If you hear any other combination or don't hear the signal, then take those two grenades and toss them down the path. That should knock out enough trees to keep anyone else from getting through too quickly and give you additional time to get out of here."

"I should go too," Greg interjected. "It is better odds. Two against three."

"No. I can manage this better alone. You stay here."

"You are spending too much time protecting me. We are supposed to be a team. Help each other."

Greg knew in his heart that Mac never thought of them as a team. He was Greg's bodyguard. Just like he had been Albie's protector. But Greg didn't want that relationship.

"What if you get hurt?" Greg asked. "And need help. I mean, you could take them out and get wounded too. I can come down and help. Stay in the back."

"Ok. Good point. A triple shot, a long pause, and a single shot. Three to one and you come help, but you don't rush in like a madman. You work it slowly with your rifle ready, understood?"

"What about those two dead bodies?" Greg then asked.

Mac sighed and shrugged.

"You can drag them even farther from the tents and start digging shallow graves for them. I can help you finish the graves when I get back. Don't worry too much about them until the shooting is over. Clean the camp, and while you do that, keep your eyes open for any sign of Albie having been here. Clothing, gear, whatever."

"Can't we just look and leave and head back? We have done what we were asked to do."

"No. We finish the job. One less bad guy, one less shipment of heroin. Believe me. We clean this all up. It protects Arthit and his people. No one knows who was responsible. No blowback to them. And the tools that these guys have been using. Throw them over the ledge, too. They are more weapons."

Mac slipped his rucksack on his back.

"Two doubles and all clear," Mac repeated and moved quickly, disappearing down the harrowing slope toward the next wave of mayhem.

CHAPTER SIXTY-EIGHT

Greg wasted no time cleaning the kitchen clearing of weapons and tools. More than a dozen shovels, axes, and saws were next to the stockpiled raw opium. He found the extra ammunition in the tents and pitched it over the ledge just as he had the rifles, knives, and handguns. Mac had already pulled both dead bodies well past the tents and near the blind spot of his descent from the ridge. Greg tossed two shovels next to the corpses, and turning, recognized from this would-be graveyard, he had a clear view of the longboats and part of the trail that led down to the lab. For a moment, he considered waiting there to see if he could get a glimpse of Mac or the three smugglers and their horses but then followed Mac's orders for positioning.

As he settled his wearied frame next to the tree, he realized just how ill-trained he was for this. He thought of the GIs, the army grunts, in Mac's gambling den. *Plumbers, mechanics, not proper soldiers.* And yet, any of them would have been better suited than he was for this assignment. Albie would have called him a *punter* for being so out of his depth. A second-rate gambler up against long odds. No chance. His throat was dry again. The first sign of fear. He pulled his backpack over and found his canteen of water. It was nearly empty, and he drained the rest.

He checked his M-16 and then removed the Colt 1991 from his backpack. He removed and reset the clip before setting it on the ground next to the two hand grenades. He wondered if he would have the courage if the signal was three to one. Would he answer the SOS? He knew he would, but to what end?

The not-knowing was haunting him. He tried to imagine how Mac would take them out. The three men had no reason to believe that there was any threat to them. Their weapons were likely slung over their back shoulders and not in a ready position. The strenuous uphill climb would fatigue them. The problem for Mac was the cover provided by the horses themselves. They would walk single file. The first man would be exposed, but the second and the third would be shielded as each walked behind a horse. In addition, the horses carried large sacks, which would provide even more cover for the man in the middle and the last one. Mac would need to get close, both for the range of the M-16 and the natural cover that the steep, winding, tree-lined track provided. His best option would be to shoot the man in the middle first. It would need to be a kill shot, and then fire on the leader before he could unpack his weapon. It would then be a shoot-out with the last man in the rear of the parade. Greg could not picture any other sequence. Mac would have the advantage of surprise and the high ground.

But what if he did it in inverse order? What if he hid in the bush, let them pass, and shot two and three from behind? The leader might be inclined to make a run up the hill to the clearing, thinking he could get help from the others who had been working up here. He could rush right into Greg's position. That is why Mac wanted Greg to be situated here. Here for cover, and a clean shot if someone came into sight from the trail.

Greg repositioned himself. Sitting and leaning on the tree was no longer an option. He shifted his items to behind the tree and adopted a prone position with the tree as cover. He propped himself on his elbows and checked his gunsight. Better, he thought. Now the only question that remained was his willingness to shoot a man in cold blood. *To kill without question, without remorse, and always without hesitation.*

He dropped his head into his bent arm and closed his eyes. He didn't sign up for this. He took a long breath. A sigh. It was so quiet up here. He could hear the river down below and the wind in the canyon. T'ang said you had to be quiet to hear the voices from beyond the thunder, so he listened now for those voices in the stillness. Another long exhalation. He was tired. Exhausted. He felt his chest rise and fall against the hard ground as he waited for the voices. Time crept away when suddenly he heard gunshots. He didn't know how many he missed. A series of single shots and then a long round. An unfamiliar sound responded, likely from one smuggler. Greg guessed it was an AK-47 like the ones he just tossed over the ridge. And then more, from what Greg hoped for, was the M-16. A series of single shots. And suddenly nothing. More silence.

Greg shifted his weight and readjusted his rifle, aiming where the trail emerged into the kitchen clearing. His breathing, only moments ago, calm, almost meditative, was now rushed, panicky. He could feel his heart pounding and his chest moving against the ground. He steadied his hands on the rifle and took two long, deep inhalations. And waited.

Finally, the all-clear message echoed from the canyon. A double, followed by a pause, and then another bang, bang. Mac was clear and heading down the path to the lab, where they too likely heard the gunfire and were arming up in anticipation.

***

Greg quickly gathered his gear, packing the hand grenades and handgun into his backpack, and rushed over to the soon-to-be burial ground, where he could get a view of the lab. His breathing was fast, in part from the sprint over to this vantage point, but also with a morbid celebration for Mac's successful kills. His indifference to the two dead bodies behind him spoke to his budding callousness.

With binoculars in hand, Greg scanned the opposite ridge, searching for movement by Mac moving down the hill or by someone mobilizing a defense near the lab. They had not discussed backup plans if anything went awry at this point. A litany of *what-ifs* now occurred to Greg. But before he could review potential scenarios, he caught sight of someone running down the hill nearing the lab. He was certain Mac would not approach the lab so recklessly. The frantic action could only be by one of the three smugglers on the trail. One of them must have eluded Mac and had made a run for the lab. Greg imagined it was number three in line.

Within minutes, the same man and the three techs, recognizable by their white lab coats, along with a fifth man with a rifle strapped across his back, were loading up two boats with processed heroin. They were wildly tossing as many bags as they could onto the boats. Greg could not hear them, but through their gestures, they were shouting and waving instructions at each other. These men had no intention of defending the lab, and Greg realized they did not know who had ambushed the three haulers on the trail. A gang of *camoys*, Xu's soldiers, or worse, Zhang Qitu. They didn't know who or how many, and they would not wait to find out.

Panic and greed worked against each other, and finally, they pushed off with half-filled boats. Mac, though still on the trail above the lab, must have seen them as well, and for good measure fired off harmless rounds in their general direction even as they headed down the river.

It wasn't long until Mac too was at the water's edge next to the remaining boats and the bags of abandoned product strewn on the shore. He looked skyward toward Greg, uncertain that Greg was even watching, and then sliced open the bags, tossed them into the water, and fired into the boats themselves, creating enough damage so that when he pushed them into the water, they sank. He left one longboat untouched.

Greg knew what would happen next, although he was surprised that it took as long as it did. As he waited for the inevitable explosion, he scanned the river's edge in both directions and unexpectedly glimpsed a tiny ledge on this side of the mountain. He refocused the lenses on the ledge and was flabbergasted to observe the legs of a man extending toward the abyss. Greg moved as far as he could to his right but could only be certain that there was a dead body on the ledge. He dropped the binoculars and rubbed his eyes with the palms of his hands. His heart sank knowing that they had finally found Albie.

CHAPTER SIXTY-NINE

The horses slowed Mac's return trip up the hill. Miraculously, none of them were hit in the crossfire. He had dumped the bags of chemicals, which the horses were carrying, tethered the animals to a tree before he continued down the hill, and then led them back to the kitchen clearing after the destruction of the heroin lab. He looked tired, and Greg guessed the amphetamine rush had worn off. Greg could not contain his enthusiasm for his discovery.

Mac insisted on providing food and water for the horses before he crossed the clearing to look at the ledge and the body on it. Greg thought it was paradoxical that he cared so much for the animals in the aftermath of killing humans. Mac, like Greg, could not identify the body on the narrow shelf. He guessed that the outcropping ledge was fifty to sixty feet below the kitchen clearing and agreed with Greg that it was so narrow that they could only see it from this vantage point. The rope, which he had used to rappel down from the ridge above them to this very spot, the spot where the two dead bodies now waited for burial, was not long enough for a similar descent to the small ledge. They searched the campsite and eventually found multiple lengths of rope on the far side of the makeshift horse pen. At least two looked like they would be long enough.

Greg returned to the site of the dead bodies and shouted directions to Mac as he moved along the top, dangling the rope over the edge. It took twenty minutes of trial and error to find the exact spot on the kitchen clearing that was above the precarious ledge and the dead body. The shelf looked smaller and smaller each time Greg looked at it through the binoculars, and the steep, vertical face of the mountainside, dropping hundreds and hundreds of feet straight down into the canyon, appeared increasingly treacherous. Finally, they found a spot where the rope hung directly to the slender outcropping. and had the good fortune of being near one of the four large trees, which remained uncut in the kitchen clearing. An ideal anchor.

Mac's shoulder was still bothering him, so this descent would be dangerous. Once again, he would have to keep the damaged arm flexed and below his head. Greg could only imagine how difficult it would be for him to climb back up. Mac began with directions again as he tied the rope around the trunk of the tree.

"We need to get moving after this. There is no telling when Fat Boy will return. We burn that massive opium pile and destroy whatever morphine product is still in those barrels. I would like to get the horses out of here. Over the hill and into that flat area, which we crossed in the night. They will be safe there until Arthit comes to get them. Then we head to the boat. If this is Albie, then we can use one horse to take him down the hill. Do you think you are strong enough to lift a dead body along the cliff's edge? Will your hand cooperate?"

"I will manage."

"Then let's get started."

***

Despite crawling on all fours to the rim of the mountain to look over its vertiginous edge, Greg lost sight of Mac almost immediately. He dropped and lay completely prone on his stomach and chest with his hand on the tightening rope and peaked over the edge but saw nothing but the abyss. He stared at the rushing brown waters of the Salween River and waited.

"It's not him," he heard Mac call out.

"Are you sure?" Greg shouted.

"It's a *farang*, for sure, but it's not Albie."

A part of Greg was relieved.

"I am going to wrap the rope around the body. Get ready to pull him up."

Greg was still lying flat on his stomach when suddenly he felt someone step onto his back, pinning him to the ground. He then heard the odious voice of the fiendish Fat Boy.

"Welcome to hell."

Removing the foot from Greg's back, Fat Boy kicked him violently in the side, knocking the air out of him and nearly propelling him over the cliff.

In the distance, he heard Mac's voice telling him to pull up the body.

Fat Boy grabbed Greg by his hair and jerked him away from the edge, pulling him up to his knees. He held a gun in his other hand and pointed it at Greg's face.

"Robber! Do you hear me? Start pulling the rope," Mac was shouting.

Fat Boy smiled menacingly and shook his head slowly. He then let go of Greg's hair and head, and while keeping the gun directed at his face, removed a small hatchet from his belt and dropped it on the ground.

"Cut the rope," he said.

Greg objected, and Fat Boy hit him with the back of his hand across his face.

"Not a word. Pick up the ax and cut the rope," he repeated.

Blood dripped from his mouth, and Greg was paralyzed with fear. Fat Boy nudged the ax closer to Greg with his foot and pulled the hammer on his gun.

"Robber? Are you still there? What the hell are you doing?" Mac called, now annoyed.

Greg tried to rush the words out of his mouth, knowing what was coming next. "Mac, I am cutting the rope." And Fat Boy hit him this time with the butt of the gun on his head, knocking him flat on the ground.

Somewhere in the distance, he heard Mac scream at him, but with tears welling in his eyes and blood now dripping behind his ear, he reached for the small ax.

"Cut the rope, or I shoot you and cut it myself."

Greg gripped the small hatchet, wondered how he could use it against Fat Boy and not get shot during the attack, and then, looking hopelessly into the gorge, swung the hatchet at the rope and cut it completely in three strikes.

Mac must have watched the rope slip down the mountainside, and called Robber yet again, but Greg lost consciousness in the explosion of pain as Fat Boy pummeled him repeatedly with the butt of his gun.

***

He came to coughing and gasping for air. Both of his eyes nearly swollen shut from the blows before and after he lost consciousness. His head throbbed while hanging down, too heavy to lift. Disoriented, shuddering involuntarily, and barely able to swallow, he discovered his hands tied together and arms extended over his head as he hung on a rope from the limb of a tree. Fat Boy had positioned a stone under his feet, which he kicked away as Greg now regained consciousness. Absent the rock, his weight fell to earth, falling just short of ground, and stretching his shoulders and arms into excruciating pain. He swallowed hard for air as he cried out loudly. He was struggling to breathe as the weight of his crucified-like body made inhaling nearly impossible.

"I thought you would enjoy this position," Fat Boy jeered. "I waited a long time for a moment like this. I never imagined that it would be so easy."

Greg tried to speak, but nothing came out.

"Don't waste your breath. No one wants to hear you." And he laughed, saying, "No one will ever hear you again."

Fat Boy took out a long knife and sliced Greg's shirt from his neckline to the bottom, letting the blade run against his skin at the same time.

Greg howled in anguish as blood dripped across his front, writhing in desperation as the rope twisted around his wrists and ripped his flesh.

"Not as precise as the bloodletting you gave to my friends," Fat Boy said, stripping the rest of the blood-soaked shirt from Greg's body.

Fat Boy then picked up a long bamboo pole and a short leather lash. He walked around in front of Greg. He fiendishly poked Greg in the groin with the pole, and Greg let out another groan. Greg now could see the awful viscous whites of Fat Boy's eyes. A face of evil. It was flushed and Greg realized Fat Boy was drunk. He was mumbling about making a choice. Past Fat Boy was the tree that anchored Mac's rope. Greg wondered what happened to Mac. How desperate he must be. How Greg deserved to die for betraying Mac by cutting the rope. He closed his eyes and prayed for forgiveness, but that too was cut short, as Fat Boy dropped the whip, and moving to the side, swung mightily and often with the bamboo stick across Greg's body. Greg cried out in anguish as Fat Boy beat him mercilessly above and below the waist, and with no relief in sight, Greg plummeted again into a tunnel of darkness.

Greg could never say precisely what happened next. But he was certain that it began with the unexpected arrival of Wes and Mary P on the scene. Fat Boy had no intention of Greg dying too quickly from asphyxia or exhaustion and had repositioned the stone beneath Greg's feet. He then exchanged his bamboo bat for the whip, and after reviving Greg with a splash of water, thrashed him on both his back and chest with the lash. Greg's screams of agony were limited to his own mind. His throat, hoarse from shouting, could not make any audible sound.

"Cut him down," Wes' voice boomed across the clearing. He was speaking in Mandarin.

"Go to hell," yelled Fat Boy and lashed yet again at Greg's back with the whip.

Greg thought he saw Wes aim his rifle at Fat Boy and yell once again to *cut him down.*

Fat Boy kicked the rock out from under Greg's feet, and Greg moaned in torment as he fell toward the earth yet again, his arms stretching beyond their limits skyward, and his lungs nearly collapsing from both exhaustion and cracked ribs.

"What are you going to do?" Fat Boy yelled at Wes. "Kill me like you did the scientist. This *farang* insulted me and killed my men. He destroyed my lab. You think Fat Man wants him to live?"

Wes fired his rifle past Fat Boy and the hanging Greg.

"I won't miss with the next one. You are one sick son-of-a-bitch. Now cut him down."

Fat Boy went over to the base of the tree that anchored the rope holding Greg and cut it with the same knife he used to slash Greg's chest when he removed his shirt.

Mary P ran to Greg and gathered him into her arms. She wiped the blood from his face and tried to talk to him in between her sobs.

Greg could hear Wes and Fat Boy continuing to argue across the clearing. He knew Mary P could not understand Mandarin. He tried to talk, to find a voice, to tell Mary P that Wes had killed Albie, to tell her he cut the rope, to tell her everything hurt, but he could only utter indecipherable noises. She kept telling him not to talk. And she left him for a minute to find water. She held his head up and helped him drink a little, but he choked immediately. He was trying to breathe more than anything else.

In the back of his mind, he heard Pancho telling him about hell. Asking him repeatedly if he knew the first rule of the jungle. But Mary P's voice kept interfering. She was wiping off the blood on his face and chest with a wet cloth. He recoiled in pain as she patted the stripes and open skin. Every touch was like fire.

Finally, Greg uttered Mac's name clearly and Mary P understood.

"Where is Mac? Greg, talk to me. Where is Mac?"

Greg spoke in gasps. "I cut the rope. By the tree. He's trapped … over the edge. Help him."

"Wes!" Mary P yelled loudly as she ran toward the cut rope. "Wes, please help. Mac is over the cliff."

Wes and Fat Boy both went over to Mary P near the tree, and Fat Boy kicked loose rocks over the rim, the falling scree directed toward Mac. Greg could not see Fat Boy's face but imagined that he smiled as Mary P explained what little she knew.

"Mac! Can you hear me? Mac! This is Wes. Are you there?"

"Where's Robber?" Mac called back.

"He is here."

"I heard gunfire. How is Robber?"

"He is banged up, but alive. Listen. I am going to throw you a rope. Tie it around yourself and I will pull you up."

Fat Boy and Wes then had yet another argument and shouting match, but Greg's head was so clouded that he couldn't understand what they were saying. He was convinced Pancho was talking to him, even while Wes showered imprecations and obscenities on the lawless Fat Boy.

He saw Wes throw the second, long length of rope over the edge, and he then looped his end around his waist, and when the slack disappeared and the rope went taut, Wes walked backward slowly, while pulling the rope with his thick, muscular arms and dragging Mac up the face of the mountain. Greg imagined Mac helped when he could by grabbing rocks and setting a foothold. A part of him wanted to believe that the indomitable, *nonpareil* hero-soldier would have eventually scaled the mountain even with his bad shoulder and without a rope.

Slowly, Wes moved backward across the clearing, farther and farther away from the edge where Mary P and Fat Boy stood waiting. Greg watched it all in horrible slow motion. He strained to shout a warning, to tell Wes to stop, to let Mac back down, but nothing but a whimper came out. His throat was dried up like baked clay. He was in tears, desperate to stop this.

But Mac's good arm appeared over the edge, and then his head, and when Mary P leaned over dangerously to help pull him up the rest of the way, Fat Boy moved in. Greg screamed, not sure if anything came out, and as Mac's upper torso reached flat ground, Mary P turned to look at Greg. She somehow avoided the full push by Fat Boy and tumbled backward, barely clear of the edge, but no one could stop Fat

Boy now from drawing his gun and shooting Mac twice in the back before he could ever lift his head or use the gun in his other hand.

Wes tugged one last time to get Mac completely away from the edge and then dropped the rope and ran to Mac and Mary P. He grabbed Mary P by the arm and threw her even farther away from the edge and to safety. He then pulled Mac clear as well, all the while cursing and yelling at Fat Boy, who stood gloating over the body.

"He was a soldier. You don't shoot a soldier in the back," Wes roared.

"He killed my men. Just like the other one, and they are both going to die."

And Fat Boy turned and headed toward Greg with his gun drawn. There was nothing Greg could do. He sat motionless, leaning against his hanging tree. His body was racked. His flesh had been thrashed. It was time. The brutality of fate had rendered its toll.

But Fat Boy suddenly stopped short of Greg as the first torrent of bullets hit him in the back. Somehow, Fat Boy turned back to Wes, who then emptied his clip into the despicable murderer. Greg watched him fall, then stared past Fat Boy's body to see Mary P holding Mac, rocking, crying, and desperately trying to stop the bleeding.

Wes approached Greg next, stepping over the dead demon and standing threateningly over Greg. Wes dropped the empty clip from his gun and replaced it with a full one.

"Listen, schoolboy. This is officially a shit show, and we need to clear out. There is a fortune here in dope. I can move this out through Mae Salong with my friends in the Border Patrol, and it can set us up for life. I need to know you are in."

Greg shook his head, no. He swallowed weakly, looked for his breath, and muttered hoarsely. "You betrayed Albie. He was your friend, and you killed him."

"You don't know what you are talking about," he said, waving his gun.

"I heard Fat Boy. I heard him say that you killed Albie. He was your friend, and you betrayed him. You lied to me about being partners with Fat Man. You lied to everyone."

"Albie betrayed me. He lied to me and then…" Mary P was shouting for Wes. "Yea, Albie knew what I was doing. We had a deal, and he broke it. He risked my life. Sometimes you don't have a choice. You just do what you have to do."

"You are a Judas. How can you live with yourself?"

Mary P's shouts to Wes continued.

"Wes, please!" she implored. "He is still alive. He is still breathing."

Wes walked over next to Mac. He knelt next to him across from Mary P. Blood covered Mac's body and Mary P's as well.

"He will never make it. He's lost too much blood already."

"We must try. We must take him to a hospital. We must try. Please," she begged, grabbing Wes' arm.

Wes shook free of her grasp and stood slowly. He still had his gun out.

"It's too far away. Sorry, Mac." And with his left arm, he pushed Mary P back and fired two more shots into Mac, killing him.

Mary P shrieked yet again and fell across Mac's dead body, but Wes just walked away and headed directly back to Greg.

"Too many dead bodies. Too much to explain to Fat Man and others. You are in or you are out, schoolboy. This is your chance. Nobody will know about another dead body in the Golden Triangle. Nobody cares."

He stood over Greg with the gun pointing at his head, but Greg looked into Wes' merciless eyes of deceit, and with his own collapsing resignation, shook his head.

"I don't care anymore. Shoot me. I deserve it. I betrayed Mac. I cut the rope. I will never help you. You've killed everyone. Eventually, you will kill me. Just do it now. You are a snake who will always end up betraying your friends."

Wes fired a shot inches away from Greg's head, and Greg winced as the resounding blast punished his eardrums, rendering one more blow to his defeated body.

Wes yelled at Greg. Yelled that Greg didn't know anything. That Greg couldn't see past his own selfish, insignificant life. Didn't Greg realize that in this game, someone always loses? He was still shouting invectives when bullets ripped through him, and he stumbled and fell to his knees before dropping on top of Greg.

Across the clearing, lying in a prone position with two hands on Mac's .45 caliber handgun, was Annie Oakley, aka Mary P.

Despite taking three bullets to the body, Wes was still alive as he draped across Greg's legs. His tattooed arm, with its prominent maxim screaming in silence about peace and war, stretched across Greg's lap.

Greg struggled to roll Wes' heavy body off and onto his back. Wes looked up at Greg almost kindly.

"I never would have hurt you, schoolboy. Never."

"Where is Albie buried? Where is his body? Tell me, Wes. Tell me where you put him."

Wes grimaced now as if trying to smile, blood and life running out of him. He coughed and spit blood onto himself as he grabbed Greg's forearm. He gripped it as hard as he could with his last bit of strength. Greg did not move, but watched life leave Wes' eyes as he uttered his last words. *He is alive.*

CHAPTER SEVENTY

The first time Greg ever told anyone anything about what occurred at Ban Su, he was in Katmandu. His audience was a heartbroken medical student from Hamburg. She and the love of her life, another woman—as if such sapphic leanings made any difference to Greg—had recently arrived at the never-to-be famous, two-star hostel, Nirvana Inn. But before they could begin their ten-day trek into the Himalayan Mountains, a discussion about karma turned into a robust disagreement and then a full-tilt quarrel, a raucous shouting match about the meaning of life. Had the squabble not taken place in the tiny bar next to the reception desk, and had the half-dozen, impenitent hippies not taken sides, cheering enthusiastically like soccer fans for Greg's soon-to-be new paramour, Gabriele, the two women likely would have reconciled and enjoyed a wonderful walk in the lower Himalayan regions.

Greg had no interest in walking anywhere but from his nondescript hotel room to this low-ceiling lounge, where he sat daily at the end of the five-person bar or one of the seven tables, most often the one in the corner, and watched the world travelers parade in and out of the bar, the hostel, and his life. Gabriele, unlike her friend, had no intention of returning to Germany until she completed her holiday, and had settled on Greg as the object of her distraction.

Gabriele was not a beautiful woman in the most obvious ways. She had a high forehead and straight brows over intense, coffee-colored eyes. She made little to no attempt to prettify herself. She shunned make-up, perfume, and adornments and was content to be hygienic in every way. In another life, Greg would have preferred that Gabriele at least shaved her legs and armpits, but such preferences and concerns had long passed.

When she learned that Greg's deep-tanned skin resulted from having spent the last six months in Bali, the prospect of going there on her next holiday intrigued her. She pressed Greg for details, but he had little to offer other than the obvious. Beautiful beaches. Great waves for surfing. Nice people. Isolated. Not crowded with WTs, as it took such an effort and expense to get there. He said nothing about the topless sunbathers or the two Australian girls who spent their days collecting seashells and their nights displaying their assets with him.

They lolled in bed until late morning, smoked hashish in the afternoon, and wandered around the narrow Katmandu streets, stopping, as their spirit and appetite moved them, to drink coffee, tea, or beer at local shops. She was convinced that order and fairness in the world were achievable. She believed everyone, without exception, could be cured. Her lost lover disagreed with her. She insisted everyone was broken and plummeting toward chaos and ruin. She said to look at the prisons, the destitution, the deaths. Humankind was incapable of changing course. She pressed Greg for his opinion, but he remained circumspect, and he took refuge in equivocation, summoned his inner Pancho, and parroted prosaic apothegms such as *you don't run out of dreams, you run out of time,* and *it's not money that is corrupt, it is the person.* She found them amusing, mildly insightful, until one sunny afternoon, while they were drinking beer at an outside café on a side street off Patan Darbar Square, the discussion turned to protests, violence, and wars, and Greg made the mistake of saying that *a bomb does not know why it explodes*, and *bullets have no conscience.*

It was then that Gabriele reached across the table, took his hand, and softly traced her finger across the marks scored on his wrists, questioning him about the scars on his body. He was never certain where to start. His clearest memory was at the end, huddled together in the kitchen clearing with a traumatized Mary P through the night. She put her face against his neck and trembled and shuddered. She wept uncontrollably, lost in the grief of becoming a killer. Her soul stained forever like Cain's. No penance would suffice. Greg tried in vain to console her. She shook hysterically. *He killed Mac. He killed Fat Boy, and he was going to kill you. I couldn't let that happen.* Her spiritual agony surpassed his physical pain. Greg hugged her as tight as his beaten body would allow, held her to prevent her from being washed away by the tide, and thanked her repeatedly for saving his life. He never believed Wes. And his seven-word message that he later sent to London said as much. *Mac is dead. No trace of Albie.*

T'ang and Arthit found them the next morning, nursed them both for a day, and transported them furtively to Chiang Rai, where he recovered, while she sought forgiveness from the priest at St. Michael's in Chiang Mai. She returned to the clinic only to say goodbye to him, and they held each other for the longest time, knowing that the journey away from happiness was unstoppable.

"Only God can save us," she said. And placing both her hands gently on his face, kissed him full on his lips, and said goodbye.

The next morning, he made a single phone call which required one stop in Chiang Mai in the middle of the night with his new driver, Prawaite, who as a recipient of two motorcycles—one severely damaged and the other in need of only minor repairs—and two thousand U.S. dollars, was more than willing to drive him covertly to Bangkok. He considered phoning Ping to inform her he would not be returning to Chiang Mai but then deemed that she was safest not knowing anything. He trusted Crissa would take care of her financially, as promised.

None of this was part of his story to Gabriele, so he started instead with how he received medical attention in Bangkok, and as he described why he and his friend Mac went to Ban Su, he decided fiction was more believable than fact. Confession remained a luxury for believers. He only needed a fabricated torture scene to satisfy Gabriele's curiosity, and a confrontation with a fictitious drug lord or a corrupt police sergeant could easily suffice. No one ever needed to hear about Mac's demise.

They were back at the hotel bar, where Greg continued his tale, himself discovering that it was a notorious gang of thieves, brigands, *camoys* in the Thai language, who ambushed their jeep and held Mac and Greg hostage, and just for cruel sport, tortured Greg. It was only through the heroic efforts of a long-time friend called Stephen Joyce that they were saved from further brutality and certain death.

With another pipe of hashish, or at least another beer or two, Greg believed he could continue with the narrative. Weave another chapter or two of fiction with just the smallest amount of truth to make it all seem real. His hopefulness, however, was cut short by the most unexpected arrival of the inimitable Elliot, who appeared at the table side with such casualness it was as if the two men had a long-standing appointment.

"Who is your friend, Greg?" Elliot asked.

But before Greg could answer, Gabriele interjected.

"I thought you said your name was Michael?"

"It is. Michael is my middle name. I prefer that," Greg lied.

She believed him, or at least pretended as much, and then with the same self-confidence she exhibited from the moment she first met Greg, aka Michael, Gabriele introduced herself to Elliot.

"What do you want, Elliot?" Greg asked gruffly.

"Just a few minutes if you can spare that. If Gabriele doesn't mind, of course," replied Elliot courteously, dismissing Greg's asperity.

"No. Not at all. It has been a long day and I need to clean up."

Elliot, always the gentleman, helped move her chair away from the table. His charm was never-ending, thought Greg scornfully.

With Gabriele's departure, Elliot settled into her chair, and as if by an act of God, two cups of steaming hot, dark Nepalese coffee, along with an expensive bottle of scotch, arrived at the table. The bartender brought two glasses as well.

"Michael, is it? Here I thought Alexander was your middle name. This lying is coming to you easier and easier. Must be the practice."

"I had an excellent teacher," replied Greg. "What did you tell me? *There are many good reasons to tell the truth, but an infinite number of reasons to lie.* How did you find me?"

"The money withdrawal," Elliot replied.

"Yeah, figured. Needed cash, and my departure was delayed."

"So, I see. Funny thing. It was your first misstep, so I wonder if it was intentional. You were much quicker to exit Bali when you used your real name there."

Greg poured the expensive whisky into the coffee.

"What passport are you using these days?" Elliot asked, not expecting an answer.

Greg said nothing and sipped the hot toddy.

"I must admit the red herring with Jack before you left Chiang Mai was clever. Your tradecraft has taken an upward trajectory. Getting a passport from him was cunning but also dangerous both for you and him. But that made it even more believable, didn't it? Although your plea to him to keep it secret, even from me, was over the top. We spent a fair amount of time tracking that passport. I assume you purchased other passports in Bangkok. If you use them over here only, you aren't likely to have any problems."

"You still haven't told me why you are here," Greg said.

"I will, but I have one or two more questions about your breadcrumbs. The letter to Ping from Hong Kong. How did you manage that? The station head there is still catching fire for missing you in his backyard."

"Charlie."

"Who?"

"I had a driver in Bangkok when I was arranging the deal with Mac. He was more than willing to take a brief holiday to Hong Kong and mail letters."

"Letters?"

"Ping and to a friend in London."

"That would be Crissa Bradley, I assume," replied Elliot.

"That's right." Greg was afraid to ask how he knew Crissa. His worst thought was that she had collaborated with Elliot. Spied on Lady Saint Clair and spied on him. No. He didn't want to know.

Elliot was silent for a moment as well, and Greg realized that Crissa never revealed the contents of his letter. Told no one. Elliot poured himself a drink into the tumbler. His coffee abandoned. He then offered Greg another shot into his half-filled coffee cup, and Greg nodded his assent.

"I was hoping you could tell me how you killed all those people," Elliot inquired.

Greg set down his coffee mug with a thud.

"Is that what you think? Is that what you think I am?"

"There are lots of missing people and you are the only one no longer missing. How do you explain the wreckage? What would you think if you were in our shoes? Why would you run so quickly out of Chiang Mai, unless you thought Fat Man would hunt you down for killing his son? No. Your disappearance—except for that midnight contact with Jack for our entertainment, and then the letter to Ping, which you knew we would intercept and which she destroyed immediately per your directions—told the Chiang Mai world that you too met your demise in the Golden Triangle."

Greg quietly took another drink.

"But that's not why you left those breadcrumbs. You know something. Or think you know something, and you are guarding that secret. Aren't you?"

Greg said nothing.

"Have you ever heard of the wilderness of mirrors? It is part of our nomenclature, our jargon. The land of spies, spooks, double agents, case officers, assets, and moles. Spycraft. Mirrors. Nothing you see in the mirror is real, apart from the time when it is. The question becomes, how do you know which is the reflection and which is real?"

Greg took a generous swallow and grimaced. Sometimes, if he gulped substantial amounts of any liquid, his throat would burn. Alcohol was the worst, but it didn't deter him. The pain remained an unremitting reminder of his betrayal, of his cutting the rope. He earned it. His other parts were healing, but he cleaved to this stinging reminder of his ignominy. The stain on his soul.

Elliot did not look any different from what he did on that night when they both played cards with Preeya. Still the same. Unruffled. Unflappable. He saw through Greg's conjured anger. Could guess that he survived a harrowing ordeal. Might even know from T'ang or Arthit that torture, not murder, marked Greg's being. He knew that the only thing Greg wanted was to disappear, but unfortunately, that could not happen just yet.

"You never told Crissa or Lady Saint Clair that Albie was dead," Elliot said with a measured tone and a precise choice of words.

"No. No, I didn't. Before Wes died, in fact as he died, his last words to me were that Albie was alive. A part of me believed him, but Wes had lied to me so often…" Greg's voice trailed off, and then he resumed. "He was exactly like your mirror."

Elliot paused, leaned forward, and placed both his elbows on the table, overlapping his right hand over the left fist, and resting his chin on his knuckles. The inscrutable mien reminded Greg of how Elliot hovered over his chips and cards.

"Albie is alive," said Elliot with certainty.

"Where is he?"

"That I don't know," he answered and sat back in his chair.

"Then why are you so certain?"

"Albie was one of ours."

"And you never told me?" Greg's voice rose with incredulity.

"There is a great deal that I never told you. Or ever will. But in this case, you deserve to know the truth."

Elliot poured them both yet another drink. If Greg had learned anything, it was that no one wants to know the truth. Some, like Mary Peyton, believe they want to confess it. Others, like Pancho, have their version of it. But it is the Elliots of the world who finally determine it.

Elliot said that he recruited Albie in Sweden at one of his environmental conferences. He was an easy recruit. Caterina had just died. He was adrift, vulnerable. Disillusioned with his government for so many things, but currently for their lack of commitment to environmental degradation. He spewed invectives at their utter ignorance of emissions from gasoline engines and coal. Despite all the warnings, no one would act. He hated his father, who had made his fortune in World War II and continued to profit from the massive energy deals he had with the government.

Albie was astute enough to know China was important and Mao running China was not in the best interests of the West. No one had to remind him that China was already surpassing all others in greenhouse emissions and pollution. Their refusal to be part of the environmental summit in Sweden was just one more reason for Albie to do what he could do.

The KMT are the guardians of the northern gate. They exist with U.S. support in part to deter and hopefully stop Chinese encroachment into Thailand. Supporting Chiang Kai-shek's rebel army was an easy connection for Albie.

The Research Station was legit, but it had two purposes. The Company agreed to fund the lion's share of the project, as well as his friends' projects in other countries. The station would do everything that the scientist intended, but it would also serve as cover for their purposes—transferring money and weapons to Xu. One more place for such transactions. With a little effort, they fashioned a decent road that led from Chiang Rai to the Research Station. Steep and serpentine in parts, as Greg well knew, but wide enough for large farm equipment and crates of weapons. Albie stored the weapons at the Research Station and then transferred them, along with cash, to Xu discreetly.

Fat Man was a problem from the very beginning. Along with other Chinese and Burmese drug lords, they had long ago divided up the villages throughout the Golden Triangle on all sides of the border, including Laos. But Zhang Qitu was building an army of insurgents against the Burmese government, and he needed the opium money and expressed little regard for any previous accords with Fat Man or others. He wanted all of Burma and had an army now to back that up. He pushed Fat Man out of the bordering Burmese villages, leaving Fat Man with the villages and opium fields in Northern Thailand.

But when Chiang Kai-shek's Fifth Army came along, his General Xu picked off dozens of Thai villages and agreed with Zhang to leave the western part of Burma to him, except for a small alley in northwest

Burma that crossed near the northern Thai border and into Laos. Xu built roads, heroin labs, and a pipeline across to Pakse in Laos, where product flew out in all directions.

Fat Man was getting squeezed out. He couldn't fight Zhang and had even less chance with Xu. He was still making a fortune. But as his ambit dwindled, he clung fiercely to his smaller piece of the opium pie, including all the villages surrounding Ban Su.

Albie set up shop with labor from T'ang and paid him generously. General Xu meanwhile figured that since Albie was in Ban Su now, he should have T'ang's opium as well. So, to keep him happy, T'ang did as directed and was again paid handsomely.

In hindsight, it was a mistake.

Greg interrupted Elliot and called over to the bartender, asking for a cold beer.

"Do you want one?" he asked Elliot.

"Sure," said Elliot.

"Two, please," Greg added loudly. "So, you made a mistake."

"Not our first, but yes. Fat Man was incensed. He took it upon himself to visit the area himself. Not one of his usual practices. He threatened everyone. So, we arranged for Thai soldiers to come into the area to protect Albie—and our interests. And to protect T'ang and Nok from Fat Man. We knew Xu would never bother T'ang and his people. He never crossed over into Thailand. Ever. Albie was the one who journeyed to him."

The beers arrived, and out of habit more than friendship, they clinked bottles.

"But then something happened," said Greg.

"Yes. It was Nok."

"Nok? What could she have possibly done? She was blameless."

"She was. The beating sent Albie over the edge. She and Albie had fallen in love. Hopelessly, madly, stupidly in love. Maybe one day that will happen to us. She was the consummate helper and village maiden. She took care of everyone. Not just T'ang."

"Ok. I understand the bit about them being in love. I knew it was his tipping point. How did Wes fit in? How did he know Albie was alive? Was he part of this?"

"No. We never trusted Wes. He had been good in the beginning, but he wasn't someone I would trust. Wes found out that Albie was helping Xu. I don't know how, and it doesn't matter. Wes knew he could expose

Albie, but Wes had been working with Fat Man for years, and blowing Albie's cover meant an end to his lucrative arrangement, if not his life. Ironically, they also liked each other and reached an agreement of silence, letting each continue in his own way.

"Wes set up Fat Man's routes. He was good at navigating through jungles and rough terrain, found the best places for the first step in the process of heroin production—cooking the opium—and found the best and most discreet paths to transfer morphine to the more sophisticated labs. The labs are the key. Xu set up these specialized labs across his route and was producing no. 4 Tiger and Globe, each package seven-tenths of a kilo and eighty to ninety-nine percent pure. Only the Double U-O globe ever comes close to that. Fat Man wanted to do the same. He had quacks from Hong Kong cooking no. 3 in Chiang Mai, but a gram of no. 4 sells for twenty times more than a gram of no. 3."

"Then it was Wes who set up Fat Man's heroin lab on the river," said Greg.

"Most likely," answered Elliot.

"It had been working well. They stayed away from Xu. They avoided the growing presence of the DEA in Chiang Mai. They got the army out of the area and closed the Research Station by amplifying the possibility of brush fires with Xu and faking gun battles. Of course, they used bribes as well. But when T'ang kept selling his opium to General Xu, Fat Man made good on his threats and hurt Nok."

"Killed her," corrected Greg.

"Sadly, yes," said Elliot.

And both men were silent for a moment before Elliot continued.

"Albie came to see me only days before Fat Boy assaulted Nok. I am sure you know that Albie always wanted her to leave the village, but she refused because of T'ang. However, when she became pregnant, she didn't want to raise a child in the hill tribe world. She knew that with an education, particularly the type that someone like Albie could provide, the child could have a different type of life. He was making plans when the attack occurred.

"He came to see me again that day with you. He was sincere about re-opening the Research Station, in large part to protect the Ban Su village and T'ang from Fat Man. Part of that meeting was an act for your benefit. Sorry, but he had been haranguing me for weeks about the threats to T'ang and Nok. He insisted we had a moral responsibility to help the people who once helped us. We could not just use people and then abandon them. He did not know our history.

"He took his jeep and our next payment for Xu and headed back up the mountain in a Gadarene dash. He had been delivering money to Xu from the beginning. The weapons' delivery ceased shortly after they completed the building of the Research Station, but there was no reason for him not to continue carrying money to Xu. He was the most dependable person we ever had. He didn't need or want money for himself and understood that we couldn't write a check for Xu.

"Albie said he was finished with us. He would make this one last delivery and then he was going to destroy Fat Man since we refused to do that. He was attempting to do that when Fat Boy caught him. Fat Boy beat him but left it to Wes to make him disappear."

Greg could not fathom how Albie survived torture and shuddered at the thought of Albie experiencing anything like what had happened to him. He understood now how easy it must have been for Wes to kill Fat Boy.

"Are you telling me Wes saved him?"

"That's right. He helped him get back to Xu. Albie had a hidden path well beyond his orchard fields that led directly into Burma. It was his delivery route. Wes probably created fake gunfire and pronounced Albie buried in swamp grass, but got him back to his jeep, which was hidden on that route. Wes told Albie that they would kill Ping, her child, and even the sister if he ever surfaced again. T'ang and others in the village as well. Wes certainly knew Fat Man and Fat Boy would kill him for betraying them and not finishing off Albie."

"If not your friends, then who can you betray?" Greg said cryptically.

"You are a fast learner," said Elliot.

"I misread Wes," confessed Greg. "At least in part. He may have saved Albie, but he killed Mac."

"So, Mac is dead?" Elliot asked.

"Yes."

"It's just that you never know until you know. Are you going to tell me how?"

"What difference does it make? Was he one of yours too?"

"No, but it wasn't from lack of trying. We keep track of his type. He wouldn't work for us directly. He had had his fill in Laos and 'Nam, but he agreed to help Albie. He was a good fit to watch Albie's six. But he had a chip on his shoulder. He knew we had a hand in the heroin traffic, and we were helping Xu. Hell, everyone knew it, but he thought we crossed an imaginary line. He watched Saigon become a cesspool, and when his friend got hooked, he said enough was enough."

"Yea, he told me as much."

"He was on his mission, blowing up labs in the gulf, and even one in central Bangkok. I guess that Mac and Wes ran into each other in Chiang Mai when Mac was helping Albie. They both knew each other for what they were. So, I am not surprised he shot Mac."

"Fat Boy shot Mac first, but he was still alive when Wes pretended to save him from suffering," explained Greg.

"And then you killed Fat Boy and Wes?"

"No. Wes killed Fat Boy and was about to shoot me when Sister Mary Peyton shot him. I shot no one." But the last swallow of his beer screamed the silent reminder that he betrayed Mac when he cut the rope.

Elliot drained his beer as well, processing what occurred in the kitchen clearing. No doubt still filled with questions. But before he asked anything else, Greg had his questions and wanted to get back to Albie.

"I have a tough time believing Albie is living with the Fifth Army or anywhere in China. He could barely communicate in Thailand," said Greg.

"I understand, but Albie spoke Mandarin. Not like you or Mac, but he studied it at Cambridge. Kept it quiet from his family. It was embarrassing back then. Chinese language. Communism. Red scare. He was smart, and for the five or six months that he poked around with Mac deciding on where to build the Research Station, he learned even more. Nok helped him, too. He played the *I don't understand tonal language* card well.

"Xu contacted us while Albie recovered. He loved Albie, and why not? He was his money man. Xu insisted Albie go to Taiwan so General Chiang Kai-shek could thank him personally. We gave Albie fresh papers, a new identity, and Xu arranged his travel. After that, I don't know. South America? He had plenty of money. He was always talking about the Amazon. A few cosmetic touches. Stop shaving his head, add facial hair and glasses, and he could be in this bar, and we wouldn't know it."

"Why didn't you tell me all this?"

"You were never supposed to be part of it. You did your job. We kept you safe and no one, not even Albie or any of them, knew about you. It was perfect. I told you that at the Night Market. You were perfect."

"Until I wanted to find out what happened?"

"Yes. You were pursuing the truth and we don't do that."

"What else are you not telling me?"

"You were the sixth man. Our bench player. Albie had just started in Thailand when I came to Oxford. Initially, I thought we would use you. Your language skills and general insouciance made you ideal. We could use Albie as misdirection or even cover, but Albie was a baller and played well from the beginning, so we kept him in the game, and we kept you on the bench. It turned out that we didn't need you. Albie played the entire game. At least until he quit."

"Why is all this so necessary? Wasn't Mac, right? Shouldn't we be stopping this and not aiding and abetting?"

"Langley believes any interruption of drug trafficking will destabilize the political situation in the Golden Triangle and Northern Thailand and that there would be serious implications for the intelligence services who have been part of it for so long."

"So Fat Man is not only still standing but wins."

"You might want one last beer," Elliot said.

CHAPTER SEVENTY-ONE

Elliot reached into the pocket of his jacket and handed Greg the white amulet. Greg turned it over in his hand and read the inscription. *Preeya* on one side and *R 3:5* on the other. Greg closed his hand tightly around the charm, flooded with memories of the most beautiful woman he ever knew.

"Jack asked me to give this to you if I ever saw you again."

Greg closed his eyes. He promised himself he would never cry again.

"The *R 3:5*," said Elliot. "It's from *Revelations*, right?"

"Yes," answered Greg. "*The one who is victorious will be dressed in white.*"

"Well, at least part of that is true."

Not too long after the carnage that resulted in the deaths of so many, both the known and unknown, the rhythm of everyday life in Chiang Mai resumed—even for those affected the most. Except for Jack, who discharged the responsibility for his casino to his second-in-command and appeared to be drinking heavily while visiting other casinos to gamble. He was quite adept, and while no one was tracking his winnings, he was doing well. His fellow casino operators were happy to collect the rakes that accumulated, and Jack was generous with tipping all the dealers.

He visited Fat Man's establishment at least weekly but shunned the high-stakes games in the private parlor with Preeya as the dealer. One evening when Fat Man sat next to him during a poker game, Jack floated the idea of another Big Game. Maybe not as international as the one Jack held a while back, but certainly a version thereof. Jack would manage the invitations because he was much more lovable than Fat Man, but the major attraction would be Preeya.

The wily Fat Man wanted to know what the *catch* was, and Jack was forthcoming. He said he wanted to find out for himself if he could hang with the best. He had watched enough for years and believed he could win against most, if not all, these heavy hitters. And then, seemingly as an afterthought, said to Fat Man that he too should finally test his skills against the best, rather than continue to beat up the local hacks and drunks in meaningless card games. Both ideas intrigued Fat Man. Aroused his cupidity. He knew he would make a fortune on the rake alone and laughing in the faces of the arrogant high rollers would be a bonus.

So, they arrived. Thirteen of the best poker players from Bangkok, Hong Kong, Penang, and Singapore joined Jack and Fat Man, who remained indifferent to wagering in his own establishment. They played for three nights from dusk to dawn, rotating to the vision of Preeya as prescribed, until the last table comprised Jack, Fat Man, Yusof, a rail-thin artist from Penang, the Singaporean Adriel, who insisted on always having a lit cigarette at his side, and a burly, tattooed, and talkative American expat who ran a bar in Pattaya.

Fat Man, in all his physical amplitude, sat on one side of Preeya and Jack on the other, while the other three circled the table. The American sat directly across from Preeya and stared at her unremittingly, to the point of neglecting his cards. The observers who filled the room said it seemed he had already won by being in her gaze.

They played for hours with the chips doing little more than exchanging hands. Jack drank, and the American did not seem to run out of breath. He wanted to know from Jack if the Russians were coming to Chiang Mai. He said that the Russian mob was easing into Pattaya. Their business interests expanded daily. He told Adriel that he was certain someone smarter than himself could create a language of numbers. He was fascinated by those who believe deeply in something and by those who want to believe, and he questioned Yusof on the meaning of his name, already knowing that it meant *God increases power and influence.* He talked and talked, and questioned everyone, except Fat Man, who glowered at him constantly, but miraculously held his tongue.

Jack, who had his bottle of Mekong whiskey next to his chips, drank and drank, and he soon required a break to use the restroom. A flagrant breach of the protocol. Untimed rests simply were not allowed. The American, Yusof, and Adriel were gracious in understanding, and Fat Man, out of gratitude to Jack for arranging this massively successful game, acquiesced.

All the gamblers stood and stretched their legs except Fat Man, whose fleshy frame remained at rest in a soft stack of antipathy. It was then that Preeya leaned over to Fat Man and whispered something to him. He looked at her with uncertainty but said nothing. When everyone had resumed their seats, including Jack, who had secured another bottle of Mekong, Fat Man announced in rasping puffs of breath that, given the high stakes, there could be no more such interruptions from here on in. It would be the original, strict rules of poker, table stakes—match each bet or fold. None of this faddish all-in rubbish. And then he added each gambler should pay special attention to always keeping their hands above the table. They were all professionals, and no one seemed to mind except the American, who said that he would do his best but that sometimes he simply had to scratch himself in the nether regions. His comment brought laughter across the table and from the gallery. However, Fat Man said that he was not joking about the hands above the table, and to make his point, he pulled out his revolver, which he placed strategically on the table next to Preeya.

Eventually, the cards fell out of favor with Adriel, and his final desperate bets left a large winning pot for Fat Man. Yusof was the next victim. He lost with a full house to the American, who unveiled a higher full house. He told Yusof that it was okay to cry, even angels wept when they saw the crucifixion.

And then there were three, although how Jack remained solvent and sober enough to continue was beyond understanding. Cards and chips crossed the worn, green, baize cloth with little favor for anyone of the remaining threesome. The American seemed obsessed with the number three. He explained that a Russian troika was a vehicle with three horses, and a Russian judiciary council of three was called a troika. He doubted that anyone at the table was Christian but that the Catholics believed that their One God consisted of three persons. They called it the Holy Trinity. Americans have a favorite expression, that *the third time is* a *charm*. Not like the one Preeya was wearing. Her charm was an amulet, a talisman. A juju. In French, they pronounced it the same but spelled it *jou-jou*. But neither should be confused with a juju man. A term made famous by an English spy with a French name. He clarified those types do not come in threes but are always alone. No one paid him much attention, as his jabbering continued one hand after another until he said he knew a juju man who disappeared in the Golden Triangle. A misshapen, three-sided, topographical splotch, lacking honest definition, and whose only gold was opium.

Fat Man told him to stop. His voice croaky, hoarse, and hostile. He had had enough. And the American withdrew into a cocoon of silence.

The rules of the final round required an increase in both the ante and the minimum bet after each hand, so each pot became larger even on non-competitive hands. Jack's luck was taking a turn for the worse until he finally hit what he believed to be a sure winner and caught Fat Man and the American believing the same. Slowly, Jack increased the bets and each of the others kept adding on. But Jack abandoned restraint, no longer trying to hide anything, and took larger drinks of his whisky in between bets. The American, still ever so quiet, folded, leaving Jack and Fat Man in a face-off. With each man's chips plainly in sight, it was clear that Fat Man held an immense advantage, so he raised the bet to such a degree that Jack could not match it. Jack was furious, but Fat Man said with a rancid smile that those were the rules, and if you can't make the bet, then you fold and lose.

Jack was bereft of reason. He had made a crucial mistake by not calling sooner. The alcohol had clouded his brain. He could not believe he would lose on such a tactic. Not when he had such a fantastic hand. Fat Man smiled malevolently. He asked Jack if he thought he could win, and Jack answered with certainty. Fat Man leaned across the table—almost touching Preeya—his large back hunched below a balding head, and slowly he pushed the gun past Preeya to Jack. Fat Man said that he was grateful to Jack for arranging this game and that in appreciation, he would withdraw his oversized bet and would remove all but two bullets. He then added that if Jack wanted to add his casino to the bet, he would remove one more bullet as well. But Preeya shook her head, reminding him you can't bet something that is not on the table.

Everyone knew that if Jack took the gun and lost the hand, then he would have to spin the chamber, put the gun to his head, and pull the trigger.

Jack dropped his cards on the table and shook his head. Fat Man erupted in laughter. He ridiculed Jack, derided him for his cowardice, and invited him to continue to drink freely at the bar, as it was the only thing he could do well.

Greg was stunned. He couldn't believe Jack and Preeya, knowing what they did about Preeya's father, would get trapped in such a fiendish endgame. And Pancho! What the hell was he thinking? Why was he there? Greg had been too much of a coward to visit him afterward. Greg worried that Mac's death would drive Pancho back to the needle.

The American acted dumbfounded by the revolver incident. He said he was flabbergasted. He said that in all his years, in all the places he had ever played, he had never seen such a diabolical and scandalous display. He had heard of such stories when he first came to Bangkok, but to witness such depravity firsthand appalled him. Fat Man was dismissive. He said some men are too afraid to win, and he suggested the American quit if the stakes were too high for him. The American looked at Preeya, who remained completely impassive, and then he requested a new deck of cards.

They played two hands and not much happened, but the chatter of the American returned and as Preeya dealt the third hand, the American reminded Fat Man that the *third time was the charm.* Both men bet heavily from the beginning and the American commented on each one, mocking the Fat Man for his meager raises. And when both men had discarded and received their new cards, Preeya folded her hands and remained sphinxlike. Fat Man could not believe his good fortune. He held a royal straight flush with a king high. He did not hide his satisfaction, knowing that there was only one possibility in the entire universe of cards that could beat him. But he needed to draw the American in slowly and not let him drop out too soon. He too had a good hand, which played into Fat Man's favor.

They bet back and forth a few more times with neither man willing to call, and then unexpectedly, while both men still had piles and piles of chips, tens of thousands of dollars in front of each of them, the American slowly counted the total of all his chips, pushed them into the center, and called the bet. Fat Man pushed all his chips in, but the American stopped him, reminded him of the rules, and insisted that he count them and match the number. If Jack had to match the number, then the American thought it was only fair for Fat Man to do the same.

Fat Man felt insulted and called the American a foul name in Chinese and loudly counted out his thousands and thousands of dollars in chips. In the end, discovering that he was exactly one hundred dollars short. A pittance compared to all that was on the table.

The entire room had been mumbling their opinions and now fell silent.

The American asked Fat Man if he wanted to recount his chips. It was a shame that he was so close and would now lose because of a meager one hundred dollars. The mockery was palpable and severe. When Fat Man did not respond, the American leaned forward and extended his arms as if to gather the entirety of his immense winnings in one swoop, but Fat Man shouted for him to stop.

The revolver had never left the table. It remained between Fat Man and Preeya after Jack declined to use it. Fat Man slid the gun into the middle toward the American. Fat Man said his hand was unbeatable, and he would bet all his chips and his life on it. The American scoffed, saying there was no such thing, and said that Fat Man was the biggest coward he had ever met, and he had met some famous ones.

Instead of being insulted, Fat Man smirked at the American and said that he would leave all the bullets in the revolver. That is how certain he was, and it was the American who was afraid to lose. But it did not persuade the American, who said the revolver bet was a farce and repeated that the cravenly Fat Man would never pull the trigger. Fat Man swore otherwise to the entire room. And the American, looking first at all the bystanders who filled the room and had been witnessing this showdown, raised his arms in mock resignation and agreed.

The entire room gasped when Fat Man turned over his cards one by one with his corpulent fingers. Never in his life had he smiled so broadly. His fleshy face quivered as he laughed. The room buzzed with hushed whispers as everyone now stared at the American, who did not toss his cards into the center admitting defeat, but nonchalantly flipped them over, revealing the same hand as Fat Man's—a royal straight flush with ace high. The only hand that could beat Fat Man.

They said that Preeya did not move when the blood splattered across her face and her white dress. Jack, who had been standing in the crowd, now appeared next to her, suddenly more sober than a monk. The American told Jack to keep the money, and walking over to Preeya, extended his hand and the two of them walked out together like old friends.

He squeezed the amulet in his hand, trying to wake himself from this clouded place of a dream. Preeya said she knew what she was doing, but he never believed her. Just like he never believed Pancho or Mary P or even Ping. Not anyone or anything.

Some nights he imagined that could still see her, sitting cool and businesslike, shuffling the deck of cards in the dark with only a splinter of moonlight slanting through the shutters. Her mind clear, registering the place of each card in every riffle and split cut. Colors and numbers, like bone and marrow. She must have paused when she caught her reflection in the pocket-sized mirror, which she kept on the ledge above the table, puzzled by what stared back at her. Time had been kind to her deceiving all who failed to see past the aura. All who could not pierce the carapace. She remembers him, one of the few that mattered, and wonders where he is now.

Misses the touch of his hand. He held her as if he always knew, knew that she was a shard of glass. Positioned right, you can see through its smooth surface, and with sunlight it can magnify, even beautify. But the jagged edges make it impossible to grasp, to embrace…unless…unless you need a weapon. Then, with grim determination, a scintilla of courage, and the coldest of blood, you pinch the smooth part perfectly between your thumb and forefinger and slice with the jagged edge.

From the shadows at the far end of the bar, an umber-faced Nepalese with scruffy facial hair signaled Elliot.

"We need to go," said Elliot. "Collect your passport and money from the front desk safe."

"Where are we going?"

"There are people who would like to meet you, hear your story."

"No thanks," replied Greg. "I am not cut out for this."

"I disagree. I don't know if I ever met anyone more suited."

"Tell that to Mac."

"That's not fair. Above all others, Mac knew that not everything worked like a script."

Elliot reached into the inside pocket of his coat and placed an envelope on the table, but Greg did not reach for it.

"What's that?" Greg asked.

"Have a look. It's payment for your pictures and story in the *National Geographic* magazine. The forthcoming cover will feature this photo," he said, handing Greg the print of Nok and T'ang together, smiling in the poppy fields. The same photo he was taking to T'ang when he discovered the beaten Mary P.

"The editors loved how you captured the moment. The resplendent background of purple, white, and green flowers, and a pristine blue sky. The sweat on T'ang's face is glistening in the picture. Impressive photography."

Greg remained silent. He sent nothing to *National Geographic.* And it was the joy, not the sweat, that made the picture.

"We cleaned up your place in Chiang Mai. You had everything organized, so it only required a little editing. There is also a generous advance from the World Geographic Association. They are one of the very few Western publications that have visa entry into China and freedom of movement. They have a place set up for you in Shanghai. It is quite nice, by all standards."

"What could I possibly do there?"

"More of the same. Take pictures. Talk to people. Make friends."

Elliot leaned forward, his elbows on the table once again.

"I doubt that you have ever heard of Pan Hannian. He is the head of Chinese counterintelligence. Until now, he has directed his efforts against the Kuomintang. Defectors, double agents, the usual. Recently, he set up residency in Shanghai, targeting international businesses and non-company types. You manufactured a perfect legend over these last months. Fake passports. Disillusionment bolstered by your debauchery in Bali and here. You won't go unnoticed. You won't even need to dangle your coattails in Shanghai."

Greg stared into the low ceiling, his studied indifference wavering. Besotted by his constant restlessness and enamored with the carapace of deceit, he had struggled to hold free of the maelstrom that was the Golden Triangle. And paid the price. And now, with redemption out of reach, he ached, not for another chance, but for something unknown, something he could trust, and if not that, then for something sweet, a woman's perfume.

The Nepalese babysitter had moved behind Greg, offering kindly to help him to his feet.

"Let's get out of this place," said Elliot. "It's time to come off the shelf. Next time, we'll get it right."

THE END

Made in the USA
Las Vegas, NV
16 December 2023

82857975R00215